I0823266

BIOGRAPHY OF A DANGEROUS IDEA

ALSO BY ANDREW S. CURRAN

Sublime Disorder

The Anatomy of Blackness: Science and Slavery in an Age of Enlightenment

Diderot and the Art of Thinking Freely

Who's Black and Why? A Hidden Chapter from the Eighteenth-Century Invention of Race
(COEDITOR, WITH HENRY LOUIS GATES JR.)

BIOGRAPHY OF A DANGEROUS IDEA

A NEW HISTORY OF RACE

FROM LOUIS XIV TO THOMAS JEFFERSON

ANDREW S. CURRAN

Other Press New York

Production editor: Yvonne E. Cárdenas
Text designer: Julie Fry
This book was set in Californian with Alternate Gothic.

10 9 8 7 6 5 4 3 2 1

 Printed in the United States of America on acid-free paper. For information write to Other Press LLC, 267 Fifth Avenue, 6th Floor, New York, NY 10016. Or visit our Web site: www.otherpress.com.

Due to the 2025 government shutdown, the Library of Congress Cataloging-in-Publication Data was not available at the time of printing.

ISBN 978-1-63542-224-5
E-book ISBN 978-1-63542-225-2
LCCN 2025030144

For my mother, aka CNC,

for helping me see

a different kind of world

CONTENTS

BIOGRAPHY OF
A DANGEROUS IDEA

VOLTAIRE'S STATUE IN FRONT OF THE ACADÉMIE FRANÇAISE, 1890

PROLOGUE

The greatest minds are capable of the greatest vices as well as of the greatest virtues.

— René Descartes, *Discourse on the Method*, 1637

In late 1941, France's Vichy government created a list of metal statues to be melted down for the German war machine. Among these monuments was a full-scale likeness of one of the country's most beloved writers, the Enlightenment philosopher known as Voltaire. That France's fascist regime chose to do away with this statue was no coincidence. Though the author of *Candide* had been dead for nearly two centuries, his name continued to be synonymous with liberty, tolerance, and freedom of thought — the values of the now-disbanded French Republic. By early 1942, the statue had been transformed into Nazi bullets and shell casings.[1]

Two decades later, in 1962, the city of Paris replaced the lost monument with a new statue of Voltaire. Sculpted by Léon-Ernest Drivier, the marble version of the writer was erected in a modest, triangular patch of land not far from the Académie Française. Ringed by low fencing and hemmed in by city streets, the statue sat undisturbed for nearly sixty years. Beginning in 2018, however, activists repeatedly slipped into the park after dark to douse the monument with red paint. One night, someone broke off the statue's nose. Judging by what was being said about Voltaire on social media at the time, the protesters had been provoked by two well-documented facts. The first was that the writer had owned shares in a trading company that trafficked tens of thousands of African captives to the New World. Even more upsetting, Voltaire had repeatedly claimed that Black Africans and Amerindians were intellectually inferior races with no biological link to Europeans.

DRIVIER'S STATUE OF VOLTAIRE IN 2022 COVERED IN GRAFFITI

THE EMPTY PEDESTAL

In August 2022, activists mounted their final attack on the increasingly degraded monument. Shortly after this last incident, the Paris government defiantly announced that Drivier's artwork would be removed for repair and reconditioning before being returned to its rightful place. Four years later, the same administrative office released a statement explaining that the monument was now too fragile to return to its park and would be replaced with an exact replica cast in resin. This plasticized Voltaire, which is more resistant to both Paris's weather and militants, now sits atop the original pedestal.

The downward spiral of Voltaire's statues in this neighborhood—from bronze, to marble, to a mixture of fiberglass, epoxy, and stone—has paralleled both the writer's *and* the Enlightenment's legacy over the past two decades. At a recent international history conference in Rome attended by over a thousand people, a double session was provocatively titled: "Should we burn Voltaire?" The French philosopher and writer is not alone in suffering such scrutiny. David Hume, Immanuel Kant, and Thomas Jefferson, along with a number of other writers and political figures from the era, are also being re-evaluated in light of their corrosive and often dehumanizing writings on race.

For many people, castigating these one-time heroes of the Enlightenment has been an act of liberation, a symbolic reckoning with a generation of men whose ideas and writing were tied to colonialism, slavery, or racism. Yet as satisfying as such retribution may feel, this act leaves a number of pressing questions unanswered. The first of these is: *Why*? Why did this generation of thinkers come to hold such racist views in the first place? And why did these ideas only come into being during the eighteenth century—more than two centuries *after* the transatlantic slave trade had begun? Such properly historical questions point to an even deeper quandary: Why did so many Enlightenment-era champions of tolerance and civil liberties work so hard to limit these supposedly universal birthrights to Europeans? This book, the first biography-driven history of race, seeks to answer these questions.

Writing or teaching about the subject of this book, the history of race, is no longer simply about the past; it is decidedly about our present. Yet it remains imperative to go back to the eighteenth century and even earlier to understand where the most dangerous idea ever invented came from.

Most people who have thought about the origins of race understand that it is deeply intertwined with two New World tragedies: the disenfranchisement and genocide of native populations and the importation of eleven million captives from West Africa to the New World, approximately 400,000 of whom landed in what is now the United States. Yet the complicated story of race is more than a centuries-long European conspiracy to justify empire and chattel slavery, as useful as the concept itself proved to be in both cases.[2]

I first became interested in this complex history when I was a graduate student at New York University during the mid-1990s. I realized then as I do now that one of the reasons that so few people are familiar with this story is because the subject is so mind-spinningly complicated. To begin with, the origins of what would become Europe's understanding of race are scattered throughout history. The first traces of this concept emerged from earlier eras, for a variety of reasons, and from a number of decidedly nonscientific sources. There are proto-biological notions related to race in writings from classical antiquity, in the Bible, in the medieval- and Renaissance-era blood laws used to chase the Jews out of Portugal, in the papal decrees regarding the enslavement of non-Christian peoples, and in the categorization of various “interracial” combinations in Spanish *casta* paintings. There are also non-European sources that filtered into this genealogy, among them Arabic writings that came into being alongside the trans-Saharan slave trade. Suffice it to say that what now functions as race in our collective consciousness stems from a variety of sources, many of which are lost in the sands of time.

What happened in eighteenth-century Europe, however, deserves particular attention. As Christianity’s hold on the human story began to falter, secular thinkers raised new questions about humankind’s differences in a range of settings, from medical schools and anatomical theaters to royally sanctioned research academies and the great universities of Scotland and Germany. By the end of the century, scientific inquiry had radically reshaped what it meant to be human. The xenophobia of the past, once based largely on anecdote or religious prejudice, gave way to anatomical “data,” deterministic sociological theories, and racial taxonomies that assigned entire populations to specific stages of development. What we now know as *race*, in short, came about in large part because of the institutions and methods invented by the Enlightenment.

The specificity of the eighteenth century, however, was not limited to the creation of racialized ideas themselves. It was also about how and to what extent these ideas were disseminated. If, by 1710 or 1720, discussions related to the emerging idea of race were confined largely to elites, by 1800 these same ideas had seeped into school curricula, geography manuals for children, works of natural history for a general public, women’s magazines, and novels. In fact, increased literacy was arguably the Enlightenment era’s greatest race maker. The more progressive a country’s educational policies, the more people were exposed to this pernicious and seemingly scientific concept.[3]

Tracking the idea of race as it evolved in various spheres of thought is perhaps the most logical way to tell this story. I have done so myself in two previous books. Several years ago, however, I concluded that I might be able to write a more accessible history by embedding the story in a group biography—by plunging into the lives and (often messy) psychologies of the people who actually *made* race. The result of such a project, I thought, might read more like a novel than a textbook.

When I pitched this idea to a friend, she suggested that each one of my chapters feature a "people–idea," a biography-driven segment that would bring to life the person and the specific concept related to race for which they were responsible.[4] This became the main conceit of the book. The characters in this book are more than simply individuals: They are also stand-ins for the wide range of theorists who helped fashion race during the Enlightenment, among them travel writers, natural historians, climate theorists, anatomists, skull-measuring quacks, classifiers, jurists, planters, kings, ministers, and presidents.

In *Biography of a Dangerous Idea*, I have chosen to chronicle the lives and evolving ideas of thirteen individuals, all of whom contributed in specific ways to the birth of race as a concept. The first figure is the most famous of French kings, Louis XIV, the seventeenth-century monarch and empire builder who commissioned the sixty-article set of slave laws known as *Le Code Noir* (1685) for his Caribbean colonies.[5] The second is a French Dominican priest and sugar plantation manager whose published account of African chattel slavery in the Caribbean became one of the most important sources of African ethnography during much of the eighteenth century.

I focus on France and France's overseas slave colonies in the early part of the book for several reasons. In addition to the fact that France's population had reached 22 million in 1700 — it was almost three times larger than that of either Great Britain or Spain — the country became the breeding ground for some of the most important developments in racial thinking. The first was the classification of the human species; the second the theory that a prototype race "degenerated" into all of humankind's varieties, or *races*.

From France, the book moves on, much like the concept of race itself, to other countries and thinkers: to Uppsala, Sweden, and the inventor of the term *Homo sapiens*, Carl Linnaeus; to Edinburgh where an astonishing group of men including David Hume, Adam Smith, Lord Kames, and William Robertson began dividing up humankind in terms of stages of development; and to Prussia and the Electorate of Hanover where Immanuel Kant and Johann Frederich Blumenbach were defining and debating the notion of race as never before. The final chapter brings us to Virginia in the 1780s, where Thomas Jefferson — the architect of American democracy, budding anthropologist, and future president of the United States — confronted the fundamental contradiction between universal human rights and what he believed to be the unfortunate liabilities of the "Black race." Jefferson is the capstone to this story and this book: He embodies both the lofty ideals of the high Enlightenment and the more brutal, clinical, and economic-based notions of race emerging in the nineteenth century.

The story that I tell in *Biography of a Dangerous Idea* is admittedly an example of what is sometimes called "top-down" history, focusing as it does primarily on the ideas and the experiences of influential philosophers, naturalists, and politicians. My intention, however, is not to produce glorified portraits of these men. Throughout the book I have tried to engage with their legacies —

good and bad—with honesty and unflinching clarity. I have also tried to remind readers that these same Enlightenment-era individuals not only helped transform the world's peoples into "races," but the fates of these same "races" as well. Ironically enough, it is Voltaire who perhaps best sums up the reason for a book dedicated to the history of race and, ultimately, its casualties: "To the living we owe respect, to the dead, however, we owe only the truth."[6]

A NOTE ON LANGUAGE

More than most academic subjects, the history of race requires careful explanation and occasional caveats. One key point involves the term *race* itself. Despite its widespread use, there is no scientific basis for identifying distinct racial categories through the study of DNA or genes. Since the 1970s, geneticists have emphasized that individuals grouped under the same racial label often differ more genetically from each other than from members of other groups. This fact creates an inherent paradox: While the concept of race has no biological foundation, its social and political effects are as real and measurable as any other concrete reality.

In addition to clarifying here what *race* is and is not, I would also like to explain what language I chose to describe the actors who were involved in this book. When I first began writing about the topic two decades ago — it was then a lonely field — most scholars did not shy away from citing the often-wounding language of the past. The approach was much more dispassionate, even though the history never was.

In *Biography of a Dangerous Idea*, I have decided to avoid or to paraphrase the worst of eighteenth-century epithets in both my text and in my translations. I do not think the reader will lose anything as a result. This said, it is also true that, at times, I occasionally conjure up the point of view of a European taxonomist or Caribbean planter by strategically using an eighteenth-century term—the word "slave" for example—as opposed to "enslaved African." Likewise, and once again depending on the context and the flow of ideas, I sometimes use a term such as "plantation owner" as opposed to the now more generally accepted term of "enslaver." I hope that it will be clear that my intention is neither to diminish the plight of the enslaved nor to somehow valorize the enslaver. My objective in such instances is to bring the reader back to a time when language reflected a very different political reality in the Atlantic world.

This brings me to the related question of capitalization, specifically how to capitalize the categories to which certain individuals belong. Style guides are divided on the subject. The American Psychological Association argues that adjectives such as *Black* and *White* when transformed into nouns, e.g., *Blacks* or *Whites*, should be capitalized like any other group, e.g., Native Americans. The same guide also recommends that adjectives modifying any given group, e.g., "White people" or "Black people," should also be capitalized as a matter of respect for all racial and ethnic groups. This generates uncontroversial sentences such as: "There are White and Black people living on the same city block." It can also lead to curious sentences: "In the United States, we find Black people, Black workers, White workers, and White supremacists." Other style guides argue that only *Black* should be capitalized as either a noun or an adjective because it is a distinct cultural and perhaps even global identity, whereas *white* should not be capitalized because it does not have the same conceptual coherence. The problem with such an approach in *this* book is that, when an eighteenth-century writer such as Thomas Jefferson refers to "whites," he is certainly conjuring a global and biological identity. According to certain style guides, this would merit a capital *W*.

Because this book moves across time periods, cultures, and geographical spaces — reconstructing the beliefs of a wide range of individuals in the process — I've chosen the terminology that, to my mind, makes the most consistent and meaningful sense. All ethnic groups referred to by adjectives of color are capitalized, e.g., Blacks, Whites, Amerindians, etc. When racial "colors" are used as adjectives, most prominently where authors are speaking about "white" skin or "black" skin and not *people qua people*, I have decided to use lower case. This rule generates word groupings such as "black resistance" and "white flight." When these same "color" adjectives are referring specifically to people, e.g., a "Black writer," or a "White politician," they are again capitalized. I have followed this format even when quoting from eighteenth-century texts, which are, on the whole, quite inconsistent on this matter.

Two final caveats. In a book with so many different thinkers and translations, I have not maintained eighteenth-century spelling, even when quoting from, for example, Robert Pierce Forbes's meticulous edition of Thomas Jefferson's *Notes on the State of Virginia*. The second forewarning has to do with anachronistic vocabulary. Purists who balk at anachronism will see that I sometimes use words that did not exist during the eighteenth century. I have sometimes availed myself of the word *science*, for example, to refer to a series of practices that were more generally described as natural philosophy or natural history during the eighteenth century. I also use the word *anthropology*, which began taking on its current meaning in Germany in the 1770s and only came into being as a "science" in the nineteenth century, to conjure up the general study of the human species (albeit often undertaken without any real contact with the actual peoples being "studied"). My final bit of shorthand is occasionally using words such as *ethnography* and *biology*, even though these concepts did not yet really exist in the eighteenth century. Suffice to say that these terms are intended to invoke the concepts, ideas, and methods that we now know by other names.

PART ONE

RACE BEFORE THE ADVENT OF RACE

The principal object of the . . . colonies
must be the glory of God.
—FATHER JEAN-BAPTISTE DU TERTRE,
Histoire générale des Antilles, 1654

The inhabitants of [Barbados] may be ranged
under three heads or sorts, to wit, Masters
(which are English, Scotch, and Irish,
with some few Dutch, French, and Jews),
Christian Servants, and Negro-Slaves. . . . The *Masters*,
for the most part, live at the height of pleasure.
—RICHARD BLOME,
A Description of the Island of Jamaica, 1672

I

LOUIS XIV AND JEAN-BAPTISTE COLBERT; DETAIL FROM PAINTING BY HENRI TESTELIN, AFTER CHARLES LE BRUN; 1667–1670

LOUIS XIV: KING OF THE SLAVES

On April 30, 1681, Louis XIV of France began his day as he always did, with the meticulously orchestrated ritual of *le petit lever*—the royal *rise from bed*. Once the "First Doctor" and "First Surgeon" had confirmed that the king was in good health, the officers of the bedchamber fastidiously washed, shaved, and dressed the forty-two-year-old monarch. Louis then sat down to a small bowl of soup, after which his wig master secured a towering mass of human hair atop his head to hide his premature baldness. By ten o'clock, cane in hand, he stepped out of his private quarters into a grand antechamber where dozens of lingering aristocrats awaited him, applauding his every movement.[1]

The remainder of the day followed a similarly regimented pattern. At midmorning, the king attended mass in Versailles's chapel, where the liturgy was interspersed with Gregorian chants and motets or other choral compositions.[2] He then returned to his chamber to confer briefly on religious matters before sitting down to a prodigious meal that typically featured a large plate of salad, a spicy soup, and sweetmeats.[3] After this midday "dinner," he escaped from the château for some blood sport. Mounting one of his 200 horses, he set off with his hunting party into the forests of Versailles in pursuit of pheasant, deer, and boar. By midafternoon, he returned to the council chambers reeking of horse and gunpowder. Waiting for him there, with several files related to France's overseas colonies, was his comptroller general, Jean-Baptiste Colbert (1619–1683).

COLBERT, PAINTING BY PHILIPPE DE CHAMPAIGNE, 1655

Colbert, the son of a clothing manufacturer from Reims, had risen to become the king's chief minister and Secretary of the Navy—the second most powerful man in France. By 1681, this long-serving policymaker was juggling a seemingly impossible array of responsibilities. In addition to overseeing the construction of Versailles, which was then entering a particularly crucial phase, he was also managing France's manufacturing sector, the country's colonial policy, and the kingdom's labyrinthine finances. The many oil paintings of Colbert that date from this era, most of which he probably commissioned, tend to emphasize his soft, cowlike eyes and disarming smile. These images, however, reveal nothing of his crushing workload. In truth, they present a misleading portrait of the man, one that belies the most single-minded and, at times, ruthless administrator in Louis XIV's government.[4]

During his meeting with the king on this Saturday afternoon, Colbert brought up a series of pressing issues related to France's colonies in the Caribbean. Managing these island settlements from 4,000 miles away tended to be exasperating, especially given how long it took to communicate with colonial administrators. When Colbert and the king sent a letter to Martinique or Guadeloupe, this same royal dispatch would first be carried by courier to either Saint-Malo, La Rochelle, or Nantes. At this point, it was entrusted to a ship captain who, once he made his way across the Atlantic, would deliver the document to the intended recipient. Responses from the islands retraced the same route; in all, an exchange of letters took four to five months.

When Colbert had first begun serving the king in the early 1660s, much of this day-to-day administration had not been under the direct supervision of the crown. In 1664, in fact, Colbert himself had delegated the oversight of France's New World colonies in Canada, Acadia, Newfoundland, and the Caribbean to a new business syndicate called the *Compagnie française des Indes occidentales* (French West India Company).[5] The hope had been that the *Compagnie* would soon become the "Master of the Atlantic," the dominant force from Canada to the Caribbean.[6] Ten years later, the debt-ridden trade syndicate was in such turmoil that Colbert and Louis assumed direct control of the French islands. It was only then the two men were wholly involved in solving an enormous array of maddening "Caribbean" problems, among them the constant threat of attack from France's Protestant rivals, tensions between colonists and the crown's administrators, and, perhaps above all, making sure that the colonies had enough laborers.

THE LARGE ISLANDS OF CUBA, JAMAICA, HISPANIOLA, AND PUERTO RICO, AND THE "LESSER ANTILLES" INCLUDING GUADELOUPE, MARTINIQUE, AND BARBADOS; C. 1680

Securing enough workers for the islands had been a challenge since Louis XIV's father (Louis XIII) and Cardinal Richelieu first decided to send colonists to Saint-Christopher, Guadeloupe, and Martinique to cultivate tobacco and cotton in the 1630s.[7] To address this problem during these early years of colonization, plantation owners and investors had hired shipping agents and labor recruiters to lure the urban poor (and sometimes petty criminals) to the islands with the promise of a small plot of land in exchange for three years of hard labor.[8] During the 1640s and 1650s, these so-called *engagés*, or indentured servants, who came from French port cities such as Nantes, La Rochelle, Bordeaux, or Dieppe, crammed themselves into merchant ships by the hundreds.[9] Once they arrived on plantations, they often worked side-by-side with enslaved Africans who had been purchased from Dutch traders in exchange for twenty or twenty-five bales of tobacco.[10] The punishing life of the *slave* and the *engagé* during these years was quite similar with one major exception: The suffering of the indentured servant was a contractual obligation limited to a specific duration.

Colbert and Louis XIV were facing a dramatically altered labor situation in 1681. The number of French farmhands or laborers willing to relocate to the islands as indentured servants had dropped off precipitously, largely because so many of the plantations were being converted to sugarcane. Reports coming back from the colonies were hardly reassuring: Sugar production was significantly more dangerous than cultivating crops such as tobacco. The cane fields were notorious for harboring deadly *fer-de-lance* snakes (*Bothrops* vipers) that lay coiled and ready to strike at ankle level.[11] And sugarcane was not a delicate flowering plant; it was a towering, dense grass, with thick, razor-sharp stalks that were difficult to cut and even harder to carry. The worst stage of sugar production, people said, took place in the mill, once the harvested stalks were hauled back to the plantation. There, workers had to feed the cane by hand into a pair of massive vertical rollers, a task that could cost them an arm or, in some cases, their life.

Not surprisingly, during the progressive conversion to sugarcane, many of the indentured servants who had finished their three-year contracts in the French islands returned to the mainland or left for other islands in the Caribbean.[12] The demographic shifts that took place in Martinique were telling. In 1664 there were approximately 1,500 White men directly involved in agricultural production on the island. Fifteen years later, when far more of

Martinique was under active cultivation for sugarcane, this number had dropped by twenty percent, to 1,200.[13]

French planters, eager to replace indentured servants with a far larger and permanently enslaved workforce, repeatedly appealed to the French crown. In 1673, Colbert and Louis XIV responded to this "need" by chartering a new trading company—the *Compagnie du Sénégal*—tasked primarily with transporting significantly more African captives to the French islands.[14] Between 1678 and 1679, French ships carried almost 4,000 slaves to the Caribbean, mainly to Martinique.[15] Louis and Colbert recognized this as the dawn of a new era. From the halls of the Louvre or Versailles, they were engineering the same demographic transformation that had already reshaped other Caribbean islands, Barbados in particular. Barbados, in fact, had foreshadowed the future of all the major sugar islands. As early as 1640, planters on the English island had purchased 6,400 slaves; by 1681, the enslaved population had swollen to 38,000 while the number of White indentured servants had plummeted to the point where the ratio of indentured servants to slaves stood at 1:12.[16]

As chief finance minister and architect of France's commercial policies, Colbert knew that larger and larger enslaved populations in the French colonies were key to improving France's maritime and, by extension, domestic economy. The advantages began with the trade in humans itself. Although transporting captives across the Atlantic had enormous risks for investors, crew, and especially Africans—up to fifteen percent of the captives perished on board—the sale of the surviving slaves in the Caribbean sometimes doubled or tripled the initial outlay.[17] The real profits, however, only began after these African men, women, and children were incorporated into plantation workforces. Enslaved laborers became the means of production for a range of precious colonial commodities: not only sugar, but also ginger root, achiote spice, cocoa, indigo, coffee beans, and cotton. These commodities, which were exported to French ports, then passed through royal customs houses, where import levies filled the royal coffers.

Benefits of the colonial enterprise extended to the manufacturing sector as well. Port cities such as Bordeaux were receiving, refining, and ultimately re-exporting a range of colonial goods at significant profit throughout France and the rest of Europe. Equally important, entirely new industries and factories were coming into existence in order to create the goods needed to supply the colonies themselves, or to be bartered in Africa for slaves. As early as 1670, Colbert had trumpeted the fact that there was "no business in the world that produces as many advantages as the trade in Negroes."[18]

It should be pointed out that neither Colbert nor Louis was under any illusion regarding the type of slavery that they were encouraging on the islands. Even their own colonial administrators sometimes recoiled at the horror of what was transpiring on Caribbean plantations. In 1672, the Governor-General of the French Islands informed Colbert that there was something profoundly un-Christian about a form of agricultural production that relied on a population of ill-fed and overworked Africans: "I have a great deal of difficulty in the matter of carrying out your orders, for slaves are human beings," he wrote, "and human beings should not be reduced to a state that is worse than that of beasts."[19] For Colbert, at least, the tremendous economic advantages of African chattel slavery trumped such moral considerations.

LOUIS AND SLAVERY C. 1680

Despite the economic benefits of slavery, the status of France's enslaved workforce in the Caribbean remained something of a nagging philosophical and religious problem for Louis during the 1670s and early 1680s. For centuries, France had prided itself on a longstanding antislavery tradition that maintained that, within its own territory at least, slavery and serfdom were not permitted. This belief had been sanctified in 1315, when King Louis X signed letters patent that forever associated the words *French* and *France* with *free* and the eradication of slavery.

According to this so-called Free Soil principle, any bonded person who set foot in French territory was decreed as free. This doctrine had been put to the test on several occasions, most famously in 1571, when a Norman ship captain returning from West Africa attempted to sell a cargo of African captives in the port city of Bordeaux. The city's *parlement*, which was scandalized at the audacity of the trader, ordered that the slaves be freed, and the owner of the African captives arrested.[20] The ruling of the parlement was unequivocal: "France, the mother of liberty, does not permit any slaves."[21]

There was one telling exception to the Free Soil principle, however. To man the huge galley warships that Louis needed to patrol the Mediterranean, he relied on forced labor provided by thousands of decidedly unfree *galériens*, galley slaves who spent most of their lives chained to the oars of his southern fleet.[22] Maintaining an army of domestic slaves in a country without slavery, as it turned out, was surprisingly easy to justify. When pressed, the crown explained that it was simply respecting a longstanding Mediterranean tradition. As the Minister of the French Navy put it in 1694, the Free Soil principle did not apply to the Muslims, Turks, and Black Africans serving in the galleys because "they were purchased in foreign countries [i.e., North Africa] where this kind of commerce is established."[23] As for the other French-born *galériens* who did not benefit from the rule — Jews, rogue Protestants, prisoners of war, and criminals who were sentenced to hard labor — it was said that they had simply lost their rights. This was also the case for a shipload of thirty-six rebellious Iroquois warriors who, during the 1680s, were dispatched (in irons) from Montreal to Marseille to spend the rest of their lives — rarely more than ten years — rowing for Louis XIV.[24]

While Louis lost no sleep regarding the legality and morality of enslaving his *galériens*, what he and his entourage thought about Black Africans was more complicated. One can make an educated guess about how the inhabitants of Versailles envisioned most Africans by consulting the 1658 *Le Monde, ou Géographie universelle* (The world, or a universal geography), which was written by the king's friend and personal geographer, Pierre Duval, for the instruction of the dauphin.

In the section dedicated to sub-Saharan Africa, Duval explains that the inhabitants of this part of the world are backward, that the men are polygamists, that the women are licentious, and that, more often than not, these godless people worship snakes and fetishes. As a supplement to this prejudicial "ethnography," which came primarily from traders and European missionaries, Duval also added the opinions of French plantation owners living in the Caribbean. This Caribbean-derived information evaluated several African ethnicities according to their uses and most suitable roles in a plantation setting:

> The Negroes [of Senegal] are very robust, and are therefore sold more than others. Those of Guinea are very good, but they are not as strong; this is why we make them domestic servants. Those from Angola are used to cultivate the land because of their strength. It is said that whoever wants to best draw service from his Negro, must give him a lot to eat, a lot of work, and many lashes.[25]

Such was the worldview that was circulating at Versailles in the 1670s and 1680s, and not only during tutoring sessions with the dauphin. As France's Caribbean territories evolved from a series of tiny outposts into one of the cornerstones of its empire, Louis and his ministers fully absorbed the vocabulary and the mindset of both slave trader and plantation owner. This was reflected in the way that the term "Negro" was increasingly being used throughout Europe. If the word *nègre* (the French equivalent of "Negro") had long indicated a dark-skinned inhabitant of sub-Saharan Africa, it was progressively becoming synonymous with that of *slave* as well. This enormously significant and seemingly racialized connotation would soon appear in the era's dictionaries.[26]

VERSAILLES IN 1682, ENGRAVING

There were surely many times at Versailles where Louis XIV and his entourage envisioned all Black Africans as potential commodities, as little more than the tools necessary to accomplish

France's colonial aspirations. And yet, there were also numerous instances during his reign where Louis, in his capacity as steward of France's foreign policy and trade in Africa, interacted with shrewd African rulers and diplomats, not only via his emissaries in West Africa, but also in France. In 1669, King Tezifon of Allada, who had heard of King Louis of France from representatives of the Compagnie des Indes, sent an emissary named Mattéo Lopes to Paris to meet the French monarch.[27]

DOM MATHEO LOPES, AMBASSADOR FOR THE KING OF ALLADA; ENGRAVING BY NICOLAS DE LARMESSIN; 1690

As was generally the case for anyone in Africa wishing to travel to Europe, Lopes was obliged to first travel to the Antilles before going back to France. In his case, he traveled on a ship called the *Concorde* carrying 432 African captives, 100 of whom died and were unceremoniously thrown into the ocean during the crossing.[28]

There is no record of what Lopes, his three wives, and his three children thought about this.

After recrossing the Atlantic, and finally arriving in Dieppe in December of 1669, Lopes was received with the pomp and circumstance reserved for any other foreign dignitary. This initial welcome was followed by the journey to Paris in a luxury carriage drawn by six horses financed by the *Compagnie*. On the day that he finally met the king at the Tuileries Palace, he was greeted by an honor guard composed of Louis XIV's Swiss and French regiments.[29] Such meetings were not altogether unusual. In both 1672 and 1686, the king of Commanda (present-day Ghana) also dispatched embassies to France to discuss new trade agreements with the French crown.[30]

The one African that Louis ultimately came to know better than all others was a man named Aniaba, the purported king of Issiny (a portion of Côte d'Ivoire), who arrived in France in 1688.[31] Aniaba became a favorite of Louis's second wife, Madame de Maintenon, and ultimately spent quite a bit of time at Versailles. Although scholars now assert that Aniaba may not have been a king's son at all, Louis not only attended Aniaba's baptism in 1691; he also granted the African "prince" a position in a royal calvary in Picardie with a (substantial) annual pension of 12,000 livres.[32] According to a report in the 1701 *Mercure de France*, Louis had even supposedly declared to Aniaba that "there is no more difference between you and me than black from white."[33] Behind all these honors, of course, were the king's strategic interests in Africa. It is quite reasonable to assume, although there is no proof, that Louis believed that Aniaba's eventual return to Africa might allow the French to establish another trading fort on an area of the coast whose slaves, according to the era's "ethnography," were believed to be the most productive in the field.[34]

FRANÇOISE-MARIE DE BOURBON, ILLEGITIMATE DAUGHTER OF LOUIS XIV, WITH HER PAGE; PAINTING BY PHILIPPE VIGNON; C. 1690

Visiting African dignitaries or princes were not the only Black people that Louis came to know during his reign. Among the thousands of servants who roamed the corridors of the Louvre or Versailles were a number of Black or mixed-race pages, footmen, and ladies' maids. Some of the king's royal family, in fact, had readily adopted the Spanish fashion of acquiring African *négrillons*—literally "small Negroes"—who became living symbols of the power and prestige of their masters. Most famously, Louis's first wife, Marie-Thérèse of Spain, was offered a young twelve- or thirteen-year-old "dwarf moor" named Nabo as a wedding present. Taken from his home in Dahomey (Benin), Nabo reportedly became a great source of amusement for the queen, generally hovering about her and entertaining her with his miniature guitar.[35]

The time that the queen spent with this young boy, who was said to be as beautiful as he was short, actually led to an unfounded rumor. According to some of the court's more *nasty tongues*, the queen had become so embittered with Louis's philandering that she had taken her teenage page as a lover and gave birth to a mixed-race baby girl in November of 1664. Those who were in attendance at the birth (these were semipublic events) were supposedly shocked to see the dark complexion of the queen's love child. To avoid scandal, the story went, Louis's valet Alexandre Bontemps purportedly whisked the queen's baby off to a Benedictine abbey outside of Paris, where she grew up as the so-called Mauresse of Moret Convent. That this dark-skinned nun (who actually existed) was somehow directly related to the royal family was given more credence in the early 1680s when the young woman, who formally took her vows, chose as her new name *Sister Louise Marie de Sainte-Thérèse* — a highly unusual combination of the king's and queen's first names.[36]

LOUISE MARIE DE SAINTE-THÉRÈSE, OR THE BLACK NUN OF MORET-SUR-LOING; PAINTING; SEVENTEENTH CENTURY

Most of Sister Louis Marie's life is shrouded in mystery due to the fact that her file at the convent has been extensively redacted. What the file does reveal is that the nun received a lifelong royal pension from the crown and regularly received visitors from Versailles, including Queen Marie-Thérèse, the princes, and on at least one occasion, the king himself.[37] And yet, more likely than not, the diminutive Nabo was not the father of this young nun, nor was the queen her mother. The more probable story is that Louis himself was the father of this child. One theory has it that the mother of this mixed-race nun had originally been hired by the king's theater troupe at the Louvre to play the role of the *sauvage* (probably with pseudo-African or pseudo-Amerindian music) in various plays or ballets.[38] And like many of the women who worked in the Louvre palace in the 1660s, she perhaps — whether by her own choice or coercion, or some combination thereof — found herself in the royal bedchamber.

What exactly Louis himself thought about Black people, in short, was shaped by the conventions and contradictions of his time. At the Louvre or Versailles, blackness was not a fixed category, but a fluid identity shaped by social class, religion, geopolitics, and economics, not to mention the king's libido. To the extent that a vague concept of race may have existed in Louis's mind in the 1680s, such ideas had nothing to do with biological determinism or racial classification.

During the 1680s, the most important factor related to the conceptual shift that Africans were undergoing was the simple fact that certain types of work were increasingly being mapped onto certain types of bodies.[39] How to manage this example of "race" before the advent of a truly biological understanding of the human species generated a five-year debate at Versailles. The legally binding document that resulted from these deliberations, the so-called *Code Noir*, would become the most famous of the era's European slave laws.

NEW WORLD BLACK CODES

Among the many letters that Louis hated receiving from his administrators in the colonies, few were as disturbing as those that conjured up the potential violence simmering among France's enslaved populations. As the ratio of Blacks to White colonists continued to increase during the 1670s, Louis and Colbert heard more and more about sabotaged equipment, work slowdowns, and the fact that some mothers practiced infanticide in order to save their offspring from a life of slavery. The greatest fear was, of course, the possibility of a murderous uprising or revolt that would not only scare off potential colonists but interfere with the colonial enterprise as a whole. In early 1679, Colbert and the king were informed that a large group of slaves had revolted in Martinique. In the same letter, the then governor, Count Charles de Courbon de Blénac, reassured the king that a dozen or so slaves had been shot and killed during the uprising, and another nine had been tortured and killed publicly, either by hanging or being broken on the wheel.[40]

Well before the 1670s, the Spanish and the English—with far larger slave-based colonies in the New World—had already faced such rebellions. The Spanish, who had imported approximately 300,000 enslaved Africans to their colonies in Mexico, Peru, Central America, and the Caribbean, had responded to such perils by establishing overseas militias and, when necessary, sending more troops. By the early sixteenth century, the Spanish government had also created slave laws that not only restricted the movement and autonomy of their Black populations in colonial America, but prescribed specific punishments for particular offenses.[41]

The British had followed suit. As early as 1636, only a few years after the first forests in Barbados had been cleared for cotton and tobacco, the Barbados Council instituted the first rules of conduct for enslaved Africans in the Caribbean. In addition to enumerating a list of infractions and punishments for the enslaved population, the English island's council took one of the first steps toward creating something approaching a theory of racial distinction by separating the islands' populations on the basis of their color and political status. Whites and White indentured servants were deemed free, whereas Africans and Indians were described as having one sole function: "to be sold" and serve their masters "for life."[42]

Twenty-five years later, the members of the Colonial Legislature of Barbados instituted an even more comprehensive codification of African enslavement, the 1661 "Act for the better ordering and governing of Negroes." Designed to regulate the relations between the comparatively small society of White colonists and a swelling population of enslaved Africans who were "prone to escape and revolt," the so-called Barbados Code listed a series of "objectionable" behaviors alongside the horrific punishments — whipping, branding, and nose slitting — that such offenses incurred. The language of the document, which soon was adopted (and adapted) in other slave-based colonies, including Virginia, also hinted at a further step in the human categorization of slaves and non-slaves. According to the act, Blacks were described as both heathens and slaves who were somehow zoologically or biologically different from their White masters. They were, as the document put it, a "heathenish brutish and . . . uncertain dangerous pride of people."[43] The word *pride*, generally used to refer to a group of animals, is one of the more telling precursors to a biological understanding of race.

By late April 1681, Louis and Colbert had decided that the time had also come for France — the most populous country in Europe by a factor of three — to join their European rivals in standardizing codes of conduct governing "black" behavior on the French islands. While French planters had been given tacit permission to make use of slave labor in the islands beginning in the 1640s, it had been the colonists themselves who had instituted their own rules related to slave management.

To address this lapse in colonial administration, Louis and Colbert composed a letter on April 30 to the crown's so-called "Superintendent of Justice, Police, and Finances" in Martinique, Jean-Baptiste Patoulet. Their directive was straightforward. Patoulet was told to study the locally established practices and rules related to slavery in the French islands and report back to Versailles with recommendations related to a new "code of conduct" for the islands' slaves. The subjects that he was supposed to cover included "interdictions, punishments, as well as the safeguarding, policing, and legal treatment of this sort of people [Negroes]."[44] Versailles's objective was clear: putting a royal and legal stamp on the institution of French slavery.

Patoulet received the king's letter sometime in June 1681. As a seasoned colonial administrator who had already served in Acadia before coming to the Caribbean, he was well placed to think through and execute this multilayered task. In addition to serving as the president of the three French islands' so-called Sovereign Councils — the legislative law courts where all the local decrees concerning slavery had originated — Patoulet was already deeply involved in a range of slave-related matters, including auctions, censuses, punishment, and the "seasoning" of newly arrived Africans.[45] In fact, he was one of the few colonial officials in the French Caribbean who had invested his money directly in both sugar refineries and the slave trade itself.[46]

From Patoulet's point of view, the most difficult part of providing a blueprint for a new slave code was not the work itself;

it was the fact that Versailles had instructed him to work closely with the only man who outranked him in the Caribbean, the aforementioned Charles de Courbon de Blénac, Governor-General of the French Islands. Blénac was a bullheaded ex-military man known for being as truculent during periods of peace as he was during times of war.[47] Both Colbert and the king were well aware that the two administrators loathed each other, so Colbert sent a second letter to Blénac instructing him to cooperate fully with Patoulet on the draft of the slave code. To a certain extent (and for several months), this imposed truce worked. During the fall of 1681, the two men consulted plantation owners to determine what slaves ate (and did not), how they were punished, and whether they had been instructed in the Catholic religion or not. Patoulet and Blénac also pored over the sometimes-contradictory decrees related to slavery issued by the Sovereign Councils on the three major Caribbean islands. When it came time to make recommendations on a given subject, such as the punishment of slaves, Patoulet and Blénac agreed to list their dissenting opinions in separate columns.

Blénac, despite his belligerent reputation, actually favored a more "humane" form of slavery. He even suggested outlawing two particularly horrible punishments that were frequently used on French plantations: whipping slaves while they were hanging by their wrists or, even more horrifying, while they were suspended by all four members.[48] Blénac also had a more lenient view of miscegenation. From his point of view, Whites producing mixed-race children with the Black population was not only inevitable given the demographics on the islands; it was perhaps necessary.

Patoulet disagreed with both these proposals. As someone with far more sympathy for the planters themselves, he saw no reason to abandon what he believed to be an effective means of discipline. He also asserted that Black–White coupling was an abomination.[49]

Patoulet and Blénac nonetheless jointly signed off on a preliminary report in December 1681. The resulting document then made its way to Versailles for review and revision by the king and Colbert, presumably during the spring or summer of 1682.[50] This timetable, however, was upended by a strange twist of fate. Sometime during the first months of 1682, Blénac discovered that Patoulet had been illegally importing watches, clocks, mirrors, and barrels of beef to sell on his own behalf. Beside himself with glee, Blénac sanctimoniously informed Colbert and the king that their "superintendent" had committed the same sort of unpardonable offense that he was supposed to be policing![51] Upon hearing this news in July of 1682, Colbert sent off a letter relieving Patoulet of his responsibilities. He also informed Blénac that he was naming Michel Bégon, who happened to be Colbert's first cousin on his wife's side, as the new superintendent.

Bégon arrived in Martinique sometime in the fall of 1682. Some six months later, the new superintendent and Blénac collaborated on a more polished version of the slavery-related document that comprised fifty suggested articles or rules related to slavery. While this second set of recommendations varied little from what Patoulet and Blénac had produced the previous year, by the time that this new document reached Versailles (in the spring of 1683), the atmosphere at the château had undergone a significant political shift, a shift that would have a measurable effect on the final form of France's slave code.

To begin with, the man who would have doubtless crafted the final language of the slave laws, the long-serving chief minister Jean-Baptiste Colbert, had both fallen gravely ill and, to a certain extent, out of favor with the king.[52] After Colbert died in September 1683, the king divided up his enormous portfolio among several ministers, including Colbert's own son, Seignelay. None of these administrators, however, would have the same influence with the king that the elder Colbert had enjoyed.

The vacuum created by Colbert's death also coincided with the beginning of a far more religiously conservative period in Louis's XIV's life. Perhaps no other event was more telling in this respect than the king's decision to marry the exceedingly devout Marquise de Maintenon in a secret ceremony sometime in October 1683.[53] Foregoing the type of politically advantageous wedding that was customary among European monarchs, Louis instead entered into the first monogamous relationship in his life, in part so that he could consummate the bond.[54] Gone were the days when his court was a pleasure palace of extravagant clothing, culture, and sexual excess, where his own cavorting had resulted in at least a dozen illegitimate children.[55] Gone also were the days when a man like Colbert could convince the king to look beyond spiritual priorities in the interest of the nation and the economy. Religion, as one courtier put it about this era, had become the fashion at Versailles. So had rooting out disorderly behavior, blasphemy, sodomy, prostitution, and gambling, many of which had been popular pastimes at Versailles.[56]

During the post-Colbert years, Louis had also decided to let nothing stand between him and his dream of ruling over a truly Catholic nation, a land defined by "*une foi, une loi, un roi*" (one faith, one law, one king). The most reckless decision along these lines came in October 1685, when Louis signed the so-called Edict of Fontainebleau (better known as the Revocation of the Edict of Nantes). This infamous document, which nullified the longstanding policy of religious tolerance toward nearly a million French Huguenots, sanctioned a two-pronged campaign of terror throughout the kingdom. In the weeks after the royal edict went into effect, the French army began razing Protestant houses of worship and padlocking Huguenot schools. A far more insidious form of terrorism was also delegated to roving bands of armed dragoons, who broke into Protestant households and presented their inhabitants with a choice: convert or go into exile. Though fleeing the country was later forbidden on pain of death, over the course of the next two decades, hundreds of thousands of French Protestants boarded ships and fled to neighboring Protestant countries.

CODE NOIR,
OU
RECUEIL D'EDITS,
DÉCLARATIONS ET ARRETS
CONCERNANT
Les Eſclaves Négres de l'Amérique,
AVEC
Un Recueil de Réglemens, concernant la police des Iſles Françoiſes de l'Amérique & les Engagés.

A PARIS,
Chez les LIBRAIRES ASSOCIEZ.
M. DCC. XLIII.

THE *CODE NOIR*, 1743 EDITION

In March 1685, a few months before Louis ordered the wholesale persecution of French Protestants, he also put his big looping signature on the so-called *Ordonnance* related to management of the slaves in the French islands. This set of regulations, which ultimately came to be known both familiarly and officially as the *Code Noir*, or *Black Code*, had as much to do with the king's aspirations to become Europe's foremost Catholic monarch as it did with the welfare and punishment of enslaved Africans. Rare indeed are the documents that reflect such a curious admixture of royal authority, New World capitalism, and supposedly irreproachable religious duty.

THE CODE OF RACE

The *Code Noir* made abundantly clear from the outset that the king's first priority was ridding the colonies of their undesirables. For years, Louis had heard from the islands' missionaries that the French colonies were polluted by a confusing mishmash of cultures and religions. The island of Martinique, as one Jesuit priest put it, was filled with "Portuguese, Castilians, Englishmen, Zealanders, Scots, Flemish, Dutch, Germans, Africans from almost the entire west coast of Africa, and [Native] Americans from both the islands and the northern and southern continent." The result, according to this same letter writer, was that Martinique had become an island of "atheists, idolaters, Jews, Lutherans, Huguenots."[57]

Among the different "types" of non-Catholics in the Caribbean, Louis had long been particularly keen on expelling the community of approximately 300 Sephardic Jews who had settled on Martinique after being driven out of the Dutch colony of Recife (Brazil) by the Portuguese in 1654.[58] Louis would surely have "purified" the colonies of this population by the late 1670s, had it not been for the ever-pragmatic Colbert, who had repeatedly convinced his king that it was not in the crown's economic interest to harass or expel these productive colonists, regardless of their religion.[59]

As the final form of the *Code Noir* took shape, however, Louis ordered that the very first of the document's regulations ban the Jews from the islands. Following up on a similar edict that he had already issued in 1683, the *Code*'s initial article stipulated that any remaining Jewish colonists "who had established residence" in the islands now had three months to leave. Having assured the forced departure of these so-called "declared enemies of Christianity" once and for all, the king then made use of the *Code* to target his other religious bugbears, the region's Protestants. Articles 3 and 4 of the *Code* outlawed any Protestant religious services, prohibited any slave from being instructed in a reformed religion, and, most effectively, barred any non-Catholic from getting married in the islands. The final disincentive to being a Protestant was the proviso that any children from a Catholic–Protestant marriage would be declared bastards.

In Louis's view, ridding the Caribbean of infidels was an essential step toward building a forward-looking empire sustained by an enslaved workforce of believers. Slavery, to his mind, was never separate from religion. From his earliest years as monarch, he had been taught that his late father had only allowed the presence of enslaved Africans on Saint-Christopher after being persuaded that slavery could serve a spiritual purpose: saving the souls of pagans. This logic not only shaped Louis's personal beliefs; it also became official policy, publicly endorsed by the crown's chief trade official in the widely circulated *Perfect Merchant* (1675):

> [The fate of Africans on our islands] appears inhuman to those who don't know that these poor people are idolatrous or Muslim, and that our Christian merchants, by buying them from their enemies, are saving them from a cruel slavery [in Africa. In the French islands, we] create a type of servitude for them that is not only more pleasant, but that provides them with knowledge of the real God, and the path to salvation thanks to the good instructions of the priests and clergy who take care to make them Christian.[60]

To ensure that this Christianization was carried out, the subsequent articles of the *Code* (many of which were based on existing practices) obliged slave owners to baptize Africans within eight days of their arrival in the islands and provide instruction in the Christian religion. Religious indoctrination even extended into the fields: Only Christian slave drivers—always of African descent—were supposed to oversee slave populations. In addition to facilitating Christianization throughout the plantation environment, the new *Code* was also designed to curb the depravity of colonial life, especially the dissolute sexual conduct of the slave owners. Theoretically, at least, White masters who had bastard children with enslaved women were to receive a heavy fine, and any resulting offspring were to be confiscated and sold by the authorities.

Louis also saw himself as a royal curb on abuse and neglect. He instructed the planter class to ensure that enslaved Africans in the French colonies had a modicum of basic necessities. Slave owners were ordered to provide a certain amount of clothing (two full sets or two meters of canvas each year) and food (cassava flour, salted beef, or fish) to each of their workers. Louis also forbade colonists from breaking up families and stipulated that sick or aged slaves should be properly cared for, receive last rites, and, if they were baptized, receive a proper burial in sacred ground. According to the *Code* (at least on paper), the king also allowed enslaved Africans to seek legal recourse against their masters if they were being mistreated. The 1685 version of the document even left open the possibility of proper Christian marriages between a free White man and his slave, in which case the enslaved woman would be manumitted and any resulting children similarly considered free and legitimate.

Well into the eighteenth century, most people looking back at Louis's decision to establish the *Code Noir* credited him with being the first great reformer of slavery, the author of "wise regulations" that were "made in favor of these miserable creatures."[61]

And yet, despite the fact that certain articles were theoretically designed to improve the lives of the enslaved, the vast majority of the *Code Noir* testifies vehemently against the supposed benevolence of its creators, not to mention the planters, missionaries, and administrators who had supplied much of its content. While the French slave laws—as they were written—implicitly rejected the single-minded mercantilism of the Barbados Code, the thrust of Louis's religion-inspired *Ordonnance* was nonetheless designed to assure the control and punishment of a society of enslaved humans through coercion, torture, and, in certain instances, murder. The long list of prescribed punishments began with some of the same penalties used in France for criminals. Slaves who gathered in a group or stole something were whipped or branded with the *fleur de lys*. Those who ran off and were subsequently captured, in addition to being branded, also had their ears cut off and, if they escaped again, their hamstring severed. Any slave who struck his or her master could be put to death.

As for the implementation of these supposedly compassionate laws, many—if not the majority—of French slave owners simply disregarded the parts of the *Code* that they found inopportune.[62] Punishments varied widely, religious instruction was generally spotty, and island planters, especially those who lived far from either legal or religious oversight, paid little attention to the sections of the *Code* that conferred limited legal rights to enslaved Africans.

Yet whether enforced or not, Louis's *Code Noir* nonetheless became the single most important testament to how the legal status of blackness was being codified within Europe's Caribbean colonies: as dehumanized, inheritable property. This was spelled out most starkly in Article 44, which clarified, once and for all, that slavery was a permanent political status passed on through the mother to her children.[63] In this sense, the real effect of the *Code*

Noir lay less in its day-to-day policing of island life than in its power to define the absolute authority of the enslaver over the enslaved.

THE KING'S CATHOLIC SLAVES

Versailles dispatched the first copies of the French slave code to Martinique in the summer of 1685. Soon thereafter it was ratified, copied, and sent to the other French islands in the lesser Antilles. Two years later, a similar adoption process took place in the burgeoning colony of Saint-Domingue (Haiti).[64] During the 1720s, versions of the slave laws also made their way beyond the islands of the Caribbean. In 1723, a revised *Code Noir* was endorsed on the islands of Mauritius and Bourbon (Réunion). The following year, the governing council in Louisiana approved a similar document.[65] As was the case with many such official documents, the edict was posted where everyone would see it, in each of the parish churches.

By the time that the *Code Noir* went into effect in New Orleans, Louis XIV had been dead for nine years. After serving as king for over seven decades, he had succumbed at Versailles to a slow and agonizing bacterial infection that had turned his leg black with gangrene. His legacy, by 1715, had darkened as well. Having been the most esteemed and feared monarch in European history, he had more recently suffered a series of stunning military defeats. In addition to a humiliating reversal in Siam (Thailand), France had recently lost the costly War of Spanish Succession (1702–1714), a confrontation which had demonstrated only too clearly that France's position as the dominant power in Europe was in jeopardy.[66]

Among the bright spots remaining in France's portfolio were its American colonies, especially those in the Caribbean. Saint-Domingue, in particular, stood on the verge of an astonishing cycle of growth that would lead to it becoming the most profitable colony in the world. Although Louis XIV did not live to see this day, he would likely have been flabbergasted by the future demographics of the French sugar islands.

PORTRAIT OF LOUIS XIV, WAX RELIEF BY ANTOINE BENOIST, C. 1705 (SEVEN YEARS BEFORE HIS DEATH)

When he and Colbert had first set out to codify slave laws for the colonies in the 1680s, fewer than 20,000 enslaved people lived under French rule. In 1715, the year of Louis's death, an additional 62,000 African captives had come under the *Code Noir*'s jurisdiction.[67] These figures, however, pale in comparison to the situation in 1848, when slavery was irrevocably abolished in the French colonies. By then — 163 years after Louis XIV signed the *Code Noir* — French ships had transported 1,200,000 Africans to overseas plantations. A quarter of a million were still alive and in bondage when freedom came.[68]

During his lifetime, Louis had envisioned slavery as involving *thousands* of people, not *millions*. And yet, he had also expected his *Code Noir* to provide a set of lasting directives for future generations, for the people whose lives would be affected by the institution of slavery in the years to come: not only French kings, French slave traders, and French plantation owners, but the as-yet unborn Africans who would serve out their lives on France's islands.

The so-called Sun King did not invent slavery. Nor did he believe that there was some specifically identifiable corporeal essence among Black Africans that justified their enslavement. Indeed, to the extent that the profoundly religious Louis XIV used the word *race*, he would have done so to refer to a family of horses or his own blue blood. Black Africans, by definition, were simply another branch of the larger human tree. They were a group of God's children that, as Louis had been told since childhood, had set off on their own after the ark landed in the Caucuses some 4,000 years before. The paradox of Louis XIV's worldview was that it had been Africans' very humanity—and their potential salvation—that had justified their enslavement and their suffering. Such was the supposedly noble intention of the *Code Noir.*

II

PORTRAIT OF FATHER LABAT, ENGRAVING, 1742

JEAN-BAPTISTE LABAT: THE PRIESTLY ETHNOGRAPHER

The state of the Negroes is much more miserable
than that of the indentured servant.
Not only because it is never-ending,
but because Negroes are subject to treatments
that would make nature herself tremble.
—Abbé Prévost, *Histoire générale des voyages*, 1747

In 1693, eight years after Louis XIV had put his signature on the *Code Noir*, a particularly bad outbreak of yellow fever cut a swath through the small population of Dominican missionaries living on the Caribbean island of Martinique.[1] Death did not come easily for the clergymen. As was often the case, once the mosquito-borne virus had taken hold in their systems, the men spent several days vomiting bile, shaking with chills, and bleeding from their eyes before they finally expired.[2]

Well before their funerals had been organized, the *Supérieur Général*, or head priest, of the island's Dominicans knew that their order was in crisis. Faced with the prospect of empty parish churches, he sent off a despairing plea for volunteers to his fellow Dominicans in France. This letter, which was copied and circulated among the order's convents, ultimately reached a restless thirty-year-old Parisian priest named Jean-Baptiste Labat.[3] Unlike most people who heard about the missionaries' plight, this tall, bully-faced clergyman decided that he was more than ready to trade his current responsibilities — teaching philosophy and mathematics to aspiring ecclesiastics — for the adventure and dangers of an island assignment. Much of this decision probably had to do with his thrill-seeking personality, which often seemed ill-suited to a man of the cloth.

Labat's voyage to the New World began in La Rochelle, one of several French ports from which merchant and warships sailed to the Caribbean islands. From the very first moment that he climbed down into the bobbing skiff that took him out to his ship, it was clear that he comported himself more like a soldier than a celebrant. Though he wore the long white cassock and black cape that signaled his membership in the Dominican order, he had a profoundly *earthly* energy. When his rowboat finally pulled up alongside the hull of the ship — a 115-foot merchantman named the *Loire* — the priest grabbed hold of the rope ladder and scampered up to the ship's deck.

Once on board, Labat marveled at the chaos. Along with all the merchandise, wine, hardware, tools, and food being lowered into the hold, there were thirty soldiers, eighty crew, and twenty-five paying passengers milling about. Space was tight. Though the priest was treated with more respect than other passengers, he was assigned a berth between two cannons. It was here that Labat stowed the trunk containing all the personal items that he would need during his time overseas. These included his vestments, a dark coat, six shirts, six pairs of underwear, twelve handkerchiefs, twelve bonnets, twelve canvas stockings, twelve socks, a hat, three pairs of shoes, and two shrouds to bury the dead. The rest of his personal affairs included books, journals, paper, pens, and two big jugs containing his allotment of liquor.[4]

Two hours after Labat came aboard, the captain gave the order to pull up anchor and head off to sea. The *Loire* was not permitted to make the crossing on its own. In the 1670s, Jean-Baptiste Colbert had enough of the Dutch and the English sinking or stealing French ships and ordered that all vessels crossing the Atlantic do so *en masse*. The *Loire* thus joined a squadron of thirty-seven other ships once it left port. By December, two of these ships had peeled off from the group and navigated toward the Straits of Gibraltar and the Mediterranean. About a week later, three so-called *négriers*, or slave ships — merchant vessels whose "tween decks" had been converted to carry African captives — sailed east toward the slave-trading island of Gorée, off the coast of Senegal. The *Loire* and the remainder of the fleet continued on toward the Caribbean, taking full advantage of the trade winds that had been propelling Europeans to the New World since the days of Columbus.

The priest was entering a perilous time in his life. Only a few days after the *Loire* had reached open sea, a lingering virus that had been bothering him in La Rochelle worsened to the point where the ship's surgeon believed that they would soon be "throwing [the priest's] body into the sea."[5] Labat ultimately recovered three weeks later, about the same time the ship sailed straight into a powerful gale that ripped the rudder clean off the *Loire*'s sister ship.

Labat learned a great deal about the dangers and cruelty of sea life during his crossing. In early January, six weeks after leaving La Rochelle, he was informed by the captain that two men had been arrested for separate offenses on the same day. The first was a soldier who had stabbed one of his shipmates; the second an unfortunate sailor who had skipped or slept through his watch, a nearly unforgivable mistake. Both seemed to have also taken the Lord's name in vain. The captain ordered that the two men be put in irons, a foretaste to the humiliating public punishment they would receive the next day.

The following morning, all of the crew and passengers were called out to the main deck to witness the spectacle. The Quartermaster, who presided over much of the proceedings, bellowed to the crew that the man who had used his knife against a fellow soldier would be stripped to the waist and tied face down on a cannon. He then ordered one of his men to administer fifty lashes, specifying that they should land on the offender's back. The punishment for the sailor who slept through his watch was more complicated. Sentenced to the so-called *bouline sèche*, or *dry bowline*, he was stripped of his clothing and attached at the waist to a cord leading to a second rope running the length of the main deck. Once this was done, the captain ordered the man to run the length of the *bouline* seven times while the rest of the crew whipped the screaming sailor with the inflexible *garcette* ropes used to secure the sails.[6]

Bearing witness to corporal punishment was not the greatest shock Labat encountered during the voyage. Two weeks later, when the *Loire* was already within eyeshot of Martinique, an English ship with fifty-four cannons closed on the French *flûte*, hoping to capture it or send it to the bottom of the sea. According to Labat's lengthy account of the ensuing naval battle, the French sailors successfully fought off the larger warship by unleashing barrage after barrage of musket balls that killed or injured perhaps sixty English sailors. At several points during the battle, the two vessels were often close enough for the priest to hear the English screaming *huzza* as the two crews fired cannons and muskets at each other before the damaged English ship ultimately pulled away.[7]

Labat's eventful sea journey to Martinique ended on January 28, 1694, exactly three months to the day after leaving La Rochelle. Arriving at dusk, the *Loire* moored in Saint-Pierre harbor, on the calmer, leeward side of the island. The next morning, the priest clambered onto the ship's deck to get his first look at the thickly forested ridges that rose from the settlement's fort toward the summit of Mount Pelée. Labat was not wrong when he remarked that this 5,000-foot volcano was "monstrous." Two centuries later, in 1902, Mount Pelée exploded, bellowing a river of burning gas and rock fragments that killed every last man, woman, and child living in the center of Saint-Pierre—27,000 people—with the exception of a prisoner who had been locked behind the thick walls of his jail cell.[8]

Labat was still marveling at the dormant volcano when dozens of enslaved Africans began rowing out toward the *Loire* in canoes and rowboats. Once aboard, these same men disappeared into the ship's hold to hoist casks of wine, tools, and crated hardware back up the ladder toward the waiting boats. Though Labat had surely seen the occasional African in Paris or in La Rochelle's port, this was his first large-scale encounter with the human chattel that toiled in France's overseas colonies. When recording the experience in his journal, the priest noted that these barefoot "Negroes" were miserably dressed and wore little more than tattered loin cloths and a cap or "ugly" hat. He also seemed stunned that nearly all of the men had thick raised scars crisscrossing their backs. Pity welled up in him at this early point in his voyage; he admitted to feeling deep "compassion."[9]

Labat's reaction to such moments evolved significantly over time. Some years later, when he once again commented on this same scene, he suggested that the more time one spends in the islands, the more "one gets used to all this."[10] Though he did not specify just what he had "gotten used to" during his years in the Caribbean, the priest was obviously alluding to two things. The first was the monumental and widespread cruelty that made the plantation economy possible. The second was the embryonic notion of a distinct and natural separation between white and black, a concept that would increasingly be referred to throughout Europe as *race*.

THE FONDS SAINT-JACQUES PLANTATION

Once on shore, Labat quickly discovered from his fellow Dominicans what life was really like on the island. In addition to the fact that the colony was under the constant threat of attack by the English — something the priest had experienced firsthand while at sea — nature herself seemed far more hazardous on this side of the Atlantic. Every few years, during the summer or fall, enormous storms called *hurricanes* ripped trees clean out of the ground and flattened all but the strongest structures. One also needed to keep an eye out for poisonous snakes, scorpions, and spiders, not to mention swarms of stinging ants or invisible egg-laying worms that bored under the skin. The only thing that Labat admitted to fearing were the snakes.

Some of the most unpleasant surprises were inconvenient rather than life-threatening. Getting from place to place on the island's mountainous footpaths took an enormous amount of time. To reach the administrative heart of the colony — Fort Royal, eighteen miles south of Saint-Pierre — Labat discovered that the best means of transportation was a water taxi operated by a free Black man named Louis Galère (whose surname means "galley ship"). Ferrying colonial administrators, merchants, and sometimes priests back and forth between Martinique's two biggest settlements had been so profitable for Galère that he had managed to purchase twenty of his own slaves to pilot a fleet of canoes.[11]

It did not take long for Labat to understand that his religious order was not merely a spiritual presence in the colonies; the Dominicans were deeply enmeshed in the secular workings of colonial life. In addition to the fact that his superiors were active participants in decisions related to land management and even military matters, the Dominicans owned and operated a sugar plantation whose profits supported their missionary activities.[12] This *habitation*, whose ruins can still be seen today on the island's northeast coast, was known as the Fonds Saint-Jacques.

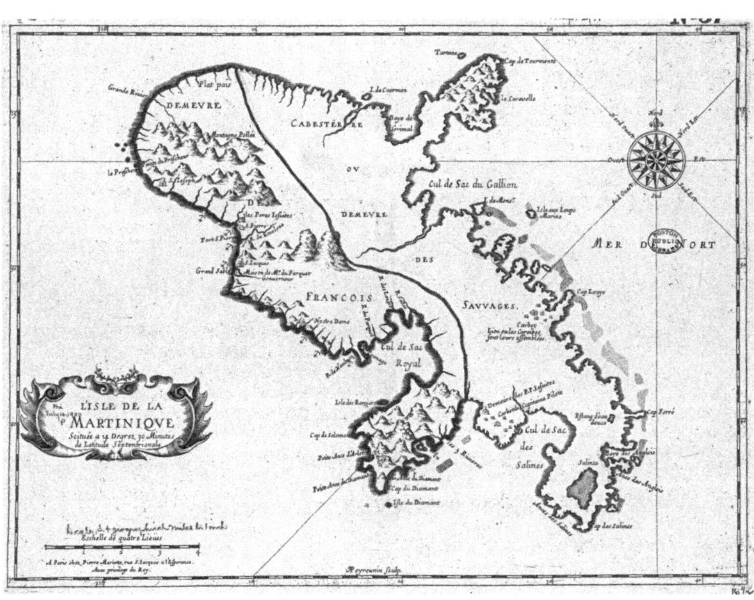

SEVENTEENTH-CENTURY MAP OF MARTINIQUE, SHOWING DEMARCATION BETWEEN "FRENCH" AND "SAVAGES"

The vast parcel of land on which the Fonds Saint-Jacques plantation was established had come as a gift—a reward for the

Dominicans' role in helping crush a rebellion of native Caribe (Kalinago Amerindians) in 1658.[13] Several years after taking possession of the land, members of the order began converting the hillside plot into a commercial enterprise. They purchased twenty recently arrived African captives from the slave market in Saint-Pierre and oversaw the clearing of seventy acres of arable land. A poorly constructed sugar mill was also built and later rebuilt. The venture was far from thriving in 1694, when Labat first came to inspect the plantation.

To make the trek from Saint-Pierre to the Fonds Saint-Jacques, Labat and another priest set off on horseback. They were accompanied by two enslaved Africans who had only recently gone through the process of seasoning after the Middle Passage. The two men carried the priests' bedding and gear on their backs, swatting the underbrush with sticks to scare away the lancehead snakes that made travel through the mountains so dangerous. Twelve hours later, around nine o'clock that same night, Labat and the three other men emerged from the forest trails above the plantation. Overjoyed to see the hazy outlines of the Fond Saint-Jacques, the two clergymen quickly identified themselves and were invited into the Dominicans' convent to have some supper.

Compared to the relatively lavish life led by the Dominicans in Paris, the priests on the plantation were living in poverty. At supper, Labat marveled when he was given a napkin that was in tatters.[14] This turned out to be a telltale sign of the state of the entire plantation. The next day, while touring the *habitation*'s grounds, he remarked that the three main buildings were "as broken down outside, as they were poorly furnished inside."[15] Even the recently rebuilt sugar mill, the most important structure at the Fonds Saint-Jacques, had grave problems. Whoever had designed the circular structure had neglected to leave space for sunlight to stream into the building. This was a dangerous situation to say the least: Without adequate light, the enslaved women who fed the sugarcane stalks into the large vertical rollers — this was generally women's work — could easily have an arm torn off.

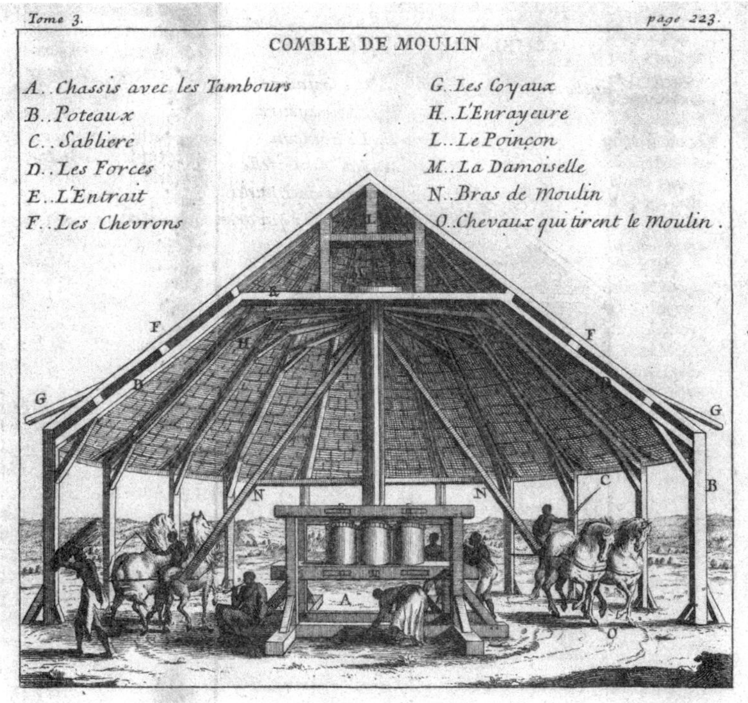

ANIMAL-DRIVEN SUGAR PRESS, OR CANE MILL;
ENGRAVING FROM LABAT'S *NOUVEAU VOYAGE*

Labat was most distressed when he crossed over the plantation's small river into the so-called Neighborhood of the Negroes: a makeshift village of a dozen or so small huts where the plantation's enslaved laborers lived. Moving from one hut to the next, Labat saw how the plantation's pitiful financial state had affected its workers. By the time that he had finished his inspection, he had counted and spoken with "thirty-five able-bodied slaves" and another "eight or ten Negroes" who were now infirm and unable to work.[16] The missionary also noted that there were about fifteen children, all of whom were desperately ill due to a lack of food, clothing, and medicine. A number of these enslaved boys and girls would soon end up in the "slaves' cemetery," just outside the southern walls of the complex.

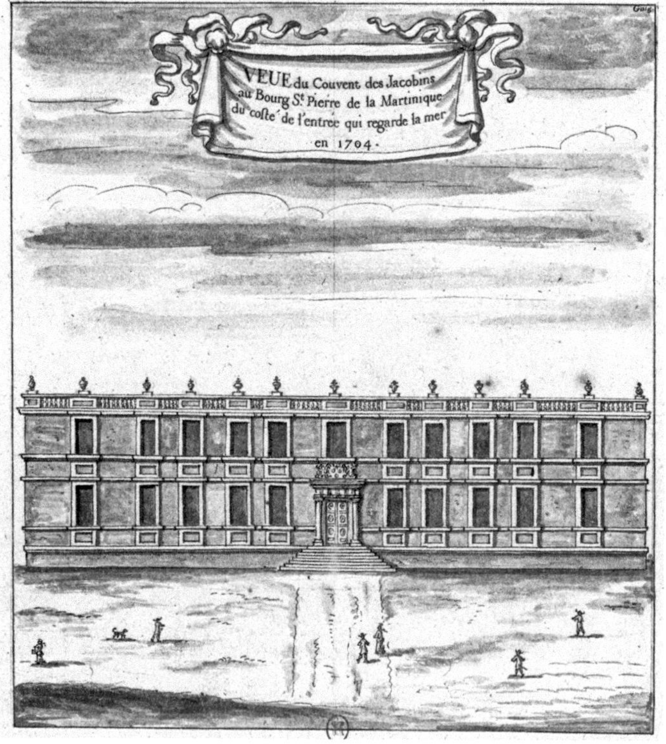

THE JACOBIN CONVENT IN SAINT-PIERRE,
DESIGNED BY LABAT AND COMPLETED IN 1704

Labat understood only too well that the many shortcomings of the plantation were all interrelated. Never one to shy from identifying ineptitude and poor decisions, he denounced the plantation's leaders for failing to build a proper curing house (where raw molasses and crystalized sugar would be poured into hundreds of refining pots), for borrowing and spending money foolishly, and for neglecting to properly nourish its labor force. In his view, the very existence of the Dominicans in Martinique was being put in jeopardy by the incompetent, short-sighted administrators at the plantation.

It did not take long for Labat's Dominican superiors to understand that this simultaneously charming and overbearing priest had abilities — including an interest and expertise in engineering and architecture related to his study of mathematics — that could be fruitfully employed in the French Caribbean. Two years after his first assignment in the parish of Macouba, Labat was asked by the Dominican *Supérieur Général* to travel to Guadeloupe to supervise the construction of a water-powered cane mill. On his return, this same *Supérieur* prevailed upon him to help build a proper curing house at the Fonds Saint-Jacques. Shortly thereafter, he was also asked to design a new convent for the Dominicans at Saint-Pierre. While all this work was transpiring, in 1696, his colleagues elected him to be *syndic*, or plantation manager, of the Fonds Saint-Jacques.

Within a few short years, Labat had transformed the formerly struggling plantation. After purchasing dozens more enslaved Africans (often on credit), he oversaw the construction of several new buildings, including a dormitory for the priests, some offices, a distillery, and a water-powered mill to press the cane. He also instituted more rational manufacturing processes and even invented a cognac-inspired method of producing rum that now bears his name.[17] The improvements helped the Dominican plantation grow into one of the most profitable on the island, employing almost 600 enslaved workers by the end of the century.[18] Today, the buildings that are still standing at the Fonds Saint-Jacques were nearly all designed and constructed during Labat's tenure as *syndic*.

RUINS OF THE FONDS SAINT-JACQUES

THE CHAPEL AT THE FONDS SAINT-JACQUES

Furthering the Dominicans' mission at the Fonds Saint-Jacques—via enslaved labor—was only the beginning of Labat's legacy. During his years in the French Caribbean, *Père* (or Father) Labat, as he came to be called, achieved mythological status. In addition to becoming one of the primary architects—both figuratively and literally—of the early French colonial endeavor, he also distinguished himself as a cartographer, botanist, zoologist, historian, gastronomist, and soldier, having routinely taken up arms when needed, including during a fifty-day defense of Guadeloupe against the English.[19] His real celebrity, however, came almost twenty years later when he published his six-volume account of how he had bought, baptized, punished, and buried the enslaved laborers working at the Fonds Saint-Jacques plantation. At once influential in its own right and emblematic of a broader turn in travel writing—one increasingly preoccupied with non-European "ethnography"—Labat's book helped furnish the raw material for the emergence of a distinctly race-based conception of humanity.

AN EVENTFUL RETURN: LABAT'S EXILE AND THE PUBLICATION OF THE *"NEW" VOYAGE*

By 1705, after spending eleven years in the Caribbean, Labat had no intention of either returning to France or publishing his memoirs. That same year, however, the Dominican *Supérieur Général* in Martinique informed the priest that he was being sent back to Europe on a secret mission: to make a formal complaint about the "affronts to which [the Dominican order] was subjected on a daily basis."[20] The target of these grievances was the island's governor, Charles-François Machault de Belmont. For over a year, the Dominicans had had the distinct impression that whenever there was a conflict among the different religious orders, the governor had favored the

Jesuits and the Capuchins over the Dominicans. Labat's *Supérieur* had been particularly furious after the governor had prevented the order from buying the land adjacent to the Fonds Saint-Jacques, an acquisition that the Dominicans needed to expand their now successful sugar-making operations.[21]

Labat's mission was complex to say the least. He was first told to rendezvous with a ship destined for Marseille, travel by coach to Bologna to seek support from the central administration of the Dominican order, and, finally, make his way to Paris where he was to complain about this hated administrator.

On August 8, 1705, at three o'clock in the morning, Labat secretly left Saint-Pierre in a canoe that took him to the *Saint-Paul*, which lay at anchor in port in Fort Royal. Three hours later, once he was aboard, the merchant ship set sail for Europe alongside fourteen other vessels. Compared to the first time that Labat crossed the Atlantic, he recorded precious little about the return voyage. One of the few things that he did note was the moment that he spied (from afar) the coast of Africa. Years later, when he published a multivolume book on West Africa, this moment allowed him to state: "I have seen Africa, but I have never set foot there."[22]

Labat's mission turned out to be even more complicated than he had expected. When the *Saint-Paul* put into port at the Spanish city of Cadiz for provisions, the crew learned that a fleet of English and Dutch ships was blocking the Straits of Gibraltar, cutting off the route through the Mediterranean to Marseille.[23] Unable to leave the Spanish port city for what turned out to be months, Labat finally gave up on sailing directly to Marseille and booked passage on a ship sailing north to La Rochelle. After arriving in the same city from which he had left for Martinique, the priest set off almost immediately toward Italy, where the Dominicans' General Chapter was waiting for his report.[24]

Having accomplished the first part of his mission, Labat then returned to Paris in July of 1706, where he had been instructed to secure an audience with Louis Phélypeaux de Pontchartrain, then Secretary of State for the Navy. This was the moment when he was supposed to orchestrate the removal of the hated governor of Martinique.[25] In the end, it was not the governor's downfall he brought about — but his own.

Well before Labat had arrived in Paris, Pontchartrain had heard from various sources that the assertive Dominican had been sent to spread lies and foment dissent. One of the dispatches Pontchartrain received claimed that Labat had a "passionate and agitated mind" and that it would be "prudent to prevent him from returning to the islands."[26] Another declared that he had a "conspiratorial" mentality.[27] News of this Dominican cabal against the colonial authority in Martinique soon reached Versailles as well. When Louis XIV heard about this troublemaker of a priest, he decreed that "Father Labat will never return to the colonies, whatever he may do to obtain permission."[28] The king then took another step: He exiled Labat to a Dominican convent in the cold, windy, and remote city of Toul, 200 miles to the east of Paris.

Depressed and bitter, Labat relocated to Toul for several months before obtaining permission to move to Italy.[29] Ten years later, after Louis XIV died in 1715, Labat came back to France — to the same Dominican convent on the rue Saint-Honoré in Paris where he had taken his vows thirty years before.[30] During the next few years, the once adventurous Labat — he was now fifty-two — transformed his Caribbean diaries into a memoir. One of his primary objectives in doing so, of course, was to set the record straight regarding the perceived injustices that both he and his order had suffered.

Sometime in 1719, Labat approached a Latin Quarter editor, Pierre-François Giffart, with a proposal to publish his now polished account of life in Martinique. Giffart snapped up the manuscript and presumably paid the priest a one-time fee of a few hundred livres for the rights. Travel-related books had, by then, become one of the most profitable genres for publishers such as Giffart. If he and his fellow printers continued to do well issuing all manner of religious books — these included prayer books, spiritual exercises, theological treatises, and the "lives" of the saints — many of his clients were now far more interested in works of geography and personal travel diaries. Readers in the 1720s were particularly hungry for up-to-date information. This explains why Giffart and Labat decided to call the book *A New Voyage to the Islands*, even though the voyage in question had begun twenty-seven years earlier.

Giffart's small shop on the rue Saint-Jacques began distributing Labat's travelogue to booksellers in late 1722. The first edition of 2,000 copies sold out immediately; larger print runs soon followed. Word of the success quickly reached Dutch editors who wasted no time printing three pirated editions for the French market. German and Dutch translations also appeared.[31] By the late 1720s, as one English periodical put it, Labat was "very well known by his *New Voyage*."[32] His travelogue had not only become a bestseller throughout Europe; virtually every major philosopher, naturalist historian, or race-based thinker associated with what we now call the Enlightenment era would have a copy on his or her shelf. Even the American Thomas Jefferson.

LABAT'S "ETHNOGRAPHY"

Much of the appeal of the *Nouveau voyage* can be attributed to Labat's often detailed portraits of Carib (Kalinago) Indians, enslaved Africans, and "Creole Negroes." Eighteenth-century readers were not put off by the priest's denigrating assessments of these non-

Europeans. Nor were they scandalized by the matter-of-fact descriptions of the regime of torture used to discipline the enslaved population at the Fonds Saint-Jacques. Indeed, his "ethnography" and the brutal vignettes of plantation life melded seamlessly into the overall exotic world that Labat was attempting to convey. This was one of the major intentions of the book: allowing readers to experience the outlandish and the alien, be it the fury of a tropical storm, eating "buccaneer turtle," "camping" with the Kalinago, or running a sugar factory for the benefit of God and country.

Labat's description of the nearly vanished indigenous inhabitants of Martinique was of particular interest to his readers. Early in his chronicle, he let his readers know that he had been hoping to meet (and presumably study) members of the native population for months before finally being able to do so. Coming into contact with the Kalinago, however, had become far more difficult in his era. Forty years before he arrived in Martinique, an armed militia of 600 French colonists had wiped out the last significant population of natives living in the northern portion of the island.[33] Those Kalinago who survived this campaign were exiled to the island of Dominica, thirty miles due north. The only times that Labat had seen any Kalinago Indians, in fact, was when they were far out at sea in their pirogues, silhouetted against the horizon.

In November 1695, Labat was delighted to learn that a group of eighty Kalinago Indians had come from Dominica to trade at the port of Saint-Pierre and quickly rushed to see them.[34] His considerable prejudices notwithstanding—like most priests Labat considered the Kalinago to be stubborn unbelievers who were unwilling to convert—the priest describes them as "well-made and well proportioned" with perfect white teeth, unlike the sugar-eating Europeans.[35] During his first, brief encounter with the indigenous population, the priest seemed most fascinated by their face paint (made with ground seeds from the achiote tree) and the group's polygamous practices, especially the idea that one man might marry three sisters. He also marveled at one of their ingenious techniques for hunting parrots: burning gum and hot green peppers under the tall pine trees where the birds were nesting, until they fell to the ground.[36]

KALINAGO MAN AND KALINAGO WOMAN, RESPECTIVELY; ENGRAVINGS FROM LABAT'S *NOUVEAU VOYAGE*

Several years later, Labat sailed from the southern tip of Martinique to neighboring Dominica with the specific intention of observing these Amerindians in their own environment. During his weeklong stay on the island, the priest shadowed members of the indigenous community from dawn until dusk. He also visited a number of their *carbets*, or large meeting houses. Much of this second account of the Kalinago was quite different from what he had recorded before. Like many other Europeans who wrote about Amerindians, be they indigenous communities in Canada or the Great Plains, Labat painted a terribly negative portrait of the men, especially regarding the way they treated the Kalinago women.[37] He claims that when these same men returned from a hunt to the *carbet*, they did not address or even acknowledge their women. Instead, they simply tossed the animals they had killed onto the ground and wandered off to sit around the fire. His description of this scene — he explains that they were "squatting . . . on their heels, like monkeys" — drips with disdain.[38] In the few instances where Labat describes other types of labor performed by the men — making baskets or bows and arrows — he asserts that they did so only "for the present need, and always in a negligent and indifferent manner" until they got bored and wandered off.[39]

Labat demonstrates far more sympathy for the industrious Kalinago girls and women, whom he portrays as spending their days waiting hand and foot on the men — rubbing them down with achiote paint and oil after their morning bath, preparing their cassava, or silently proposing various things to drink or eat while the men sit idly by.[40] At the end of this assessment of gender roles, the priest states that the industriousness and silent respect that these wives showed for their husbands might be a good example for "Christian women."[41]

Although Labat's readers certainly appreciated his assessment of the Kalinago, his extensive and multifaceted presentation of enslaved Africans drew more attention. That he, a Dominican priest and representative of God on Earth, took it upon himself to explain how African chattel slavery functioned in the Caribbean world was seen as perfectly normal by his readers in the 1720s, especially by the French Catholic public. True to both the general ethos of the era and the *Code Noir*, Labat repeatedly makes clear that Africans had a dual status as both "meubles" (property) *and* redeemable humans blessed with a soul. Nowhere in his account does he feel it necessary to explicitly reconcile the soul-crushing terror of chattel slavery with the common humanity and universalism that was one of the foundational ideas of the Gospel.[42] Instead, he explains the phenomenon of slavery from his point of view as a religious historian, ethnographer, and ultimately prison warden. While a true biological or scientific concept of *race* is not yet present in his writing, every Black African Labat conjures up in his book had nonetheless lost his or her specific "ethnic" and geographical identity to the mechanical logic and processes of the slave trade.[43]

Labat begins his overall assessment of slavery and enslaved Africans with an often-repeated historical anecdote, informing his readers that King Louis XIII (1601–1643) had initially been uneasy about human bondage until he realized that the practice was an "infallible way of inculcating belief in the only one true God [in Africans]."[44] After crediting this "pious" and "wise" monarch, Labat provides a sanitized account of the purchase and transport of African captives.

In French port cities, according to the priest, slave ships are loaded with merchandise that will be of particular interest to African merchants: These include iron bars, guns, ammunition, cloth, paper, textiles, and cowry shells (purchased in the Maldives).[45] Once these vessels arrive on the west coast of Africa, a delegation from the ship meets with local merchants and exchanges their wares for African men, women, and children.

After describing the purchase of these captives as little more than a simple barter of "goods" (in a naturally occurring African market), Labat then explains that these enslaved Africans belong to four different categories. Some were supposedly criminals who were sold off as part of their punishment (a familiar idea given the existence of *galériens* in France). Others were purportedly prisoners who had been captured during what Labat describes as the state of "perpetual war" among various African kingdoms. The third category of captives, he continues, had simply been unlucky enough to be traded by a king or prince who "owned them." The final and largest group of these slaves, which Labat seems to admit almost as an afterthought, had been kidnapped, stolen from their villages.[46] Whatever the source of captives, however, Labat puts the responsibility of enslavement squarely on Africans themselves, not on the unquenchable European thirst for enslaved labor.

In subsequent paragraphs, Labat does not burden his readers with a description of how this human cargo was subsequently shackled to a ship's tween deck for as long as four months. Instead, he picks up the narrative once these African captives arrive in the islands, at the "end" of the Middle Passage. Casting himself as an enlightened voice at this point in the story, he counsels his fellow planters to avoid the mistake of putting their newly arrived Africans to work without giving them time to recuperate. Rather than being sent directly to the cane fields, he suggests that these new captives should be bathed in the sea, shaved to be rid of lice, and, finally, rubbed down with palm oil. The delay is worth the trouble from Labat's paternalistic point of view: These same men, women, and children not only survive in greater number, but will become affectionate and loyal. Indeed, Labat claims that such kindnesses might even lead a slave to sacrifice his or her life for their master.[47]

In addition to giving practical advice to his fellow planters, Labat writes at length about the Africans themselves. Presenting himself as an expert on the subject — he makes sure to emphasize the fact that he learned Arada, the most commonly used African language on the island — he introduces his readers to a number of enslaved individuals.[48] This intimacy leads to one of the most distinctive aspects of the *Nouveau voyage*: Labat's unsettling *humanization* of the *dehumanized*. In contrast to the far more brutal theoreticians of race who wrote during the latter part of the eighteenth century — Edward Long and his 1774 *History of Jamaica* comes to mind — Labat often claims to care deeply for his enslaved workers, particularly the children at the Fonds Saint-Jacques.

In one of the most heart-wrenching moments in his chronicle, Labat recounts how an enslaved boy who had just arrived at the plantation was so despondent that he committed suicide by ingesting a large quantity of dirt. Shortly after the child was buried, Labat discovers that the child had ended his life because he and his brother had been auctioned off to different *habitations*. The even worse conclusion of the story comes when Labat discovers that the other brother had also killed himself in the same fashion. The priest laments the fact that, had he known that the boys felt this way, he could have easily arranged for the children to spend their life together, albeit in bondage.[49]

This harrowing anecdote underscores the profound moral divide between Labat's eighteenth-century readers and us today. In recounting this episode, Labat was neither condemning the potential horrors of Caribbean slavery nor illustrating the resistance of enslaved people. Instead, his aim was quite different: to depict plantation managers like himself as compassionate individuals working under difficult circumstances. Paradoxically, the story of these agonizing deaths was meant to reassure his audience, offering the comforting illusion that men like Labat sought to improve the conditions of the enslaved in the French islands.

Throughout the *Nouveau voyage*, Labat's presentation of his enslaved Africans alternates between anecdote and more general observations. In the most famous section of the book, which the priest entitled "The Black Slaves that we use in the Colonies," he shares a series of pointed proto-racial reflections regarding the African "type" and "mindset." While his own experience (and narrative) underscores the profound differences he sees among individual Africans on both the level of ethnicity and "psychology," he also claims that there is, overall, a specific African temperament — a series of universal traits — shared by all "Negroes."

Some of Labat's observations, at first glance, seem quite positive. "All Negroes," he writes, "have a deep respect for their elders." They are "very community minded and work well in groups."[50] Upon reflection, of course, such traits correspond exactly to the characteristics that Labat was seeking to inculcate in his enslaved workforce: a passive and subservient mentality that was supposedly perfectly suited to obeying the master of the plantation or the *commandeur* in the cane fields.

Not surprisingly, Labat also writes at length about the alleged liabilities of the Black African. As a rule, he claims Blacks are "vainglorious" and prone to mocking everybody, especially *Whites*.[51] He also claims that every single African loves gambling, wine, and liquor.[52] Drinking and gambling apparently bothered Labat far less, however, than what he claims is Africans' "favorite passion," the *calenda*, a drum-driven dance during which the men and women engage in what he describes as wild jumping, twirling, "thigh-slapping," and stomach-bumping to the tune of a banjo-type instrument made of gourds.[53] The whole spectacle of the *calenda*, Labat claims, is both "lascivious" and "immodest." Such comments were very much related to his understanding of African sexuality, which he considered to be unbridled. In his opinion, the powerful lure of the erogenous *calenda* can only be explained by a *physiological* tendency specific to Africans: It is the natural result of a "heated complexion" that made the men addicted "to women."[54] This is as close as Labat gets to putting forward a biological conception of race.

Regardless of the source of Africans' supposed hypersexuality, Labat asserts that these behaviors merit specific corrective measures. To combat the powerful and supposedly primal lure of the *calenda*, he recommends teaching slaves a range of French dances that are less suggestive and sensual. Learning how to dance the French minuet, the *passepied*, or any number of *branles* or "round dances," Labat claims, would allow slaves to "jump around as much as they want" without the same indecency. The policing of the sexual habits of unmarried Africans necessitated a more proactive approach in his opinion: To prevent out-of-wedlock sex from taking place among the enslaved (not to mention between African women and the White planters who Labat admits invariably prey on them), the priest suggests arranging marriages among even very young Africans.

Generally speaking, the corrective measures that Labat suggests here are moderate. His reaction to the persistence of magic or healing among baptized "slaves," however, is exceedingly brutal. In 1698, during his tenure as plantation manager of the Fonds Saint-Jacques, Labat stumbled upon a ritual being performed in the "Neighborhood of the Blacks" by a medicine man from a neighboring plantation. Explaining that he initially spied on the ceremony from outside the cabin, he relates in detail how the "sorcerer" placed some pitch or tar into a gourd with a small candle, causing the hollow vegetable to erupt in light. According to Labat, the same man then placed a clay figurine in the fire and began communing with a spirit in order to give advice to a dying woman who was lying on the floor.

Expressing his horror that this "sorcerer" has dared violate one of the central sins of Christianity — idolatry — Labat then presents himself as a Christian hero in the story. According to his version of events, he and seven other men burst into the room and dragged the screaming man out to the plantation's main courtyard. He then boasts that he ordered the offending African stripped of his clothes and given 300 lashes in front of the community.[55] At the end of this ghastly anecdote, Labat congratulates himself for his sadism, relating how he then ordered that the man be put in irons and rubbed down with a *pimentade*, a mixture of crushed hot peppers and lemons.[56]

Labat follows up on this distressing torture scene with a specific recommendation to the planter community: Anyone in a position of power over the enslaved Africans or "Creole Africans" should never ever threaten to punish. Instead, they must have the guilty parties disciplined immediately for fear that the accused person run off and join one of the maroon communities that lived independently in the mountains. It may have been the account of this incident, or others like it, that ultimately gave rise to a new adjective in French Creole — *perelèba* ("Père Labat") — which means someone who is "mean-spirited."

Labat's description of plantation life in Martinique sparked extensive debate for decades. What most readers never understood was that his book was well out-of-date on the day it was published. When Labat returned from Martinique in 1705, there were 15,000 enslaved Africans scattered throughout the island's *habitations*. By the time that the *New Voyage* appeared in print, in 1722, French slave traders had imported another 25,000 captives.[57] These numbers accelerated even faster between 1722 and mid-century, by which point another 76,000 men, women, and children had been sold off at auction to harvest sugarcane on newly created plantations. What happened during these same years on Saint-Domingue (Haiti) was even more dramatic. In the twenty-eight-year span between the publication of Labat's book and 1750, France's largest Caribbean colony took delivery of 150,000 African captives.[58]

Labat did update the book one final time in the 1730s, but he never alluded to how much the French islands must have changed over the course of three decades. Instead, he added a new chapter relating the history of early colonization, as well as a discussion of coffee, sugar, and indigo production. He also included a list of the governors and intendants who had worked on each of the French islands. The one substantive change that he made regarding the reality of slavery in the islands was erasing any mention of the marriages that had taken place between Whites and Blacks.[59] Some of the colonists who had read one of the previous editions of the *New Voyage* had written him to say that they did not want to continue to see this in print.[60]

PERELÈBA AND PÈRE LABAT

The publication of the *New Voyage* changed the course of Labat's life. By the mid-1720s, after several editions of his book had been published, the now sixty-two-year-old priest reveled in his Europe-wide reputation. Having been libeled, disgraced, and exiled from Paris, he had risen like a phoenix to become the era's most famous "Caribbean" writer. Labat was never one to rest on his laurels, of course. After the success of the *New Voyage*, he set an even more ambitious goal for himself: becoming his era's greatest *Africanist*. Beginning in the mid-1720s, he began working on a series of books that he hoped would provide his readers with a complete "description of Africa" and its peoples. His sources were varied: archival documents provided by a French trading company in Europe;

previously published travelogues; and interviews with voyagers (e.g., slave traders) who had spent considerable time in West Africa. The irony of this undertaking was that Labat, as he had himself admitted, had never set foot in Africa. This was anything but a disqualification in his view, especially when it came to discussing Black Africans themselves. As an expert on New World slavery, he was convinced that he was already an expert on *all Africans*.[61]

Over the course of six years, Labat published three books on Africa, each of which was the same length as his Caribbean travelogue. His first, *A New Relation of West Africa* (1728), provided his readers with a sweeping history of French colonization in the region, as well as the nature of the different African "nations" with which traders interacted in the Senegambia region.[62] Two years later, he brought out a second *Africanist* work recounting the adventures of the slave trader Reynaud Des Marchais in Sierra Leone, Cameroon, and Cayenne.[63] His third and final book on Africa, the 1732 *Historical Relation of West Ethiopia*, became his best known and, arguably, most notorious work on Africa. Translating and adapting selections from the memoirs of a seventeenth-century Italian missionary named Giovanni Antonio Cavazzi, Labat portrayed Africans as, on the whole, living in the "shadows of paganism."[64] Among other things, the *Historical Relation* helped disseminate the belief that there was a group of cannibalistic warriors named the Jaga living in the kingdom of the Kongo that prepared themselves for battle by crushing newborns in a mortar and then applying the grease to their skin.[65] Such lore not only provided implicit justification for the Caribbean slavery that Labat had described when writing about the Caribbean; it actually inspired mapmakers to dot the African landscape with indications that, in the deep interior of dark Africa, there were numerous tribes of *anthropophagic humans*.[66]

By the time that the once-indefatigable Labat died at the age of seventy-five, on January 6, 1738, the priest had published more pages on West Africa than anybody else during the eighteenth century. His *Africanist* books, along with his famous *New Voyage*, were now essential works within the era's burgeoning repository of information related to Black Africans. What Labat did not know, however, was that his books (and all such travelogues) were being reinterpreted by an increasingly "anthropologically" minded generation—a generation of men whose orientation, methods, and preoccupations differed significantly from those of a Dominican priest.

PALM TREE, WITH SCENE OF CANNIBALISM; ENGRAVING FROM LABAT'S *RELATION HISTORIQUE DE L'ÉTHIOPIE OCCIDENTALE*

These thinkers—the Buffons, the Kants, the Voltaires, and the Jeffersons of the world—were less interested in Labat's love of exoticism and anecdotes. They pored over his and various other travelogues related to non-Europeans in order to answer several pressing "anthropological" questions that would become nothing short of obsessions during the rest of the century.

> Assuming that there is only one human species, who were the original members of this group?
>
> If all humans are somehow related, what caused the other human varieties, especially Africans, to diverge from this same band of humans?
>
> Exactly how many human types can we identify? And what method should be used to do this?
>
> And finally, is it possible to create some sort of rational taxonomy to understand the human species in the same way that naturalists divided animals into species and *races*?

Such classificatory considerations would never have occurred to Father Labat. Although he may have heard the word *race* being used to refer to humans by the time he died, it was still very rare for someone of his generation to identify Amerindians, Asians, or Black Africans in this fashion. And yet, even before Labat left for the Caribbean, the first inklings of what would become racial classification had been theorized by a world traveler named François Bernier. Ironically enough, he had done so only a few blocks away from the Dominican convent on the rue Saint-Honoré where Labat, as a young seminarian, was studying to become a priest.

PART TWO

THE NEW ANIMAL: MAN

Man is a sociable animal.
—MONTESQUIEU,
Persian Letters, 1721

Man is a reasonable animal . . .
the most noble of all the animals.
—*Dictionnaire de l'Académie Françoise*, 1740

Man is a ferocious animal.
—DIDEROT, "Ferocity,"
L'Encyclopédie, 1756

III

PORTRAIT OF A FRENCH DOCTOR, PERHAPS BERNIER;
SEVENTEENTH-CENTURY INDIAN PAINTING

FRANÇOIS BERNIER: THE FIRST CLASSIFIER

The first time that a group of people discussed the concept of *race* in public presumably took place on a Tuesday.[1] Tuesday was the day of the week when, during much of the 1670s, a brilliant, witty, and alluring thirty-year-old Huguenot woman named Marguerite de La Sablière opened her Paris townhouse to the capital's most celebrated thinkers and conversationalists.[2] Frequent guests at her weekly *salon* included the legendary playwrights Racine and Molière; the witty savant Bernard Le Bouyer de Fontenelle; the fabulist Jean de La Fontaine; and the celebrated writers Madame de Sévigné and Madame de Lafayette.

Despite all the puffed-up overskirts and long curly wigs (the latter worn by the men) at Sablière's salon, these occasions were far more than an excuse to showcase the season's latest fashions. Topics of conversation on the rue Neuve-des-Petits-Champs often reflected the hostess's uncommon interest in physics, mathematics, and astronomy — subjects that she had studied with the guidance of several friends who were members of Paris's Royal Academy of Sciences. Of the 250,000 women living in Paris in the 1670s, Sablière was almost certainly the only one to have a telescope on her rooftop.[3] She was also the first woman in history to encourage a new racial categorization of humankind.

MARGUERITE DE LA SABLIÈRE, PAINTING BY CHARLES AND HENRI BEAUBRUN

The use of the word *race* to identify human categories had been the brainchild of one of the most admired attendees at her salons, her good friend François Bernier. In addition to the fact that Bernier was tall and fine-looking, this medical doctor (and roaming spirit) had an irreverent sense of humor that all but the most pious found entrancing. "Abstaining from pleasure," Bernier once quipped, "appears to me to be a mortal sin."[4]

The real reason for his notoriety, however, had come from the fact that he had spent thirteen years of his life traveling in the "Orient." Sablière and her entourage jokingly called Bernier "the Mughal" in honor of his service to the emperor of India.[5] In an era when most people would never even witness a seascape, Bernier could conjure up what it was like to stand in front of the pyramids, the Taj Mahal, and the amazing peacock feather throne belonging to the emperor of India. His favorite tales included the time he snuck into a harem; how the Indian court entertained itself by watching elephants and their riders fight to the death; and how he convinced a poor Indian widow that she did not need to perform suttee — burning herself alive on her husband's funeral pyre. His anecdotes seemed endless.

François Bernier and Madame de La Sablière are now remembered primarily for a short essay that he shared with her salon over 350 years ago. We do not know who was present, but one can nonetheless imagine that, true to what generally occurred in such settings, Bernier rose from his seat, opened a folded manuscript, and read his "A New Division of the Earth according to the Different Species or Races of Men" to the group of perhaps fifteen people. This presentation — which contained the *first* ever classification of the human species using the term *race* — probably took him ten or fifteen minutes to deliver. Discussion and debate, as was often the case at the salon, likely lasted hours.

Most of the great ideas, chitchat, and tittle-tattle exchanged at Madame de La Sablière's salon evaporated into the ether. Bernier's unusual theory of human races almost did as well. Yet, a decade or so after he first read this paper at Sablière's salon, the now sixty-four-year-old Bernier decided to submit the "New Division" to Jean-Paul de La Roque, the editor of the *Journal des savants*, the premier scientific journal of the era. La Roque was intrigued and published Bernier's article as the lead in the April 24, 1684, issue alongside a letter on mathematics, the account of a woman who gave birth to nine babies, and two book reviews.

Almost exactly one year after Louis XIV had signed the *Code Noir* (and 166 years after Europeans first began transporting captive Africans across the Atlantic), copies of Bernier's radical reconceptualization of the human species began making their way across Europe. The race genie had escaped its bottle.

That François Bernier (1620–1688), the impoverished son of a tenant farmer, would change the course of history in this way was as improbable as the rest of his life. Born in Joué-Etiau, a remote village of mud houses nestled in France's Loire Valley, Bernier would have undoubtedly spent his life tending to livestock, wheat, and field beans had his father not died when he was a child. Sometime after this grievous event, it was decided that the five-year-old boy would leave his house and become the ward of his father's brother, a priest in the neighboring village of Chanzeaux.

Bernier's early years, both before and after he came under his uncle's care, are a document-less desert. There are no letters, reminiscences, or any material traces of his life other than an unrevealing entry in a baptismal register. One thing is sure, however: Like every other child in the village, the young boy began learning formally about God and the one, holy, Catholic, and apostolic Church around age seven. Much of the Latin liturgy that Bernier heard during his early years would have washed over him. His real introduction to the tenets of the faith surely came in catechism class where, week after week, he sat huddled alongside the other village children memorizing answers to questions such as: What is the only comfort in life and death? What is true faith? Are all men saved by Christ?

The message that Bernier was supposed to glean from his weekly sessions was really quite simple: that he belonged, body and soul, to God, and that this same deity was an all-powerful and potentially vengeful being who was carefully surveilling and evaluating him for admission to heaven. Whether at home or at church, he would have also heard that it was imperative to avoid earthly temptation or unholy activities—fornication, "pollution" (masturbation), and gluttony, not to mention the twin evils of theater and dancing. In this milieu, life's highest calling was turning away from the pleasures of existence.

Catechism also provided Bernier with his first notions of biblical "anthropology," referred to at the time as "sacred universal history." After internalizing the story of how God had created mankind some six thousand years before, young François heard how the Lord had become enraged at mankind's sins and willed the Great Flood into existence, wiping out the entire human race, except for Noah and his family. This spine-chilling example of divine wrath led to the more hopeful story of how Noah's three sons and their wives, after the floodwaters receded, spread out over the globe and became the ancestors of every one of the current inhabitants of the planet.

The specifics of humankind's *coloration*, not to mention how long this process took, were not covered in catechism. Bernier did learn, however, that Noah's son Shem became the father of Abraham and the Israelites, that Japheth provided the rootstock for the Greeks, and that the maligned Ham—who had seen his father Noah naked—was the father of the Africans. Neither Bernier nor anyone else in his village paid any attention to one of the Bible's curious omissions: There was, for example, no mention of the New World and its "beardless" native peoples.

Despite the type of education one would have received in Chanzeaux, becoming the ward of a literate ecclesiastic had been a gift. Thanks to his uncle (or a tutor hired by his uncle), Bernier studied both French and Latin grammar in addition to his religious training. He may have even received the beginnings of a humanistic, philosophical, or theological education assuming his teacher was so inclined. Whatever the exact form of instruction, literacy made him eligible for admission to school. His uncle surely expected that his charge would follow in his footsteps and become a priest.

It was during the early 1630s that the prospect of further education opened up for Bernier. While still at school in Chanzeaux, Bernier had so impressed a rich member of Parlement with his wit and intelligence that this same man sponsored the boy's education in a Jesuit *collège* (secondary school) in Paris. Sometime after this offer was tended, Bernier boarded a carriage in the neighboring city of Angers and made his way over the rut-and-root-infested roads leading to Paris, the largest city in Europe.

Coaches from Angers entered Paris—then a walled city—via the large stone gate at the southwestern rampart. From there Bernier would have crossed through some of the poorest and most populous neighborhoods in the city, the stench of which tended to turn the stomach of people arriving from the comparatively airy countryside. Bernier's destination, the Collège de Clermont, was situated in the heart of Paris's Latin Quarter.

As was the case for all students enrolled in one of the country's Jesuit schools, the 2,000 students at Clermont followed a multiyear program known as the *ratio studiorum*, a humanities-based regimen of Greek and Latin, rhetoric, and philosophy. During this rigorous course of study, Bernier began each school day with prayers, followed by five or so hours of classwork and six more hours of assigned studying, where he was expected to memorize notes that he needed to recite on Saturdays. Students who excelled at the end of the week were rewarded. Those who did not received some form of physical punishment, be it a slap on the wrist or a more serious paddling with a leather strap.[6]

Life at Clermont in the 1630s left much to be desired. The food was monotonous and rarely served warm, bedbugs and diseases were endemic, and students were forced to sleep two-to-a-bed. Even the rich boarders could not secure better separate living quarters with individual fireplaces, as was the case in some other schools.[7] Bernier's years as a boarder came to an end when the same benefactor who was paying for his education—his name was François Luillier—asked Bernier if he wanted to move to his far more luxurious Parisian townhouse in the Faubourg Saint-Germain. Bernier happily accepted. In addition to relocating to a far warmer residence with a better bed and far better food, Bernier discovered that the generous Luillier had also hired one of the greatest minds of the seventeenth century to instruct both him and Luillier's illegitimate son, Claude-Emmanuel Chapelle. This teacher was a freethinking philosopher-priest by the name of Pierre Gassendi (1592–1655).

THE EMPIRICAL PRIEST AND THE METHOD OF RACE

By the time that Pierre Gassendi had begun teaching philosophy to Bernier in Luillier's Parisian townhouse in 1641, the forty-nine-year-old clergyman had already become one of Europe's most important thinkers. In addition to exchanging ideas with Galileo, Kepler, and Hobbes, Gassendi had famously entered into debate with René Descartes, refuting the latter's belief that certain ideas can be considered as true because they can be perceived by the mind to be "clear and distinct." From Gassendi's point of view, the rationalist elements of Descartes's philosophy, including his famous *cogito ergo sum*, were little more than unfounded abstractions. This refutation of Descartes's rationalist understanding of the universe was more than a simple disagreement: It was a turning point in early modern philosophy. By rebutting Descartes's idea that the mind could seize truth on its own, and by arguing that the senses were the sole means of gathering reliable information from the outside world, Gassendi became the first philosopher to put forward a "modern model of knowledge," one that not only relied solely on the workings of the senses, but was entirely "integrated with a physiological account of perception."[8] Thirty years before the Englishman John Locke wrote *An Essay on Human Understanding* (1689), Gassendi had already advocated for an entirely material explanation of the workings of the human mind.[9]

Gassendi's teaching had an enormous effect on the twenty-year-old Bernier, including how the young man would ultimately conceive of the human species. When Bernier finally got around to writing about humankind in the 1670s, he had already learned from the skeptical priest to separate belief in God from scientific practice. Indeed, Bernier had been taught to envision the functioning of the world from an entirely naturalistic point of view, whether he was studying astronomy, the intelligence of animals, or the different types of humans found on the planet.[10]

In addition to everything else that he gleaned from Gassendi, Bernier also embraced his mentor's belief that wide-ranging travel was among the most philosophical of pursuits.[11] This idea, rooted in the skeptical tradition passed down by Montaigne, held that such voyages not only allowed people to understand other perspectives, but also freed them from the bondage of custom.[12] Bernier took this maxim to heart and, by the late 1640s, he had already traveled to Holland, Germany, eastern Europe, and Italy. His most significant voyage, however, began in 1652 when he and Gassendi journeyed throughout France in order to conduct various experiments, including studying both solar and lunar eclipses from the hills of Provence.[13] It was also during this trip that Bernier, who had been studying anatomy under Gassendi for years, enrolled briefly at the University of Montpellier in order to obtain his doctoral degree in medicine.

PIERRE GASSENDI, ENGRAVING BY CLAUDE MELLAN, C. 1637 OR 1638

Bernier and Gassendi returned to Paris in 1653. As voyagers inevitably do, they presumably began thinking about their next trip. Gassendi, for one, had long hoped to travel to Jerusalem and the Orient to indulge his antiquarian fascination with the Levant.[14] This, however, became an unfulfilled dream. During the winter of 1655, the sixty-three-year-old philosopher fell gravely ill with a recurrent lung ailment. By October, his condition had worsened to the point where the only treatment that a phalanx of doctors could agree on was to bleed the famous man thirteen times. Bernier never wrote about this desperate scene, but a witness to Gassendi's final moments recounted how Bernier remained at his mentor's bedside throughout the ordeal, finally drawing Gassendi's eyes shut after he died.

Several months later, the now twice-orphaned Bernier decided to fulfill his and Gassendi's dream of exploring the Orient. In early 1656, he traveled to Marseille, where he boarded a ship destined for Egypt, the first stop on a far longer solo journey. Unlike most other Frenchmen who left France for faraway lands during the 1650s, the one-time farm boy was not a merchant, slave trader, colonialist, missionary, or ambassador operating on behalf of Louis XIV. Though he surely did not realize it, he had become one of the era's first philosophically minded European travelers, the type of person who sought to understand other countries, cultures, and peoples from the same critical and empirical point of view that was at the basis of his philosophy of nature.

THE ORIENT

Over the course of his thirteen years traveling through the "East," Bernier became increasingly fascinated by the different types (and colors) of humans he encountered. Early in his trip, however, he was simply attempting to stay alive. Not long after his arrival in Egypt, sometime in the summer of 1656, the thirty-six-year-old doctor trudged into Rosetta, a small city in the north of Egypt whose redbrick buildings looked down over the final stretch of the Nile. Like all French travelers who made their way to Rosetta, Bernier proceeded directly to the "French Quarter," a large, cloister-like series of buildings where one could cadge a hot meal. It was here that Bernier discovered that several Frenchmen in the compound, including the French Vice-Consul, were suffering from horrible fevers, crushing headaches, and agonizingly swollen lymph nodes: the telltale symptoms of plague. Bernier quickly attended to the men and, not surprisingly, he too came down with the disease.[15] Although he did not dwell on the specifics of this episode in his book, he claimed to have saved one person, lost another, and only rescued himself from the horrible malady by lancing his own swollen glands with a scalpel.

EGYPTIAN PYRAMIDS, ILLUSTRATION BY OLFERT DAPPER, 1670

By 1658, Bernier had tired of his travels in Palestine, Syria, and Egypt — he claimed to have been unimpressed by the pyramids — and booked passage on a 100-foot galley ship in Suez. The vessel, which was powered by two rows of slaves chained to their oars, proceeded south through the 1,400-mile Red Sea toward Mokha (in present-day Yemen). Here, he had planned to find another ship that would take him to Gondor (present-day Ethiopia), from where he was going to set off on a search for the source of the Nile.[16] Once he finally made it to Mokha, however, he met an Armenian slave trader who informed him that the likelihood of a Christian returning from a voyage to the interior of East Africa was slim to none. It was at this point that he impulsively decided to change plans and board a ship bound for Surat, on the west coast of India.[17]

Few Frenchmen had traveled to India before Bernier arrived in the 1660s.[18] Most were merchants who crossed the Arabian Sea to trade before returning to Europe shortly thereafter. Bernier's intention, on the contrary, was to explore the subcontinent. After spending a few days in Surat — a busy port with a seemingly endless matrix of mud and bamboo houses rising from the docks — he purchased a cart and three oxen and set off for adventure through the city's gates. Little did he know that he would soon be witness to the fratricidal civil war that would determine the fate of the Mughal Empire, an enormous hereditary monarchy whose population — c. 150 million — was more than double that of western Europe.[19]

Not long after leaving Surat, Bernier came across a battle-weary 2,000-man army led by Prince Dara Shukoh, the elder of two brothers claiming to be heir to the Mughal throne. Suddenly surrounded by a group of soldiers, Bernier was taken to meet the prince himself, at which point the Frenchman revealed — presumably in rudimentary Persian — that he was a physician traveling through the country. This news was received favorably and, within minutes, he was pressed into service to care for the prince's entourage, and in particular one of his wives, who had seriously injured her leg.

For the next few days, Bernier had no choice but to accompany Prince Dara's army, which was advancing slowly toward the city of Ahmedabad with the hope of securing provisions and reinforcements. Before arriving at this fortresslike enclave, however, the prince and his troops discovered to their horror that the governor had pledged loyalty to Dara's brother and had closed the city gates. Most of the now-starving troops deserted en masse, while Dara, who still possessed two elephants laden with gold and silver, convinced a small contingent of 500 men to join him on a desperate march to Kabul to continue the fight.

Bernier, at this point, was left behind with his books, maps, cart, valet, driver, and one dying ox. Already filthy and exhausted, he then began an arduous 600-mile trek to the seat of the Muslim-led Mughal Empire in Shahjahanabad (Delhi), during which he was detained for more than a week by a band of roaming thieves, or *kulis*. By the time that the French doctor arrived in Delhi, he was nearly penniless and physically depleted.

Having nonetheless understood that his medical expertise was highly appreciated in Mughal society, he made his way to the palace occupied by Dara's brother, Aurangzeb, who had by then cemented his position as Great Mughal, or Padishah of Hindustan. Remarkably, despite having served Aurangzeb's rival and brother, Bernier was immediately appointed personal physician to the emperor—a position that would give him unprecedented access to the highest spheres of the empire.

From his first weeks at court, Bernier realized that he had far fewer affinities with Aurangzeb than he had had with Prince Dara. While Dara was thoughtful and intellectual—even on the run—his brother, the emperor, was authoritarian, dogmatic, and ruthless. This impression was confirmed after Aurangzeb's army finally captured Dara and brought him back to the capital. To fully humiliate his defeated brother and demystify him in the eyes of the city's population, Aurangzeb ordered that Dara be tied to an elephant and paraded through the streets, before finally commanding that he be decapitated in his jail cell. To ensure that Dara was dead, he then demanded that his brother's head be delivered to him—quite literally—on a platter.

PORTRAIT OF AURANGZEB, WATERCOLOR, C. 1653–1655

Despite Bernier's distaste for some of the emperor's violent methods, living and traveling with Aurangzeb's court for the next eight years allowed the Frenchman to experience and record life on the subcontinent in a way that no other Westerner had yet done. Much of Bernier's insight into Indian customs and religions came from his lengthy and frequent discussions with a Persian nobleman, philosopher, and Mughal lord named Daneshmend Khan. Khan, who had hired Bernier a year or so after he arrived at court, was one of the most powerful men in India: simultaneously secretary of state for foreign affairs, Grand Master of the Horse, and governor of Delhi under Aurangzeb. Over the course of six years, the two men fell into a pleasant routine. Bernier's "Agha" or "Master" generally spent the morning occupying himself with courtly duties, but after the midday meal, this genial and relativistic interlocutor engaged with Bernier on a number of philosophical subjects. Among other things, Bernier claims to have translated both Descartes and Gassendi for Khan. It was also presumably from Khan that he learned about the racial hierarchy that characterized the Muslim Mughal empire. To be a Mughal, Khan told Bernier, it was best to be, like Khan himself, "a white foreigner and a Muslim, and thus distinct from the Hindus who are brown and heathen."[20]

During his time in "the Orient," Bernier recorded encounters with an astonishing palette of human phenotypes: dark-skinned and light-skinned Africans, Arabs, Baluchi, Barabras, Bohemians, Chinese, Dutch, Fundji, Georgians, Indians, Jews, Kashmiris, Mughals, Pathans, Persians, Poles, Portuguese, Rajputs, Tartars, Turks, and Uzbeks. He also traveled from one end of the Indian subcontinent to the other, from what is now southern Afghanistan and Pakistan to Golconda, in southern India. The most stunning travel account in his book was his trip to Kashmir, when he accompanied the court and Aurangzeb's 45,000-man army on a long trek north to this green and fertile basin surrounded by the snow-capped Himalayas. Much of this geographical, political, and ethnographic information was presumably recorded in the manuscripts that Bernier took back with him to France.

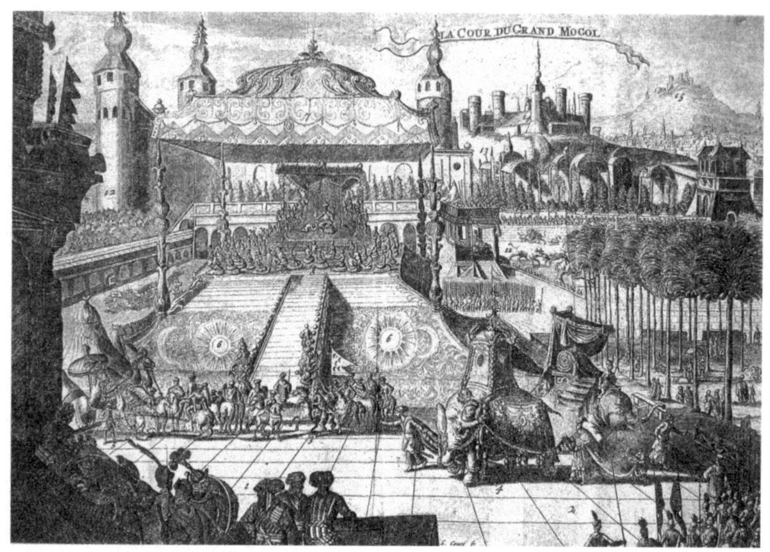

"THE COURT OF THE GREAT MOGUL," ENGRAVING FROM ROMEYN DE HOOGE, *LES INDES ORIENTALES ET OCCIDENTALES*, 1710

During the three years that it took to return to Europe, Bernier circumnavigated the entire Indian subcontinent from Bengal to Surat, before continuing on to Shiraz, Persia (Iran), and eventually Constantinople (Istanbul, Turkey), capital of the Ottoman Empire. From there, he secured passage on a French merchant vessel bound for Toulon. After sailing more than 2,000 nautical miles, the ship passed through the two stone forts guarding the entrance to the French port. Much like the French harbor from which he had departed years earlier, Toulon was crowded with merchant vessels, galleys, and hundreds of fishing boats. Along the waterfront, dockworkers moved bales of cotton, raw wool, and silk imported from Asia. The look of a French port had not changed in his absence. He, however, had aged considerably during several lifetimes of adventure.

THE RETURN TO PARIS

Before Bernier had even set foot on French soil, some of the letters that he had sent back from India had begun to circulate widely, winning him a certain notoriety in Paris and at Versailles. In particular, Jean-Baptiste Colbert, Louis XIV's chief minister and the engineer of France's imperial projects, was eagerly waiting to hear what Bernier had to say about Indian politics, agriculture, and history.[21] This type of fame was a welcome change for Bernier. To the extent that his name had been mentioned at court prior to his departure for the East, it had not been favorable.

In the early 1650s, the then-unknown Bernier had entered into a nasty public fight with a well-known mathematician and astrologer by the name of Jean-Baptiste Morin (1583–1656). Morin had committed a cardinal sin in Bernier's opinion: He had mocked Gassendi for supporting Galileo's theory that the Earth revolved around the sun. Bernier had riposted on his mentor's behalf by publishing two highly satirical books directed against Morin, the titles of which played off the similarity between Morin and the Latin word for mouse, *muris*. The resulting books—*Anatomy of a Ridiculous Mouse* (1651) and *The Ashes of a Ridiculous Mouse* (1653)—so incensed Morin that he wrote to Louis XIV's then-chief minister, Cardinal Mazarin, demanding that Bernier be questioned about his supposed heresy "under threat of the noose or the galleys."[22]

All this was forgotten by the time that the coach carrying Bernier arrived in Paris during the fall of 1669. Returning to the capital with 10,000 silver rupees bestowed upon him by the Great Mughal (c. 15,000 livres), Bernier now had the means to begin a far more distinguished writing career. Many of his aspirations would ultimately be facilitated by Madame de La Sablière, who not only provided Bernier with lodging, but invited him to think through what his adventures meant in the larger scheme of things.[23]

In the months after Bernier moved into Sablière's townhouse on the rue Neuve-des-Petits-Champs, he transformed his travel notes into a vast travelogue (and European bestseller) entitled *Voyages dans les états du Grand Mogul* (Travels in the Mogul Empire).[24] Over the course of the next few years, Bernier also composed a seven-volume synthesis of Pierre Gassendi's philosophy, a book which he created, in large part, for Madame de La Sablière herself.[25]

Given that Bernier was a fixture at Madame de La Sablière's famous salon, her entourage had certainly read him or at least knew about the books he had composed. Yet on the fateful day during the 1670s when Bernier decided to share his racialized "Division of the Earth," the audience may have been disconcerted, to say the least.

To understand just what Bernier was proposing — in an era where the notion of race remained as foreign as the yet undiscovered theory of gravity — several concepts need a bit of explaining. The first is the history of classification itself. Bernier was obviously not the first person to suggest that people could assign their fellow humans to specific groups. Every single ethnicity or community that has ever existed has probably produced some form of folk taxonomy with themselves as the ur-category — positioned at the center of the world or superior to other human groups. Europe and Europeans, of course, were no exceptions to this rule. During antiquity, the Greeks and the Romans distinguished themselves from the rest of the world's supposed rabble by designating themselves as civilized whereas all other human types were labeled barbarians.[26] Just who these barbarians were depended on one's perspective of course. The Greeks initially assigned the term to all non-Greek-speaking peoples, including Africans, Persians, and even Romans. Several centuries later, Romans tended to use the term to refer to the northern "tribes," including the Saxons, Goths, and Vandals — anyone who was not part of the Greco-Roman world. The term barbarian was still in use in the 1670s as well, and was sometimes applied to anyone who did not seem to have "laws or politeness," be they Iroquois, Highlanders, or Tartars.[27]

Bernier's taxonomy, however, did not attempt to divide the world in terms of its civilization or lack thereof; his innovation was dividing the world based on physical criteria. In this regard, he was tapping into a concurrent tendency that had begun when Aristotle broke down the world and its creatures into manageable, rational categories in his *History of Animals* (c. 350 BCE). Among the many stunning innovations in Aristotle's book, the Greek philosopher combined detailed observation with inductive reasoning. After studying the physical "data" that characterized the animal kingdom, he proposed two major categories: enaima (red-blooded animals — vertebrates) and anaima (invertebrates without blood). For each of these two classes, Aristotle then further inferred five genera, classing humans among the viviparous quadrupeds, four-limbed creatures who were born alive, which is to say not in eggs.[28]

Aristotle's classification scheme had two lasting — and somewhat contradictory — effects on the way that both animals and humans were understood over the next two millennia. First, he helped inspire the desire to categorize the natural world — to organize its flora and fauna within a rationalized system of taxonomy. Second, he envisioned humankind as a distinct and unified species, despite its many varieties and political statuses. While it is certainly true that Aristotle famously claimed that some people were slaves "by nature" and that women were naturally inferior to men, he did not divide the human species into distinct groups based on specific nations, geography, or skin color.[29] From his point of view, humanity was best understood as a whole: a species of rational beings who shared similar physical features and who collectively occupied the highest position in what would later be known as the Great Chain of Being—an immense hierarchy stretching from inanimate rocks through plants, animals, and humans, culminating, in the Christianized version, with angels and the deity.[30]

Humankind's special status as unclassifiable—as a unique species situated between animals and God—also meant that humans were necessarily of one *type* according to Aristotle. A similar understanding of humankind undergirds what we might call a biblical conception of the species. Consider how Paul describes the relationship of the deity to the world's peoples in Athenians. Far from reigning over a set of diverse and different humans, according to Paul, God "giveth to all life, and breath, and all things; and hath made of one blood all nations of men for to dwell on all the face of the Earth" (Acts 17:26).

Given Bernier's generally skeptical point of view, he presumably paid very little attention to "biblical anthropology." In this, he was not alone. By the 1670s, both freethinkers and biblical scholars alike had begun to ask why so many of the world's newly discovered nations or peoples—especially Native Americans—had not been mentioned in the Bible. As puzzling as the sheer variety of human beings was the fact that huge geographical distances and obstacles separated these same human groups from each other, not to mention from Europeans. The orthodox explanation that the descendants of Noah's three sons had somehow managed to migrate to Antarctica or Australia on foot, donkeys, or in some primitive boat seemed hard to believe.

Bernier studiously avoided taking up the dangerous question of human origins when talking about races in his "New Division of the Earth." He had, however, briefly alluded to this nagging problem in the seven-volume *Summary of the Philosophy of Gassendi*, which he first began publishing in 1678. Interestingly enough, Bernier never revealed what Gassendi himself thought about sacred history in this sprawling homage to his mentor. Instead, he began the discussion by conjuring up and then attempting to eliminate the "doubts" that certain philosophers—in all likelihood his free-thinking friends and maybe even himself—had voiced related to the Bible's account of humankind's origins:

> Regarding the doubt that some people have related to the settlement of various humans [in the various antipodes of the world], I will first leave to the side those Philosophers who have imagined that men could have originated all over the world; I will also leave aside those Philosophers who believe that our world is eternal, and that it is changing constantly and imperceptibly from land into ocean and ocean into land, and that the original men had no real origin, and that by some repeated reproduction they settled all over [the Earth] where we see them today and where they found nourishment; I am leaving these Philosophers to the side.[31]

There are two scandalous anthropological theories embedded in this paragraph, theories that will become far more important in subsequent decades. The first is the belief that the most geographically isolated and "unusual" types of humans—Africans and "Laplanders" (the Sámi)—were actually unrelated to Europeans and had distinct origins. This "separate origins theory" obviously contradicts the aforementioned Christian notion that all humans, whatever their size, shape, or color, had been created and blessed by an all-seeing and powerful deity.

Different versions of this so-called *polygenism*—literally a theory of multiple human geneses—had been circulating in certain circles since the Swiss physician and alchemist Paracelsus claimed in 1520 that there were actually two Adams, a White one who came into existence in Asia and a Native American one, the latter of whom God had created in the New World after the flood. Seventy years after Paracelsus, the Italian philosopher Giordano Bruno had added his own take on this theory. In Bruno's opinion, Africans had obviously come from a Black "Adam" or a separate pre-Adamite race.[32]

The most influential theory of polygenesis, however, had been published during Bernier's lifetime by a French traveler, diplomat, and biblical exegete by the name of Isaac de La Peyrère. La Peyrère's 1655 *Praeadamitae*, or *The Pre-Adamities*, contradicted the traditional Genesis story by maintaining that God had actually produced human groups on two different occasions. Basing his theory on his careful (if fanciful) study of the Bible, he claimed that, before God created the Jews, he gave life to the tribes of Gentiles (Native Americans, Eskimos, Africans, South Sea Islanders, Chinese, Europeans, etc.), all of whom initially lived in a brutish state of nature reminiscent of Hobbes's *Leviathan* (1651).[33]

The greatest irony about all of these polygenist theories was that their early proponents were all deeply religious, although heterodox thinkers. La Peyrère, for example, had hoped to reconcile the existence of humans who were not mentioned in the Bible with Scripture itself. His intention, in other words, was to shore up the coherence of sacred history with what he believed was a more logical (polygenetic) explanation for the physical, cultural, and geographical dissimilarities among the Earth's humans.[34] Subsequent generations of philosophers and naturalists who dabbled with the theory were far less interested in bothering with biblical exegesis. Indeed, most future polygenists — among them Voltaire — simply streamlined the theory by claiming that Whites, Blacks, and Native Americans had separate origins.

Bernier was well aware of the danger of discussing polygenesis in detail, so, regardless of what he may have thought about it himself, he dismissed it quickly before moving on to the second and even more radical explanation for humankind's origins: Namely, that it was not God, but rather the aimless bubbling of nature that eventually gave rise to the human race after countless attempts, failures, and generations. Bernier knew that defending or developing such a heretical idea—which flowed either directly or indirectly from the Roman poet Lucretius—could have easily meant being sent to the Bastille. Accordingly, in addition to righteously disagreeing with this theory, he reminds his readers of the orthodox "anthropology" of the Church: "[W]e are obliged to believe that all men draw their origin from one man who was formed in the Ancient World, and in Asia."[35] This language, which does not reveal exactly what Bernier himself thinks, only what one *must* think, is intriguing.

Identifying exactly what Bernier believed about the origins of humanity is, of course, impossible. And yet, while writing about Gassendi's life and philosophy, he nonetheless revealed how he would ultimately tackle the puzzling question of humankind's variants—by adopting the four-step empirical approach that Gassendi had taught him to use in his philosophy classes. According to the *bene cogitandi*, or the art of thinking well, that Gassendi preached, one would first need to imagine the topic to be discussed intelligently (without affirming or denying anything, including Scripture.)[36] Secondly, one would need to put forward solid propositions based on evidence from the senses. And third, one would need to deduce or infer an answer from the available evidence. And finally, one must order the findings. This is precisely what gave rise to the first paragraph of the "New Division" and a new theory of race:

> Hitherto, geographers have only divided the Earth into its respective Countries and Regions. But my own observations during my lengthy travels gave me the idea of dividing it in another way. Although one can easily associate men with the different areas of the world in which they live by looking at the external form of their bodies — especially their faces — and while people who have traveled widely can often distinguish one nation from another without a problem, I have nevertheless observed that there are four or five Types of Race among men that are so obvious that they can justifiably serve as the basis for a new division of the Earth.[37]

It was, in short, an empirical method of drawing a conclusion only after combining observation and one's own experience — and not by relying on the authority of Scripture — that gave rise to the novelty of the "New Division." It is amazing to think that this short paragraph heralded a revolution in the way that scientific-minded thinkers would soon begin perceiving the human species.

MAPPING PEOPLES, DIVIDING HUMANS

Despite the significance of the "New Division," Bernier's taxonomy of the human species has little in common with the dogmatic, skull-based classification schemes that would come into existence a hundred years later. One of the more intriguing and "candid" aspects of Bernier's salon-generated musings is his frank admission that he was initially unsure if there were four or five distinct races. This hesitation stemmed from the puzzling status of far-off Native Americans. Were they a separate group? Were their features, including their supposed "beardlessness," different enough to constitute a separate race? Or, on the contrary, were they cousins — linked to the larger group of humans living on the other sides of the huge oceans that separated them from the rest of the world?

Ultimately, with a quick stroke of his quill at the end of his article, Bernier chose to lump Amerindians in with the first "race" of humans, dividing the world's peoples into four major categories rather than five. This decision created the most enormous racial assemblage in the history of classification — an umbrella that encompassed a bewildering range of phenotypes, religions, and cultures, including: a) the indigenous nations of South, Central, and North America; b) the inhabitants of "France, Spain, England, Denmark, Sweden, Germany, Poland, and the whole of Europe in general except for part of Muscovy"; c) North Africans living "between the kingdoms of Fez and Morocco, Algiers, Tunis, and Tripoli as far as the Nile"; d) and the various peoples found in "the Empire of the Great Khan with the three Arabias, the whole of Persia, the realms of the Great Mogul, the Kingdom of Golconda, that of Bijapur, the Maldives, and part of the Kingdoms of Arakan, Pegu, Siam, Sumatra, Bantam, and Borneo."[38]

The size of this ostensibly related group of humans presumably left his audience gobsmacked. Bernier had stated in his preamble that he was breaking down humankind into separate groups. Yet his first race actually brought together a vast array of peoples and nations who had been separated from each other for centuries due to geography or ethnic or religious hatred, oftentimes both. Though Bernier never spelled it out in quite this way, he was asserting that everybody living in Europe — be they German, "Gypsy," or Jew — were members of the same race alongside "tawny" Turks, North Africans, Arabs, and Indians, as well as the inhabitants of some Asian islands! What was more, he had grouped different nations with a stunning range of pigmentation, from the whitest

Norwegian to dark-skinned Egyptians and Indians. Bernier's first race, in short, could not plausibly be called "white."

Bernier's study of human phenotypes produced different results when he assessed the three other categories of humans: Asians, Black Africans, and "Laplanders." Of these remaining races, he had precious little to say about Asians, apart from the fact that they were found in China, Japan, Burma, Vietnam, Turkestan, Nepal, upper Russia, and Mongolia, and could be identified by their "large shoulders, flat faces, snub noses, and oval-shaped eyes." Significantly, Bernier claimed that this was the sole race that was universally "white."[39]

BERNIER'S NEW DIVISION OF THE EARTH			
RACE 1	RACE 2	RACE 3	RACE 4
Amerindians, Europeans, North Africans, Middle Easterners, Indians, Southeast Asians	Sub-Saharan Africans	East Asians, Northeast Asians	Sámi peoples

BERNIER'S TAXONOMY OF HUMANKIND

The comparatively benign portrayal of the Asian "race" found in "New Divisions" contrasts markedly with Bernier's discussion of what he deemed to be the world's two truly inferior races, Black Africans and the so-called Laplanders. The latter of these two "races"—more appropriately referred to as the Sámi peoples of Northern Finland, Norway, Sweden, and parts of Russia—had only recently become a preoccupation for European thinkers. Although medieval- and Renaissance-era travelers had mentioned the existence of the inhabitants of these northern lands, there had been comparatively little written or known about "Lapland" or the "Laplanders" before the 1670s. As one writer put it at the time, Lapland was not the northern portion of Europe — it was a "new world," geographically close but seemingly the antithesis of European civilization.[40]

Bernier had two sources of information for his classification of the "Laplander" race. The first was Johannes Schefferus's *Lapponia* (1673), an "authoritative" account that laid the foundation for two centuries of belittling ethnography. Schefferus described the Sámi as a diminutive group of men who rarely reached "three feet tall," a condition he attributed to their meager diet of raw fish and the harsh, frigid environment they inhabited.[41] In his view, the Sámi were not only physically stunted, but also profoundly unattractive — generally stooped over with disproportionately huge heads mounted on their tiny bodies. Worse yet, morally speaking, they were supposedly superstitious, cowardly, and fearful, more devoted to devil worship than to the Christian God being introduced to them by evangelizing missionaries.

Bernier's second source of information came from his own experience. Establishing his credibility as an expert in Laplander "ethnography," he explained that he had personally met two members of this "race" while traveling through Danzig. As such, he assured his readers that everything he had seen confirmed everything he had read: They were indeed "villainous animals" with heads that resembled those of bears.[42]

As dehumanizing as Bernier's assessment of the Sámi was, his description of this seminomadic people remains on the level of basic xenophobia. Far closer to a deterministic, biological explanation of "race" is his view of the Black African. Bernier saw or met numerous Black Africans in his travels, all of whom had been the unwilling victims of the East African slave trade.[43] Some of these enslaved men worked the galley ships that took him across the Mediterranean. Others served in the Great Mughal's armies. There were also Black African eunuchs who had been purchased and subsequently emasculated in order to work in Persian and Indian seraglios.

Bernier's assessments of these transplanted or captive Africans reveal his training as a physician as well as his overall physiological orientation. As he does in his discussion of the Asian race and the Laplander race, Bernier cites the supposedly distinguishing features of Black Africans, e.g., their textured, "wool-like" hair and their "thick lips and their snub noses."[44] Most salient, however, is his view of African pigmentation. In stark contrast to what he affirms when discussing the skin color of Indians, Bernier rejects climatic explanations for African pigmentation. Instead, he argues that "blackness is [Africans'] essential trait" and that it is in no way caused by "the heat of the sun."[45] His rationale for this notion was based on what he believed to be empirical evidence: "[I]f you transport a Black man and a Black woman to a cold country, their children will continue to be black and so will all their descendants until they intermarry with White women."[46]

Blackness, for Bernier, has conceptual and taxonomical significance. Far more than a surface trait, it signals the fundamental stability of the African category. Bearing this in mind, Bernier inferred that the source of the Black race's "essential" traits, including supposedly oily skin, must be sought out on a deeper physiological level: in their "sperm" and in "their blood."[47] This explanation for blackness functions on two levels. Not only does this elemental and heredity-based understanding of African physical features prop up the taxonomical reality of the African category; it allows Bernier to conclude that all phenotypes or races must stem "from the nature of semen which must vary with specific races and types."[48] Here in one simple phrase were the basic ingredients for a biologically based racial classification.

These were not Bernier's final words on the African race, however. Having spent the first third of his article separating the world's peoples into four main categories, Bernier concludes with a strange anecdote regarding African women that was more smutty than scientific. Drawing nostalgically from his adventures in the Orient, where he had come across (and perhaps slept with) a wide range of women "types," Bernier assures his readers that female beauty sometimes has the ability to transcend European norms. "[B]eautiful and ugly women," as he puts it, "are found everywhere."[49] This phenomenon, he claims, is most pronounced among the African race.

To prove his point, Bernier conjures up an afternoon he had spent at a slave market in Mokha (Yemen). Strolling through the city's bazaar, where East African traders often arrived with caravans of young African girls to be sold, he was struck by the fact that some of these enslaved Black Africans—who had been stripped naked for inspection—lacked the supposed physical characteristics that Bernier believed *defined* the Black race. Indeed, he was so besotted by several of these enslaved girls that he compared them to a famous Roman-era marble statue called the *Venus Callipyge*. The choice of artwork was hardly innocent. In addition to the fact that Venus (or Aphrodite) was the Goddess of love, the *Venus Callipyge* was quite literally the "Venus of the beautiful buttocks."

> Seven or eight of [these enslaved Black girls at Mokha] were of a beauty so surprising, that in my opinion they eclipsed the Venus of the Farnese palace at Rome. The aquiline nose, the little mouth, the coral lips, the ivory teeth, the large and ardent

> eyes, that softness of expression, the bosom and all the rest, is sometimes of the last perfection. I have seen at Mokha many quite naked for sale, and I may say that I have never seen anything lovelier in the world.[50]

VENUS CALLIPYGE, STATUE, C. 200–100 BCE

Who knows what Bernier was thinking when he wrote these words. Did he realize that he had effectively undermined his own deterministic understanding of race, one that was supposedly passed on in semen and blood? Or did he believe that these young, enslaved girls—who were as subjugated as they were sublime to him—were the living exceptions to the Black race that nonetheless proved the rule? Whatever his intention or mindset, his assessment of African women contrasts markedly with how the majority of the era's travelers and philosophers envisioned blackness in the late seventeenth century.

THE LEGACY

Like many pioneering articles from which writers expect a big reaction, Bernier's "New Division" fell flat when it first appeared. Most seventeenth-century readers of his essay were presumably confused when this self-declared "famous traveler" referred to different types of humans with the word "race." Contemporary dictionaries, including Antoine Furetière's authoritative *Universal Dictionary* (1690) of the French language, did not reflect this innovation. In common parlance, "race" continued to be used to refer to different types of soulless animals, such as dogs, or bloodlines, such as the members of an "illustrious family" or several generations of kings. While late seventeenth-century French men and women had no problem identifying Blacks, Amerindians, Jews, Chinese, or Laplanders as their moral and perhaps even their physical inferiors, it remained uncommon to sort humankind into strict *racial* categories.[51]

Bernier did not forget about the "New Division," however. A few years after he first published his race theory, in June of 1688, he dispatched a letter and a slightly modified version of his text to Madame de La Sablière. By the late 1680s, he was no longer living in Sablière's house on the rue Neuve-des-Petits-Champs and had resumed traveling, this time to England and Southern France. As for the once worldly Madame de La Sablière, she too had moved on. In addition to disbanding her salon and converting to Catholicism (surely to avoid persecution after the Revocation of the Edict of Nantes in 1685), she ultimately retired to the Feuillants Convent on the rue Neuve-Saint-Honoré, where she lived until her death.[52]

In his note to Sablière, Bernier tries to amuse his friend by telling her that he hoped his little present would "draw her out of her solitary life for fifteen minutes."[53] But he also reveals why he had sent the already published "New Division" to her in the first place: He wanted to acknowledge the fact that it had been Madame de La Sablière's vibrant and effervescent mind that had helped give birth to this novel theory of human races. It had been she, in point of fact, who told him that "it would be wonderful to know if those peoples who lived in the middle of Africa, Australia, and other places that are almost unknown [to Europeans] would be different enough from us to be a type of different race."[54]

Three months after he sent his letter to Sablière, the sixty-eight-year-old Bernier, who had returned to Paris, was on his deathbed, acutely aware that the symptoms he was experiencing meant that his days or hours on Earth were numbered. On September 18, 1688, the worldly doctor summoned a notary, to whom he dictated his last will and testament. Only hours before he died, the once-vibrant traveler leaned painfully over the bed and signed the document in a shaky scrawl.[55]

During his last days on Earth, Bernier presumably received last rites from a parish priest and may have been convinced to think hard about eternal salvation. As likely, the freethinking skeptic may have looked back over his own astonishing life, perhaps wondering if posterity would remember him for his famous travelogue and massive summary of Gassendi's philosophy. As it turns out, however, his legacy stems from his breakdown of the Earth's inhabitants into "races" or "types."

Bernier's reputation as an early anthropologist began to solidify some thirty years after his death. By 1722, there had been enough talk about his curious essay that the *Mercure de France*, one of the most important literary journals in Europe, republished the "New Division" for an entirely different audience.[56] Bernier's thirty-eight-year-old breakdown of the human species, which now seemed exceedingly chatty by eighteenth-century standards, nonetheless invited a new generation of naturalists to better organize centuries of xenophobia into more logical categories.[57] As it turned out, this traveler and salon-goer had anticipated the Enlightenment's desire to bring order to the messy category of the human species. This quest, which ultimately evolved into the racialization of every last human living on the planet, took a significant step forward in 1735, when a young Swedish physician named Carl Linnaeus published one of the most influential books in history, his *Systema Naturae*, or *System of Nature*.

IV

CARL LINNAEUS, PAINTING BY ALEXANDER ROSLIN, 1775

CARL LINNAEUS: THE BOTANIST WHO TRANSFORMED MAN INTO AN ANIMAL

The unbounded dominion which Linnaeus
has assumed in the animal reign,
must upon the whole appear disgusting
to many persons.
—HALLER, "Letter to Johann Gesner," 1746

I am always astonished to find man . . .
under the category of quadrupeds.
What a strange place for man!
—BUFFON, *Histoire naturelle*, 1753

I read you, I study you,
I meditate on you, I honor you,
I love you with all my heart.
—ROUSSEAU, "Letter to Linnaeus," 1771

By the time that Carl Linnaeus reached his early sixties, the world-renowned naturalist realized that the time had come to evaluate the most impressive specimen he had ever encountered: *himself*. Over the course of the next two years, when he felt inclined, he worked on a 150-page manuscript that he called his *Vita*, or his *Life*.[1] Much of the early portion of the narrative recounts his childhood, his education, and how he eventually became a professor at the University of Uppsala. Toward the end of the story, however, Linnaeus finally assesses his many contributions to the field of natural history. Listing what he believes to be the highlights of a long career—in the same way that he might describe the characteristics of an unusual flower—Linnaeus sums up (in the third person) how important he believed he was, not only compared to his predecessors, but his contemporaries as well.

> "No one has been allowed to penetrate the secret recesses of nature but Linné."
>
> "No person has ever had a more solid knowledge of all the three kingdoms of nature."
>
> "No person has proved himself a greater botanist or zoologist."
>
> "No one has ever so completely reformed a whole science, and created therein a new era."
>
> "No one," he concludes, "has ever become so celebrated all over the world."[2]

Linnaeus also claims in these same pages, ironically enough, that he is "averse" to any behavior that bears "the appearance of pride." Modesty, however, was not appropriate in his case. Over the course of his forty-year career, he gave names to an astonishing 7,000 species of plants and 5,000 animals. His countrymen called him the

"Prince of Flowers." The French and the Dutch referred to him as the "Pliny of the North." Even in faraway North America, where European science was slower to take hold, some people dubbed him "the favored priest of nature."[3] His highest honors, however, had come from his own monarch. By the 1750s, King Adolf Frederick of Sweden had realized that Linnaeus was the most famous Swede to have ever lived and dubbed him the "Knight of the Order of the Polar Star." Several years later, the king took another step and ennobled Linnaeus, changing his name to *Carl von Linné*.

Linnaeus's long and, at times, prideful self-assessment actually downplays or neglects some of his most innovative and simultaneously provocative accomplishments.[4] In addition to the fact that he had developed a revolutionary classification system that allowed naturalists from around the globe to systematize all of nature, Linnaeus was the first person to declare unequivocally that humankind was a member of the animal kingdom, right next to the great apes. As novel as this idea was, he had also made one more unmentioned contribution to taxonomy. Within his schematic classification of the *three kingdoms of nature*, he had divided the human species into distinct groups or *varieties*, thereby becoming the first true *scientific* theoretician of race.

ORIGINS

The man who would become the "Great Linnaeus" was born in a humble, turf-roofed house located in Råshult, a remote locality in the Swedish province of Småland. One can still visit a replica of this house — the original burned down — where a museum guide dressed as the famous botanist informs guests that Christina Linnaeus delivered her firstborn son here at one o'clock in the morning on May 23, 1707. Reproduction or not, this austere one-story dwelling conveys the honest simplicity of what must have been a deeply religious household. Linnaeus's mother, born Christina Brodersonia, was the pious daughter of the rector in the neighboring parish of Stenbrohult. Her husband, Nils Ingemarsson Linnaeus, was also a man of the cloth, and had met and ultimately asked for Christina's hand in marriage while working for her father.

Several years after their wedding, by which point the young family had moved to the neighboring village of Stenbrohult, Nils Linnaeus began inculcating in his son a love of nature's wonders.[5] From Linnaeus's earliest years, he was taught that earthly and heavenly realms were intertwined, that the world was suffused with celestial intelligence and design. One of the greatest examples of this divine engineering, of course, was the stunning variety of flora found on Earth.

By the time that Carl could walk, he was already spending a lot of time in the parsonage's garden, where his father grew fruit and vegetables.[6] By age four, he had also begun accompanying Linnaeus senior on long, botanically focused walks into the forest. According to an anecdote Linnaeus later recounted, during one of these excursions he and his father were picnicking beside neighboring Lake Möcklen while discussing the orchids, honeysuckle, and devil's bit that were blossoming around them. Throughout the outing, Carl repeatedly asked his father to identify the plants and flowers that they encountered, only to forget each name as soon as he heard it. Eventually, as the story goes, the elder Linnaeus grew tired of answering the same questions and told the so-called little botanist that, from then on, he would "refuse to answer him unless [Carl] would promise to remember what was told him."[7] It was at this point in his life, Linnaeus recalled, that he began resolutely committing the names of each of these plants to memory so that he "might not be deprived of his greatest pleasure."[8]

From his parents' point of view, Linnaeus's obsession with flowers and plants started off as an endearing quality. By the time he was seven or eight, this diversion had become a source of constant familial friction, especially with his mother. Much of this had to do with her expectation that he become a Lutheran priest, like her father and her husband.

Linnaeus's supposed path to the clergy began at Wexiö school, some thirty miles away from Stenbrohult, at age nine.[9] The boy was certainly bright enough to excel at the religion-based curriculum that led to life as a pastor, but he was far more interested in plants than he was in theology, rhetoric, or ancient Greek. In an era where knowledge of the plant world was often seen as a distraction from more serious pursuits, Linnaeus was mocked and ridiculed. This trend began with his first tutor, whom Linnaeus later described as a violent brute better suited to "extinguishing a youth's talents, than . . . for improving them."[10] Several years later, his instructors at the Katedralskolan or "cathedral school" in Växjö were similarly frustrated with Linnaeus, and apparently did not hesitate to cuff him or any other student who did not memorize their lessons. By his teenage years, Carl had nonetheless managed to move on to *Gymnasium*, or high school. True to form, the now-eighteen-year-old skipped classes and wandered "around the outskirts of town," making "himself accurately acquainted with all the plants he could find."[11] By late 1726, Carl's father received the disappointing news that his boy might be best suited to making shoes or barrels.

Despite this pessimistic assessment, there was one professor at Växjö, a physician named Johan Rothmann, who understood that Linnaeus's inability to excel in school had little to do with his real potential. In spring of 1726, he let Nils Linnaeus know that Carl was perhaps ill-suited to the priesthood. But he also suggested that the boy begin medical studies since botanical knowledge was such a key aspect of the profession.[12] To help facilitate this abrupt career change, Rothmann volunteered to tutor Linnaeus in *physics*—a discipline understood quite broadly as the study of the natural world—in order to prepare him for university.[13] The gambit worked. In 1727, Linnaeus matriculated at Lund University, where he continued both his formal and informal study of botany and even had occasion to visit sick patients alongside an elderly doctor with whom he was lodging. The following year, he decided, upon Rothmann's suggestion, to transfer to the University of Uppsala to pursue his interest in botany and medicine.[14]

Linnaeus was buoyant as he set off for what was supposedly the best university in Sweden. Before he left, Rothmann had extolled the university's superb botanical garden, its extensive library, and what he claimed were the country's best professors.[15] Much had changed, however, since his professor had left the university. An English traveler who passed through Uppsala shortly before Linnaeus began there described the institution as anemic. Not only had the university's student body decreased to 150 or 200 students, but, according to this same Englishman, its library paled in comparison to that of a decent English grammar school.[16]

Linnaeus, too, realized that Uppsala did not live up to Rothmann's acclaim. Upon his arrival, he discovered that offerings related to both anatomy and botany had all but disappeared from the curriculum due to retirements. Even more disheartening was the fact that the botanical garden, which was surrounded by a number of foul-smelling tanneries, had degenerated into a weed-infested tangle of perhaps 200 plants, of which "not more than a hundred [were] of any interest."[17] The few students who had come to Uppsala to study botany and medicine at the university—there were perhaps a dozen in all—were effectively on their own. This became painfully clear to Linnaeus and his fellow medical students when they had to arrange and pay for a ten-hour coach ride to Stockholm in order to attend their first human dissection. Ironically enough, the only person who helped facilitate the careers of these would-be doctors was the city magistrate responsible for law and order in Stockholm: He kindly delayed the execution of the future cadaver in question — a female prostitute or thief? — so that her body would be fresh when the students finally made it to town.[18]

In addition to the challenges posed by the university, Linnaeus received a letter informing him that his parents' financial state prevented them from further funding his education. The young man was so destitute during his first months at the university that he frequently needed to borrow money from friends to eat or, on one occasion, to have his shoes resoled. His luck finally changed on an autumn day in 1729, when an elderly clergyman with long stringy hair and a short beard came upon Linnaeus in the university's botanical gardens. After quizzing the young man on botanical specimens, during which time Linnaeus stunned the man with his plant knowledge, his inquisitor revealed that he was none other than Olof Celsius, a famous doctor and botanist who, while no longer teaching at the university, still wielded enormous influence in the community.[19] This chance encounter changed Linnaeus's life. Within a year, the medical student was not only living in Celsius's house, but had received two fellowships, had found a number of paying private students, and had penned a short treatise on identifying plants by means of their sexual organs. This last essay had so impressed yet another professor that Linnaeus soon received an offer to give lectures in the botanical gardens.[20]

It was also during the late 1720s that the full scale of Linnaeus's ambitions began to materialize. Disappointed by what he believed to be haphazard classification systems employed by other naturalists, he began dreaming of a new and comprehensive *system of nature* that would extend to the mineral and animal realms, as well as to the more familiar botanical kingdom.[21] To do so was to challenge the millennia-old skepticism of Aristotle who, despite the fact that he had proposed his own taxonomy, nonetheless acknowledged the limitations of drawing clear and permanent distinctions within the grand *flux* of nature.[22] Linnaeus, in short, was confronting one of the greatest quandaries of science, a problem that seemed as insolvable as it was eternal: how to identify a single characteristic or set of characteristics in a fish, rock, or plant that would allow naturalists to place this same "taxonomic unit" within a coherent series of ordered divisions.[23]

In these early years, Linnaeus worked on this project with Peter Artedi, an advanced medical student who shared the belief that all existing taxonomies were misleading and arbitrary.[24] In the late 1720s and early 1730s, Linnaeus and Artedi began constructing their own classificatory system. Artedi took charge of the complicated world of reptiles, amphibians, and fish; he also claimed jurisdiction over plants with parasol-like flowers such as wild carrots or hemlock, the so-called *umbellate* plants. As for Linnaeus, he concentrated on birds and insects and provided a framework for the rest of the plant world. Both men shared the herculean task of breaking down quadrupeds.[25]

Looking back on these heady days, Linnaeus recalled that the two friends worked extremely well together despite the fact that, as he saw it, they were as different as chalk and cheese. Artedi was far taller, thinner, and handsome; the brown-eyed Linnaeus was shorter, darker, and stockier, with less "aristocratic" features. There were also big differences in demeanor. Artedi had a very serious and "deliberate" way of relating to life, whereas Linnaeus admitted that he was far more impetuous and enthusiastic, even "hasty" and "sanguine."[26]

After several months of work where the two men began to see real progress on their system, Linnaeus and Artedi vowed to carry their important task to completion, even if one of them should die prematurely. This was a distinct possibility. In 1732, Linnaeus announced that he planned to undertake a dangerous solo voyage to Lapland and the Arctic Circle to seek out and identify new specimens of uncataloged flowers, mosses, lichens, rocks, and birds from interior Lapland (as well as to make a name for himself).[27]

To finance this expedition, Linnaeus did what most scientists must do at some point in their careers: beg for money. Presumably championed by Celsius and Olof Rudbeck—the latter of whom had traveled to Lapland in 1695—Linnaeus requested funding from Uppsala's Royal Society of Science. In his letter to the Society, Linnaeus proposed exploring this frozen and potentially perilous land in search of heretofore unknown animals, minerals, and—of particular interest—plants, that might prove useful in medicine.[28] He also asserted that he would conduct ethnographic research on the territory's nomadic fishermen and reindeer herders, populations whose way of life seemed so different from that of the average Swede. Although the Society rejected his first request, they ultimately financed the expedition with a relatively modest grant of 400 dalers.[29]

In May of 1732, the twenty-five-year-old Linnaeus bought some used leather breeches at auction and set off on horseback from Uppsala on a four-month journey covering some 3,000 miles. His log indicates that he packed light: In addition to a heavy coat and gloves, he brought along a pigtailed wig, a woven cotton cap, a nightcap, and several shirts of various lengths. The leather bag he toted with him also contained his pen and ink, notebook, paper, magnifying glass, spyglass, letters of introduction, and his manuscripts on ornithology. A small shotgun and a sword, both of which were draped over his shoulders, were his only means of defense.[30]

During the first eleven weeks of his trip, Linnaeus followed the comparatively well-traveled dirt (or muddy) roads that ran parallel to Sweden's lake-filled east coast, staying in posthouses along the way. Once he left "civilization," he began crossing through conifer-dense forests that—even today—are famous for their particularly aggressive gnats, flies, and mosquitos. By the time that he had reached the northernmost areas of Lapland—during the season of the midnight sun—he was hiking on rock-filled plateaus and, eventually, up and over several snow-covered Scandinavian mountains. Overwhelmed at what he was seeing, he declared that he had entered a world whose plants and soil were so different that he might as well be in "Asia or Africa."[31]

During much of this voyage, Linnaeus relied on the native Sámi (he called them Laplanders) for food, shelter, and, on occasion, to shepherd him across or up the many rivers that poured into the northern Gulf of Bothnia. It was during these moments that Linnaeus recorded his ethnographic musings in his diary-like travelogue. Unlike the majority of eighteenth-century travelers and naturalists who published their views on the Sámi, Linnaeus generally avoided dehumanizing language. A man of his time, he nonetheless focused on customs that he found primitive, exotic, or otherworldly. He marveled at the fact that they smoked juniper berries, ate beaver feet, and strained their reindeer milk through the "tufts of hair from a cow's tail."[32] This prurient Lutheran was also fascinated by the way that the Sámi lived in their four- or six-sided teepee-like *kodda* (*kåta* in Swedish), or huts. "The inhabitants sleep quite naked on skins of reindeer, spread over a layer of branches of Dwarf Birch (*Betula nana*), with similar skins spread over them. The sexes rise from this simple couch, and dress themselves promiscuously without any shame or concealment."[33] Though Linnaeus admitted that there were aspects to the Sámis' existence that seemed brutally backward—he constantly wondered why they did not make use of all the excellent wood to make houses instead of wandering around the country in pursuit of fish—he also marveled at their tranquility of mind, their uncanny ability to run quickly over any terrain, and their ability to provide unusual food for themselves, be it reindeer cheese or bread baked from pine bark.[34]

SÁMI SHELTER, ENGRAVING BY WILLIAM HOGARTH IN AUBRY DE LA MOTTRAYE'S *TRAVELS THROUGHOUT EUROPE, ASIA AND INTO PART OF AFRICA*, 1724

In his notes, posthumously published in 1811 as *Lachesis Lapponica*, or a *Tour in Lapland*, Linnaeus painted the Sámis' unfettered existence as something of a "Golden Age," the "pastoral state as depicted by Virgil."[35] Prefiguring elements of the "noble savage" trope that Rousseau would make famous in the 1750s, Linnaeus compared the endless churning of European existence—he was clearly thinking of the harried existence that he himself was leading as student, naturalist, and teacher—to the bucolic life of freedom and happiness that he had seen among the Sámi.

Linnaeus's trip to Lapland was undoubtedly the most meaningful voyage of his life. Toward the end of his journey, he was so moved by the experience that he composed a prose poem in which he attempted to summarize both the emotional and geographical states he had experienced. Recollecting the flowers that he had seen as "waving to him in friendship," he mused that he had climbed "six miles into the skies," "passed through clouds," "visited the ends of the world," and witnessed "the sun's overnight refuge." What he did not mention in this lyrical summary of his travels was a different epiphany: his discovery of a revolutionary new way of organizing the world's quadrupeds, among them the human species.[36]

This Newton-like revelation had happened when Linnaeus stumbled across a horse carcass rotting on the side of the road, about a month after his departure from Uppsala. As he stared down at the animal's skull, he noticed that the creature's "under jaw" had "six fore-teeth, much worn and blunted, two canine teeth, and at a certain distance from the latter twelve grinders, six on each side."[37] This cursory assessment of the horse's bones and dental structure suddenly led to the comparative anatomy insight that would help him think through his ongoing study of classification: "If only I knew how many teeth and of what kind every animal had, how many teats and where they were placed, I should perhaps be able to work out a perfectly natural system for the arrangement of all quadrupeds."[38] This is precisely what he would attempt to achieve upon his return to Uppsala, not only for quadrupeds but for the whole of nature.

THE ORIGINS OF THE *SYSTEM OF NATURE*

In October 1732, four months after leaving Uppsala, Linnaeus returned to his adopted city. The twenty-five-year-old traveler did not shy away from the notoriety that his voyage had generated. Upon his return, he sometimes paraded around town in a strange assemblage of Sámi clothing that included a big flowing tunic, fur-lined boots, a woman's hat, various weapons, and one or two musical instruments draped around his neck. The combination, of course, would have made the Sámi laugh in derision. In later years, he added a "magic" drum to this collection, which is now on display in his house in Uppsala.[39]

PORTRAIT OF LINNAEUS IN SÁMI CLOTHING,
PAINTING BY MARTIN HOFFMAN, 1737

When not engaging in these jovial moments of self-promotion, Linnaeus holed up in a small room that he rented near the university in order to write. Surrounded by a mishmash of bird skins, animal bones, and botanical specimens that he had tacked on his walls, he dashed off a series of scientific papers on subjects related to his trip. These included the mysterious death of cattle, the use of the poisonous wolf's bane (aconite) as food, and how to create a "makeshift bed in the wilderness."[40] In these same months, Linnaeus also continued working with Peter Artedi on what would become his life's work: dividing the natural world into logical categories based on observable phenomena.

Linnaeus was only too aware that they were far from the first people to give new names to the world's animals, vegetables, and minerals. He also knew that each attempt at doing so muddied the discipline of natural history. In addition to the fact that each world language had its own terminology, European naturalists had put forward a number of competing and conflicting ways of identifying and organizing plants and animals. Linnaeus himself joked that zoology before his time was a horrific mess, an "Augean stable, filled with tables and nonsense, and far from being a science or a system."[41] Diderot's *Encyclopédie* also summed up the situation. Any eighteenth-century naturalist who wanted to make order of the world was working in a discipline characterized by "chaos and confusion"; it was a "vague science without order or principles."[42]

Just what kind of "chaos and confusion" could result in eighteenth-century natural history is best seen if one looks at one of the era's zoological riddles: the family of large seagrass mammals now known familiarly as manatees.[43] Sailors had encountered these slow-moving aquatic creatures in Africa, the Pacific, North and South America, and the Caribbean. The Portuguese called them "cow fish"; the Italians "fish women"; and German naturalist

Georg Wilhelm Steller, who was actually referring to the whale-sized (and now-extinct) *Hydrodamalis gigas*, dubbed them "sea cows."[44] Jean-Baptiste Labat also added to the confusion, calling manatees a "fish" or "a marine cow."[45]

Linnaeus, who was speculating on the status of these animals from remote Uppsala, hesitated. Indeed, he even wondered if some of these creatures were actually the *sirens*, or *mermaids*, referred to most famously by Homer in the *Odyssey*. After some indecision, he ultimately added these creatures to a category of beings he called *paradoxa*, strange creatures that natural history had not yet understood or that he believed were perhaps *phantastic*.[46]

The inevitable contradictions and misunderstandings that came about due to the world's diverse systems of classification and nomenclature had been less of a problem when few people traveled. Earlier savants who organized nature into a "system" were addressing themselves to relatively localized audiences, as Aristotle and Theophrastus had done for the Mediterranean world.[47] All of that changed with the European outthrust. Beginning in the fifteenth century, European ships were returning from Asia, Africa, and the New World on a regular basis with descriptions (and actual specimens) of thousands of heretofore unknown plants and animals. Earlier reference books of natural history from antiquity or the Middle Ages generally were of little help in figuring out what these plants and animals were.[48] Linnaeus himself tended to malign these early works, filled as they were with vague descriptions without illustrations or, worse, peppered with mythology-laced images of terrifying beasts: "[I]f we examine [these old] zoologies," he wrote, "we shall find for the greater part nothing but fabulous stories, a vague way of writing, [and] pictures by the copper engravers. There are very few indeed, who have tried to reduce zoology to genera and species according to the rules of systematics."[49]

THE COMPARATIVELY SPECULATIVE OUTLINE OF THE AFRICA COAST IN SEBASTIAN MUNSTER'S MAP OF AFRICA, 1554

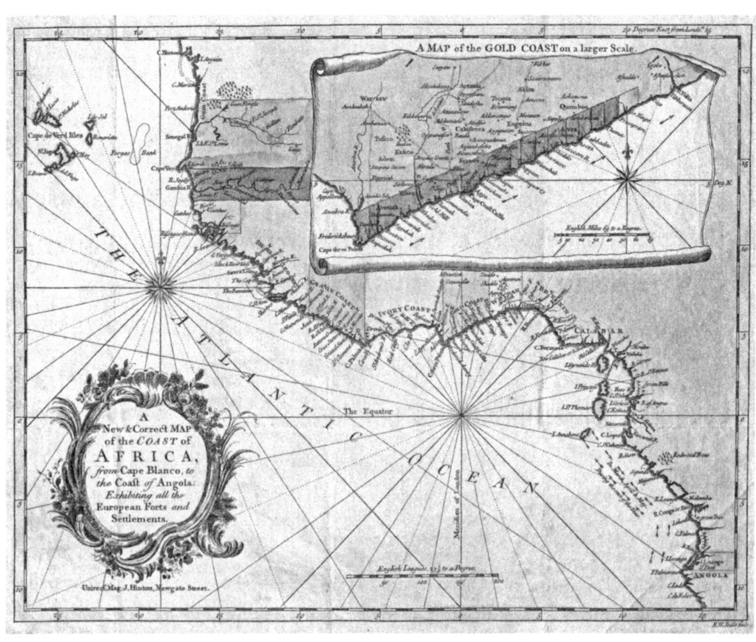

MAP OF THE AFRICAN COAST, C. 1750, REFLECTING THOUSANDS MORE VOYAGES AND LANDFALLS

To anybody trying to decipher the world's botanical and zoological mysteries, nature seemed to be a Tower of Babel. Yet Linnaeus was not only convinced that nature held a true order, but that it was also his calling to identify new categories that would actually produce real, demonstrable knowledge regarding the essence of and links among natural phenomena.[50] Part of his conviction that such an insurmountable task was possible stemmed from the fact that he believed that nature's many species had always been exactly as he saw them before his eyes; they were perfect, immutable, and timeless categories, extensions and signs of God's splendor and intentions. Linnaeus summed up this principle as an axiomatic conviction a few years later. As he put it: The "same truly begets the same." Needless to say that the far more fluid idea of nature that was increasingly being theorized — especially in France — had no place in his worldview.[51]

Linnaeus continued working on his classification scheme in Uppsala for two more years. Around 1734, his plans changed after his fellow classifier Peter Artedi left for London with the intention of studying natural history for a year or so before relocating to Holland to obtain a medical license. Linnaeus, too, had always known that the time would come when he would be obliged to temporarily relocate to Holland if he wanted to become a doctor because universities in Sweden did not offer a specific degree in medicine. The need to obtain this diploma — and the gainful employment that it might produce — became even more pressing after Linnaeus proposed marriage to a blond-haired, sixteen-year-old girl named Sara Elisabeth Moraea from the neighboring province of Dalarna. On the day that he asked for her hand, he donned his Sámi costume, presumably to remind everybody concerned (including Sara Elisabeth's skeptical parents) of his greatest accomplishment: risking life and limb in Lapland in the interest of natural philosophy.

Sara Elisabeth's mother and father were anything but enthused about welcoming Linnaeus into their family. Compared to the many other possible suitors for their daughter, this ragtag botanist had little money and seemingly even fewer prospects.[52] Her father, a very successful doctor practicing in Falun, ultimately relented under one condition: Linnaeus needed to finish his medical degree within three years. Linnaeus accepted these terms and, six months later, set off for Harderwijk, Netherlands, a small provincial city whose primary claim to fame was having a university known for its quick delivery of diplomas. By June 1735, he had successfully defended his doctoral thesis, which attributed the cause of malaria in Sweden to drinking water contaminated with small particles of clay.[53]

By acquiring medical credentials, Linnaeus had fulfilled his obligation vis-à-vis his fiancée (and her father). Yet rather than returning to Sweden to be wed and establish a medical practice, he decided to devote himself more fully to botany for several years in Leyden and eventually in Amsterdam, the latter city a metropolis more than twenty times bigger than Uppsala (c. 240,000 versus c. 11,000 inhabitants).[54]

Once Linnaeus had found lodging in the Dutch capital, the still-nearly-penniless doctor wasted no time seeking out the most famous scientists and naturalists in the city with the intention of sharing his new *system of nature*. As was often true, his enthusiasm and self-confidence were initially off-putting, yet in virtually every case, his knowledge and charm ultimately won out.[55] One of the first people he met in Amsterdam was Johannes Burman, the director of the city's botanical garden. During one of their conversations, Burman decided to test the young Swede by asking him to identify a rare plant specimen. Linnaeus first inspected and then licked the sample, quickly announcing that it was a *cinnamomum*, or cinnamon plant. Soon thereafter, Burman invited Linnaeus to lodge with him in exchange for his help on a book related to the plants of New Zealand.[56]

Several months later, the two men received a visit from one of the richest men in Holland, the Anglo-Dutch banker and director of the Dutch East India Company, George Clifford (1685–1760). When Clifford discovered how talented and knowledgeable Linnaeus was, he excitedly invited Burman and his "lodger" to come see his enormous collection of plants and zoological specimens at his estate in the neighboring village of Heemstede.

Several weeks later, the carriage carrying Burman and Linnaeus pulled up in front of Hartekamp, the late seventeenth-century Dutch château that Clifford's father had bought in 1709. Linnaeus was overwhelmed. Hartekamp's gardens included an orangery and four large tropical hothouses that a contingent of garden boys kept warm by burning enormous quantities of wood.[57] For the first time in his life, Linnaeus was able to come in contact with hundreds of tropical plants from the two Indies — East and West — that he had only read about in books or, when he was really lucky, had seen as dried specimens. As obsessed as he was with these botanical specimens, Linnaeus was even more overwhelmed by Clifford's aviary and menagerie, where he was able to see (and study) tigers, apes, monkeys, warthogs, antelopes, peccaries, pheasants, falcons, teals, coots, buntings, parrots, and far more.[58] Hartekamp's collections were not only a testament to the Enlightenment-era fascination with the living world; they demonstrated how the enormous wealth generated from the colonial trade was translating into new knowledge.

Clifford ultimately convinced Linnaeus to stay on as house physician and gardener for two years.[59] While living in this botanical and zoological laboratory, Linnaeus worked unremittingly, producing a catalog of Clifford's garden and publishing three major works related to classification. The first was his *Fundamenta Botanica* (Fundamentals of botany), which explains his rationale for updating the taxonomy of the plant world in the form of 365 aphorisms.[60] In his second work, *Flora Lapponica* (Flora of Lapland), Linnaeus demonstrates how his new understanding of botanical nomenclature could be used to sort the native plants he encountered in the north of Sweden.[61] The most significant work that he had prepared for publication, however, was the first edition (1735) of his *Systema Naturae*, a fourteen-page book—typeset in an enormous folio-size edition—that schematically rendered Linnaeus's breakdown of nature into three kingdoms and their respective *classes*, *orders*, *genera*, and *species*.

FRONTISPIECE OF *FLORA LAPPONICA*, 1737

CAROLI LINNÆI

I. QUADRUPEDIA. *Corpus* hirsutum. *Pedes* quatuor. *Feminæ* viviparæ, lactiferæ.

ANTHROPOMORPHA: Homo, Simia, Bradypus.
FERÆ: Ursus, Leo, Tigris, Felis, Mustela, Didelphis, Lutra, Odobænus, Phoca, Hyæna, Canis, Meles, Talpa, Erinaceus, Vespertilio.
GLIRES: Hystrix, Sciurus, Castor, Mus, Lepus, Sorex.
JUMENTA: Equus, Hippopotamus, Elephas, Sus.
PECORA: Camelus, Cervus, Capra, Ovis, Bos.

Ordines. Genera. Characteres Generum. Species.

II. AVES. *Corpus* plumosum. *Alæ* duæ. *Pedes* duo. *Rostrum* osseum. *Feminæ* oviparæ.

ACCIPITRES: Psittacus, Strix, Falco.
PICÆ: Paradisea, Coracias, Corvus, Cuculus, Picus, Certhia, Sitta, Upupa, Ispida.
MACRORHYNCHÆ: Grus, Ciconia, Ardea.
ANSERES: Platea, Pelecanus, Cygnus, Anas, Mergus, Graculus, Colymbus, Larus.
SCOLOPACES: Hæmatopus, Charadrius, Vanellus, Tringa, Numenius, Fulica.
GALLINÆ: Struthio, Casuarius, Otis, Pavo, Meleagris, Gallina, Tetrao.
PASSERES: Columba, Turdus, Sturnus, Alauda, Motacilla, Luscinia, Parus, Hirundo, Loxia, Ampelis, Fringilla.

III. AMPHIBIA. *Corpus* nudum, vel squamosum. *Dentes molares* nulli: reliqui semper. *Pinnæ* nullæ.

SERPENTIA: Testudo, Rana, Lacerta, Anguis.

PARADOXA.

Hydra. Rana-Piscis. Monoceros. Pelecanus. Satyrus. Borometz s. Agnus Scythicus. Phoenix. Bernicla s. Anser Scoticus & Concha Anatifera. Draco. Automa Mortis.

SYSTEMA NATURAE, 1735

By the mid- to late-1730s, Linnaeus's reputation as a naturalist and botanist had spread well beyond both Sweden and Holland, largely thanks to his *Systema Naturae*. But not all of his fame came from his publications. While living at Clifford's estate, Linnaeus also made headlines for coaxing fruit from the famed *Musa* — the banana tree — making him the first in Northern Europe to do so.[62] His success lay in replicating the tropical conditions in which the *Musa* thrived. Coordinating his efforts with Clifford's "garden boys," he raised the temperature in the hothouse by burning logs around the clock and alternatively drenching and depriving the plant of water based on his understanding of jungle rainfall patterns. After months of attending to the rare specimen, Linnaeus was overjoyed to see the appearance of the first blossoms and, eventually, the sweet banana fruit. "Causing the fine *Musa* to flower in Holland for the first time," Linnaeus said later, "was looked upon through the whole country as a wonder."[63]

Linnaeus described this period of his life at Hartekamp as paradise-like. Though he exhausted himself by working on multiple projects simultaneously, he finally had a proper salary and laboratory in which to conduct his research. What was more, his reputation was such that some of the most well-known people in Holland were offering him prized positions — provided he stay in the country.[64]

Clifford had hinted that, were his lodger to remain, he would surely come to occupy the chair in botany at the University of Utrecht. The world-famous doctor and botanist Herman Boerhaave also had proposals. Although he had initially refused to meet with Linnaeus when the Swede first arrived in Holland, he now offered to send him on a research expedition to South Africa, during which time he promised that the young naturalist could collect specimens from the other side of the world. After Linnaeus declined, Boerhaave proposed yet another idea in 1738: arranging to have him named the Ordinary Physician of the Dutch slave colony of Surinam, a post that would come "with some tons of gold."[65] Linnaeus politely passed up all of these opportunities.

Linnaeus's Dutch colleagues had clearly understood that the author of the groundbreaking 1735 *Systema Naturae* was in the process of accomplishing something remarkable for the discipline of natural history. Although his first chart-like breakdown of all of nature may now seem simplistic, forced, and unnecessarily reductive, the Swede had opened the door to a new and all-encompassing way of systematizing all natural phenomena. The most significant category to be absorbed into this enormous enterprise was, of course, the at-one-time *unclassable* human species.

RE-THINKING *HOMO* AND ITS VARIETIES

It was during the late 1730s that Linnaeus began to describe himself as an "oracle." And yet, if much of Holland had fallen under his spell, this was not the case throughout all of Europe. As Linnaeus's classificatory writings became better known, an increasing number of people understood that he was advocating for the overthrow of all previous systems of nomenclature and classification. In Britain, naturalists were reluctant to abandon their own classificatory pathfinder, John Ray. In Leipzig, Germany, Christian Gottlieb Ludwig sent Linnaeus a letter stating flatly that it was foolhardy to attempt to revamp the discipline of botany because German botanists would never abandon "well-established" plant names.[66] There were also more censorious attacks. In Sweden, the religiously oriented Johann Georg Siegesbeck published a book that lambasted Linnaeus for using sexualized metaphors to describe pollination (e.g., bed, husband, and womb). Mocking what he called Linnaeus's "fictitious matrimony of plants," Siegesbeck asked how anyone could recommend such a system, particularly given that botany was often taught to children.[67]

It was, however, placing humans squarely within the animal kingdom — a move of stunning impudence — that incited the fiercest criticism from as far as Saint Petersburg.[68] In assigning the genus *Homo* to the same plane of being as other animals, Linnaeus seemingly turned his back on a series of biblical truths, namely: 1) that man had been made "after [God's] likeness"; 2) that man stood apart from the rest of the animals; and 3) that "all flesh is not the same flesh [that] there is one flesh of man, and another of beasts, and another flesh of birds, and another of fish."[69] For the most religious thinkers, Linnaeus's worst sin was neglecting to mention the sine qua non of the species, the idea that the first man, Adam, and all those who came after, were given souls.[70]

Linnaeus, who was himself a firm believer in the astonishing power of God, had anticipated such objections. He had even tried to counter them in advance in providing a short text that accompanied his 1735 classification chart. As he put it, the breakdown he was proposing was anything but outrageous. It was as simple as the fact that:

> "Minerals grow"; "plants grow and live"; and "animals grow, live, and feel."[71]

Given this simple division of the natural world, where else would one place humankind? A few years later, when this idea became the subject of even more criticism, Linnaeus stated his position even more forcefully:

> No one has the right to be angry with me . . . , [m]an is neither a stone nor a plant, but an animal, for such is his way of living and moving.[72]

This second declaration is as much about Linnaeus's method as it is about the resulting categories. The naturalist is explaining to his readers that he is simply subjecting humankind to the same modus operandi that he had employed for the other creatures living on Earth. If certain types of fish are grouped by dint of the morphology of their fins, certain species of insects by the configuration of their wings and antennae, and select subgroups of amphibians by their cold body and "naked" skin — humans should logically be lumped in those animals with four appendages. The term he used to bring these animals together was *Quadrupedia*, a category first coined by Aristotle two thousand years before.[73]

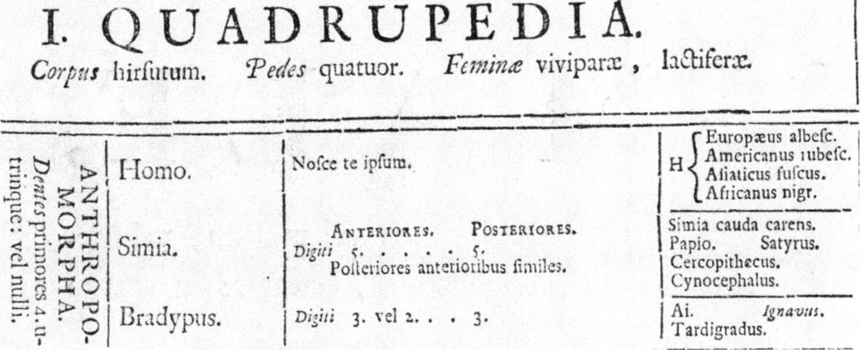

I. QUADRUPEDIA.

Corpus hirſutum. *Pedes* quatuor. *Feminæ* viviparæ, lactiferæ.

ANTHROPOMORPHA. *Dentes* primores 4. utrinque: vel nulli.			
	Homo.	Noſce te ipſum.	H { Europæus albeſc. Americanus rubeſc. Aſiaticus fuſcus. Africanus nigr.
	Simia.	ANTERIORES. POSTERIORES. *Digiti* 5. . . . . 5. Poſteriores anterioribus ſimiles.	Simia cauda carens. Papio. Satyrus. Cercopithecus. Cynocephalus.
	Bradypus.	*Digiti* 3. vel 2. . . . 3.	Ai. *Ignavus.* Tardigradus.

QUADRUPEDIA* DETAIL FROM *SYSTEMA NATURAE

According to Linnaeus, humans and all members of the class of Quadrupedia have several distinguishing features in addition to the number of arms and legs. Their bodies are covered with hair; the female members of Quadrupedia produce live-born children (as opposed to eggs); and they breastfeed their young. This reduction of the human species to a series of anatomical criteria and mechanical functions was already sufficient to merit scorn from a number of religious thinkers. Yet Linnaeus went further by situating humans under a second taxon, Anthropomorpha. This category, which brought together animals that were *man-shaped*, not only included the genus *Homo*, but two other genera as well: *Simia* (apes) and *Bradypus* (sloths), the latter because female members of the species have a pair of pectoral teats.

If comparing sloths to humans seemed like a joke to some people, associating humans with apes was a terrible insult. Yet Linnaeus felt like he had no choice; he had been overwhelmed by the staggering *humanness* of the primates he had seen during his life. In Holland, he had marveled at the apes and monkeys who lived in the zoo at Clifford's estate; he had also interacted with the clever and hilarious monkeys that ran freely around Blue John's Tavern in Amsterdam.[74] The most important scholarly influence, however, had come from an English anatomist named Edward Tyson, who had documented the profound similarities between apes and humans in his 1699 *Orang-Outang, sive Homo Sylvestris: or, the Anatomy of a Pygmie Compared with that of a Monkey, an Ape, and a Man*. In this pioneering work of comparative anatomy, Tyson had published detailed renderings of a dissected chimpanzee (he called it a pygmy) whose undeniable similarities with far-better-known human anatomy had shocked naturalists throughout Europe.[75]

Bringing together sloths, apes, and humans under the same class was far from the only controversial innovation in the 1735 *Systema*, however. In contrast to the way he treated other animals—by identifying them with certain physical traits—Linnaeus defined the genus *Homo* or *Man* by the Delphic maxim *Nosce te ipsum*, "know thyself." The very *definition* of the human species is thus a great and universal imperative: a command. Linnaeus not only imposed a self-reflective task upon the whole species; he effectively positioned himself as the supreme arbiter (and subject) of this anthropocentric enterprise.[76] Linnaeus, in short, had claimed the responsibility of explaining the status of the entire species to the rest of humankind.

If the basic thrust of Linnaeus's *Systema* was assigning a given species to larger orders and even larger classes based on shared anatomical traits, it is also true that he sometimes broke down certain species into specific "varieties," as he called them. Consider his treatment of apes. After assigning the ape species, most generally, to the enormous category of animals, then to the kingdom of Quadrupedia, and then to the order of Anthropomorpha, he goes on to further separate the species into apes without tails, apes with tails, and dogface baboons. This was precisely what he did when classifying the human species, breaking down the genus *Homo* into four varieties: *Europaeus albus* (white), *Americanus rubescens* (red), *Asiaticus fuscus* (dusky, dark), and *Africanus niger* (black), which he expressed in descending order.

Though Linnaeus said nothing more about how he arrived at this color-based breakdown of humankind, his vertical chart nonetheless conveyed two critical ideas. The first is that the four varieties of human belong to the larger unified species. Unlike François Bernier's somewhat hesitant *New Division of the Earth*, Linnaeus's categorization of humankind seems unambiguously *monogenetic*, and is perfectly compatible with the orthodox view that God had created one species of man. But there is also another, perhaps unintentional, idea lurking within Linnaeus's grouping of humankind in this same 1735 edition. He had created what looked like an explicit hierarchy, with the *Europaeus albus* listed first and the *Africanus niger* listed last. Even more dramatically, especially to the casual observer who did not know that Linnaeus believed that all species were *distinct*, was the fact the Black subspecies of man seemed to occupy a place in this taxonomy that was only slightly above *Simian caudal carens*, or "monkey without a tail."[77]

TOWARD A SCIENCE OF RACE

The simmering question of where and how to classify the human species was only one of many of Linnaeus's concerns during the late 1730s. This was especially true after he returned from the continent to Stockholm in 1738. Re-entry into Sweden was challenging, especially for his ego. Though his work had certainly provoked criticism on numerous fronts, much of the scientific community abroad had effectively canonized him. In addition to all the honors he had received while in Holland, he had traveled to London in 1736, where he was warmly received by the leading British natural historians, including the English doyen of the discipline and president of the Royal Society, Hans Sloane.[78] The following year, while he was visiting Paris, the French had also accorded him the highest scientific honor possible: electing him as a member of the Paris Royal Academy of Sciences.

Few people in Sweden, of course, cared about these foreign accolades. In fact, to the extent that his work as a botanist was known by his fellow countryman, Linnaeus had continued to endure a good deal of disparagement from theologians and naturalists alike. Had he not been in love with Sara Elisabeth, he later wrote, he would certainly have packed his bags and gone abroad again."[79]

In addition to everything else, Linnaeus was once again in financial trouble. Unable to obtain the type of exalted university post that he had been promised in Holland, he was trying to make ends meet (and earn enough money to marry) by establishing a medical practice in Stockholm. Patientless for quite a time, Linnaeus ultimately began frequenting taverns and other public establishments in search of paying clients. His first customers turned out to be sailors suffering from gonorrhea, a clientele he treated with mercury ointment and Rhine wine. His success in curing what he called *Castris Veneris* — translated as "wounded in the camps of Venus" — brought him numerous new patients.[80] Later that same year, he also used his knowledge of "physic herbs" to help dozens of people afflicted with smallpox.

By the late 1730s, Linnaeus's abilities as a physician became so renowned that he was being well paid by the country's elite for treating various ailments. In addition to the fact that this had finally allowed him to marry Sara Elisabeth in June of 1739, he was also given a royal appointment as Physician to the Admiralty. Several months later, Mårten Triewald, with whom Linnaeus had founded the Royal Swedish Academy of Sciences, asked him to serve as the institution's first president. The culmination of this string of victories came in May 1741, when he was named professor of medicine and botany at Uppsala.

It was from this new and exalted position that the thirty-four-year-old Linnaeus continued to revolutionize the discipline of natural history. To do so, he first had to transform the university where he worked. Delegating the teaching of medicine to another colleague, he concentrated his studies (and lectures) almost exclusively on botany, zoology, and classification. He also began improving the university garden, which had fallen into a terrible state under the care of his late mentor Olof Rudbeck. (Linnaeus later honored the man by bestowing the Latin name *rudbeckia* on the North American flower known familiarly as the *black-eyed Susan*). Two years after arriving at the university, by 1743, Linnaeus had already supervised the construction of a new greenhouse and redesigned the botanical garden. This "teaching portion" of the grounds, which was situated just outside his residence on Svartbäckgatan Street, featured a path that cut through twenty-four raised beds. Each of these areas was planted with one of the different classes of plants that Linnaeus had identified according to the number and form of their reproductive organs.

Part of Linnaeus's plan was bringing the rest of the world's vegetation to Uppsala. By the end of the decade, his reputation inspired scholars and naturalists across the globe to send him seeds or crates of plants on nearly a daily basis. Some of these packages were sent by his former students — his "apostles" — whom he had dispatched to China, Egypt, Lapland, Spain, North America and Canada, Africa, South Europe, and Gothland. The living specimens that flowed back to Uppsala entered into the university's gardens; the dried flowers were quickly incorporated into Linnaeus's own press books. All of this new information was ultimately absorbed into subsequent versions of the *Systema Naturae*.[81]

LINNAEUS'S GARDEN TODAY

Linnaeus's increasing repute also stemmed from the fact that he was a remarkable pedagogue and lecturer. On Wednesdays and Saturdays during the spring and early summer, he led two hundred or so paying students (and some ordinary Uppsalians) into the woods on a mission to explain nature — an activity that mirrored what he was attempting to accomplish on a global scale.

During these twelve-hour *Herbationes Upsalienses*, men and (a few) women armed with "field microscopes, magnifying glasses, notes, nets, insect pins, and various knives" entered Linnaeus's "outdoor classroom," not only gathering specimens under his watch but hanging on the famous professor's every word.[82] Soldierly order was apparently de rigueur during these treks: The men, some of whom were charged with shooting birds and other small animals, were obliged to wear a "short jacket, loose trousers, hat, and umbrella."[83] Outings generally came to an end around nine o'clock, when Linnaeus's army of budding naturalists returned triumphantly to the city streets, accompanied by the trumpeters and the drummers who had also trudged through the forest.[84]

Linnaeus's quest to hunt down nature's still undiscovered creatures, be it in the woods with his students or in his home laboratory, had accelerated tremendously since he first began classifying the world. In 1735, he had identified 569 animal species.[85] By 1749, he had inventoried 10,000 plants, 2,000 worms, 10,000 insects, 300 amphibious animals, 2,000 fishes, 2,000 birds, and 200 quadrupeds.[86] Contemporary scientists now estimate the number of species is probably somewhere between ten and fourteen million.[87]

Linnaeus may not have understood just how many species remained to be discovered in 1749, but he had certainly realized that the task of identifying and sorting nature had expanded well past what one person could accomplish in several lifetimes.[88] Establishing the proper method for classification for those who came after him thus became a priority. He took his biggest step toward this method in 1753, when he proposed yet another system for naming plants in his *Species Plantarum*. Replacing the long, drawn-out Latin names that often seemed more like run-on sentences than anything else, Linnaeus gave organisms what essentially amounted to a first name and a last name (or a noun with an adjective), making the natural world both orderly and accessible.[89] It was what we now know as the binomial classification system that eventually gave rise to Linnaeus's most significant treatment of humankind, a species he now began calling *Homo sapiens*, or wise man.

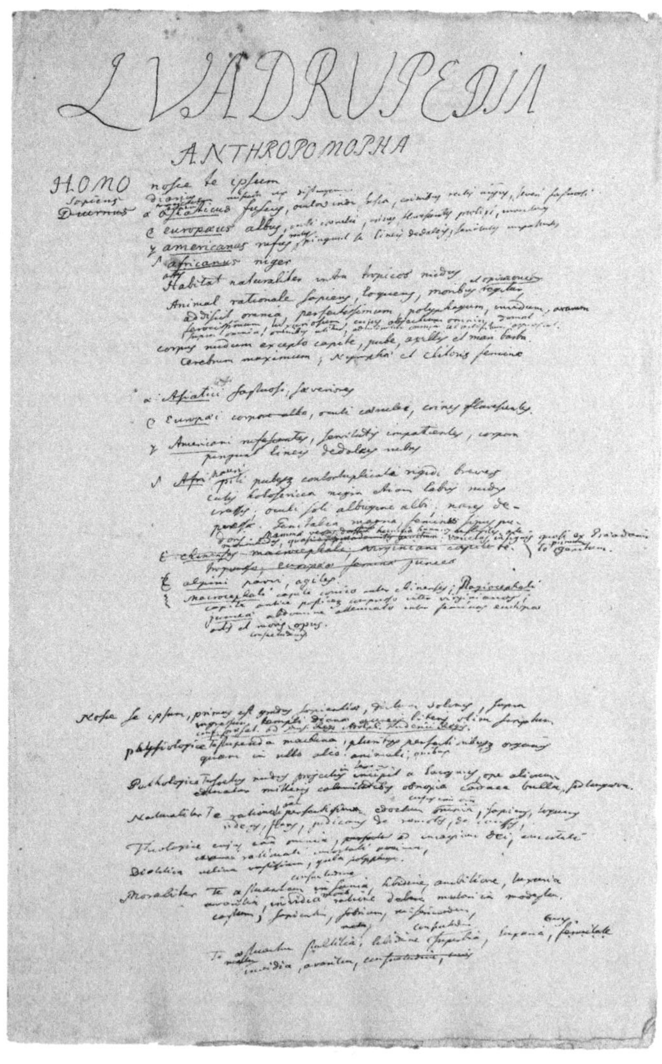

THE ORIGIN OF THE NEW TERM *HOMO SAPIENS*

THE FINAL CLASSIFICATION OF *HOMO SAPIENS*

By the 1750s, naturalists throughout Europe had begun turning their attention to a series of anthropological questions, many of which touched humankind's different varieties. Some of the era's thinkers focused on properly *biological* matters, such as: What caused the development of humankind's many *types*? Others were concerned with finding specific anatomical features among non-Europeans, such as "dark" African blood or textured hair. And then there also were those more historically minded anthropologists who sought to create comprehensive and race-based theories explaining what was increasingly seen as Europe's domination of the world. By the 1750s, virtually all of the era's most famous figureheads, including Montesquieu, Hume, Buffon, and Voltaire, had published their own theories regarding the relative worth of Europeans and non-Europeans.

Linnaeus, who was deeply immersed in the botanical world during the 1740s and early 1750s, had not actively participated in any of these debates. He was, however, quite aware of the "anthropological" turn in natural history. By the 1740s, the so-called disciples he had dispatched to Africa, Asia, and Latin America were not only sending back collected specimens; they were sharing new information concerning the diverse peoples of the world.[90] It was perhaps with this in mind that, in 1758, Linnaeus returned to the question of the human species with dramatic effect.

Some of the modifications Linnaeus made in the tenth edition of the *Systema* simply addressed the valid criticisms that people had levied about his view of the human species. He abandoned the ambiguous and capacious category of *Quadrupedia* and replaced it with *Mammalia*, which applied to all milk-producing creatures regardless of physical features (e.g., the type of toes or the placement of mammary glands). He also dropped the term *Anthropomorpha* or "man-like," and coined the now-familiar expression *Primates*—meaning *first among the animals*—for humans and apes. This created an even more direct link between these two categories.[91]

Linnaeus's understanding and presentation of the genus *Homo* had evolved as well. By the mid-1750s, he had decided that he would extend the binomial system he had created for plants to the animal world, which led to the new binominal taxon *Homo sapiens* and a fuller racialization of the human species.[92]

	TENDENCY/ POSTURE	TRAITS		TREATMENT	
AMERICANUS	Red, choleric, straight	Striaght, black, and thick hair; gaping nostrils; [freckled] face; beardless chin	Unyielding, cheerful, free	Paints himself in a maze of red lines	Governed by customary right
EUROPAEUS	White, sanguine, muscular	Plenty of yellow hair; blue eyes	Light, wise, inventive	Protected by tight clothing	Governed by rites
ASIATICUS	Sallow, melancholic, stiff	Blackish hair; dark eyes	Stern, haughty, greedy	Protected by loose garments	Governed by opinions
AFRICANUS	Black, phlegmatic, lazy	Dark hair, with many braids; silky skin; flat nose; thick lips; women [with] elongated labia; breasts lactating profusely	Sly, sluggish, neglectful	Annoints himself with fat	Governed by caprice

LINNAEUS'S HUMAN CLASSIFICATION SCHEME

Linnaeus divided humankind into six major categories, or varieties: *Americanus*, *Europaeus*, *Asiaticus*, *Africanus*, *Homo sapiens ferus*, and *Homo sapiens monstrosus*. The penultimate category, "ferus," referred to wild children who lived by themselves in the woods. The final category, "monstrosus," reflected Linnaeus's belief that certain groups of people had been twisted and deformed by their customs and the environment in which they lived. This last taxon, interestingly enough, came to include the Sámi, the northern peoples whom Linnaeus had previously praised as living richer lives than many Europeans given their proximity to nature.[93]

The most significant change in the 1758 edition of the *Systema*, however, was not the inclusion of the world's supposedly environmentally deformed humans. It was the fact that Linnaeus had decided to move beyond his earlier, comparatively benign, categorization of humans based on color and geography, such as *Africanus niger*. For this new edition, Linnaeus now cited distinct morphological traits including nose shape, temperament, the treatment of skin, and even each group's political orientation.

Eighteen years before he published this version of the *Systema*, Linnaeus had seemingly rejected this type of schematic breakdown of humankind in his *Critica Botanica* (1737). Starting from the premise that the deity had created one sole "human," he claims here that focusing on specific traits would fool naturalists into thinking that there were "thousands of different species of man." Consider the fact, he continues, that humans had "white, red, black, and grey hair; white, rosy, tawny, and black faces; straight, stubby, crooked, flattened, and aquiline noses." Size, too, he argues, defies rigid categorization. After all, one can find "giants and pygmies, fat and skinny people . . . humpy, brittle, and lame people" within the same population. Linnaeus had even concluded with a powerful, anticlassificatory question: "[W]ho with a sane mind would be so frivolous as to call these distinct species?"[94]

Interestingly enough, the source of Linnaeus's new classification had little to do with the advances in natural history taking place in the rest of Europe; it had actually come from antiquity, from a version of the ancient Greek theory that maintained that a given individual's health, aptitudes, and potential could be explained by the body's dominant humor, be it blood (which produced sanguine people), choler (which produced anger), black bile (which produced melancholy), or phlegm (which produced phlegmatic or lazy people).[95]

White Europeans clearly benefitted the most within this revised typology: Linnaeus portrayed *Homo sapiens Europaeus* as sanguine (wise, optimistic), blue-eyed, muscular, vigorous, very intelligent, inventive, "covered by tight clothing," and governed by laws. The other categories, in his view, had far more liabilities. He characterized *Homo sapiens Americanus* as beardless, ill-tempered, impassive, and stubborn, with wide nostrils and a harsh physiognomy. The traits of *Homo sapiens Asiaticus* were noted as very similar to those of the Amerindians, though Linnaeus claimed that the entire type was "melancholic, strict, haughty, greedy, covered by loose garments, and governed by opinion." The last of the four major varieties, *Homo sapiens Afer*, seemed the furthest away from the obvious European ideal. Based on a mishmash of prejudicial information that conflated the purported habits and anatomy of the Khoi people of South Africa with the rest of sub-Saharan Africa, Linnaeus depicted the continent's inhabitants as "silky-skinned, sluggish, slow, lazy, crafty, careless," with flat noses, thick lips, and, among the women, elongated breasts and a genital flap or "apron" covering the labia.[96] The rest of the description was even more dehumanizing: Africans were covered by grease and ruled by caprice.[97]

Linnaeus never tampered with the 1758 classification during the last twenty years of his life. He was far more preoccupied with the nonhuman world, spending most of his time cataloging heretofore unnamed species of mollusks, sponges, and insects. His last publications, which included writings on the Swedish queen's natural history collection and intoxicating medicines, also steered clear of any new information on *Homo sapiens*' different varieties. In 1767, he simply reproduced this same taxonomy in the final 2,400-page version of the *Systema Naturae*.

The last edition of the *Systema* to appear during his lifetime was published in 1772. It was also during this year that his failing health forced him to begin pulling back from the university. Given all that he had achieved — among other things, he had been serving on and off as the university's rector since 1750 — he was asked to give a farewell speech in the city's enormous redbrick cathedral in December.[98] Several months later, having settled at his estate in the Swedish countryside at Hammarby, Linnaeus suffered the first of several strokes. A friend who visited in 1775 recorded Linnaeus's reduced capacities. Linnaeus still "drinks and smokes tobacco like a healthy man but cannot speak . . . also cannot walk or write legibly; memory and right thinking are lost."[99] By 1777, Linnaeus had entered the final stage of life, regressing to the state of a toothless child, exactly as he had described the end of life in the *Systema*. Six months later, in January 1778, after returning to his house in Uppsala, he finally succumbed after a prolonged bout with a convulsion-producing fever.

That Linnaeus had spent so much time thinking through life in terms of *stages* had perhaps led him to carefully dictate what would happen to his lifeless body. Unlike many Enlightenment-era figureheads who asked that they be dissected in the interest of science, Linnaeus instructed his family to immediately place his unwashed and unshaven body in a sheet and a coffin so, in his words, "my frailty is not seen."[100] He also specified that there should be neither condolences nor eating during the memorial service. As a final wish, he requested that a medallion with the Latin title "*princeps botanicorum*" be placed on his grave.[101] In death, he had crowned himself "prince of the botanists."

CAROLI LINNAEI
EQVITIS DE STELLA POLARI,
ARCHIATRI REGII, MED. ET BOTAN. PROFESS. VPSAL.
ACAD. VPSAL. HOLMENS. PETROPOL. BEROL. IMPER.
LOND. MONSPEL. TOLOS. FLORENT. SOC.

SYSTEMA
NATVRAE
PER
REGNA TRIA NATVR
SECVNDVM
CLASSES, ORDINES,
GENERA, SPECIES,
CVM
CHARACTERIBVS, DIFFERENTIIS, SYNONYMIS, LOCIS.
TOMVS I.

PRAEFATVS EST
IOANNES IOACHIMVS LANGIVS
MATH. PROF. PVBL. ORD. HALENS. ACAD. IMP. ET BORVSS. COLLEGA.

AD EDITIONEM DECIMAM REFORMATAM HOLMIENSEM.

HALAE MAGDEBVRGICAE
TYPIS ET SVMTIBVS IO. IAC. CVRT. MDCCLX.

LINNAEUS PICTURED AS THE "NAME GIVER"
IN THE FRONTISPIECE OF *SYSTEMA NATURAE*, 1760

Linnaeus had believed on his deathbed that he would be remembered, primarily, for his contribution to the classification of plants. But his quest to make order of the natural world in general had also led him to utterly transform the status of his own species. Treating the category of the human like any other animal with its own subspecies, he carved *Homo sapiens* — us — into four color-coded "varieties," among them the supposedly clever and inventive blue-eyed *Europaeus*. In comparison to the tens of thousands of natural history taxons that Linnaeus invented during his lifetime, *Homo sapiens Europaeus* surely had the most pernicious afterlife. Though Linnaeus had no inkling of what he had done, he had established the classificatory basis for what would come to be known as the Teutonic or Aryan branch of the human species. That the most influential classifier of humans was anything but an Übermensch — he was short, stocky, dark-eyed, and brown-haired — was conveniently overlooked by the racial taxonomists who built on his legacy.

PART THREE

RACE GETS A HISTORY

Earth nurses not man alone; she presses
all her children to one bosom,
embraces all in the same maternal arms; and,
when one changes, all must undergo change.
—JOHANN GOTTFRIED HERDER,
Outlines of a Philosophy of History of Man, 1784

[I]nstead of going on to further perfection,
as the theory of modern philosophers
would lead us to suppose, we find that mankind
degenerated in a most astonishing degree.
—*Encyclopedia Britannica*, 1810

V

BUFFON, PORTRAIT BY DROUAIS, 1761

BUFFON: THE MAN WHO PUT HUMANS IN TIME

In 1744, nine years after Linnaeus first published his *Systema Naturae*, Parisian bookshops began selling a French edition of the Swede's increasingly famous work. Among its most critical readers was a tall and elegant aristocrat named Georges-Louis Leclerc, better known as Buffon. Appointed by Louis XV in 1739 to oversee the kingdom's vast botanical and zoological collections, Buffon was determined to stay at the forefront of the life sciences—even if it meant poring over the work of a hated rival who was attempting to overthrow the entire discipline of natural history.

Buffon was not only unimpressed by Linnaeus's so-called *Systema*; he was enraged by it. Though he typically avoided public confrontations, he vowed to refute Linnaeus's work in the multivolume *Natural History* that he was preparing for publication at that very moment. In the short term, however, he gave a lecture at the Paris Academy of Sciences, where he lambasted Linnaeus for giving birth to "an infinity of false relationships between natural beings."[1]

The Academy was apparently not the only time where Buffon passed judgment on Linnaeus. According to an apocryphal story, the French naturalist also took up the subject of Linnaeus's system with Voltaire and some other friends in a more intimate setting. Mocking Linnaeus for lumping humankind in with apes, sloths, and apparently horses, Buffon supposedly concluded with a joke: "*Cheval toi-même* Linnaeus," meaning "you're the horse, Linnaeus."[2] The anecdote ends with Voltaire returning with a far wittier retort: "You must agree with me, Monsieur Buffon, that if Monsieur Linnaeus is a horse, he is the first of all the horses."[3]

Whether this yarn is true or not, Buffon was finally able to vent his disdain for Linnaeus's system when his *Natural History* appeared in 1749. In addition to reducing the Swede's classification of the animal kingdom to what he mockingly called "teeth" and "teats," Buffon asked a very pointed question: "[W]ould not it have been simpler, more natural, and more truthful to say that a donkey is a donkey, a cat is a cat, than to hope, without knowing why, that a donkey is a horse, and a cat a lynx?"[4]

Linnaeus and Buffon never met. Yet it is patently clear that their mutual hatred, which endured for decades, was real. Buffon's animosity toward his northern rival was such that he derided the entire Swedish nation. When describing the parts of the world where the highest expression of humankind seemed to flourish, Buffon declared that the northern border of this favorable zone stopped abruptly in northern Germany, which did not include Sweden.[5] As for Linnaeus, he could not help but return the favor. On the subject of Buffon — by now the most celebrated naturalist on the continent — he remarked: Monsieur Buffon "is not particularly learned, but since he is rather eloquent, that must count for something."[6] Linnaeus's best revenge took place, however, on the level of taxonomy. When naming a type of long, stringy, and foul-smelling plant from Macaronesia, he chose the term *buffonia*, whose Latin root means *toad*.

The source of these exchanged insults—egos aside—stems from the fact that these two men were locked in a battle about the status of nature itself. Linnaeus was the greatest organizer of nature's diversity to ever set foot on the planet. He created groups of species, enormous taxonomical tables, and sought to share the splendor of a divinely engineered nature with his readers by *defining* and categorizing each type of living creature.[7] Buffon, on the contrary, rejected what he believed were subjective classifications that taught people very little about the animal and plant world. His method was more *descriptive* than classificatory. By painting a vivid word portrait of each species of plant or animal and by including an enormous collection of accompanying illustrations, Buffon sought to bring the staggering variety of nature to life, consciously replacing Linnaeus's clinical categories with his exquisite writing style and evocative imagery.

Colorful prose was not the only aspect of the *Natural History* that distinguished Buffon's worldview from Linnaeus's. The Frenchman also rejected the idea that one could classify animal and plant species as fixed and immutable entities. The whole of *nature*, for Buffon, was anything but static; it was in a constant state of flux, subject to an ongoing process of transformation and even destruction.[8] This radical understanding of nature even held, Buffon would make clear, for the supposedly sacred and unique human species.

THE PATH TOWARD NATURAL HISTORY: "NATURE'S GREATEST WORKER IS TIME."

Given the ill will between Linnaeus and Buffon, it is one of the delightful ironies of the *history* of natural history that the two men came into the world in the same year, 1707. There are several other similarities as well. Both were initially disappointments to their fathers before rising to prominence and being ennobled by their respective monarchs. (Linnaeus was made Carl von Linné in 1761 and George-Louis Leclerc became Comte de Buffon in 1773.) One other shared aspect was the fact that both men hailed from small, obscure villages — in Buffon's case from the tiny Burgundy hamlet of Montbard.

Early eighteenth-century travelers who passed through Montbard had little good to say about the stream-side settlement where Buffon grew up. One travel writer claimed that it consisted of little more than the ruins of a 600-year-old château, a primitive four-bed hospital, and a handful of houses that had sprung up along the watercourse.[9] This same author did admit, however, that the village's dogskin gloves were of the highest quality.[10]

While there was not much to Montbard, Georges-Louis Leclerc, the future Comte de Buffon, was born in its most privileged family, a family whose ancestors had skillfully climbed the provincial social ladder. His great-great-grandfather, a peasant farmer, had sent his son to university to become a barber-surgeon. The surgeon's son went to law school and eventually held the position of village mayor. His boy — Buffon's father — continued the upward ascent. In addition to purchasing both a seat in the Burgundy Parlement and a position as local administrator of the king's (hated) salt tax, he also acquired the title to the neighboring village of Buffon, thereby securing his family's right to the aristocratic *de Buffon*.

Georges wrote little about growing up in Montbard, which is hardly surprising. Later in life, he dismissed the stage of childhood altogether, insisting that "one must consider the first fifteen years of [one's] life as *null* . . . worthless."[11] The one clear opinion that emerges from his early years is that he loathed his overbearing father. As an adult, he not only stated that he had preferred his mother's company, but that he had inherited all of his creativity and intelligence from her. This conviction was ultimately transformed into "science" in the *Natural History*. When identifying the source of the "intellectual abilities and moral qualities" of children, he claimed they came uniquely from one's mother.[12]

If Buffon's intelligence theoretically came to him *matrilineally*, it was nonetheless the patriarchy that structured his life. As the oldest male of five children, Georges had been groomed from birth for the same type of illustrious career that his father had enjoyed.[13] After being sent to Dijon's Jesuit school, he enrolled (or was compelled to enroll) in the city's faculty of law.

By the time Buffon had half-heartedly completed his degree, he had soured on the law. This change of heart was due in large part to his first true intellectual mentor, the humanist and jurist Jean Bouhier (1673–1746). Buffon became closely acquainted with Bouhier through the latter's weekly salon, held in his elegant seventeenth-century *hôtel particulier*. It was here, surrounded by a vast library of 30,000 volumes, that Buffon was introduced to Enlightenment philosophy and the natural sciences, especially Leibniz's systematic view of nature, Locke's empiricism, and Newton's theory of universal gravitation.[14]

In 1728, when Buffon was twenty-one, he announced to his father that, given his new interests, he had decided to leave Dijon for the University of Angers to study mathematics and the natural sciences. The implications of this choice were not lost on the patriarch: In his view, his son had opted for a self-indulgent folly, a caprice that would reflect poorly on the family. Buffon, however, was now able to study complex mathematical problems and attend courses on botany (and perhaps anatomy) at Angers' medical school.[15] He would have likely continued to study here, had he not gotten into an illegal duel and been forced to return to Dijon.

During the next few years, Buffon traveled to southern France, Italy, and England. By 1732, after finally securing the rights to a colossal fortune that he had inherited (at age seven) from his mother's uncle, he moved to Paris to pursue a scientific career.[16] Establishing himself as a *savant* in the capital, he understood, was as much about cultivating relationships as it was about producing actual science. With this in mind, he arranged to live with a member of the Paris Royal Academy of Sciences and the king's personal apothecary, a man who had deep contacts at Versailles. The aspiring naturalist also plunged headlong into Paris's social and scientific scene, joining a group of important Newtonian mathematicians, among them Madame du Châtelet, Pierre-Louis Moreau de Maupertuis, and Alexis Claude Clairaut.[17]

While Buffon's mathematical accomplishments (including authoring a famous article on geometric probability) would ultimately earn him a coveted spot within Paris's Academy of Sciences, it was his willingness to tailor his scientific experiments to the needs of the state that most facilitated his career.[18] Not long after Buffon arrived in Paris, he had heard that the Minister of the Navy was asking the country's botanists to undertake experiments related to the density of wood, in particular how to cultivate timber that would be more resistant to the rigors of transatlantic voyages.[19] Given that Buffon owned substantial plots of land on his estate in Montbard, he readily took up the challenge and began a series of successful experiments in *dendrology*, or industrial forestry.[20]

By 1739, news of Buffon's research had reached Versailles. Later that same year, Louis XV summoned Buffon to his palace at Fontainebleau to discuss how the improved cultivation of trees might help the French navy produce far stronger and longer-lasting ships. During their discussion, the king was impressed by Buffon's knowledge and ultimately asked the young man if he would accept a position as overseer of his own extensive woodlands. While Buffon respectfully declined this offer, he had nonetheless earned the king's admiration.[21] This worked to his advantage in July of the same year when Louis XV tapped the thirty-one-year-old provincial scientist to become the *intendant*, or director, of the Jardin du Roi—the royal botanical gardens, located on the eastern frontier of Paris.

THE ROYAL BOTANICAL GARDEN IN 1636, ENGRAVING

In the weeks before Buffon was chosen for this role, he had been focusing on both mathematics and forestry. Overnight, he inherited supervision over a multidisciplinary organization whose botanists, zoologists, and mineralogists were occupied with studying specimens that were flowing back to Paris from around the world.[22] The institution had also developed a famous public lecture program that was quite unlike what one might find at the comparatively rearguard university of Paris. At the King's Garden, one might stumble on a seminar on botany, a lecture on conjoined twins, or even a chemistry demonstration, the latter of which was frequently as dangerous as it was exciting.

VIEW OF THE NATURAL HISTORY CABINET, ENGRAVING 1835

The biggest draw at the garden, however, was the king's Natural History Cabinet, a gallery of perhaps eighty wooden and glass armoires filled with an "abridgment of the whole of nature," as Buffon's assistant Louis Jean-Marie Daubenton once described it.[23] The first section of the cabinet contained the institution's huge collection of human remains: skulls, fractured bones, stillborn fetuses (both normal and "monstrous") preserved in eau-de-vie alongside a significant number of injected écorchés, or preserved human specimens in wax. The cabinet also featured an ethnographic component composed of various weapons and tools employed by "savages" across the world. The quantity and range of objects held by the Jardin was such that, once Buffon began filling the gaps in the collection, he was obliged to give up part of his apartment to make more room for fish heads and birds.[24] Buffon's friend Denis Diderot claimed that more than 1,500 people came to see the spectacle each week.[25]

Buffon was acutely aware that this jumble of shells, rocks, and skulls revealed very little about nature itself. Indeed, like all such collections, the king's cabinet lacked an underlying logic or a proper description of its contents. To address this shortcoming, Buffon approached his direct superior, the Count of Maurepas—France's Secretary of State—and proposed that the crown fund a complete inventory and catalog of the king's natural history holdings. Maurepas agreed.[26]

In 1749, Buffon published the first tomes of what would become the thirty-six-volume *Natural History*—arguably the greatest example of "bait and switch" in the history of biology. Although the work did include a straightforward inventory and description of the king's cabinet—as promised—its most compelling and often controversial sections offered a radically new vision of nature, one where flora and fauna could change over time, go extinct, or even give rise to new life forms! This bold reconceptualization was a pivotal moment in the field of natural history. Buffon was providing the first real *history* of nature—one that included an account of the origins of the human species, its races, and its varieties.

GOD, METHOD, AND THE BIRTH OF HUMAN HISTORY

In the opening pages of the *Natural History*, Buffon states that, in stark contrast to the reductive classifiers or "simple observers" of nature, he will be presenting a complete assessment of each species.

He promises that his readers will find out how each animal is born and grows; about its respective "structure"; and how it is "used."[27] This was exactly how he wrote about the human species as well.

While Buffon never gave Linnaeus credit for anything, he nonetheless began his study of the human species by stating unequivocally (very much like his Swedish rival) that anyone who studies humankind must recognize a "humiliating truth": that we humans must categorize ourselves "among the animals."[28] To a large degree, this was simply a matter of self-scrutiny, the inevitable result of the "know thyself," or *nosce te ipsum*, dictum that Linnaeus had endorsed in 1735.

Buffon, however, did not define humankind by a series of physical traits—certain types of teeth, an ability to produce milk, or a specific number of appendages. Rather, he underscored the "fact" that humans have a soul, an ability to be moral beings, and perhaps most important, the capacity to *reason*. It is this specific capacity—that Aristotle first identified as synonymous with humankind—that separates the human species from the rest of the world's animals in Buffon's view:

> Man is a reasonable creature; the animal is a being without reason; and since there is no intermediate point between the positive and the negative, [and] since there are no intermediate beings between the reasonable being and the being without reason, it is obvious that man is a being entirely different from that of the animal, and that he only resembles animals on the exterior, and to judge him by this material resemblance, is to let oneself be deceived by appearances.[29]

Having identified the human species as the only *reasonable* animal, Buffon then provides a 130-page portrait of what it means to be an individual member of the species. This story, which charts the phases of our lives, begins with the precarious existence of the human infant.[30]

According to Buffon, each individual human begins life as a pain-wracked newborn, "weaker than any other animal," "unable to make use of [its] organs," and ready to die at "any moment." If a baby is lucky enough to live through infancy, he states, he or she must then navigate a childhood that is filled with life-ending diseases before finally entering puberty and adulthood, a happier stage that corresponds both to the highest goal of the species—reproduction—as well as the beginning of an inevitable decline.[31] As soon as the human body arrives at "its point of perfection," Buffon states, it begins "to perish."[32]

One of the principal reasons that Buffon provides this "history of the individual" is to emphasize the fact that every person on the planet experiences these same milestones: be they a "European," a "Negro," a "Chinaman," an "American" [Amerindian], a "civilized" person, a "savage," a "rich man," a "poor man," a "city dweller," or a "person living in the country." Although people and groups may be "so different in terms of everything else," he adds, all of these different categories "resemble each other" when it comes to how they move through life.[33]

After describing the human condition in such sweeping, universalist terms, Buffon turns to a more global examination of the human species. In a book-length section of the *Natural History* titled the "Varieties of the Human Species," the French naturalist details the morphology, the skin color, and the customs of the world's diverse peoples. It is in this section, in short, that he begins to engage with ideas that closely resemble what we now think of as *race*.

Buffon's extensive assessment of humankind's "varieties" was the first of its kind. Consciously rejecting the type of schematic breakdown of the human species proposed by Bernier and, especially, Linnaeus, this enormous section describes hundreds of different phenotypes organized geographically, many of which, not surprisingly, reflect European prejudices and xenophobia. Readers of Buffon are now often shocked by his fundamental lack of relativism and, in certain cases, what we would now consider explicitly racist stereotypes.

The *Natural History*'s catalog of humankind begins in the north, with a remarkably unsympathetic assessment of the band of Nordic peoples living in the Arctic regions of the world, among them "Laplanders," northern Danes and Swedes, Moscovites, Samoïedes, Greenlanders, and the indigenous inhabitants of what is now northern Canada, including the so-called Eskimos (Inuit, Iñupiat, and Yupik). Drawing from the texts of a range of travelers and explorers who wrote about this part of the world — they generally tended to echo each other — Buffon affirms confidently that these diminutive and "flat-faced" Arctic peoples were little more than misshapen offshoots of the human species. Using the term *race* here to indicate a biological lineage, he defines the "Laplander race" as a "particular type whose individuals are little more than abortions."[34] This startling indictment was not the worst thing he wrote about the Sámi people of Sweden and Finland, however. From Buffon's view, the best way to distinguish among the individual members of this particular category was identifying them on the basis of who is "more or less deformed."[35]

As Buffon moves on from the northernmost parts of the world, he describes the peoples of Asia, the South Pacific, the Indian subcontinent, the Middle East and Central Asia, Southern and then Northern Europe, North Africa, sub-Saharan Africa, and the Americas. Though rife with reductive assessments, not everything Buffon writes in "Varieties of the Human Species" points to an unambiguous ideology of European superiority or racial hierarchy. Indeed, during much of his imagined stroll across the planet, the naturalist does not associate pigmentation with any specific traits or "racial" potential. This is even the case, to a certain extent, for the one category of human — the "Negro," or the Black African — around which the notion of race crystalized during the eighteenth century.

Buffon spent a great deal of time studying what had been written about the peoples of sub-Saharan Africa. To organize this discussion — tellingly — the naturalist proceeds along the same basic "route" that European ships (and slave traders) did when sailing to and around West Africa. His first "landfall" comes in Senegal, where he discusses the physiology, mores, and customs of the *Jalofes* (Wolof), the northwestern Senegalese ethnicity first encountered by Europeans in the 1450s.

Unlike much of what he writes about Black Africans elsewhere, Buffon basically had only good things to say about these first "Negroes." In addition to being "well proportioned, with beautiful bone structure and an advantageous height," he describes the Wolof as "less hard faced than other Negroes." While it is true that Buffon tosses off a number of disparaging comments regarding the inhabitants' comparative "nakedness" and supposed hypersexuality, he also claims that these people were very much like Europeans. They were, in his opinion, far superior to the "Negroes of Guinea," whom he describes as dissolute, lazy, and subject to a comparatively early death.

Buffon then continues his inventory of sub-Saharan Africans by descending along the coast to places such as Juda (Ouidah, Benin), the Kongo (Congo) region, and South Africa, before briefly moving back up the east coast to Ethiopia. In addition to providing the era's most complete (and most cited) repertory of the continent's ethnicities, Buffon also establishes a pigmentation-based definition of the term *nègre*, or Negro. From his point of view, the blacker Africans were, the more they were a "Negro." "True Negroes," as he puts it, "were the blackest."[36] The light-skinned Cafres or "Hottentots" (Khoisan peoples of South Africa) were not; nor were the Ethiopians. For Buffon, at least, the term "Negro" was not equivalent with slave; it was a marker of pigmentation.

Like many European naturalists who attempted to rationalize the great range of African "types" during the eighteenth century, Buffon derived his information from two main varieties of sources. The first were reports written *in* Africa by European traders or explorers. These travelogues, although often extremely xenophobic and belittling, nonetheless describe autonomous Africans living their own lives. While such "ethnography" is hardly trustworthy, it includes extensive information on religious rituals, specific forms of government, food, clothing, sexual mores, and various other day-to-day details about African life. Even when such accounts were written by slave traders, this Africa-related "ethnography" tends to be less racially oriented than the utility-based views of Africans originating in the Caribbean.

The Caribbean planters, explorers, and missionaries that Buffon quotes generally describe Black Africans very differently. The "Negroes" that they portray had been stamped, often literally, with the mark of heredity-based servitude, a political status guaranteed by European slave laws such as the Barbados Code, Virginia Code, and *Code Noir*.[37] Buffon ultimately conveyed a great deal of "ethnographic information" from these Caribbean writers as well, particularly what they had said about the economic worth of several different types of Africans in the colonial setting. Whether he realized it or not, Buffon was passing on a typology of bondage in what would become the most influential book of natural history written during the eighteenth century:

> On our islands, we prefer the *nègres* from Angola to those of Cape Verde for the strength of their bodies, but they smell so awful when they become hot, that the air in the places where they pass is contaminated for over fifteen minutes; those from Cape Verde do not have an odor nearly as horrible as those from Angola, and they also have the more beautiful and darker black skin, a better proportioned body, less harsh facial features, a better disposition, and a more advantageous height. Those from Guinea are also very good for farm labor and for other large undertakings; those from Senegal are not as strong, but they are the better suited to domestic service, and more capable of learning trades. Father Charlevoix says that of all the *nègres*, the Senegalese are the best looking, the easiest to discipline, and the best suited to domestic service; that the Bambaras are the biggest, but that they are thieves; that the Aradas understand agriculture the best; that the Congos are the smallest in stature, that they are good fishermen, but that they run off easily; that the Nagos are the most human; that the Mondongos are the most cruel, and that the Mines are the most determined, the most capricious, and the most likely to despair.[38]

While we may never know exactly what Buffon was thinking as he composed his assessment of Black Africans' comparative utility in the colonies, he quickly shifted tone in the lines that followed, turning his critique toward the very planters who had supplied the so-called ethnography:

> I cannot write [the] story [of Black Africans] without being moved by their situation. Are they not already unhappy enough as slaves, without being required to work every day without the possibility of ever acquiring anything at all? Is it also necessary to overwork them, and treat them like animals?[39]

This short outburst of sympathy toward the suffering African—though it now may appear condescending and wrongheaded—numbers among the first instances in which an Enlightenment figurehead took the time to question the brutality and cruelty of the extremely profitable Caribbean plantation system.[40] Buffon's readers, however, did not pay much attention to this call for an "improved" form of slavery when it first appeared in 1749.

Far more influential at the time was the naturalist's explanation of the cause, or *origin*, of blackness to his readers. This was part of a far larger theory of how humankind came into being. When composing this portion of the *Natural History* in the mid to late 1740s, Buffon knew that it would have been too dangerous to publish an entirely "material" or physical explanation of the species' origins. Yet he ultimately managed to signal what he believed to be humankind's origin by scattering his ideas throughout the book.

If we were to *speculatively* reconstitute Buffon's history of humankind (along with all living creatures), we might begin with his belief in spontaneous generation. Like many contemporary naturalists, Buffon had become fascinated with the work of John Tuberville Needham, a microscopist who had discovered the presence of microorganisms thriving in a drop of water.[41] Both Needham and Buffon were convinced that these tiny beings emerged spontaneously and proved that animal life could arise without divine intervention. One can infer from Buffon's musings in the *Natural History* that he believed that humans, too, had somehow arisen organically from fermenting matter, eventually stabilizing as a species and developing the ability to transmit hereditary traits.

An extreme version of what Buffon may have believed regarding humankind's origins can be found in a remarkable passage written by his good friend, Denis Diderot, in 1749. Diderot's "narrator" here is a congenitally blind man who claims that he is a monster, a fluke, a living example of the mistakes that happened when nature produced the first humans. He then claims that the apparent order that one sees in the world only came about through some sort of natural selection, when "nature" finally exterminated its losers and identified its winners. This same sightless narrator concludes by stating that this dynamic and godless origin story is not only the case for all creatures, but for all the universe's *worlds* as well:

> [W]hen the universe was hatched from fermenting matter, my fellow men [blind men] were very common. Yet could not [this] belief about animals also hold for worlds? How many lopsided, failed worlds are there that have been dissolved and are perhaps being remade and redissolved every minute in faraway spaces, beyond the reach of my hands and your eyes, where movement is still going on and will keep going until the bits of matter arrange themselves in a combination that is sustainable?[42]

Buffon and Diderot surely shared a number of these ideas.[43] Yet the *Natural History* was not the place to expose a dreamlike vision of failed worlds and freakish human prototypes. What Buffon chose to do was put forward a dynamic explanation of human origins that was more or less compatible with Scripture. The idea to do so may have come from the polymath and esthetic theorist Jean-Baptiste Dubos, who was among the first major thinkers to reconcile the Bible with the type of climate-based explanation of human differentiation that had been circulating since antiquity:

> [The difference] between a Negro and a Muscovite is enormous. Yet given the fact that both descended from Adam, their

> differences can only be caused by the air where their ancestors moved. The first men who moved to areas near the equator had children that were barely different from the descendants of the first parents who moved near the Arctic pole. The grandchildren of the people at the pole and at the equator . . . would resemble each other less. And finally, with each generation, their resemblance would diminish.[44]

Buffon's version of this theory, however, made no real reference to Scripture or biblical genealogy.[45] Instead, he simply told a tale of how the many types of humans on the planet had come about as a result of environmental and social factors.

Before relating this new story of human differentiation, however, Buffon needed to answer the big question that loomed in climate theory: *Which was the first human type or race*? In 1744, Buffon's friend and fellow academician, Pierre-Louis Moreau de Maupertuis, announced that he had solved this question by studying what he believed to be a cross-racial human, the albino. In an era where eighteenth-century naturalists initially believed that albinism (hypopigmentation) only occurred among Blacks, people with the condition were referred to as *White Negroes*.

In his tremendously influential *Dissertation physique à l'occasion du nègre blanc* (Dissertation on the White Negro), Maupertuis claimed that the occasional appearance of "albinos" born among black-skinned populations was a clear indication that the original population was *white*, and that these albinos were throwbacks to their primal state. "White," he concludes, "is the color of the first men, and it is only through *accident* that black became a hereditary color among those vast families who populate the Torrid Zone."[46]

Buffon not only accepted this explanation; he used the idea of human *accidents* to explain his vast new degenerative chronicle of humankind: "As soon as [the first group of White humans] began to move around the world and spread from climate to climate, [their] nature was subject to various alterations. . . . [T]hese changes were minimal in temperate regions, [the same lands] that [Europeans] presume to be the place of [humankind's] origin," but were much more severe when "continents had been crossed." Time, too, was a factor for Buffon. It was only over the course of centuries, he believed, that the effects of climate, food, and specific behaviors gave rise to the enormous palette of colors, phenotypes, and, ultimately, degenerated "human varieties" that are found on the planet.[47]

As appalling as this may now sound, the theory of degeneration allowed Buffon to strike a blow against the increasingly popular (Linnaean) notion that one could categorize people into fixed categories or *races*.[48] There is, in short, a reason why he calls this section of the *Natural History* the "Varieties of the Human Species": His intention was to emphasize an interrupted and enormous continuum of color varieties beginning with the whitest of whites and ending with the darkest of darks.[49]

Degeneration also had another strategic advantage: It allowed him to challenge what he saw as the most vile and misguided anthropological theory of his time—the polygenist claim that "the Negro, the Laplander, and the White [are all members of] different species."[50] Although Buffon readily acknowledged that people living "in extreme climates" had "degenerated" significantly, he was also careful to emphasize that these shifts were "in no way original [or distinct]"; they were "only on the exterior"; "only superficial."[51]

This commitment to a "single origin" theory of humankind culminates in one of the most universalist declarations in the *Natural History*:

> [I]t is [in fact] certain that all humans are nothing more than the same man who has been adorned with black in the torrid zone and who has been tanned and shriveled by the glacial cold at the Earth's pole."[52]

For Buffon, dividing humankind into separate species was not only scientifically unfounded; it was intellectually lazy. To properly understand the human species and its varieties, he argued, one had to look beyond skin color to a far more essential criterion: the ability of human groups, degenerate or not, to reproduce with one another. *Interfertility*, he argued, provided definitive proof that all humans belonged to a single, though variable, human species.

THE 1770S: HUMANS, RACE, AND THE EPOCHS OF NATURE

Having published the majority of his thoughts on humankind by 1749, Buffon spent much of the remaining four decades of his life writing about the rest of nature — animals in particular. Much of this work took place at his château in Montbard, 200 miles to the south of Paris.

Buffon's daily routine varied little when he was in Montbard. The first moments of the day for the naturalist were often the most unpleasant. Unable to wake on his own but determined not to waste daylight, Buffon made a pact with his valet, Joseph. If his servant could rouse him before six — even if that meant pulling the sheets off his bed or drenching him with water — he would earn a few extra *sols*. Buffon later claimed that he "owed two or three volumes of his *Natural History* to Joseph."[53]

There were other rituals at Montbard as well. After awaking, Buffon had his feet washed in a silver tureen, his hair curled, and his clothes laid out by Joseph. Once dressed, he typically dictated a few letters through his secretary before trudging up the hill from the house to a small stone office behind the ramparts of the old château.[54] At nine o'clock, a servant delivered his breakfast to him: generally, two glasses of wine and a piece of bread.[55]

BUFFON'S DESK

It was in this quiet retreat, surrounded by over a hundred framed aquatints of birds and various quadrupeds, that Buffon composed hundreds of exquisite anthropomorphic portraits of the animal kingdom. The range of animals that Buffon eventually brought to life here — including the dignified and regal lion, the intelligent elephant, and the amoral and nasty hyena — now seems unfathomable.

If one were to break down his writing activities by "category of animal" after mid-century, one might say that quadrupeds absorbed much of his life during the late 1750s and 1760s, and the bird world took up the majority of the 1770s. Finishing or delegating the remaining sections dedicated to the world's reptiles, fish, and minerals was a race against time. According to the mortality statistics that Buffon himself had published early in his career, a man who was lucky enough to make it to age sixty (he had turned sixty-three in 1770) could expect to die within nine or so years.

Buffon had made completion of the *Natural History* even less likely in 1767, when he began composing an ambitious "supplement" called *The Epochs of Nature*. Published a decade later, this speculative history of the Earth sought not only to explain the origins of life but also to offer new theories on the emergence of the human species. It quickly became the most popular — and the most controversial — volume of the *Natural History*.

Like many philosophically minded members of his generation, Buffon did not believe that an all-powerful divinity created the world with a wag of a divine finger. Although he invariably cited God as the ultimate source for the "Creation" in the *Natural History*, he was anything but a traditional believer, assuming he believed at all. Anyone who paid attention to what Buffon was asserting in the early volumes of the *Natural History*, including the censorious theologians at the Sorbonne, could find a series of heterodox notions scattered in his text. Throughout his book, he claimed that nature has a certain autonomy; that organisms shift and mutate over time; that all phenomena could and should be reduced only to physical analysis; and that humankind's varieties came about as the result of progressive mutation or degeneration.

In the 1740s and 1750s, Buffon had carefully avoided synthesizing these theories into a naturalistic account of the Genesis. To do so would have meant challenging the Church's authority on sensitive questions including: the age of the Earth, the nature of life at its origin, the emergence of animals and humans, and how the theory of humankind's "degenerated" varieties fit into the larger story of the planet. Buffon's investigation into these matters in the *Epochs of Nature*, tells a different story.

The first question that Buffon sought to answer in this *Supplé ment* to the *Natural History* was the age of the Earth. Convinced that the planet had originated as a fiery mass ejected from the sun, he described in minute detail how he resolved this puzzle by conducting an ingenious experiment at the ironworks, or *forge*, at his country property in Montbard.

On several occasions in 1767, Buffon instructed his master blacksmith to place iron spheres of varying sizes into the forge's glowing hearth. Once the spheres reached peak temperature without melting, they were pulled out with tongs and set on a stone table. Next came the slowest part of the experiment: watching the color of the spheres change from incandescent white, to red, to mottled black and white, and finally to a dark soot. (The biggest ball, as it turned out, almost took nine hours.) Though there was no way to measure the spheres' actual temperature, Buffon nonetheless recorded two key details: the time it took for each sphere to be cool enough to hold for a second without burning, and the time it took for each to reach the same temperature as an unheated sphere. From these observations, Buffon inferred that the Earth had begun as a fireball 74,000 years before — a "Creation" date that was approximately twelve times more than what theologians had maintained.[56]

MEN AT WORK IN AN EIGHTEENTH-CENTURY FORGE,
DRAWING BY ANTONIO ZUCCHI

Several years later, Buffon also attempted to determine the age of the Earth through geological means, by calculating how long it must have taken for layers of sediment to accumulate in the Alps. His conclusion, which he recorded in an unpublished manuscript, stunned him. He now believed that the Earth was perhaps seven million years old (or older). Revealing such a number in the *Natural History*, however, was out of the question. Why provoke the theologians at the Sorbonne or shock his readers? When he finally published the *Epochs*, he retained the far shorter estimate—74,000 years.[57]

Buffon had nonetheless made his point: The more that people replaced a biblical worldview with experimentation and observations, the closer they could come to scientific truth. And the "truth" that Buffon ultimately put forward in the *Epochs of Nature* began with the tale of a blisteringly hot, virtually molten planet. This, he proposed, was the first epoch of the Earth. Buffon then claimed that, over the course of the next thirty-five thousand years, the new but unstable globe began to cool while simultaneously producing new mountain chains. That period, he continued, was followed by a 15,000-year-long third epoch marked by a great flood—one during which the first life forms—fish and plants—sprang spontaneously into existence. During the fourth epoch, dated to only 20,000 years before Buffon's era, the Earth's churning interior gave rise to tremendous volcanic activity, which both dried some of the Earth's surface water and contributed to the formation of the continents. By the fifth epoch, Buffon suggested, some of the largest animals known to man, such as elephants and rhinoceroses, came into being in cold regions including Canada and Siberia. (He carefully added here that human beings were also *created* by God at this time.)

During the sixth, or penultimate, epoch, according to Buffon, the continued cooling of the Earth obliged both animals and humans to migrate south, where it was warmer. And finally, during the seventh and current epoch of nature, he asserted that humankind—at least certain varieties of humankind—had invented the tools and technology necessary to "dominate nature."[58]

Buffon's version of the human story had changed significantly over the course of three decades. In the mid-1740s, he had simply proclaimed that an original group of meandering White humans had morphed into a wide range of varieties as a result of climate, food, and customs. Thirty years later, in the 1770s, he recounted a story that was far less compatible with the idea that Noah's three sons and wives left the Ark and spread out over the Earth 4,000 years before. According to his new version of events, the first race of humans was somehow created — or came into existence — during an epoch when the Earth was still spewing a tremendous amount of heat and lava from its volcanoes. This, Buffon insisted, was a brutal time for the first humans. The pitiful lives of these people, as he put it, were spent "quaking [with fear] on an earth that was shaking under their feet."[59]

Buffon did not assign a specific race to these first men in the *Epochs*. Yet in the same basic era that he was composing his revised history of the Earth, in another section of the *Natural History*, he overturned everything he had written about degeneration in 1749. Once again theorizing that the world had been far hotter than it was currently, he asks a question. Since, as he puts it, "heat has the least bothersome effect on Negroes . . . should we not truthfully conclude that . . . their race could be older than that of White men?"[60]

In stark contrast to everything that he had written earlier about the primacy of the white prototype, Buffon now entertained the possibility that darker-skinned Africans had constituted the original human "race" from which all others had come. This assertion, which modern genetics has since confirmed, was deeply unwelcome among Buffon's peers. By the last quarter of the eighteenth century, too many of his contemporaries had already accepted the "Buffonian fact" that the White race was the first race, and that the

Black, Brown, and Native peoples were mere offshoots — human distortions produced by environmental extremes. One nineteenth-century edition of the *Epochs*, in fact, dismissed Buffon's speculation as one of the rare instances where the great naturalist had gotten things completely wrong.[61]

THE LAST YEARS AND BEYOND

Buffon turned seventy-three in 1780, surviving well past most members of his generation.[62] Although his eyesight was beginning to fail, years of strenuous exercise at Montbard had kept him fit and presumably allowed him to work on the *Natural History* past age eighty. During these last years of toil (and occasional soul-searching), Buffon came to the conclusion — quite correctly — that his writings had transformed the world. In 1785, he looked back on his career and proclaimed that there were only fifty or so books that one needed to read, among them the *Natural History*. He then concluded that recent history had only produced five geniuses: Newton, Bacon, Leibniz, Montesquieu, and himself.[63] Posterity had clearly become a comfort for Buffon as he moved into the final stage of life. Very much the stoic, he stated that if he only had three years to live, he would do so happily, "knowing full well that immortality" was his.[64] This estimate turned out to be doubly prophetic. Three years later, after he died in Paris on April 16, 1788, 20,000 mourners turned out for his funeral procession.

Immortal or not, during the last two decades of his life (and well into the nineteenth century), Buffon's *Natural History* drew considerable criticism. This was especially true for his theory of degeneration. The most famous debate had pitted him against Benjamin Franklin and, especially, Thomas Jefferson. Both of these Americans had written letters to the French naturalist, rejecting his theory that the animals in North America were smaller and more diluted than their European prototypes due to the colder, swampier, and more humid New World climate.[65] Jefferson, who actually visited Buffon at Montbard, also disputed the idea that the continent's Whites and indigenous inhabitants—its Amerindians—were similarly degenerated, stupid, and weaker.[66]

As Buffon's critics went, the two Americans remained very respectful. Not all of Buffon's faultfinders entered into such courteous disagreement with him. As early as the 1760s, a younger generation of European naturalists, all of whom had grown up reading his *Natural History*, tended to modify or flat-out reject his theories. Some offered their own far more pessimistic and racialized versions of the degeneration theory that he had popularized. Among the most influential of these men was the now-forgotten Cornelius de Pauw, a Dutch physician, philosopher, geographer, and diplomat writing (in French) while living at Frederick the Great's court in Potsdam. In stark contrast to Buffon's understanding of degeneration, de Pauw asserted forcefully that the mutation of Earth's more "extreme" varieties or races of humans was far more than a simple change in complexion. Degeneration, in his view, had been both pathological and debilitating for non-Europeans; it was a state from which there was no return or redemption and left certain races in a permanent "childhood."[67]

The only redeeming aspect of de Pauw's anthropology was that he had not refuted the idea that all human groups were related. More contrarian thinkers rejected Buffon's theory altogether, and advanced the heretical idea that the world's non-White races had never changed; they had emerged separately and had no biological link to Whites. The most vocal proponent of this polygenist theory was none other than Voltaire, the most famous writer in all of Europe by the 1760s. In stark contrast to naturalists like Buffon, who had claimed that humankind had a single origin, Voltaire claimed in his characteristically sardonic style that anatomical differences proved that Blacks and Whites (along with other "races") were, in fact, entirely separate species. Though most of the scientific community mocked the "poet" and "playwright" for engaging in a matter far beyond his expertise, Voltaire's simple and brutal explanation of humankind would ultimately gain traction, setting the stage for the far wider acceptance of polygenist thought throughout Europe and North America.

VI

SKETCH OF VOLTAIRE AT AGE 81, ETCHING BY DOMINIQUE VIVANT DENON, 1775

VOLTAIRE: THE PHILOSOPHE WHO MADE RACISM *DRÔLE*

In the winter of 1773, the seventy-nine-year-old Voltaire had been laid low for several months by an enlarged prostate that prevented him from emptying his bladder. The shudder-inducing pain of this so-called *strangury* was soon followed by infection, high fever, and sepsis, which caused his legs to swell to the size of "wine casks."[1] On the rare occasion that Voltaire felt well enough to concentrate, he asked to be propped up in his bed so that he could dictate the beginnings of an essay or a final note to a friend. In one of few poems he composed during these months, he versified that he was "on the brink of his own grave."[2]

News of his impending death spread quickly. The French Jesuits, whom he had mocked for decades, fantasized about denying him a proper burial. Voltaire had taken this threat seriously and had even hired an architect to design and build a pyramid-shaped tomb for himself on the grounds of "Ferney," his beloved neoclassical château located on the Swiss border.[3] Though he probably did not believe in the afterlife, he nonetheless felt that his body deserved better than to be tossed into a "common grave" with thieves and prostitutes.[4]

As it turned out, the old writer had prepared to die too early. Over the course of the next few months, his health improved to the point that he was able to shuffle over to the château's sun-filled office and library. Delighted with his new lease on life, he decided that the time had come to provide his public with a published assessment of his stunning literary career. He had, after all, produced the equivalent of 200 books, among them a national epic called *The Henriade*, an assessment of Newtonian physics, a "philosophical" dictionary, a *second* philosophical dictionary, a pioneering work of global history, a string of already classic plays, and the most famous philosophical short story of the eighteenth century, *Candide*.

Composing an autobiography, especially the type of self-aggrandizing autobiography that Voltaire had in mind, was considered very bad form in the eighteenth century. Accordingly, after publishing his so-called *Historical Commentary of the Works of the Author of "The Henriade"* in 1776, he vehemently denied that he had anything to do with it. Indeed, in the first pages of the book, he (in his capacity as anonymous narrator) claimed that Voltaire cared little for his reputation and even less about "his own [published] works."[5]

Readers of the *Historical Commentary* were not deceived by the false humility or the anonymous third-person authorship. Not only was the book characterized by Voltaire's distinctive prose style and sharp wit, the "author" had even slipped up a few times, and used the pronoun "I" in the text.

To Voltaire's closest friends and associates, it was obvious why he published the ninety-six-page work. Having been banished from Paris for twenty-four years, he was desperate to persuade Louis XVI — and his young wife, Marie Antoinette — to revoke his exile and allow him to return to the capital.[6] To achieve that goal, Voltaire had presented a version of himself that was both familiar and sanitized, a carefully curated portrait that focused on his least controversial works, especially his tragedies and historical writings. He made little or no mention of his antireligious philosophical treatises, political broadsides, or satirical fiction.

Voltaire also carefully avoided confronting his own contradictions — arguably the most revealing puzzle pieces of his psychology. As a political thinker, he had repeatedly denounced absolute power while eagerly cultivating relationships with Europe's most authoritarian monarchs. As a social critic, he had decried the economic inequalities of the ancien régime even as he reveled in his own vast wealth — and sometimes mocked the lives of commoners. And, finally, as staunch defender of belief in God against the rising tide of atheism, he had devoted extraordinary energy to ridiculing the religious practices of his fellow countrymen.

Such inconsistencies — assuming he was aware of them — would not have bothered Voltaire in the least. He was convinced that luminaries such as himself would inevitably have both their champions and their detractors. Several years before writing his *Historical Commentary*, in fact, he had published an essay that provided several examples of great men whose legacies were contested. Caesar, from Voltaire's point of view, was now being portrayed as both a "*débauché*" who plundered "the public treasury of Rome" *and* a man whose "valor, and whose intelligence equaled his courage."[7] He also cited the case of Thomas Cromwell, the statesman who helped engineer the English break from the Catholic Church. Voltaire was clearly amused that some people were now calling Cromwell a "rogue," a fanatic, and the "judicial assassin of the king" while others claimed that he was a "profound" politician and "brave warrior."[8]

In his final years, Voltaire may have thought that his legacy, too, would be similarly split. And so it has proven to be. But what has divided posterity is not his scorn for the Church or his cultivation of the rich and powerful. It is the chasm between two radically different Voltaires: on the one hand, the Enlightenment icon who championed tolerance and universal human rights; and on the other, the race theorist who helped legitimize the division of humankind into separate *species*.

To a large degree, Voltaire actively cultivated the contradictions and the mystery associated with his legacy. Well aware that an enigma can be an essential element within a good story, he actually began the *Historical Commentary* by casting doubt on his own birthday: "Some people claim that François de Voltaire was born on February 26, 1694, others say November 20 of the same year."[9] Voltaire followed up on this perplexing detail with another novelistic tidbit. Rather than admit to being the biological son of a treasury official, he claimed to be the product of an illicit affair between his beloved mother and an aristocratic poet and musketeer named the Chevalier de Rochebrune. This romanticized paternity seems to have pleased the writer to no end. In addition to allowing him to attribute his lyrical genius to Rochebrune (and not his "mediocre" father), this supposed aristocratic lineage added a glow to the name — de Voltaire — that he had invented for himself when he was in his twenties.

Voltaire's real name — whether he was a blue-blooded bastard or not — was François-Marie Arouet. Known to all as "Zozo" during his childhood, François-Marie grew up in what can only be called a luxurious and rarified milieu. His (presumed) father, also named François, had had such a successful career as a notary that he was able to purchase a lucrative post as collector of the spice tax in 1692. By 1701, his father's commissions from collected levies had swollen to the point that the family was able to relocate to a ten-bedroom house with a private garden on the south bank of the Île de la Cité. Situated within a stone's throw of the relic-filled Sainte Chapelle and the Palais de Justice, Voltaire's childhood home stood in the middle of the sacred and secular center of the country.[10]

A few months after the Arouet family moved to this neighborhood, Voltaire's mother, Marie Marguerite d'Aumart, died unexpectedly at age forty. Of the five children to whom she had given birth, three were still alive at the time of her death. Armand, the brother whom Voltaire would later describe as a religious "fanatic," was destined to replace his father as the receiver of the spice tax.[11] His sister Catherine, who had just turned fourteen, was soon married off. This left young François, or Zozo.

The cooks, servants, and tutors who worked for the Arouet household presumably invested more time in Zozo after Madame Arouet died. But the boy learned his most important lessons in these early years from his godfather, François de Castagnère. Castagnère, who was referred to by his ecclesiastic and aristocratic name — the Abbé de Chateauneuf — was a freethinking ecclesiastic who initiated Zozo into the joys of skepticism and irreverence.[12] At some point during Zozo's early childhood, the good abbé supposedly had the boy memorize a poem entitled "La Moïsade." This would have been an unusual assignment to say the least. "La Moïsade" was a scandalously impious short poem in which a charlatan named "Moses" uses religion to take advantage of a credulous population. Sections of the poem sound very much like the future Voltaire's creed: "With empty sophism thou shall not my reason fool nor try. The human mind wants proof more clear, than any priestly platitude."[13]

By age nine, Zozo — who was now calling himself *Arouet* — began life as a boarding student at the collège Louis-le-Grand, the largest and most prestigious Jesuit boarding school in Paris. Attended by the elite members of the aristocracy and bourgeoisie, this school not only allowed boys of the so-called "first quality to draw their initial taste of religion," but also to prepare for life's "biggest endeavors," such as a career in the army or at court.[14] While certain professions were closed off to the bourgeoisie, the nonaristocratic parents who sent their sons to Louis-le-Grand were also well aware that the school taught their progeny "noble manners"—how to function at the highest levels of society.[15] These affectations were as important as the lifelong friendships that lower caste boys forged with young nobles at the school. Voltaire certainly was no exception to this rule. By the time that he left school, he counted the future Minister of War and the president of the Paris Parlement among his friends.[16]

It was also at Louis-le-Grand that the talented young boy discovered a love for classic literature, winning prizes for his Latin translations. His favorite moments at the school, however, were spent on a makeshift stage acting in the plays that the students put on for their parents and teachers. Years later, the anticlerical Voltaire downplayed this aspect of his education and claimed that he, like everybody else with a Jesuit education, had wasted much of his childhood memorizing theological nonsense or praying for things that did not happen. What was more, he railed against the physical abuse that children suffered in such institutions. Decades after leaving Louis-le-Grand, when writing the article "Verge" (stick) for the *Questions sur l'Encyclopédie*, he claimed that some of the masters beat their students with "long rods to such a point that they left them bloodied with excessive welts on their groins."[17] One time at the dinner table, while still in England, he even accused the Jesuits of sodomizing their charges, including him: "Oh! Those damn Jesuits buggered me to such a degree that I should never get over it as long as I live."[18] Anything he could throw at the church—true or not—was fair game.

Voltaire walked out of his school for the last time at age seventeen. Independence suited the future writer, but it also brought increased conflict with his father, who not only insisted that Voltaire pursue a career in the law, but that he do so in Caen, far from the dissolute group of freethinkers and poets that his son had claimed as friends. This forced vocation did not take, and Voltaire either purposefully failed or simply dropped out of law school. The following year, in 1713, his father arranged for the now-nineteen-year-old "Arouet" to once again leave Paris and serve as secretary to the Marquis de Châteauneuf, his godfather's brother and ambassador to The Hague. This venture also flopped spectacularly.

Voltaire actually managed to create an international scandal by seducing a beautiful young Protestant refugee named Olympe Du Noyer, who went by the name Pimpette. This highly irregular relationship was quickly discovered both by Pimpette's outraged mother and the French ambassador, the latter of whom immediately ordered Voltaire to remain within the embassy walls. As was Voltaire's nature, he reacted to this confinement as if he were a character in an outlandish eighteenth-century novel, climbing out of a window and sneaking off with Pimpette for some more lovemaking.[19] By the time the lovesick boy was finally sent back to Paris in disgrace, his father had had enough. Not only did he officially disinherit Voltaire; he requested and obtained a *lettre de cachet* from the king—an extraordinary measure that gave him the right to have his own flesh and blood locked up at the Bastille.

Ultimately, though, it was not the father who would incarcerate his son. It was the Regent of France, Philippe II, the Duke of Orléans. Voltaire had already run afoul of the Regent shortly after his return from Holland by circulating epigrams and poetry that accused the Regent of enslaving Frenchmen without authority. In the spring of 1716, the then-ruler of France had become so annoyed by one poem in particular — strangely enough Voltaire was not the author — that he banned Voltaire from Paris for several months. In October, Voltaire struck back with a Latin satire that accused the Regent not only of poisoning the royal family on his way to the throne, but also of having had an incestuous affair with his own daughter. Even more foolishly, the loose-tongued Voltaire also joked to one of the Regent's many spies that the Duchesse de Berry, the Regent's daughter, was pregnant and being hidden outside of Paris. Not long after, in May of 1717, gendarmes showed up at Voltaire's apartment and dragged this "satirical poet" to the Bastille, where he remained for eleven months.

Voltaire was released from the Bastille on April 10, 1718. Before walking out the big wooden door of the prison, he was informed that his liberation was a testament to the generosity of the eight-year-old King Louis XV (who was of course acting on the Regent's recommendation). He was also told to reflect on the ways in which he might improve his dubious reputation.[20] This, in fact, he did. In addition to now officially rebaptizing himself "Monsieur de Voltaire," he finished writing a tragedy on the subject of Oedipus, a tragedy that was accepted by the Comédie Française and premiered on November 18. The subject of the play — which tells the tale of an incestuous affair between a son and his mother — was a daring one for someone who had just gotten out of prison for accusing the Regent of a similar transgression.[21]

Yet the truly audacious part of this play was not the incestuous backdrop; it was the piquant anticlerical observations embedded within this rewrite of Sophocles's famous tragedy. In one particularly famous scene, Queen Jocasta describes how the Gods not only seem unjust and vengeful, but also the nefarious role that religion plays in society: "Our priests are not what the foolish people imagine; their wisdom comes from our credulity."[22] The play was a triumph, and the first indication of Voltaire's sixty-year mantra: *écrasez l'infâme* — crush the Church and free humankind from the strictures of religion at whatever cost. It was, as it would turn out, this all-consuming anti-biblical and anticlerical orientation that would simultaneously set Voltaire on the path toward a radical race-based breakdown of humankind into separate species.

A GOOD BEATING AND THE METHOD BEHIND RACE

The long story behind Voltaire's unusual "anthropology" began, one might argue, on the night of February 4, 1726. At the time, the twenty-eight-year-old Voltaire surely believed that his novelistic youth was a thing of the past. In addition to enjoying a reputation as an acclaimed dramaturge — the queen herself had recently praised him for a new comedy called *The Indiscreet* — he had succeeded in producing a brilliant nationalist epic poem called *The Henriade* that sang the praises of Henri IV, the beloved king who brought the country together in the late sixteenth century during the religious civil wars.

Voltaire's fame had also given him access to the highest spheres of royal society. One of his best friends at the time was the Duc de Bourbon, who was acting prime minister. He had also been invited to Louis XV's wedding and had become a fixture at court, particularly among the new queen's inner circle.[23] This all changed on a winter night in February 1726, when Voltaire was in attendance at a supper party in the Duke of Sully's splendid *hôtel particulier* on the rue Saint-Antoine, just west of the Bastille.

During the meal, one of the household valets approached the table with a message for the young writer: Someone was requesting to speak to him outside the *hôtel* on a matter of great importance. Voltaire quickly excused himself and made his way outside onto the dark street, at which point three men grabbed him, tossed him to the ground, and thrashed him with canes and cudgels for several minutes. During this walloping, the man who had ordered the beating, the Count de Chabot (aka the Chevalier de Rohan) looked on with pleasure from his coach. In apparent deference to Voltaire's status as a great playwright, Rohan was supposed to have laughingly screamed to his henchmen: "[D]on't hit him in the head" in case he might still write another play.[24] As the blows rained down, Voltaire surely regretted mocking the chevalier publicly at the opera several weeks before.

After the beating, Voltaire was helped into a carriage, moaning in pain as it took him across the capital to his apartment on the rue Saint-Martin.[25] When he awoke the next morning, he felt like he had fallen from a tall building. The raised black-and-blue marks that throbbed all over his body conveyed an unmistakable message: However famous he had become, however well connected he thought he was, he remained a commoner — a *roturier* — and had no business insulting his social superior.

The story of the beating quickly made its way from Paris to Versailles, likely recounted with satisfaction by the Chevalier de Rohan himself. While a few members of court privately admitted that the chevalier had perhaps overreacted, the majority stood firmly with their fellow aristocrat.[26] As for Voltaire — bruised in both body and pride — he only made matters worse by letting his friends know that he intended to challenge the chevalier to a duel. The Rohan family, who could not countenance losing their son in such an idiotic turn of events, prevailed upon the authorities to once again lock Voltaire up in the Bastille.[27] The king agreed and signed yet another *lettre de cachet* with Voltaire's name on it. Not long after the ink was dry on this document, the young poet was once again carted off to the enormous gray colossus of a building to the east of Paris.

PORTRAIT OF VOLTAIRE IN 1718,
PAINTING BY NICOLAS DE LARGILLIÈRE

This second incarceration, although it lasted only two weeks, ultimately had a bigger effect on Voltaire's life than the first.[28] After some negotiation with the king's minister, the Count de Maurepas, Voltaire was told he would be released on the condition that he leave France for a previously planned trip to England.[29] He immediately accepted.

Voltaire arrived in London in August of 1726. During the next two years, he set about learning English while also creating a network of friends and colleagues. In addition to obtaining an audience with King George I in January 1727, Voltaire also came to know or meet some of the important literary figures of the day, among them Alexander Pope.[30] For several months, he even seems to have shared a house with Jonathan Swift, the author who had published *Gulliver's Travels* the year before Voltaire arrived.[31]

The young Frenchman's greatest discoveries, however, came while reading the critically important works of natural philosophy written by Francis Bacon, John Locke, and especially Isaac Newton. All three would remain in Voltaire's pantheon until his dying day. From Bacon, he learned about the power of empiricism, induction, and the imperative to free oneself from one's "idols" before engaging in any scientific endeavor. From Locke, he absorbed a deeply held belief in the limits of human understanding: that our ideas come from sensation and reflection, and not from some innate grasp of the world. But it was Newton's stunning mathematical explanation of the universe that had the greatest effect on him.[32] Voltaire had actually hoped to meet Newton during his trip to England, but the great physicist had died in May 1727, shortly after the Frenchman's arrival.[33] That same year, however, Voltaire managed to speak with Newton's niece, who told him how her uncle had conceived the theory of gravity when an apple fell upon his head. It was Voltaire's later account of this "discovery" that made the story famous.[34]

Interestingly enough, the Newtonian cosmology that Voltaire first came to know while in England had a major influence on how he conceived of both celestial *and* human bodies alike. This was linked to the English physicist's overall understanding of nature. Newton had not only generally claimed that nature was exceedingly simple and in perfect harmony with itself—*natura est sibi consona*—but that it was essentially unchanging.[35] The mathematical beauty of this principle, whose highest expression was the principle of gravity, led Voltaire to conceive of the entire universe as a giant clock set in motion (and subsequently abandoned to its own mechanisms) by a faraway and indifferent God.[36]

It was this lifelong belief in an immutable "world-machine" denoting a divine design that led Voltaire to assert that all categories or species of living beings—be they species of trees, fish, or dogs—had remained unchanged since they were first created. "Nothing that now grows as a plant or that is alive," Voltaire wrote several years later, "has changed. All the species have remained invariably the same."[37] From here it was only a short step to asserting that different types of humans had remained constant, and were, thus, biologically distinct from each other. This *fixist* idea would take shape under his pen several years later in what was Voltaire's first foray into race theory, his *Treatise on Metaphysics*.

BACK IN FRANCE: RACE IN THE TREATISE ON METAPHYSICS

Voltaire finally arrived back in France via Dieppe in the fall of 1728. Well aware that a phalanx of spies, censors, and Sorbonne theologians would be surveilling him upon his return, he nonetheless thrust himself back into the public eye. On the positive side, he garnered tremendous acclaim for his tragedy *Zaire*. Yet he also managed to enrage both the Church and Versailles by disseminating an irreverent poem (in manuscript) that recounted the life of Joan of Arc (c. 1412–1431).[38] This "burlesque epic," which he called "The Virgin" or the "Maid of Orleans," lambasted Christianity for its asceticism, religious fanaticism, and unhealthy obsession with the afterlife.[39]

It was the account of his stay in England, his 1733 *Letters Concerning the English Nation*, that really struck a nerve, however.[40] In this series of pithy and often hilarious letters, Voltaire criticized France as bigoted and scientifically backward while simultaneously praising England as a country that — on the whole — enjoyed the benefits of both enlightened scientific method and a less repressive constitutional monarchy. The book, in short, had something to offend virtually everybody in France, be they members of the Catholic clergy, the monarchy, or Gallic philosophers wed to Descartes's worldview.[41] By June 1734, the book had generated a general condemnation by the Paris Parlement, not to mention yet another *lettre de cachet* for Voltaire's arrest.

Voltaire, however, managed to avoid a third stint in the Bastille by preemptively fleeing to a drafty, run-down château in Cirey-sur-Blaise, 122 miles east of Paris.[42] Alone, except for his valet, he nonetheless tried to maintain his normal writing routine. Upon rising in the morning, he put on a dressing gown and consumed his daily glass of milk — he was partial to donkey milk — before dashing off several letters.[43] The main project preoccupying him during the spring was a short pamphlet-like book that he tentatively called the *Treatise of Metaphysics*. Despite the painfully dry title, the manuscript was a philosophical love letter of sorts, an intellectual tribute to the soulmate he had left behind in Paris, the brilliant and seductive Émilie du Châtelet.

Voltaire had fallen in love with the alluring du Châtelet the year before because, among other things, she was more than his equal. A natural philosopher and mathematical prodigy — she reportedly could divide a nine-digit number by a nine-digit number in her head — she was far more deeply involved in real science than her infamous boyfriend.[44] Yet Voltaire certainly believed that the love of his life, this brilliant woman who would go on to provide an illuminating translation (with commentaries) of the advanced calculus behind Newton's *Principia*, might nonetheless benefit from his own assessment of the biggest philosophical questions of the day, among them: the existence or nonexistence of God, the question of the soul, the relationship between humans and animals, and the problem of human origins.

ÉMILIE DU CHÂTELET, ENGRAVING

To the extent that Enlightenment writers of his generation dared speak of such things, they tended to do so in a roundabout way so as to distract or deceive the royal censor. This was not the case in the *Treatise*. Voltaire had no need to hide the dangerous, almost sexual, titillation of unbridled freethinking that he was sharing with Madame du Châtelet because he had no intention of publishing it. The introductory ode he dedicated to her made this clear:

> The author of this book of *Metaphysic*
> Now placed before your knee
> Deserves to be burned in the *place publique*
> But he burns only for thee.[45]

Voltaire then began by tackling the most anthropocentric question in the most anthropocentric of centuries: What is man? In his introduction, before answering, he claims that most people alive in the 1730s had no idea. A typical Christian peasant, he jokes, is "a two-footed animal . . . who articulates a few words, cultivates the land, pays tribute, without knowing why, to another animal called *king* . . . and gathers together on certain days to sing prayers in a language that he does not understand."[46]

It was also in this initial chapter, however, that Voltaire developed a sneering "anthropological" assessment of the different species of humans found on the planet. Voltaire had not held such trenchant views about humankind when, as a teenager, he had first met several French-speaking Chinese boys who, like him, attended Louis-le-Grand.[47] Nor did he maintain, in 1716, that the mixed-race daughter of Louis XIV whom he had visited in the Moret Convent was a different *type* of human. Indeed, the only thing that he noticed when he stared into the eyes of the dark-skinned nun was that she very much looked like her father, the Sun King.[48]

Voltaire's encounters with different "types" of humans nonetheless left a lasting impression on his later writings. When he was just shy of thirty, Voltaire visited the king's court at Fontainebleau, where he met and questioned four Amerindians from Mississippi who had been brought to France. Fascinated by their distinctive "beardlessness" — which he later cited as evidence of a different human species — Voltaire was also under the false impression that Amerindians were cannibals. He claimed to have asked several questions about their supposed *anthropophagic* practices, to which one native woman coldly replied "yes, as if this were an ordinary question."[49]

On another unspecified occasion, Voltaire had also questioned a number of enslaved Africans "belonging" to Bertrand-François Mahé de la Bourdonnais, an explorer and officer of the Company of the Indies. Once again, Voltaire had an agenda: He wanted to know if these men had seen any humanlike creatures with tails in the jungle — possible evidence, in his mind, of a new species of humans. (At the time, the myth of tailed men lurking in the forests of Africa and Asia was firmly rooted in the European imagination.) According to Voltaire, the men answered yes. Whether they were indulging him, or mocking him, is anyone's guess.[50]

Many of Voltaire's curious "anthropological" ideas can be found in the *Treatise*. To explain his overall theory of human differentiation, he asks his reader — du Châtelet — to imagine that the book's narrator is an extraterrestrial anthropologist interested in identifying what type of man lives on Earth. Foreshadowing the structure of philosophical short stories such as *Zadig*, *Micromégas*, and *Candide*, his alien-narrator then sets off on a voyage of cosmic relativism across this "small piece of mud," in other words, all around the Earth.[51]

Voltaire's first malicious joke in the text appears when he (speaking as the alien) announces that he has landed in Cafferia (basically South Africa) in "search of a man." Here, the alien encounters "monkeys, elephants, negroes" all of whom seem to have an "imperfect capacity to reason."[52] The alien's first reaction is that, among all these animals, it appears that the elephant is the most reasonable and, thus, perhaps . . . *a man*. Upon further inspection, however, the alien admits that it is the "negro animal" that has slightly greater capacities than the other animals and thus he announces that he has successfully identified an Earth man, whom he now classifies as follows: "Man is a black animal who has wool on his head and walks on two feet almost as adroitly as a monkey. He is less strong than other animals of his size, has a few more ideas than they do, and more of an ability to express them."[53]

From Africa the alien then proceeds to the East Indies (perhaps Thailand or Borneo), where he is surprised to find that the humans are "entirely different"; they are a "beautiful yellow" color, have black "horsehair," and "ideas" that are entirely different from those of the "negroes." This leads the extraterrestrial to declare that there appears to be "two species of men" on Earth.[54]

The alien's journey continues. From the East Indies, he heads off to the major marketplace city of Goa, India, where he encounters more human phenotypes, including dark-skinned Indians, Amerindians without any facial hair, and blond-headed Europeans with beards. The most remarkable person he meets, however, is a Christian missionary who claims, following Scripture, that all "these different men are all born from the same father."[55]

Voltaire's extraterrestrial is flummoxed by the missionary's assertion. Reasoning out loud, the alien states that if these men are supposedly all members of the same human family, then it must be true that one "species" of man should be able to give birth to another species of man: "Is it then true that a Negro and a Negro woman sometimes produce White children with blond hair? and that bearded people produce people without beards? and that Whites sometimes produce yellow children?" Finally, he asks if different races mutate when they move to different climates: Namely, do "Negroes" who are "transplanted" in Germany turn white?[56]

The answer to all of the alien's questions is an unequivocal no, at which point Voltaire takes the narrative over and proclaims (to Madame du Châtelet) that it seems obvious that the different species of men are like different types of trees. Consider the fact, he continues, that "pear trees, pine trees, oaks, and apricot trees do not come from the same tree." In his view, this is just like "Whites with beards, Negroes with wool, Yellows with horsehair, and beardless men." Clearly, he concludes, they "do not come from the same man."[57]

When Voltaire later takes up the question of *why* there are different species of men, he simply states that this was what God did: He created different types of human beings, each with its own abilities, and each with its own spot in a natural hierarchy: "Some men," he writes, "appear superior to Negroes, in the same way that Negroes are superior to monkeys and in the same way that monkeys are to oysters."[58]

When Voltaire completed his anthropological musings for Madame du Châtelet in the spring of 1734, he knew that he had staked out a radical position. No philosopher had ever put forward such a brutal *polygenetic* explanation of humankind — an explanation that not only asserted that the humans on Earth had separate and distinct origins, but that they had different aptitudes, and perhaps different destinies as well.[59]

We do not know how Madame du Châtelet reacted to the details of the *Treatise*. What is certain is that she told her paramour that he must avoid sharing it with the public at all costs. For once, Voltaire took the advice. The manuscript was only discovered years later among her papers, well after both Voltaire and du Châtelet had died. It had been labeled "to be burned."[60]

1744: THE ALBINO: WHITE NEGRO OR WHITE MOOR?

For the next decade, Voltaire remained silent (at least in print) regarding his unconventional belief that humankind's races had separate origins. In 1744, however, the philosopher would be prompted to reveal his position on humankind when an enterprising colonist from South America arrived in the capital with a four- or five-year-old albino boy named Mapondé who had presumably been taken away from his parents in the interest of "science." This small child was an example of what the era referred to as a *Nègre blanc*, or "White Negro." The very term indicated a phenomenon that Voltaire considered an impossibility: an entirely White person being born of Black African parents.[61]

Voltaire had first heard about the appearance of Mapondé in the winter of 1744. In early January, the frightened boy had been taken to the King's Library in the Louvre, where twenty or so members of the Academy of Sciences had come together to examine this so-called White Negro. Hovering around Mapondé, the men took turns scrutinizing the boy's pale eyes, his white eyelashes, and milky skin, as well as his seemingly incongruous "African" features. Though the archives do not reveal what was discussed, some of the academicians surely claimed, as was commonly believed at the time, that Mapondé's skin disorder was a type of leprosy or smallpox. Others probably attributed the small "White Negro's" color to an improperly stimulated maternal imagination, which was to say that the child's Black mother may have been thinking of a White man during the moment that the baby was conceived.[62]

MAPONDÉ, PAINTING BY JEAN-BAPTISTE PERRONNEAU

Among all the people present during this "viewing," the most visionary was the recently elected director of the Paris Academy of Sciences, Pierre-Louis Moreau de Maupertuis.[63] As well as being a brilliant mathematician, geometrician, physicist, and world explorer—he had nearly made it to the North Pole in 1737—Maupertuis was equally fascinated by heredity and the transmission of abnormal physical features from generation to generation.[64] The presence of the albino child at the Academy, in fact, prompted him to publish (anonymously) a groundbreaking book on reproduction and embryology in 1744 entitled the *Dissertation physique à l'occasion du nègre blanc*. This book, as I made clear in the previous chapter, had enormous consequences for the notion of race.

Among its most revolutionary aspects, Maupertuis's *Dissertation* targeted the widely accepted belief in *preformationism*, the most prevalent and biblically compatible embryological theory of the era. Preformationism maintains that, since God had produced all things at the beginning of time, small versions of each person or animal lay dormant, or *preformed*, in either human eggs or in human sperm. Partisans of an egg-based theory of preformationism were called *ovists*; supporters of the sperm-based version *animaculists*. Both embryological schemes, however, gave credence to the idea that either human eggs or human sperm had existed since the moment that the deity had created the universe.

Maupertuis not only rejected both versions of *preformationism*, he produced a new understanding of embryology and "generation" that contained several radical ideas: 1) to reproduce, the human body draws from its various parts to manufacture the requisite generational elements (sperm and egg); 2) reproduction is a dynamic process involving both parents *in the present*; 3) donception always contains an element of chance; and 4) humans and animals can sometimes produce something *new* and perhaps unexpected each time they have offspring.[65]

In addition to advancing this revolutionary model of "generation" or reproduction, Maupertuis put forward another influential idea related to the albino in the revised version of the *Dissertation* that he published the next year. In this new book, which he called the *Vénus physique*, or *Earthly Venus*, he claimed that the unexpected birth of a "White Negro" was not simply a matter of chance; it indicated a recessive characteristic—whiteness—that had lain dormant in certain Black individuals for generations. This turned out to be one of the most influential claims made about human reproduction and race during the eighteenth century. From Maupertuis's point of view, the fact that certain black-skinned humans occasionally produced white-skinned offspring proved that the original human type or race was *white*.[66] Over the course of the next several decades, many naturalists and philosophers agreed with Maupertuis that the "White Negro" provided the first "scientific" confirmation that all human varieties or races — even Black Africans — had come from an original white rootstock.

Voltaire, who had also had the opportunity to examine Mapondé at a friend's house in the Marais, scoffed at the idea that this was a cross-racial being. Indeed, from his point of view, the term people were using to describe Mapondé — "White Negro" — was a misnomer. According to his Newton-inspired view of the living world, there were White people on this Earth and there were Black people on this Earth, period. While he acknowledged that Blacks and Whites might produce a "mulatto" child, he mocked both the idea that Blacks might give birth to Whites as well as the belief that such freak occurrences were proof of Black peoples' ancient *whiteness*.

In 1745, Voltaire published a short screed on the subject entitled "Relation touchant un maure blanc" ("Account of a White Moor"). The first thing Voltaire did in this essay is create a brand new term for albinism. Rather than calling Mapondé a "White Negro" — which implies the idea of two races somehow existing simultaneously — he labels the boy a "White Moor from Africa." This new term both denies Mapondé's relationship with "Negroes," and suggests that he is a member of a distinct species (akin to men with tails).[67]

Voltaire's second rhetorical move in the essay is to contradict the boy's provenance. Though everybody knew that this child had been born of two African (Black) parents in South America, he nonetheless claimed that Mapondé had been kidnapped from a race of white-skinned people living somewhere deep in the jungles of Angola. (For his theory to remain coherent, he knew, he needed to affirm that only albinos could give birth to albinos.)

Voltaire's writings on the albino did not have the effect he wished. Few, if any, contemporary naturalists accepted his fixist view of nature and species. Even fewer believed, as he had asserted, that there was a strange group of "White Moors" living and producing similar children in Africa. Indeed, by the time that Voltaire had published his remarks on the albino, most French philosophers and naturalists had abandoned the notion that nature—and humankind—was static and unchanging. Instead, a new generation of thinkers was increasingly drawn to far more fluid, environmental explanations of human diversity.

The first major figure to introduce this idea in print was Montesquieu. In his tremendously influential *Spirit of the Laws* (1748), the philosopher maintained that varied world climates had changed the world's peoples, dividing them into cold, temperate, and warm bodies—each with particular dispositions or psychological traits that not only shaped their minds and *spirits*, but also determined their suitability for a given political system, be it democracy, republic, monarchy, or despotism.[68] An even more dynamic understanding of nature and the human species appeared in Buffon's *Natural History* in 1749.

Voltaire was particularly disturbed by his old friend's theories.[69] The first volumes of Buffon's massive project, from Voltaire's perspective, advanced an overreaching, unempirical, and entirely wrongheaded theory of nature—one that contradicted his own view of the universe in three critical ways. First, Buffon the geologist argued that the Earth had undergone a series of enormous geological changes since it was ripped from the sun. Second, Buffon the embryologist (borrowing some ideas from Maupertuis) affirmed that chance and permanent changes could be introduced in particular groups at the embryonic level and passed on to future generations. And finally, Buffon the anthropologist claimed that an original White group of humans had degenerated into all of the world's peoples over the course of centuries as a result of their interaction with different environments.[70]

Buffon's recasting of nature as an enormous *history*, a chronicle of change, chance, and mutation, is one of the most important epistemological paradigm shifts to take place during the Enlightenment era.[71] For Voltaire, however, this dynamic understanding of nature was a threat; it laid waste to his view that the world and its inhabitants were a finished work, a masterpiece created by a divine clockmaker to be "contemplated and admired . . . rather than something to be presumptuously pried into."[72] What was at stake for Voltaire was a coherent, stable, and ordered physical universe—one in which racial separateness was not an accident of history, as Buffon had maintained, but a sign of providential design.[73]

By the early 1750s, by which time the *Natural History* had become a runaway bestseller, Voltaire had presumably understood that he was ill-equipped to go head-to-head with the likes of Buffon in the scientific arena. It was perhaps for this reason that he chose to fight back in a forum where he exerted a singular dominance: the realm of history. It was here that Voltaire's racism—there is simply no other word for it—had its greatest impact and reached its biggest audience.

UNIVERSAL HISTORY AND RACE

In 1745, only a year after he had examined the so-called White Moor, Voltaire published a few preliminary chapters from what would become his best-known work of history, the *Essai sur les mœurs et l'esprit des nations* (*Essay on the Manners and the Spirit of Nations*).[74] This was an early version of a much larger project in which, among other things, he identified what he believed to be the biologically distinct species of humans living on the planet.

Voltaire had still not brought out the definitive version of this book nine years later. Much of this had to do with how his life had changed. In 1749, he fell into a deep depression after Madame du Châtelet died during childbirth. Despondent after losing the love of his life, he had accepted a longstanding invitation from the King of Prussia, Frederick II, to take up residence at the German monarch's court in Potsdam. Less than a year later, as was often the case with Voltaire, his sharp tongue had gotten him into trouble, and he was obliged to flee under duress.[75] Denied permission to return to France, Voltaire and his niece — Marie-Louise Mignot, who was now his new lover — traveled to Geneva where he published a finished version of the *Essay* in 1756.

Voltaire's *Essai sur les mœurs* is a watershed in universal history — a transnational account of human development over time. As Voltaire explains it in his preface, to the extent that earlier historians had attempted to think globally about history, they were generally so awestruck by the brilliance of the Roman Empire that they "treated other men in our universal histories as if they had not existed."[76] He, on the other hand, consciously began his chronicle of humankind with discussions of the most ancient "civilized" peoples, the Chinese, Indians, Chaldeans, and Egyptians, before moving on to Rome and Europe.[77] This long tour of world history was not entirely disinterested or arbitrary of course. As Enlightenment specialist Robert Darnton points out: "Voltaire surveyed the history of humanity going back to ancient China, and the closer he got to his main subject — Europe since the time of Charlemagne — the more he delighted in exposing the barbarity of the past as if it were an argument against abuses in the present."[78]

Among the other innovations that characterize the *Essay*, Voltaire painted ethnographic portraits of the people who composed the world's nations, not only the monarchs who ruled over them. World history, Voltaire believed, should be more than memorizing "in what year an unworthy prince succeeded a barbarian king in an uncouth country."[79] From his point of view, an accurate rendering of the past needed to include the state of civilization, the morals, and the "spirit" of particular nations, a mixture of what we might now call cultural history, ethnography, and ethnology.[80] This sweeping approach, as it turned out, generated a causal and comparative typology of the world's peoples, including Chinese, Europeans, Arabs, Indians, Amerindians, Africans, Laplanders, Jews, and strange "races" of men including the Albinos. In many ways, the scope of Voltaire's world history is a rejoinder to Montesquieu's *Spirit of the Laws* and Buffon's *Natural History*. Contemporary readers may also be reminded of Jared Diamond's *Guns, Germs, and Steel* and, at times, Herrnstein and Murray's notorious *Bell Curve*.

One of the biggest questions that Voltaire seeks to resolve in the *Essay* was the supposedly astonishing "discovery" of Amerindians in the New World, a group of people not mentioned in the Bible. This intellectual shock, which reverberated across Europe two hundred years before Voltaire was born, had raised troubling questions for theologians and naturalists alike: Had these "beardless men" somehow migrated to the Americas and changed in the process? Or had they always been there? Voltaire's response to this puzzle, which appeared in a chapter entitled "On the Population of America," begins by ridiculing one of the prevailing origin theories — the correct one as it turns out — that the ancestors of the Amerindians had come across the Bering Strait:

> According to [a very bad author of universal history], one of Noah's descendants had nothing more pressing to do than to establish [a household] in Kamtschatka, in northern Siberia. His family, having nothing to do [either], went to visit Canada, either by setting off on ships, walking for pleasure through all the ice and snow, or across a small bit of land that we have not yet found. People then began to have children in Canada, and soon this beautiful country could not feed the prodigious number of its inhabitants, so they went and populated Mexico, Peru, and Chile; and their great granddaughters gave birth to giants near the Strait of Magellan.[81]

After rejecting the idea that Americans were simply a group of wandering Siberians, Voltaire then supplies what he believes to be a far simpler answer: This was God's doing. Amerindians had been put in the New World by the same divine being "who made trees and grass grow there."[82] A few pages later, he elaborates on this theory in typical Voltairean fashion, which is to say by providing a mocking analogy that made his reader either side with him or feel as thick as two short planks: "[I]f we are not surprised that there are flies in America, it is a stupidity to be surprised that there are men there. The master of nature peopled and varied the whole world."[83]

Voltaire's God-based response to the "Amerindian" question did not lead to further metaphysical speculation. He did not, for example, state that Amerindians along with all other "races" were God's children. On the contrary, Voltaire engaged in speculative anthropology, explaining what he believed happened to the different races in the so-called state of nature.

Looking back into time, Voltaire initially agreed with his hero John Locke that "in the beginning, all the world was America."[84] In other words, all of the world's peoples, very much like Amerindians, had begun their existence in a barbaric state characterized by difficult physical variables and challenges. In the best of cases, Voltaire continued, these same peoples developed a more sophisticated relationship with the exterior world. The Germans and English, for example, had originally lived exactly like the Amerindians. They had covered themselves with animal skin, they had shared their women, they had lived in huts, and they had tattooed themselves before finally pulling themselves up and out of the state of nature (and barbarity).

In his view, certain human groups — certain species of humans as he saw it — were unable to make the transition from barbarism to civilization. Amerindians and other primitive peoples, he writes, have remained "plunged in a state closely resembling that of brutes for a long succession of centuries."[85] Voltaire was even more uncompromising when it came to Black Africans. The "Negroes," he pronounces, are "submerged in . . . stupidity, and will remain huddling there for a long time."[86] Africans, in his opinion, lacked humankind's defining essence: an ability to reason and thus an ability to participate meaningfully in their own existence. They are "not capable of great attention [spans]; they combine [ideas] very little, and do not seem made for either the inconveniences or the advantages of our philosophy."[87]

To further substantiate what he believed to be Black Africans' limited cognitive abilities, Voltaire refers to the supposed anatomical distinctiveness of this "species." This was not a new idea. Beginning in the early seventeenth century, anatomists had begun identifying (and often disagreeing about) the specific characteristics of African anatomy. In 1618, the Parisian anatomist Jean Riolan was able to study "Ethiopian" skin by using a blistering agent on the tissue sample and separating it into two layers. He noted that the outer skin of the African in question was white, whereas the inner skin was dark.[88] This led him to conclude that this second layer of African skin had simply darkened, the result of living in the Torrid Zone.[89]

Voltaire's information regarding African anatomy, however, had come from Marcello Malpighi, an Italian anatomist who had made a stunning "discovery" in 1666 when examining a number of different tissue samples, including one that had come from a deceased "Ethiopian."[90] While looking at this snippet of decomposed African skin under a microscope, Malpighi discovered what he believed to be a heretofore-unidentified stratum of dark skin lying between the innermost layer of the epidermis (exterior skin) and the underlying dermis. Since the darkish material in this skin layer—we now know it as melanin—appeared mucus-like and seemed to resemble some sort of web or network, he named it the *rete mucosum*, or mucus network. His published announcement that he had found a new layer of skin unique to Africans quickly became a revelation for doctors and anatomists throughout Europe. This supposedly Ethiopian-specific structure—which exists in all humans of course—soon became known as the Malpighian layer.[91]

Voltaire had seen a preserved sample of this "African" *reticulum mucosum* in 1722 while visiting the famous Dutch anatomist Frederik Ruysch in Amsterdam.[92] The experience marked him. For the rest of his life, Voltaire not only claimed that this distinct anatomical structure was the "obvious cause of the inherent and specific blackness of the Negroes"; it was the irrefutable proof that there was absolutely no biological link between white and black (and therefore between Whites and other races).[93] What was more, the *rete* seemingly conferred a deeper meaning to the African's other "liabilities," e.g., their morphology and supposedly subpar intelligence.

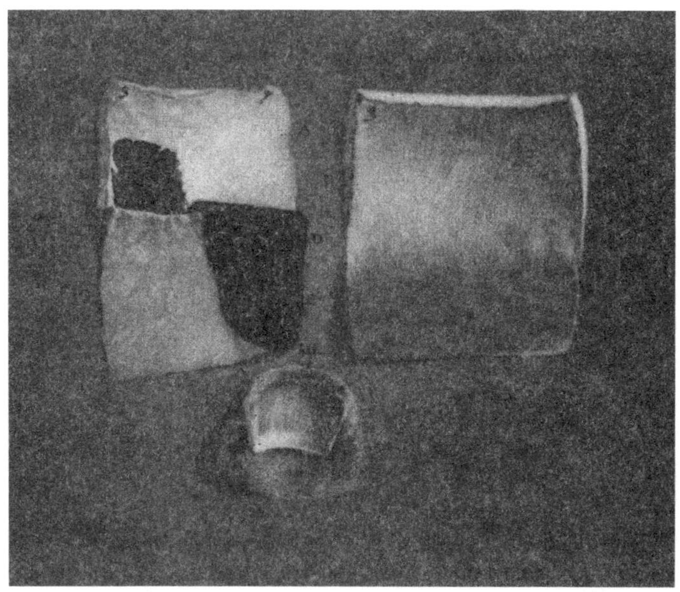

SKIN SAMPLES INCLUDING A DETAIL OF THE MALPIGHIAN LAYER

But by far Voltaire's most disturbing assessment of the Black African is related to the institution of chattel slavery. Having discussed the physical and mental state of the "Negro," Voltaire concludes that Blacks' unfortunate fate in the world economy is to be expected. Africans themselves, he writes, believe that they are "born in Guinea in order to be sold to Whites to serve them."[94] This resignation to a life of slavery is more than a simple matter of conviction in Voltaire's view. It is a sign of their "national character": "[T]here is in each species of man, as is the case with plants, a principle that distinguishes them. Following this principle, nature [has created] different types of genius and national characters that we rarely see change. It is by this principle that Negroes are the slaves of other men."[95] Among all the ghastly things that Voltaire wrote about Africans, this was perhaps the worst. In one terrifying sentence, he asserts that Nature (or perhaps God himself) had destined this category of human to be chattel within the extensive European plantation system.

VOLTAIRE, *CANDIDE*, AND INVESTING IN RACE

Only two years after publishing the *Essay*, Voltaire once again took up the question of slavery in *Candide*. Absent from this darkly comedic short story, however, was Voltaire's natural history voice: the voice that affirmed that Africans were a particular species constitutionally suited for enslavement. Instead, the now far more humanistic writer — the voice of Voltaire with whom so many people identify — lambasts the cruelty of slavery as a crime against our common humanity.

Slavery was not the primary focus of *Candide* of course. The notion appears in one brief but significant episode within a far larger examination of one of the era's most pressing philosophical and religious questions: *theodicy*, the problem of evil on a planet ostensibly created by a benevolent God. Voltaire had certainly taken up this question before, but this was the first time that he used a puppetlike protagonist — the eponymous Candide — to lay bare the cruelty masked by optimistic or religious systems of thought.

The sad story of Candide begins with his own fall from grace. Having resided happily at the baron Thunder-ten-Tronckh's court for years — in "the most beautiful and pleasant of all castles in the world" — Candide had hoped to remain in this idyllic setting forever with the love of his life, Cunégonde.[96] Yet when he is caught kissing the fair maiden by her father the baron, Candide is kicked "in the butt" and exiled along with his tutor Pangloss, a man who misses no opportunity to interpret their subsequent misfortunes by the light of *providentialism* — the belief that no matter what happens on Earth, one can easily rationalize such suffering with an axiom such as Leibniz's famous "All is well in the best of all possible worlds."

After Candide is exiled and Cunégonde kidnapped, Voltaire's guileless hero travels around the world in search of his lost love. Crossing several continents in the process, he comes face to face with torture, religious intolerance, forced conscription, sexual diseases, rape, natural disasters, the Inquisition, civil wars, executions, and murder (some of which Candide commits himself). Toward the end of his woeful voyage, he also confronts the reality of chattel slavery when he arrives in the Dutch colony of Surinam, where he encounters a "Negro" slave lying on the ground who has had both his left leg and hand amputated. Visibly affected by this scene, Candide asks the suffering Black man who could have possibly done such a horrible thing. The "Negro" replies that it was his master, Mynheer Vanderdendur ("dur" means hard or mean in French), and that the treatment that he has received is anything but unusual: "When we work at the sugar-canes, and the mill snatches hold of a finger, they cut off the hand; and when we attempt to run away, they cut off the leg; both cases have happened to me. This is the price at which you eat sugar in Europe."[97] As he stares down at this pathetic man, he is moved to tears. Significantly, it is one of the few moments in the book that is not relayed in a flippant tone.

Although the unnamed "Negro of Surinam" is hardly a postcolonial figure, the fact that an enslaved African speaks for himself in this chapter was reflective of a new era in the embryonic antislavery movement. To the extent that earlier philosophes had spoken out against slavery, they had generally limited themselves to accusing slave traders or planters of murderous cruelty and greed. In *Candide*, Voltaire had gone one step further: He had the so-called Negro of Surinam force European consumers to acknowledge that they, too, are directly implicated in a killing machine, an enterprise that only functions by "making men perish," as Voltaire put it elsewhere.[98] Fifteen years after *Candide* appeared in print, when abolitionist thought had become far more prevalent, the pitiful story of the "Negro of Surinam" cemented Voltaire's reputation as one of the era's greatest champions of the unfairly bonded.[99]

CANDIDE AND CACAMBO MEET THE "NEGRO OF SURINAM,"
ENGRAVING, 1759

Not surprisingly, readers familiar with Voltaire's racial views—and not just *Candide*—have found his overall stance on Africans and African chattel slavery puzzling. Some of this uncertainty arises from the facts and falsehoods related to his investments in the slave trade.[100]

Voltaire's first investments in the business of slavery came about passively: At age twenty-seven he inherited several shares in the French Compagnie des Indes—the monopolistic trade company that, in addition to transporting textiles, teas, coffee beans, metals, woods, and various exotic luxury goods across various oceans, was, for a certain time, the sole business allowed to carry slaves to France's colonies in the Caribbean and Indian Ocean.[101] Yet neither he nor his peers would have seen such investments (passive or not) as specifically financing the slave trade. At the time, possessing Compagnie stock was akin to having shares in a large bank involved in various foreign transactions and investments.

More damning, perhaps, were the colonial ventures in which Voltaire played a more active role. Recent archival research has revealed that, between 1749 and 1754, Voltaire invested the colossal sum of 400,000 livres with the Gilly Brothers' or "Gilles Frères" Society, a private trading company operating out of Cadiz, a port on the southwest tip of Spain.[102] In general, the Gilly Brothers did not arm slave ships; they were far more interested in chartering ships involved in direct trade with Asia or the Americas.[103] And yet, in one of the rare cases where the Gilly Brothers armed a slave trading voyage, they did invest 10,000 livres of Voltaire's funds in the *Saint George*, presumably without his knowledge given the way that such companies operated.[104] The ship set sail in December 1752, bought nearly 300 enslaved Africans at various *comptoirs*, or trading "factories," along the African coast, and ultimately delivered 251 African captives to a slave market in Buenos Aires.[105]

Voltaire's greatest fault was not his financial complicity in the slave trade. His supreme failing was his tireless promotion of contemptuous ethnographical portraits of supposedly inferior non-Europeans, virtually until his dying day. It is this legacy that most clouds his otherwise deservedly humanistic reputation. As one early nineteenth-century writer put it, Voltaire may have scoffed at "slavery, but he also scoffed at the slave."[106]

This was not the only area where Voltaire's acidic racism lived on well after his death. In the same way that he had repeatedly maligned Black Africans and Amerindians, to name but two categories, Voltaire left behind a staggering number of comments regarding European Jewry that nineteenth- and twentieth-century antisemites eagerly embraced. Although he never really claimed that Jews constituted a separate biological race, Voltaire nonetheless described them as "the most detestable nation that has ever soiled the earth," a sect of religious zealots whose comportment and beliefs were incompatible with his vision of an "enlightened Europe."[107] In the article "Jew" that appeared in the posthumous edition of his *Philosophical Dictionary*, one finds the following assessment: "[Jews] are an ignorant and barbarous people, who have combined for ages the most sordid greed with the most detestable superstition and the most invincible hatred for the people who tolerate them."[108] He concludes this statement with what can be read either as a sick joke or an indictment of the Inquisition: "[O]ne should not burn them, however."[109]

Voltaire's glib remark regarding the centuries-long practice of persecuting Jews underscores another aspect of his thought that sets him apart from his peers. Among all the naturalists, philosophers, and travel writers who contributed to the progressive racialization of humankind during the eighteenth century, he was the first to make racism *humorous* with his astonishing verbal energy, comic comparisons, and examples of reductio ad absurdum, all of which were designed to make serious points. The amount of race-based humor in Voltaire's writing is stunning. To mock the theory of degeneration, Voltaire suggested that only a fool could claim that Blacks are nothing more than "a race of Whites blackened by the climate."[110] To emphasize the seemingly huge chasm between Whites and Blacks, he wisecracked that "the race of Negroes was as different from Whites as the race of spaniels is from that of greyhounds."[111] The most appalling joke came when Voltaire was discussing the supposedly specific anatomy of Africans by inviting his readers to peer into a black body for themselves: "[W]hoever wants to have a Negro dissected (I mean after his death) will find that [the] mucus membrane [known as the *rete mucusom* found in African skin] is black like ink from head to toe."[112]

To the extent that "serious" eighteenth-century naturalists—chief among them Buffon—heard about Voltaire's fixist views of the human species, they did so while rolling their eyes. And yet, by the early- to mid-nineteenth century, at which point polygenism had emerged as the dominant theory on the origin of humankind, Voltaire's reputation among race theorists would change dramatically. Prominent anthropologists including Jean-Louis Armand de Quartrefages de Bréau, the chair of ethnography at the Museum of Natural History in Paris, marveled that "Voltaire's jokes [regarding polygenesis] have now been taken up in the most serious way possible."[113] While his racial "science" often seemed laughable during the eighteenth century, it had become deadly serious fifty or so years after his death.

VOLTAIRE AND LEGACY

Although Voltaire believed that "great men" such as himself often failed to achieve a singular, unambiguous legacy after their death, he likely assumed that he would be remembered primarily for spreading the gospel of Enlightenment — for championing progress, science, human rights, and tolerance. After all, throughout his entire career, he had been a tireless *reformer*, one of the most powerful humanist voices of his generation.

This was precisely why Versailles had wanted to keep this old and dying man at bay in the mid-1770s. Voltaire, however, refused to languish in exile. In 1778, at age eighty-three, he decided to return to the capital to die, regardless of what the king or anyone else had declared. In mid-January, he and his secretary climbed into his deluxe star-spangled carriage and set off on a bumpy, six-day journey to the capital. Upon arriving at one of the gates leading into Paris, a custom official asked if Voltaire had any contraband in his coach. Never missing the opportunity for a one-liner, he replied dryly, "the only contraband is me."[114]

Allowed to proceed through the city's stone portal, the writer soon arrived at his destination, a sumptuous *rive gauche* town house located on the rue Baune. Over the course of the next few months, he pumped himself full of his favorite colonial products — opium and coffee — and managed both to work on his final play and hold court. In addition to finally meeting with the great encyclopedist Denis Diderot, he received old friends and luminaries, including Benjamin Franklin.[115] On March 30, despite suffering from what was now an advanced form of prostate cancer, he announced that he felt well enough to venture out to the Comédie Française to attend a performance of his recently completed play, a tragedy entitled *Irène*.[116] The evening turned out to be one of the most moving of the writer's long life.

When the audience saw Voltaire arrive in his loge, they exploded in spontaneous applause for more than an hour. Each person at the Comédie Française clapped for the Voltaire that he or she loved. Theater-lovers cheered for the man who was often on the Comédie Français's playbill one night out of four. Others clapped for the historian, the writer of short stories, the enemy of the church, or the first internationally known public defender of free speech and human rights. The commotion was such that the actors could not even take the stage until, at the mob's insistence, a ceremonial crown was placed on the old man's balding head. Several weeks after this apotheosis, the old writer finally succumbed to his cancer — a malady that he described as the worst of the "eighty-two diseases" that had plagued the "eighty-two" years of his life.[117]

THE CROWNING OF VOLTAIRE, ENGRAVING, C. 1780

Two hundred and fifty years after his death, much of what Voltaire accomplished — and what he represented — has been forgotten. He is now best known for his *Candide* and, to a lesser extent, for his fierce attacks on ideological intolerance and religious fanaticism. Each time a terrorist organization justifies violence in the name of its religious beliefs, commentators invoke Voltaire's heartfelt condemnations of the zealots who incite their followers to commit unspeakable atrocities. The most famous and succinct of these barbs is: "Those who can make you believe absurdities, can make you commit atrocities."[118]

Alongside these lacerating critiques runs a heartfelt plea for tolerance — for the acceptance of human difference in all its forms. In his most generous moments, Voltaire even extended this courtesy to the categories of humans he maligned elsewhere. In a chapter of the *Philosophical Dictionary* that he entitled "Universal Tolerance," he proclaims: "I tell you that one must regard all men as our brothers. What! My brother the Turk? My brother the Chinaman? The Jew? The Siamese? Yes, of course."[119]

There is, of course, no full redemption in such a sentence. While Voltaire called upon his vast readership to treat the world's "others" as brothers in this short essay, elsewhere he was denying the humanity of these same people. This is by far the most discordant note within one of the most daring, brilliant, and humanistic of writing careers. It is perhaps for that reason that some of his admirers have sought to shield him from such reproaches by arguing that these racial views are simply a reflection of his time.

Yet Voltaire's particular form of "anthropology" cannot be explained away as nothing more than the prejudices of his generation. On the contrary, whereas Buffon, Diderot, Montesquieu, Maupertuis, Kant, and Blumenbach all believed that humankind was a single human species shaped by climate, geography, and migration, Voltaire stood virtually alone in putting forward a rigid racial hierarchy, placing a superior White "race" at its apex and treating other groups as wholly separate and unrelated species.

The only Western writer of comparable stature to advocate such a stark racial theory — and to face comparable censure today — is David Hume, often described as the most beloved philosopher ever to write in the English language.

VII

DAVID HUME, KEEPER OF THE LIBRARY, PRESIDENT OF THE SELECT SOCIETY (1754), PAINTING BY ALLAN RAMSAY

THE SCOTS AND STAGE THEORY: DAVID HUME, ADAM SMITH, LORD KAMES, AND WILLIAM ROBERTSON

The inhabitants of Great Britain and France
were as savage two thousand years ago,
as those of Africa and America are at this day.
—JAMES BEATTIE, *An Essay on the Nature and Immutability of Truth*, 1778

Over half the habitable parts of the world
remain populated by two-legged animals
living in a ghastly state
of almost unadulterated nature,
barely able to feed and clothe themselves,
barely capable of speech.
—VOLTAIRE, *Questions sur l'Encyclopédie*, 1771

Shortly before seven p.m., on Wednesday, December 11, 1754, David Hume huffed and puffed his way up several flights of stairs to the top floor of Edinburgh's Parliament building. The six-foot philosopher, who was tall and quite portly by eighteenth-century standards, then entered the Advocates Library where, during the day, he was employed as the keeper of 30,000 law books and manuscripts.[1] Hume was not here to work, however; he had come for one of his favorite weekly activities, a meeting of the so-called Select Society, the elite debate club of which he was president.

INTERIOR OF THE ADVOCATES LIBRARY, ENGRAVING, 1743

Not long after the room's candles were lit — the winter sun had gone down shortly after three-thirty — a succession of wig-clad gentlemen began strolling into the library, laughing affably and looking forward to an evening of both discussion and drinking.

One of the things that seemingly united each member of the Select, whether philosopher, historian, minister, professor, lawyer, natural philosopher, or artist, was a love of the bottle.[2]

Debate clubs along the lines of the Select or London's famous "Robin Hood Society" had begun to emerge several decades earlier, in the 1720s. What set Edinburgh's club apart was the concentration of luminaries among its members. In the first few years that the organization met, the most prominent member was arguably Lord Kames (aka Henry Home), the self-taught judge, philosopher, and agricultural theorist who also happened to be David Hume's distant cousin. Some of the other affiliates included Adam Ferguson, often considered the founder of modern sociology; Lord Monboddo, the father of modern linguistics; and Allan Ramsay, the internationally celebrated portraitist. There was also another member who would ultimately become as famous as David Hume: the soft-spoken economist, moral philosopher, and future author of *The Wealth of Nations*, Adam Smith.[3]

Hume claimed that the prominence of the club in the 1750s was such that it had become an obsession in Scotland. As he put it, "Young and old, noble and ignoble, witty and dull, laity and clergy, all the world are ambitious of a place amongst us [here in Edinburgh]."[4] In this dark and remote capital that was increasingly being called the "Athens of the North," the members of the Select felt like they had created something along the lines of Plato's Academy.[5]

The intellectual fervor in Edinburgh (and at the Select) was part of a broader Scottish transformation. The country had become lousy with geniuses over the previous decade for a simple reason: More so than any other European country, it had consciously encouraged education, social progress, and (relative) economic and intellectual liberty. This program of national self-betterment had begun shortly after the country had fused with England into a "United Kingdom" in 1707. In the first years after unification, Scottish municipal authorities opened libraries in cities and villages, while local parishes took responsibility for providing basic schooling to Scotland's children. By the 1720s and 1730s, this country of just over one million inhabitants—home to some of Europe's best universities—had achieved the highest literacy rate in Europe, if not the world.[6] Scotland, in short, had become a crucible not only for philosophers and writers, but scientific pioneers including James Hutton, the founder of modern geology; James Watt, the inventor of the steam engine; and Joseph Black, the chemist who had helped pioneer artificial refrigeration.[7]

Not surprisingly, the topics taken up by the Select Society often reflected the country's ongoing quest for progress and self-improvement. Some of the Wednesday evenings were thus spent examining economic questions: "Are moderate taxes a discouragement to trade, industry, and manufactures?" There were also debates on contemporary social issues, among them the effect of "the institution of slavery" and the permissibility of "divorces" if agreed to "by mutual consent." According to the club's bylaws, the only truly off-limits subjects were those having to do with revealed religion or liturgical matters. This guideline was presumably enacted not only to reassure those members of the club who were affiliated with the Kirk (or Scottish Church), but to keep the anticlerical Hume out of trouble.

Hume, however, had no intention of debating the existence of God or anything of the sort on this cold December night. He was far more interested in "kindl[ing] the fires of genius" of his fellow members in relation to an "anthropological" question that had fascinated him for two decades.[8] After calling the meeting to order, Hume announced the specific topic in his thick Scottish burr, namely, whether "the difference of *national characters* be chiefly owing to the difference of natural climates, or to moral or political causes."[9] Put more simply, he was asking the members of the Select if the general characteristics of the world's nations were caused by the physical environment in which people lived or resulted from the effect of customs, professions, or a particular form of government.[10]

How exactly each of the men present at the Select club would have interpreted Hume's use of the term "national character" may have varied a bit. In general, it is fair to say that they would have all assumed that there were real and demonstrable qualities that held true for each nation or people. This was not a new idea; the expression "national character" had been circulating in various European languages for decades. As early as 1678, the French traveler Jean Gailhard had published a breakdown of European national characters that evaluated the French, the Spanish, the Italians, and the Germans on a variety of subjects. Regarding the category of "behavior," for example, he asserted that the French were courteous, the Spanish lordly, the Italians amorous, and the Germans clownish. As for the art of "conversation," Gailhard continued, the Spanish were supposedly troublesome, the Italians complying, the Germans unpleasant, and the French jovial. In each of these instances (and in many other examples), the Frenchman maintained that his countrymen were far superior to the other national types.[11]

Gailhard's seventeenth-century typology amounted to little more than caricature — a whimsical catalog of dress, customs, and temperament. By the 1750s, however, the idea of national character had begun to acquire a harder edge. Across Europe, thinkers were increasingly treating perceived behaviors or characteristics as clues to something deeper or hereditary, and perhaps even as a sign of mental capacity. This was certainly the way that Hume had described the concept of national character in one of his recently published essays.

Hume's provocative question about the origins and implications of national character — posed just as the concept was taking on a more deterministic cast — sparked a lively debate at the Select. Although the archives reveal little about what was said that night, the topic had clearly struck a chord; the club took up the same question in February 1755 and again in 1757.

In subsequent years, the effort to explain "national characters" would become something of an obsession for many of the men at the Select. Several of the most prominent members eventually published their own views on the relative cognitive abilities and potential perfectibility of the world's various nations and races. David Hume, whether he knew it or not, had transformed the Select Society into an incubator for a new vision of race.[12]

1748 "OF NATIONAL CHARACTERS"

In his early twenties, Hume began to explore the philosophical questions — some of them anthropological — that would shape his life's work. After abandoning the study of law and losing a clerkship in Bristol (reportedly for correcting his master's grammar), he left for France in 1734. There, in the small Loire Valley town of La Flèche, he immersed himself in a rigorous program of classical and contemporary reading and drafted what would become *A Treatise on Human Nature*, one of the most influential works in the history of philosophy.[13]

In the *Treatise*, whose two-volume edition first appeared in 1739 and 1740, Hume argued that the "experimental" method made famous by Isaac Newton could be applied to human nature. Akin to how a physicist might examine "the sun and the climate" — which is to say, without recourse to Scripture or previous speculative philosophy — Hume recommended that his era's philosophers and naturalists study the human species by carefully observing its passions and its habits, as well as its historical variability.[14] It was just this approach that led Hume to identify (in the *Treatise*) what he believed to be a real problem related to his era's environmental explanations of "national character": the fact that the people living in certain regions of the world had changed significantly over the centuries despite the fact that other variables such as "the soil and climate" had remained precisely the same.[15]

Hume was far from the only person to be pondering anthropology-related questions in the late 1730s and 1740s. Numerous European thinkers had begun discussing subjects including humankind's "moral" differences, varied coloration, and possible "categorization." Indeed, in the same years that Hume was writing the *Treatise*, a variety of books related to "national character" and/or humankind's physical features had begun circulating. The fact that many of these theories tended to contradict each other had not really discouraged anybody from speculating even more deeply about what was becoming race. Rampant guesswork about humankind's differences would only inspire more people — including Hume himself — to try to identify the actual truth about the species.

One of the most important moments in the early formation of race had come in 1735, when Linnaeus had divided humankind into four distinct categories, or *varieties*. This revolution in taxonomy, which came five decades after François Bernier had first suggested that one could fruitfully partition humankind into distinct races or types, had inspired (or overlapped with) a whole new set of generally negative theories related to non-Europeans, especially Black Africans.

Another critical intervention came from Montesquieu, the political philosopher, magistrate, and member of the Bordeaux Academy of Sciences. Writing from a port city that was home to hundreds of enslaved Africans, Montesquieu put forward a proto-racial view of humankind that combined elements of ancient climate theory with more contemporary "discoveries" related to human physiology in his *Spirit of the Laws* (1748).[16] In Montesquieu's estimation, the world's climates had produced wildly dissimilar types of people whose "minds" or "spirits" were suited to specific political systems. The most telling example of the power of the climate, for Montesquieu, was how the brutal heat and humidity of the Torrid Zone had supposedly created an unfortunate predisposition toward slavishness and laziness in the nations near the equator. This environment-based view of human potential had a logical corollary of course: White Europeans, who lived in a far more temperate zone, not only had superior intelligence; they were better suited to "higher" forms of government.[17]

Only months after Montesquieu brought forth his global breakdown of the world's peoples, Buffon published an even more influential climatological explanation of humankind. Taking his readers back to the initial centuries after the human species had come into existence, the naturalist claimed that the first group of humans was white and had migrated throughout the globe, taking on new colors, behaviors, and changing shape as a result of the environments in which they found themselves. This dispersion of the species, according to Buffon, had had a deleterious effect on the groups who settled in the less temperate zones. Compared to the original (White) humans, some of these migrants became weaker, uglier, less white, and perhaps less intelligent. Although various climatological explanations of the human species had been circulating since antiquity, Buffon's new and authoritative account of humankind's coloration—which was published under the auspices of Louis XV himself—quickly became the dominant theory of human difference.

Not everybody agreed with various forms of climate theory. Well before either Montesquieu's or Buffon's views on the effects of climate appeared in print, Voltaire had already ridiculed the supposed environmental causes of human difference in an unpublished manuscript. By the 1750s, he had also begun directly attacking Buffon's theory of human degeneration. His most vociferous criticism came later, in the 1768 *Singularities of Nature*. Only an "ignoramus," Voltaire writes scornfully, could believe that "Blacks were a race of Whites blackened by the climate."[18] The far more plausible explanation for humankind's diversity, in his opinion, was that "inferior" races such as Africans and Native Americans had simply come into existence separately on their respective continents.

Although Hume never exposed his anthropological speculation as dogmatically as Voltaire did, he tended to think similarly about such questions. In 1748, he finally returned to the subject of "national characters" while serving as secretary to General James St. Clair (1688–1762).[19] Traveling with this military envoy to the courts of Vienna and Turin, among other cities, had allowed Hume to come into contact with various "national types" and races that he would not have encountered otherwise. It had been this voyage, perhaps, that had prompted him to compare contemporary members of a particular national variety—Italians for example—with descriptions of their ancestors, the ancient Romans. These musings ultimately gave rise to a 6,000-word manuscript on the subject of national characters.[20]

For whatever reason, Hume initially had no intention of publishing this short treatise. Yet while he was choosing the articles for a new version of his *Essays, Moral, Political, and Literary* (first edition

1741), a friend convinced him to leave out a potentially incendiary political essay on the "Protestant Succession"—a touchy subject having to do with the exclusion of Catholics from the English throne.[21] Hume took this advice and replaced it with the recently written "Of National Characters." Engaging in racial stereotypes was far less inflammatory than taking up religious topics in 1748.

Like other theoreticians of "national character," Hume believed that there were *real* traits or mindsets that held true for particular countries. To demonstrate the fact that "each nation has a peculiar set of manners," he claims that one could probably expect that the "common people in Switzerland have . . . more honesty than those of the same rank in Ireland." More insidious (and commonly accepted) stereotypes appear in this text as well. It is clear, Hume writes, that "the Jews in Europe, and the Armenians in the east, have a peculiar character. And the former are as much noted for fraud, as the latter for probity."[22]

Despite the fact that Hume's primary intent in this essay is to put forward a typology of national characters, the first two sentences of the 1748 publication begin in typical Humean fashion—with a great deal of skepticism. The philosopher warns his readers that they, like he, should avoid facile conclusions regarding national stereotypes:

> The vulgar are apt to carry all national characters to extremes; and having once established it as a principle, that any people are knavish, or cowardly, or ignorant, they will admit of no exception, but comprehend every individual under the same censure. Men of sense condemn these undistinguishing judgments.[23]

To this cautionary opening, Hume adds several counterexamples to national stereotypes, most famously: "We have reason to expect greater wit and gaiety in a Frenchman than in a Spaniard; though

Cervantes was born in Spain."[24] Ultimately, however, Hume comes back to the fact that there are indeed undeniable similarities among the members of specific nations. "Each nation," he writes, "has a peculiar set of manners."[25]

The method behind Hume's "Of National Characters" is a perfect example of the increasingly secular interpretation of human origins emerging at mid-century. To understand human differentiation, Hume asserts, one needs to evaluate the supposed effect of both *physical* and *moral* variables on the world's nations and peoples. These two terms might now appear quite vague to us, but for Hume (and the members of his generation), the difference between *physical* and *moral* causes conjured up something quite specific. By *physical* causes, he was indicating the climate; whereas by *moral* causes, he simply means nothing more than the effect of a given nation's laws, habits, customs, government, and religion on human bodies and minds.

As he had already hinted at in the *Treatise on Human Nature*, Hume objects to the millennia-old and still most popular explanation of human differentiation, climate theory. How is it, he asks, that two groups of people who live just across a national border from each other (and who experience the exact same climate) have wildly different *characters* or ways of relating to the world? The answer, of course, is that it *cannot be* climate. To add to this point, Hume also compares "historical" and contemporary ethnography of the same nations and peoples. Consider the Greeks, he says. In his estimation, the people living in this country were at one time the most civilized to have ever lived. Now, he claims, they are little more than a despicable group of cowardly cheats, despite living in the same climate as their noble ancestors. The Chinese provide Hume with another counterexample to climate theory. Based on knowledge that he derived from the era's travelogues, he asserts that the country's inhabitants have a surprisingly identical mindset despite living across huge swaths of land with wildly different climates.

Hume's final objection to climate theory is a satirical bit of (anticlerical) ethnography concerning Jesuit missionaries. Though this religious order had established missions in freezing and torrid climates throughout the world, he asserts, their missionaries do not change. To a man, they tend to promote the "spirit of superstition, by continued grimace and hypocrisy," wherever they might reside.[26]

Jews and Catholic clergy are far from the only "groups" to come under attack in Hume's essay. In 1753, when reworking "Of National Characters" for yet another new edition of his *Essays*, Hume added an ill-famed footnote regarding the intellectual potential of non-Whites. His discussion begins with a hesitant introduction: "I am apt to suspect . . ." The remainder of the note, however, is much more dogmatic.[27]

Footnotes typically serve as ancillary remarks appended to a main text. This addendum, however, contains Hume's most significant thinking on race. Non-Whites, he states, are "naturally inferior" to Whites, meaning that there is something essential, deep-rooted, or "biological" that explains their presumed lesser capabilities. To this blanket denigration of the vast majority of the world's humans, Hume then appends one of the eighteenth century's most powerful expressions of white supremacy: "There scarcely ever was a civilized nation of any other complexion than white, nor even any individual eminent either in action or speculation. No ingenious manufactures amongst them, no arts, no sciences."[28]

Such thinking was relatively rare in 1753. Hume was asserting that Amerindians, Indians, Asians, and Black Africans remained trapped in a primitive state of being. In his view, non-Whites were unable to excel in scientific or artistic endeavors; they did not give birth to the type of individual geniuses (such as a Newton) that might help improve the group as a whole; and they were incapable of achieving the status of civilization.

To further substantiate this point, Hume then compared the supposed historical trajectory of non-Whites to that of Whites. Members of the White race, he claims, differ from the other categories in that their primitive ancestors had the innate ability to improve their lot. As he puts it, even "the most rude and barbarous of the whites, such as the ancient GERMANS" or the "present TARTARS" have "something eminent about them, in their valor, form of government, or some other particular."[29] The White peoples of the world, in Hume's view, have distinguished themselves because they—and they alone—have been able to pull themselves out of their backward past; they were *perfectible* and benefited from an innate ability to move toward civilization, whereas other groups did not.

Hume's conviction that there was only one category of humans capable of achieving the highest level of civilization dovetails with his belief that humankind can be broken down into "four or five" "species" of men. When one examines the question of national characters and human history, from his point of view, one understands that the "uniform and constant difference [between human groups] could not happen, in so many countries and ages, if nature had not made an original distinction betwixt these *breeds* of men."[30]

Such unsubstantiated statements, Hume knew only too well, left him open to objections. To rebut any possible counterexamples to his race-based view of humankind—for example, Black Africans who had excelled in areas that he had associated with white civilization—Hume proactively dismisses the possibility of advanced reasoning, literacy, or intellectual refinement among the African "species." "NEGROE slaves," he explains, are "dispersed all over EUROPE," but none has shown the "symptoms of ingenuity."[31] To further this point, Hume also belittles the accomplishments of the

Jamaican poet, scholar of Latin, and astronomer Francis Williams (c. 1690–1770): "[T]hey talk of one negroe as a man of parts and learning [in Kingston, Jamaica], but 'tis likely he is admired for very slender accomplishments, like a parrot, who speaks a few words plainly."[32]

PORTRAIT OF FRANCIS WILLIAMS,
PAINTING, C. 1745

Why Hume chose to publish this footnote has long been a subject of debate among both his critics and apologists.[33] Was this simply part of his larger frustration with the illogical side of climate theory? An extension of his argument against biblical "anthropology"? Or did it come simply from some deep-seated racism? Whatever Hume's specific motivation, in subsequent years proslavery thinkers understood perfectly well how useful the famous philosopher's footnote could be. To name but one notorious example, several years after Hume had published the second edition of "Of National Characters," the Barbados planter and politician Samuel Estwick (1736–1795) congratulated the Scottish philosopher for identifying "the difference betwixt the several species of men by sorting out them out according to their innate abilities to exert their 'rational powers, or faculties of the understanding.'"[34] The enslaver then went on to draw a conclusion that was implicit in Hume's essay: Black Africans had "nothing of humanity about them but the form."[35]

Given the membership of the Select Society in December of 1754, it is easy to imagine that some of the men who debated the source of national character disagreed with Hume's extreme views. Indeed, it is quite possible that the benevolently minded Adam Smith or Adam Ferguson took Hume to task for his belief that non-Europeans were incapable of achieving what white civilization had accomplished. It was common knowledge, after all, that Arab cultures had effectively invented math, that Indian architects had designed and built architectural marvels such as the Taj Mahal, and that the Chinese had invented gunpowder, papermaking, and the printing press itself. It may have been such arguments, in fact, that convinced Hume to rethink his position when he was re-editing "Of National Characters" one final time.[36] Crossing out what he had said regarding the supposed inability of *all* non-White races to achieve the state of civilization, he now concentrated his most brutal comments solely on the world's "Negroes," identifying them as the most inferior and uncivilized of all races or species:

"I am apt to suspect the negroes, and in general all the others species of men (for there are four or five different kinds) to be naturally inferior to the whites. There scarcely ever was a civilized nation of that complexion nor even any individual eminent either in action or speculation . . ."[37]

ADAM SMITH

Even if the members of the Select did not agree with Hume's anthropological views, the provocative issues he raised at the club—the question of human origins, the changes of the species over time, and the possibility of some sort of biological or racial taxonomy—had a profound effect on the society's members. If we are to judge by some of the racial theories that members of the Select ultimately published, the major question that preoccupied most of these men had to do with the history and the evolution of the human species. Were certain groups "stuck" in time? Were others advancing and outpacing others? How was one to measure or identify the different stages in which groups found themselves? Or, as some would have it, including Hume, were these differences somehow elemental, original?

The most prominent and influential person to take up such questions, as it turned out, was Hume's best friend, Adam Smith (1723–1790). Twelve years younger than Hume, the future author of *The Wealth of Nations* grew up in Kirkcaldy, a small city that drew its lifeblood from maritime commerce. Smith's father, in fact, had worked as Comptroller of Customs for the British crown in Kirkcaldy's "tollbooth," a large warehouse near the docks where he spent his days inspecting goods and levying market dues on the tools, food, and industrial products that flowed into port from abroad. It was likely in this setting, which brought Smith Sr. into contact with sailors coming from as far as the Baltics, that the forty-year-old customs agent contracted tuberculosis, the disease that took his life in January 1725. His son—who would go on to champion international trade—was born a few months later.

ADAM SMITH, ENGRAVING

According to Smith's friend and biographer, Dugald Stewart, the fatherless Smith was "inform and sickly" in his early years and "required all the tender solicitude of his surviving parent."[38] Little more than this is known about Smith's childhood, with the exception of a bizarre (and perhaps apocryphal) tale about his being kidnapped. At age three, while on a trip with his mother to visit his uncle John in the neighboring Fife countryside, Smith was apparently whisked away by a group of "Tinkers," lowland Scottish "Gypsies," or Travelers. Luckily for the boy, his uncle, "who had heard about these vagrants," set off to the neighboring town, found his nephew, and rescued the boy. In concluding the story, Stewart remarks that this act of bravery "preserved to the world a genius."[39]

Another early biographer joked that the sickly child and future economist would certainly have made a "poor Gypsy."[40]

In the years after this momentous event, Smith began a proper Presbyterian education in a local two-room schoolhouse on Hill Street. As precocious and dedicated to his schoolwork as he was apparently absent-minded, he took classes in Latin translation, English grammar and composition, mathematics, and, of course, catechism. By age fourteen, he set off from Kirkcaldy for the University of Glasgow, where he studied "logic, metaphysics, math, Newtonian physics, and moral philosophy."[41] Three years later, in 1740, he was named a Snell exhibitioner, or scholarship student, at Balliol College in the University of Oxford.

Being simultaneously Scottish and Presbyterian did not make life easy for Smith during his six years at Oxford. The professors and students at the university tended to be blinkered Tories and High Church Anglicans who had little interest in the young Scot from Kirkcaldy.[42] Years later, in *The Wealth of Nations*, Smith described the famous university as rearguard and "intellectually stagnant" compared to the University of Glasgow. Indeed, he added that he had found it virtually impossible to learn anything from the Balliol faculty who, he claimed, had "given up altogether the pretense of teaching."[43]

Smith seemingly sublimated any frustrations he may have had at Oxford by dedicating himself to his own self-imposed task: studying both ancient and contemporary texts related to the political history and morals (viz., customs and behaviors) of the world's peoples.[44] Smith's most critical intellectual discovery at Oxford, however, came when he stumbled across the work of his elder countryman, David Hume. While the two men would not meet in person for eight or so more years, scholars now assume that Smith had had access to Hume's *Treatise of Human Nature* as well as his *Essays Moral and Political*, both of which had appeared by 1742.[45] The confirmation that Smith was familiar with Hume's writing comes to us in the form of an intriguing anecdote. Sometime in the early 1740s, the "heads of college" at Balliol were conducting an inspection of Smith's room and were horrified to discover that the young Scot was reading Hume — a thinker whose views on religion were considered heretical to say the least. Though the Oxford dons apparently chastised their Scottish fellowship student and confiscated the book, this did not dissuade Smith from continuing to read his countryman's works. Indeed, by the time that Smith returned to Edinburgh, he had become a "committed Humean."[46]

Whether at Oxford, or shortly after his return, Smith became enticed by several of Hume's most revolutionary ideas. Chief among these is the assertion that human reason operating by itself was unable to generate certain knowledge, as most philosophers had believed since antiquity. In Hume's view, humankind's comprehension of the perceived world is better understood as an assemblage of ideas brought together by the imagination and the passions.[47] This naturalistic and skeptical assessment of our ability to grasp reality became a given within Smith's worldview. Yet Smith also added a more hopeful, nuanced, and constructive addendum: the belief that our moral conventions are determined through a process of shared sensibility and sympathy. According to this contextual understanding of morality, each society produces ethical standards that emerge from their specific sentiments and experiences.[48]

Hume's theory of mind necessarily pushed Smith to think deeply about the origins of language, jurisprudence, and various economic and political systems. Some of these topics, as Hume himself had demonstrated, raised questions that were related to the origins of national characters or race. Smith, however, was less interested than Hume in the significance of pigmentation or human morphology. Rather, he was fascinated by something that Hume had hinted at but not yet fully developed: a stage or stadial theory of the human species that would explain how the world's great civilizations — Europeans in particular — had slowly evolved from more primitive phases of human development to where they were in the 1750s, to a stage that Smith would call commercial society.[49]

Smith was not the first early modern philosopher to think about humanity in terms of such epochal changes. Sixty years before he had begun reflecting on such ideas, John Locke had implied that the ancestors of the Earth's current civilizations had all emerged from the backward state of nature within which Amerindians now found themselves.[50] Other social and political theorists had also looked back to imagined states of nature where primitive humans struggled as well. Most famously, Thomas Hobbes had claimed in his 1651 *Leviathan* that the first humans had lived in a state of continual warfare and violence that only ended when they had decided to sacrifice their individual liberty and become the subjects of a powerful monarch.[51] Whatever the vision of humankind's origins or original nature — benevolent or violent — seventeenth- and eighteenth-century social contract theorists such as Grotius, Hobbes, Pufendorf, Locke, or Rousseau conjured up the deep past in order to speak more effectively about the political present. As a group, their primary focus was putting forward normative theories of political authority. The Scots, however, were undertaking something entirely different: They were generating (speculative) historical accounts of humankind's evolution by drawing on what they believed to be empirically valid "anthropological material."[52]

Smith revealed early versions of his stage theory of humankind in the lectures that he gave at the University of Edinburgh between 1750 and 1751.[53] That same year, after assuming the chair of moral philosophy at Glasgow, he added similar ideas to the classes he taught on natural theory, ethics, and jurisprudence.[54] Smith's students, who described their professor as being terribly absent-minded — often staring off blankly into space or mumbling to himself — were nonetheless fascinated by a vision of history that explained, among other things, how they as Lowland Scots had pulled themselves out of a state of barbarism on their way to the stage of civilization.[55]

Smith told his students that humankind as a species could be categorized according to one of "four distinct states." To convey this idea in his lectures, he asked his audiences to imagine a group of people who had been shipwrecked on a deserted island. He then described how this isolated and deprived population made significant progress over time. Initially, he explained, the marooned passengers regressed to the stage of hunter-gatherers, seeking out "the fruits which the soil naturally produced, and the wild beasts which they could kill."[56] As time went on, however, this same shipwrecked group was able to "tame" some of these same animals.[57] Having now achieved the stage of shepherds, they then noticed that the island produced "considerable quantities of vegetables of its own accord," and began cultivating the earth. At this point, agriculture became the island's "prevailing employment."[58] The next stage of development, the so-called age of commerce, was by far the most significant. During this final period, surplus production of food coupled with the ability to fabricate new material goods not only gave rise to new trading mechanisms, but new governmental structures, better education, and even taxation. As Smith later explained this final stage of society in *The Wealth of Nations*, commerce was a civilizing force, the sine qua non for achieving the highest form of human society.[59]

Smith's version of stage theory, which charted humankind's evolution from "rudeness to refinement," historicized every living human being on the planet, be they "lawless" Amerindian "savages" or the sophisticated members of the Select Society.[60] This chronicle of the human species did far more than to simply separate people by stage of development. It also provided a comparative study of cognitive abilities and inclinations.[61]

In the 1759 *Theory of Moral Sentiments*, Smith argued the precarious and dangerous lives of savages prevents them from having the same degree of sympathy as people in more advanced societies. The "hardiness" of their existence, he writes, "diminishes their humanity."[62] Smith elaborates on the liabilities of living "in the first ages of society" even more forcefully in a posthumously published article entitled "Of the Origin of Philosophy" (1795). In this short piece, he contends that savages lead lives devoid of "law, order, and security." The "impotence" of their minds, he concludes, also prevents them from conceiving of an all-powerful Creator. To the extent that they are even able to hold religious beliefs, he claims, they bow down superstitiously and fearfully before natural phenomena they do not understand, like childlike animists.[63]

There is undoubtedly a powerfully deterministic side to Smith's understanding of the human species, one that identifies people's intellectual potential according to the stage of society (hunter, herdsman, farmer, member of commercial society) in which they find themselves. Yet Smith's anthropology differs markedly from the trenchant categorizations of humankind that his friend David Hume (and others) were advancing at the time. Far from believing that differences in perceived achievement were predetermined or somehow attributable to a biological notion of race, Smith repeatedly reminded his students and readers that all humans had similar aptitudes, passions, and drives when they were born.[64] The relative levels of human intelligence, he asserted, are not determined by a fixed or innate form of "national character"; they were the result of one's lot in life, one's habits and education. The implications of this idea were far-reaching: Regardless of the stage in which people found themselves, in Smith's view, they could move forward into a higher sphere of being if placed in the proper environment and given the appropriate stimuli.[65]

Not everyone made use of stage theory to hint at humanity's higher potential. Indeed, it was perhaps inevitable that such a powerful notion would generate what amounted to a new way of classifying humankind: one where the so-called savages of Africa and America were assigned to a far more primitive and *permanent* phase of being, whereas Europeans were crowned as having moved through to the most sophisticated stage of humanity. Some of Smith's best friends, in fact, would do just that.

LORD KAMES AND SIR WILLIAM ROBERTSON ON THE WORLD'S "RUDE NATIONS"

If the Select Society (and the many clubs that succeeded it) were arguably the most important venues for Scottish race-making, the city's taverns arguably ran a close second. It was here, in dark and windowless establishments such as the Potterrow, that Hume, Smith, and an evolving cast of Edinburgh's intelligentsia came together on a regular basis to engage in "literary guzzlement—open-ended discussion over bottles of claret or dram."[66] Exactly who was present and when, as well as what subjects were taken up during these evenings, cannot be found in any archive. Yet what we do know is that Hume and Smith often found themselves in the company of men who used stage theory to advance their own histories of humankind. Two of these men, the jurist Henry Home (Lord

Kames) and the historian and cleric William Robertson, were the most important contributors to what became a racialized use of this approach.[67]

PORTRAIT OF HENRY HOME, LORD KAMES, ENGRAVING, 1794

The more well-known of these thinkers, Henry Home (1696–1782), was a remarkable polymath.[68] A self-taught lawyer who never attended school or university, Home came to Edinburgh from Berwickshire at age sixteen to train to be a solicitor.[69] After being admitted to the bar and establishing a successful legal practice in the 1720s, he began an extensive publishing career, writing first on legal theory before expanding into the realms of history, ethics, aesthetics, natural religion, and even the modernization of Scotland's forestry, farming, and textile industries.[70] In 1752, Home was appointed to Scotland's supreme civil court, the Scottish Court of Session, which earned him the title to which he is now generally referred, Lord Kames.

By the 1750s, Kames was not only one of the first members of the Scottish Enlightenment (along with Smith) to describe humankind's "progress" through time according to a series of stages; he was the first to publish a version of the theory in his 1758 *Historical Law-Tracts*. Although Kames did not identify the same four classic stages that became the hallmark of the theory as it was later spelled out by Adam Smith, he asserted that humankind moved from savagery (hunting and gathering), to animal domestication and husbandry, to the establishment of villages and ultimately cities. This chronicle of "the gradual progress of manners, of laws, of arts, from their birth to their present maturity" had a deep effect on the Edinburgh literati.[71] Particularly influential was his belief that the cultural evolution of humankind had actually generated varying geniuses, by which he meant different types and even levels of intelligence.

Kames developed a far more racialized version of stage theory in his best-selling 1774 *Sketches of the History of Man*. Despite the fact that he introduces this two-volume book as little more than "various speculations that occasionally amused the author and enlivened his leisure hours," the tone that he chooses to speak about non-Europeans in his *Sketches* is neither lighthearted nor skeptical.[72]

Much of Kames's anthropology can be understood as a revision of Buffon's theory of monogenesis and climate-induced degeneration. Echoing some of the views of his cousin David Hume, Kames argues that environment and complexion do not always map onto each other. Consider the fact, he argues, that there are groups of Chinese people living in extreme heat who remain white, and Ethiopians who are "tawny" despite living in some of the hottest climates in the world.[73] Kames follows up on this idea by stating that national character is far more than something that is acquired; it depends on a "permanent and invariable cause."[74]

This sentence pushes Kames's notion of national character to its logical polygenetic end. In his view, the differences between Amerindians and Europeans are so great that it is highly unlikely that they are of the same race.[75] Black skin, in particular, is the compelling proof of this essential difference in his opinion. "The colour of the Negroes . . . affords a strong presumption of their being a different species from the Whites."[76]

To explain how the different human species that he evokes came into being, Kames does not rely on degeneration. On the contrary, borrowing elements from Voltaire, he asserts that an all-powerful deity must have created biologically distinct "Adams and Eves" for the specific climates in which they now found themselves.[77] Humans, he claims, are akin to the canine species. While they might be able to interbreed, they must have been originally unrelated: "[T]here are different races of men as well as of dogs: a mastiff differs not more from a spaniel, than a White man from a Negro, or a Laplander from a Dane . . ." Kames follows up on this analogy with another Voltaire-inspired comparison. Moving from zoology to botany, he explains that the different species of plants found on the world's continents are akin to the different types of humans: They are biologically unrelated and came into existence separately because they were designed for specific environments: "[P]lants were created of different kinds to fit them for different climates, and so were brute animals."[78]

In Kames's opinion, the only human type or category that has been constitutionally able to move through the various stages of development and, thus, achieve humankind's full potential is the European.[79] The overwhelming evidence, in his opinion, is that most other peoples or groups have languished in their evolution. Much like Hume and Voltaire, he was equating geography and pigmentation with a specific racial destiny.

PORTRAIT OF WILLIAM ROBERTSON, PAINTING BY JOSHUA REYNOLDS, 1772

Kames's assertion that Africans, Asians, Amerindians, and Europeans constitute separate species appeared at a time when other members of the Select were advancing their own, less *zoological*, versions of stage theory. The most important of these men was an eloquent and sharp-witted minister of the Scottish Kirk (or Church) named William Robertson (1721–1793).[80] His influence, which has generally been forgotten, was enormous, especially in the United States.

Like many members of the Select, Robertson's fascination with history, law, rhetoric, and travel literature had drawn him into the era's anthropological debates. As early as 1757, at age thirty-six, he volunteered to preside over the Select Society's discussion of Montesquieu's view on climate and its alleged effect on humankind. Two years later, he reviewed Kames's *Historical Law-Tracts* — the first published account of stage theory — for the *Edinburgh Journal*. By the mid-1760s, he began integrating the theory into his own historical works.[81]

As a practicing Christian with no interest in disseminating heresy, Robertson was understandably far less inclined than his friends — Hume and Kames — to divide up the world's peoples into separate biological races. Indeed, before discussing the state in which Amerindians found themselves, he had felt compelled to underscore his own belief in biblical monogenism: "We know, with infallible certainty, that all the human race spring from the same source, and that the descendants of one man, under the protection, as well as in obedience to the command of heaven, multiplied and replenished the Earth."[82]

In some ways, the foundation of the minister's anthropology was more in line with that of the other "initiator" of stage theory, Adam Smith. Like Smith, Robertson claims that all humans share similar capacities and that, whenever the human mind "is placed in the same situation, [it] will, in the ages the most distant, and in countries the most remote, assume the same form, and be distinguished by the same manners."[83] This orientation not only emphasizes a certain commonality, but the idea that every human group might find a path to God, commercial society, and civilization.

Despite such universalist ideas, Robertson ultimately developed a brutal version of stage theory in his *History of America*. How and when this book came into being, given its profoundly complicated publication history, merits a bit of explanation. During the early 1770s, after publishing *The History of Scotland* (1759), *A View of the Progress of Society in Europe* (1769), and *The History of the Reign of Emperor Charles V* (1769), Robertson began work on yet another massive historical project, a chronological and comparative account of the Spanish and British "colonizations" of the Americas. One of the not-so-subtle goals of *The History of America*, as he had originally conceived it, was glorifying the superior way the British had managed their possessions in the New World.

By 1776, however, the unfortunate "civil war" taking place in the North American colonies had convinced Robertson that it made no sense to continue his work. How, indeed, was one supposed to provide a triumphalist account of the British colonization of the region when the colony in question was being torn apart by colonial insurgents? "America," as he wrote at the time, "is now lost to the Empire and to me."[84] Several months later, Robertson shelved the manuscript pages he had written on North America and only published what he had written about Spanish America. He then turned his attention to other endeavors, including a book-length study of ancient India."[85]

Some years later, after the old minister died of liver failure in 1793, his son — another William Robertson — decided that the time had come to publish the "American" manuscript. In 1796, after a bit of editing, the previously unpublished history of Virginia and New England was added to an expanded edition of *The History of America*. This larger work, which now included both the chronicle of British colonization in the area and a stage theory view of history, allowed readers to envision the settling of the region in ethnological terms.

Anyone reading Robertson's *History* understood that the contact between Europeans and Indians was not simply a clash between people from two different parts of the world. According to the minister's version of stage theory, it was a mismatch between the most technologically advanced humans on the planet (who had already achieved the summit of civil society) and a class of hot-tempered, illiterate, and supposedly cannibalistic "savages" whose only redeeming features were a highly developed sense of community and fairness, a fierce sense of independence, and remarkable courage, especially when tortured.

Courage notwithstanding, the vast majority of Amerindian tribes from Robertson's point of view corresponded to the "rudest form in which we can conceive [humankind] to subsist."[86] They were "communities just beginning to unite" existing only "in the infancy" of society, "a naked, feeble, and ignorant race of men" who, alas, were seemingly stuck in time.[87]

Among the many aspects of native life that flummoxed Robertson, it was his understanding of male Amerindians' gender and sex drive that seemed to bother him the most. Robertson describes native men as smooth-skinned like women, lacking any real facial hair, and insensitive to "the charms of beauty, and the power of love."[88] The Amerindian male, he writes, "views his female with disdain, as an animal of a lesser noble species."[89] This supposed deficiency in sexual vigor leads to a cross-cultural comparison that denigrates two "races" at the same time. In Robertson's view, the sex drive of the "savages of America" is far inferior to that of the "Negro" race, a group of people who "glows with all the warmth of desire natural to his climate."[90]

The most damning critique that Robertson levels at the typical "savage" mind, however, was not a feeble sex drive: It was the tenuous grasp that the native mind had on existence itself. In his view, the intellect of the Amerindian is devoted primarily to chasing the next meal, a fact that has a terrible spiritual downside. Since, as he puts it, the range of Amerindians' activities and ideas are so "narrow," they do not have the wherewithal to grasp the complex idea of a supreme deity.[91]

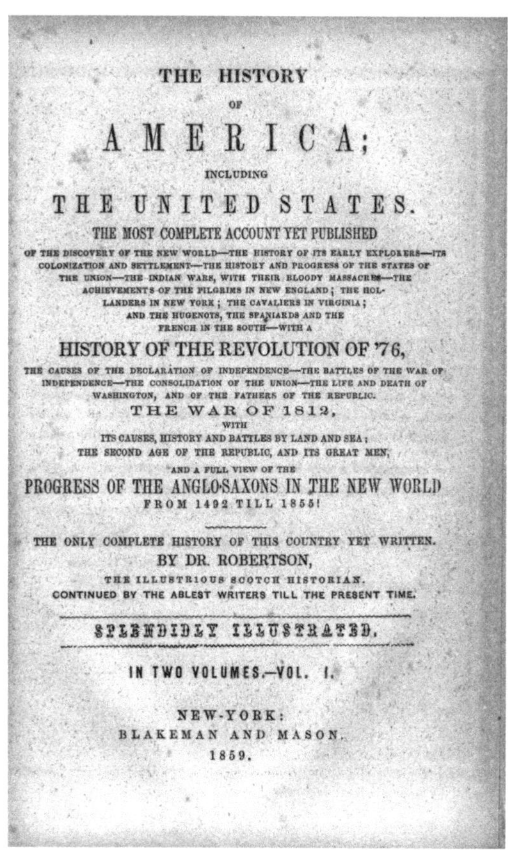

THE HISTORY

OF

AMERICA;

INCLUDING

THE UNITED STATES.

THE MOST COMPLETE ACCOUNT YET PUBLISHED

OF THE DISCOVERY OF THE NEW WORLD—THE HISTORY OF ITS EARLY EXPLORERS—ITS COLONIZATION AND SETTLEMENT—THE HISTORY AND PROGRESS OF THE STATES OF THE UNION—THE INDIAN WARS, WITH THEIR BLOODY MASSACRES—THE ACHIEVEMENTS OF THE PILGRIMS IN NEW ENGLAND; THE HOLLANDERS IN NEW YORK; THE CAVALIERS IN VIRGINIA; AND THE HUGENOTS, THE SPANIARDS AND THE FRENCH IN THE SOUTH—WITH A

HISTORY OF THE REVOLUTION OF '76,

THE CAUSES OF THE DECLARATION OF INDEPENDENCE—THE BATTLES OF THE WAR OF INDEPENDENCE—THE CONSOLIDATION OF THE UNION—THE LIFE AND DEATH OF WASHINGTON, AND OF THE FATHERS OF THE REPUBLIC.

THE WAR OF 1812,

WITH

ITS CAUSES, HISTORY AND BATTLES BY LAND AND SEA; THE SECOND AGE OF THE REPUBLIC, AND ITS GREAT MEN,

AND A FULL VIEW OF THE

PROGRESS OF THE ANGLO-SAXONS IN THE NEW WORLD

FROM 1492 TILL 1855!

THE ONLY COMPLETE HISTORY OF THIS COUNTRY YET WRITTEN.

BY DR. ROBERTSON,

THE ILLUSTRIOUS SCOTCH HISTORIAN.

CONTINUED BY THE ABLEST WRITERS TILL THE PRESENT TIME.

SPLENDIDLY ILLUSTRATED.

IN TWO VOLUMES.—VOL. I.

NEW-YORK:

BLAKEMAN AND MASON.

1859.

TITLE PAGE OF WILLIAM ROBERTSON'S *HISTORY OF AMERICA* (1859)

Among the many books having to do with race produced by the members of the Select Society, Robertson's *History of America* wielded perhaps the most profound and lasting influence. The first version of the *History*, which included Robertson's views of Amer-indians, was quickly translated into Dutch and German in 1777 and French in 1779. Posthumous editions, with the new section on North America, were published in Italy, Russia, Spain, and the

United States (the first American edition appearing in 1798).[92] Not surprisingly, it was in the fledgling United States where Robertson's stage theory account of New World peoples had its most significant impact.[93] By the 1820s, Robertson was considered the most famous historian in the United States.

In addition to the multiple editions of *The History of America* that were circulating in the United States, *Harper's Magazine* sold a very popular adapted version that was used in schools across the country well into the 1850s.[94] Another revised edition of the *History*, with a series of new chapters written by America's "ablest authors," also appeared after mid-century.[95] This rendering fully racialized Robertson's stage theory. Henceforth, his *History* was no longer the story of the Spanish, the British, and the Amerindians; the book's subtitle promised something different—a chronicle of "the progress of the Anglo-Saxons in the New World." According to the authors, the real heroes of the American saga were the "Caucasian," the "Norman," and the "Anglo-Norman." These peoples—best embodied in the Protestants of New England—were portrayed as the source of "the great thoughts, and the great deeds of man."[96]

Long after Robertson had died, at a time when the borders of the United States were being extended almost daily, his ideas (both original and adapted) helped fuse God, the new American nation, and race into a story of historical inevitability. Although he himself had lamented the victory of the American revolutionaries, his *History* lent itself perfectly to the aspirations of the country that they had created.

THE SCOTTISH LEGACY

By the time that William Robertson died in 1793, most of the towering figures that had given rise to the Scottish Enlightenment had disappeared. David Hume was the first to go, famously dying in 1776 as a godless stoic might—with a smile and without regret or last rights. Six years later, the so-called spiritual father of the movement, Henry Home, or Lord Kames, also breathed his last.[97] In the 1790s, the philosopher Thomas Reid, the writer Hugh Blair, and Adam Smith all died as well. One of the longest-lived members of the group, Adam Ferguson (who used stage theory to diagnose the moral decline occurring in certain "advanced" civilizations) departed this life in 1816.

To the extent that people now evoke the Scottish Enlightenment, they tend to remember the two major figureheads of the era, Hume and Smith. It is often said that the men had distinct legacies. Hume is portrayed as the ponderous philosopher primarily interested in "abstract metaphysical and epistemological questions," among them the nature of self-consciousness or the limits of our understanding of reality. Smith, on the contrary, is cast as the "hardheaded economist focused on practical matters," the man who first theorized the measurement of economic input (GDP), the division of labor, and the theory of the "invisible hand."[98] Within the universities that now keep the ideas and the legacies of the two Scots alive, Smith has generally fallen under the jurisdiction of economists, and Hume under that of the philosophers.

Hume and Smith—both inveterate bachelors as well as the best of friends—actually had far more in common than this artificial division would lead us to believe. In particular, both men saw *history* as the gateway to a new and naturalistic science that could shed light on humankind's past as well as its present. Smith's economic system, as well as his theory of moral sentiments, was built upon the idea that history "teaches people how a plurality of forces informs our moral and economic actions."[99] Hume agreed. History, he explains, is not only "the great antidote to the arrogance of the present"; it gives us access to "the remotest ages of the world," to a time where we can "observe human society, in its infancy, making the first faint essays towards the arts and sciences." History, in sum, allows us to understand how it was that certain groups came to perfect the art of conversation and establish sophisticated forms of government.[100]

There was also one other "advantage" that Hume did not spell out: The particular form of history that he and others were practicing allowed its partisans to situate human types within a continuum. Whether writing about the "European," the "Asian," the "African," the "Amerindian," the "savage," the "Highlander," or the "Ancient Briton," many of the thinkers associated with the Scottish Enlightenment tended to identify the world's races, peoples, or nations in relation to either unrealized or realized potential.

One should note, however, that there was never one mutually agreed upon form of "conjectural history" or stage theory among the Scots. Although a number of the country's theoreticians endorsed or made use of the concept, there was actually little consensus. They disagreed on the effect of climate on both the "primitive" and "civilized" peoples of the world; they were divided on the actual causes and origins of human diversity; and they argued about the specific triggers that incited progress (or a lack thereof) among peoples whom they perceived as less advanced than they were. As a group, the literati of Edinburgh never produced a universal or universally accepted history of humankind, they just believed that there had to be one.

The wrangling and disagreement that presumably took place among these men did not prevent stage theory from becoming one of the most compelling ways of envisioning human difference during the late eighteenth and nineteenth centuries. Regardless of how the concept was applied, the method allowed Europeans to understand themselves as the racialized winners of a cognitive and commercial competition. The political theorist and conservative pundit Edmund Burke understood this perfectly. In a letter to William Robertson, he wrote that the theory provides a "great map of mankind" — a map on which one can locate every "state or gradation of barbarism" and every "mode of refinement" that exists in the entire world.[101] Burke's metaphor is telling. If Linnaeus had classed the human species vertically, with Europeans on top, the Scots had achieved the same result horizontally, by identifying their own variety (or race) as the winner over time.

Engaging in this new form of race-making — which divided and often denigrated the world's peoples according to cultural and economic achievements or perceived aptitude — was anything but contentious during the eighteenth century. The only thing that was potentially problematic about this or any form of anthropology, especially in Scotland, was the hidden naturalistic or godless orientation that underpinned much of the methodology. Most members of the Scottish Enlightenment, unlike their counterparts in France, studiously avoided acknowledging the naturalism and the philosophical skepticism (especially vis-à-vis religious ideas) that had made their anthropological ideas possible in the first case. The only Scottish thinker, in fact, to trumpet his skepticism alongside his anthropology was, not surprisingly, David Hume.

In the mid-1750s, when Adam Smith and Lord Kames were concocting the first versions of stage theory, Hume had already used a type of "conjectural history" in his *Natural History of Religion* to explain (or explain away) the origin of supernatural or religious ideas. Adding to his dubious reputation as a nonbeliever — he had already questioned the existence of miracles, the veracity of sacred texts, and the sanctioned proofs of God's existence — Hume charted the "progress" of the human species from the earliest stages of "vulgar polytheism" to present day Christianity, the supposedly highest form of monotheism. Along the way, Hume also made abundantly clear that the birth of "real" religion, like any belief system, had stemmed from a universal psychological need: a yearning for a reassuring answer to our fears of mortality. It is, as he states, our "anxious concern for happiness that begets the idea of these invisible, thinking powers."[102]

DAVID HUME, ENGRAVING, 1764

It was precisely this type of religious skepticism—and not his racial views—that defined Hume's legacy in the decades after his death. This controversy began almost immediately. Before his remains were laid to rest in the Roman-style mausoleum built for him in 1777, his family was forced to post guards at his temporary grave to prevent it from being vandalized.[103]

The significance of Hume's antireligious views has of course diminished in our era. In 1963, the same University of Edinburgh that passed over this heterodox philosopher for a teaching position finally recognized their most famous alumnus by inscribing his name on the facade of a 140-foot-tall building on George Square. Twenty-five years later, in 1997, his "presence" in the city received another boost when Alexander Stoddart's nine-foot bronze statue of the philosopher was erected in front of St. Giles Cathedral, on Edinburgh's Royal Mile.

Hume's recently elevated status in the city has been short-lived.[104] In 2019, protesters began hanging placards around the neck of his statue, drawing attention to the racist comments found in "Of National Characters." The university, which reacted to this and other forms of protest in 2020, ultimately voted to rename "his" tower by its street address: 40 Georges Square.

Reconciling Hume's raciology with his far more universalist writings has left even his staunchest admirers confounded. It now seems inconceivable that, in the same month that Hume published his "Of National Characters" (1748), he also brought out his far more influential *An Enquiry Concerning Human Understanding*. Here, Hume does not talk about humankind's differences; he turns his attention to the human species in general, writing at length about humanity's will, humanity's passions, humanity's imagination, and humanity's ability to reason. Most importantly, and in stark contrast to what he affirms about national character elsewhere, Hume also describes a universal human species.

> It is universally acknowledged that there is great uniformity among the actions of man, in all nations and ages, and that human nature remains still the same, in its principles and

> operations. . . . Ambition, avarice, self-love, vanity, friendship, generosity, public spirit; these passions, in various degrees and distributed through society have been, from the beginning of the world, and still are the source of all the actions and enterprises which have ever been observed among mankind.[105]

Four years later, during a discussion of the "populousness of ancient nations," Hume goes even further, asserting that "the stature and force of body, length of life, even courage and extent of genius" have been "in all ages, pretty much the same."[106] This seemingly egalitarian view of the species serves as a preamble to an even more unprejudiced claim in the same book: "[T]here is no universal difference discernible in the human species."[107]

In recent years, scholars have increasingly debated Hume's inconsistent understanding of the human species. They, however, are not the first to draw attention to these seeming contradictions. The eighteenth-century abolitionist James Beattie, who attacked Hume on numerous fronts in his 1770 *Essay on the Nature and Immutability of Truth*, expressed a salient thought about the philosopher's legacy in general: "[W]hy is this author's character so replete with inconsistency! Why should his principles and his talents exert at once our esteem and detestation, our applause and our contempt?"[108]

It was, perhaps, Hume's destiny to be a man out of time. During his own lifetime, this affable and fearless skeptic faced various forms of persecution for daring to question the most fundamental religious beliefs of his era. Today, however, it is not his anticlericalism that qualifies him as rearguard; it is his denigrating understanding of non-Europeans, particularly Black Africans.

Hume, as is the case for many of his friends at the Select, has a complicated legacy. As one of the greatest advocates of human enlightenment, he and his ideas continue to infuse contemporary debates on the human mind, the source of our morality, and the validity of certain types of inductive reasoning. But it is also true that, whether he intended it or not, Hume had a profound impact on the race theorists who came after him. One of these people was the German philosopher Immanuel Kant. If, in 1781, Kant famously credited Hume for awaking him from his "dogmatic slumber" — for motivating him to undertake one of the most critical examinations of human existence in the history of philosophy—it was also Hume's "anthropology" that helped inspire the German philosopher to define — for the first time in history — the heretofore ambiguous notion of race.

PART FOUR

RACE AND THE ENLIGHTENMENT

Let us try to propose the best way
of classifying man into races...
—EBERHARD AUGUST WILHELM VON ZIMMERMANN,
Geographische Geschichte des Menschen, 1779

Although the human species would appear to be single,
since the union of any of its members produces individuals
capable of propagation, there are, nonetheless,
certain hereditary peculiarities of conformation...
that constitute what are termed races.
—GEORGES CUVIER, *The Animal Kingdom*, 1817

VIII

KANT IN 1768, PAINTING BY JOHANN GOTTLIEB BECKER

KANT AND BLUMENBACH AND THE GERMAN DEFINITION OF RACE

On the first day of the University of Königsberg's 1756 summer semester, a wispy-haired professor with the torso of an adolescent walked into his classroom and nodded to the students. Standing as straight as he could at just over five feet tall, he then introduced himself as Herr Immanuel Kant. Those students who had not yet met him marveled at his compact size.

Like many part-time lecturers, or *privatdozents*, Kant's ability to eat, pay his rent, or buy a new pair of breeches was directly linked to how many paying students he attracted to his courses.[1] Establishing a reputation as a compelling lecturer was thus of immense importance, and Kant had excelled at doing so. While he lacked the lung power of some of the thick-chested orators at the university, he had been so effective at the podium that the university's full professors assigned him twenty-five hours of class a week. By the time he was in his early thirties, he was covering fields as varied as metaphysics, ethics, logic, pyrotechnics, military fortifications, and the era's understanding of the natural world, otherwise known as "physics."[2]

Judging from the *nachschriften*, or lecture notes, that are now part of the archive, Kant's students clearly hung on his every word, dipping their quills and furiously scratching down the day's lecture—whatever the class may have been.[3] Even in the days before Kant had become famous, the men in his classes presumably had an inkling that they were in the presence of a thinker of towering intellect. Unlike the other privatdozents, who generally followed established lecture notes, Kant preferred to think on his feet, juggling his ideas in front of an audience while simultaneously commenting on the era's most provocative thinkers, be they Hume, Buffon, or Jean-Jacques Rousseau.

As compelling as Kant was in the classroom, few of the students present would have guessed that this sharp-featured blond would soon transform nearly every subfield of philosophy. This revolution would also extend to the subject he was lecturing on that day: "Physical Geography."[4]

During the first two-hour session of this class, Kant explained that he would be taking his students on an imaginary tour spanning four continents. But rather than simply describing topography and climate, he promised a systematic comparison of the world's peoples "in respect of their differences in natural shape," their "color," as well as their respective intelligences—what he referred to as their ways of "thinking."[5] He closed the lecture with a striking promise: The students in the seminar would become *weltbürger*—world citizens equipped to understand why they, as European men, occupied their lofty position within a naturally occurring human hierarchy. Geography and *rasse*, or *race*, he explained, had determined their destiny.[6]

A CRAFTSMAN'S SON

Kant's path to the academy had not been an easy one. His late father, Johann Georg Kant (1683–1746), had been a master harness-maker who fabricated (and also repaired) the complicated straps, loops, and lines that were fitted on draft horses. Like all tradesmen involved in the city's foul-smelling leather industry—including the tanners who transformed animal carcasses into salable hides—Kant senior had set up shop in the less-than-chic merchant and manufacturing section of Königsberg. It was in this same neighborhood, in a narrow, three-story building looking out over a small meadow, where Immanuel was born and spent his first years.[7]

Kant did not write extensively about his own childhood. Like many people during the eighteenth century, he believed that children were little more than irrational animals who could only see as far as their "immediate desire and want."[8] Yet on those rare occasions where Kant did mention his early family life, he made abundantly clear that his mother and father valued hard work, discipline, charity, and the religious self-reflection that was the very definition of the German version of the Lutheran religion known as Pietism.[9]

What distinguished the Kant household, however, was the extent to which the family valued education.[10] By age five or six, young Immanuel began attending the state-sponsored neighborhood school. When he turned eight, his parents decided that he should continue his education at Königsberg's Collegium Fredericianum, where he studied Latin, Greek, Hebrew, calligraphy, poetry, geography, history, antiquity, and theology.[11] The school, however, offered no classes in natural history or natural philosophy, and virtually no instruction in mathematics. The Pietists who ran the school not only saw these subjects as distractions, but as threats to the biblical truths that they sought to instill in their students.

When Kant looked back at his early education, he lamented that his teachers spent most of their time relating useless Bible stories or urging their students to seek out any signs of depravity or sinfulness within themselves. To attend the Gymnasium, as he put it, was to endure the "pedantic and gloomy discipline of the fanatics" who not only viewed life through the narrow lens of Lutheran dogma but also believed that their highest calling was preparing the next generation of young men for a career in the church, regardless of the human cost.[12]

Religious zealotry was not the only downside of Kant's teenage years. Not only did his beloved mother die when he was thirteen, but his father's once-thriving harness business had begun to fail, putting the entire family at risk. By the time that Kant finished his schooling at the Gymnasium, the household had been labeled "poor" on the city's registers, a designation that meant that they benefited from lower taxes and a substantial discount on burial fees.[13]

Domestic upheaval did not interrupt the plans that the family had for Immanuel, at least initially. After leaving the Collegium at age sixteen, he was able to enroll at the University of Königsberg.[14] Given his family's precarious financial state, the burden of providing Immanuel with a small allowance fell on his uncle, a shoemaker. Kant supplemented this meager stipend by tutoring his friends in exchange for rent money or, in some cases, for "coffee and white bread."[15]

Food insecurity notwithstanding, Kant was delighted to study new disciplines, including experimental physics and natural philosophy. It was also during these first years at university that he developed a persona that was very much unlike those of his classmates. In an era where most students apparently took their drinking and bar fighting as seriously as they did their studies, Kant became increasingly regimented, fastidious, and studious.[16] Far from a hermit, however, he apparently spent a great deal of time conversing with friends or his professors in taverns. He also delighted in billiards, not surprisingly a game of precision.[17]

By his fourth year at university, Kant had established himself as one of the most brilliant students in his classes. Life, however, conspired against finishing a degree within the usual timeframe. In 1746, following the death of his widowed father, Kant assumed responsibility for managing the household and caring for his younger siblings. By 1748, it became clear that he needed to pause his university studies and earn a proper living. For the next six years, he found work tutoring the children of Königsberg's aristocracy.[18]

In 1754, Kant had finally earned enough money to return to university.[19] Years of pent-up energy and frustration were quickly sublimated into writing. Still lacking a university diploma, Kant published three essays over the course of the next year, each of which contributed to a specific debate related to the natural world.[20] The first examined possible changes in the rotation of the Earth; the second treated the possible causes of the so-called ageing of the planet. In the third and most ambitious of these forays into the public sphere, Kant provided an all-encompassing theory of how the cosmos—meaning both the movement and materiality of the universe's suns, planets, moons, and comets—came into being. The title of this third work is as assertive as it is provocative:

> *Universal Natural History and Theory of the Heavens, . . . or an Essay on the Constitution and Mechanical Origin of the Whole Universe*

Much like the other two texts, the title of Kant's *Universal Natural History* seemingly had nothing to do with his burgeoning interest in geography or what he would later call *anthropology*. Yet the dynamic cosmology at the core of this article certainly hinted at what he thought about the world's supposed *races*.

1754: EXTRATERRESTRIAL ANTHROPOLOGY AND THE SUBLIME

The *Universal Natural History and Theory of the Heavens* appeared in print in early spring 1755. Kant dedicated the book to Frederick II, Prussia's so-called philosopher king. After praising his "most gracious King and Lord" and belittling himself for being unworthy of such an ambitious subject, Kant nonetheless admitted that he hoped to "achieve the highest pleasure of his Monarch."[21]

Frederick, who was busy ruling over Prussia from Potsdam—300 miles to the southwest of the remote city of Königsberg—probably did not hear about this book or its dedication. Yet the fact that Kant published the *Universal Natural History* in his honor reveals something about German intellectual culture in the 1750s. Frederick, who had been on the throne for fifteen years, had established himself as Europe's first enlightened despot, not only encouraging the arts, the sciences, and the first hints of a meritocracy, but also giving refuge to several freethinking exiles.[22]

Currying favor with such a ruler was potentially a smart way to protect oneself from the repercussions of what was contained in the *Universal Natural History*. In seeking to explain nothing less than the creation of the universe, Kant seemingly drew more from Lucretius's *De rerum natura* (*On the Nature of Things*) than he did from the Bible. While he admits in the book that God is responsible for producing "basic matter itself," he also describes the universe's inception as little more than the spontaneous coalescing of unorganized masses of nebula. The real first mover in this cosmos, in short, was less a divine hand than the ceaseless churning of gravity, of Newtonian forces coupled with *time*.[23] From Kant's perspective, it had taken "a number of millions of years" before Earth assumed its present form.[24] Similar head-spinning ideas appear regarding the future of the cosmos as well. Conjuring up spans of time that would have boggled his eighteenth-century readers' minds, the young philosopher claims that over the course of "millions of centuries" the universe will see the rise of an infinite number of "new worlds and world-orders."[25]

The audacity of Kant's overall understanding of the cosmic shifts within deep time are best encapsulated in two memorable aphorisms. The first openly contradicts the notion of a seven-day Creation:

> Creation is never complete.[26]

The second is a Promethean challenge:

> Just give me matter, and I will build you a world out of it.[27]

It was this type of unbridled freethinking, interestingly enough, that led Kant to speculate on what he believed to be the hierarchical nature of the human species.[28]

Kant's first anthropological musings emerge during a broader discussion about life on other planets. After confidently asserting that most planets in the universe are already inhabited, he proposed a striking method for comparing the rational capacities of these extraterrestrial beings: by considering how far they were from the sun and, by extension, the amount of heat they receive.[29] According to this theory, beings from faraway, colder planets (like the inhabitants of northern Europe) are thought to possess sharper intellects and a natural ability to form clear and vivid concepts. In contrast, the inhabitants of hotter planets (much like Black Africans) are presumed to lack these intellectual advantages.

To illustrate his theory, Kant turns to the cases of Saturn and Jupiter, planets far colder than Earth due to their greater distance from the sun. He imagines that the Saturnians and Jovians would belong to a "sublime class of rational creatures" blessed with minds so powerful that even Isaac Newton, Earth's greatest genius, would appear as little more than a simple "ape" in comparison. On the other end of the spectrum, Kant asserts that aliens living on worlds closer to the sun would be so mentally stunted that, according to this hypothetical scenario, even a "stupefied African Hottentot" would be considered "a Newton" among them.[30] While Kant may not have been the first thinker in the 1750s to claim that heat had a direct effect on the intelligence of different human groups, he was certainly the first to make this point through extraterrestrial ethnography.

TOWARD A SUBLIME NOTION OF RACE

Of all the books that Kant ultimately published during his lifetime, the 1755 *Universal Natural History* had the worst luck. Shortly after the first review copies had been dispatched to various journals, the publisher went bankrupt. Bailiffs then showed up at the press and impounded every single book at the printing press—including the copies of the *Universal Natural History*—before transferring the lot to a warehouse.[31] Weeks later, this same building went up in flames, presumably destroying most of the print run of the ill-fated book.[32]

Setbacks notwithstanding, Kant had entered into a time of feverish productivity in the spring of 1755. Only months after his book was reduced to ashes, he handed in his master's thesis. (Ironically enough, this was a study of combustion entitled "Some Meditations on Fire.") By September, he defended another dissertation—this time on the subject of metaphysical cognition—

thereby earning his *Magister legens*. It was this second degree—which had conferred upon him the title of *Privatdozent*—that made him eligible to lecture at the university level.

By the 1760s, Kant's growing financial stability allowed him to adopt the polished personal style—he was partial to colorful waistcoats, breeches, and coordinated vests—that earned him the nickname "elegant Magister" at the university.[33] During these same years, his intellectual reputation was growing as well, thanks in large part to a series of increasingly influential and well-received essays.[34]

Kant wrote the most successful of these works, the *Observations on the Feeling of the Beautiful and the Sublime*, during the summer of 1763 at a "friend's house in the woods."[35] Published the following year, this foray into aesthetic theory remains Kant's most accessible piece of prose. Designed to be both waggish and incisive, the essay overflows with pithy comments and aphorisms that allowed Kant to distinguish between the title's two related esthetic concepts: the *beautiful* and the *sublime*. Yet most of the essay was an excuse to evaluate the entire human species according to what he believed were varying aesthetic orientations, capabilities, and supposed shortcomings. It is his first real examination of the question of race.

A student of Locke, Hume, and basic eighteenth-century epistemology, Kant asserts from the outset that perception is entirely relative: Two people can experience the exact same exterior experience or "object," yet one might feel "joy" while the other reacts with disgust or "repugnance."[36]

The paradox, however, is that Kant also insists that categories such as the "beautiful" and the "sublime" have real conceptual integrity. Flowers, low hedges, trimmed trees, and a sunny day, for example, generally produce the feeling of beauty and a sensation of "gaiety."[37] Such pleasing experiences or *feelings*, he continues, are quite different from the much more intense sensation produced by mountain ranges, horrific storms, and the darkest moments before dawn; these latter experiences are catalysts of the sublime. This "finer feeling," as he describes it, is serious, stunning, and may even give rise to "dread."[38]

As Kant gets deeper into the subject, he develops a series of concise and memorable comparisons to help make his point:

> The sublime touches, the beautiful charms.
>
> Understanding is sublime; wit is beautiful.
>
> Sublime qualities inspire esteem, but beautiful ones inspire love.
>
> The sublime must always be large; the beautiful can also be small.
>
> The sublime must be simple; the beautiful can be decorated.[39]

Just who has access to these aesthetic experiences — and to what extent — constitutes the rest of the essay.

Kant begins his typology of *aesthetes* (and *non-aesthetes*) by breaking down humankind according to antiquity's humoral dispositions (sanguine, melancholic, choleric, and phlegmatic). Should someone have a melancholic temperament, he is supposedly drawn to the sublime. A sanguine character, which he describes as being "fickle" and "given to amusements," generally has "a dominant feeling" for the beautiful.[40] People with a choleric tendency, he continues, seek out a type of sublime best described as *magnificent*, although they supposedly do so in a way that is artificial, self-serving, and sometimes even hypocritical. As for the "phlegmatics" — who Kant believes are cold-blooded and apathetic — they are so undemonstrative that they simply do not have an ability to understand either of the two finer feelings, be it beauty or the sublime.

This categorization of humankind according to humoral tendencies initially seems like it might apply to any individual, regardless of the "group" or "category" to which he or she belongs. Yet in the remainder of the *Observations* Kant proceeds to assign specific aesthetic orientations and capabilities to women and men, the world's nations, and finally its races. It is at this point that the essay utterly shifts from a discussion of how individuals engage perceptually and aesthetically with the exterior world to a study in comparative cognition.

This breakdown begins with women. In part three of the *Observations*, Kant claims that the "fairer sex" views the world through a lens of love and kindness—with an "innate feeling for everything that is beautiful, decorative and adorned."[41] This somewhat lyrical misogyny soon leads to a far more serious assertion: Women simply do not have the capacity to participate meaningfully in the serious, noble, and sublime pursuits experienced by men, nor should they *try* to do so. Evoking the Marquise du Châtelet, the late mistress of Voltaire whose brilliant translation of Newton's *Philosophiæ Naturalis Principia Mathematica* is still being used in France to this day, Kant proclaims that she "might as well wear a beard."[42] Women, he sums up caustically, should content themselves with the finer feeling of the beautiful, and leave "abstract speculation or knowledge . . . to the industrious, thorough, and deep understanding" of men.[43]

After presenting his breakdown of the world according to gender, Kant shifts his focus to the aesthetic abilities of various "nations."[44] This assessment is strikingly reminiscent of David Hume's 1748 work "Of National Characters." Turning his gaze on Europeans to start, Kant claims that the Italians and the French can be grouped together because they "distinguish themselves in the feeling of the *beautiful*." The Germans, the English, and the Spaniards, he continues, are more inclined to "appreciate the feeling of the *sublime*," whether it be it the "terrible," "noble," or "magnificent" variety of the feeling.[45] Unsurprisingly, in his comparison of these nations, Kant asserts that only the Germans have achieved a "happy mixture" of both the sublime and the beautiful in their aesthetic sensibilities.[46]

As Kant moves on to those countries outside of Europe, this same catalog of European tendencies provides him with *archetypes* — points of reference for his discussion of other nations. The Arabs become the "Spaniards of the Orient." The Persians are "the Frenchmen of Asia." The Japanese, given their purported "steadfastness," should be considered "the Englishmen of this part of the world" despite the fact that they "demonstrate few marks of a finer feeling" toward the sublime or the beautiful.[47]

Kant's breakdown of the world according to aesthetic temperament moves from the category of "nations" to that of "races" when he speaks of Amerindians and Black Africans. Of these two groups, the indigenous inhabitants of North America fare far better than "Negroes" under Kant's pen because he believes that these "nomadic" peoples have a taste for the sublime. In addition to the fact that Amerindians are constantly seeking out "wild adventures hundreds of miles away," they supposedly have a highly developed sense of "honor," "a sublime character of mind," and a fortitude that makes them impervious to any form of torture. The primary liability of the Amerindian, Kant adds in passing, is the fact that they lack a sense of the "beautiful in the moral sense."[48]

Compared to his relatively generous understanding of Amerindians, Kant's view of Black Africans is contemptuous. Not only does he deny "Negroes" any capacity to understand the sublime or the beautiful; he claims that, given their "religion of fetishes," they clearly have "no feeling that rises above the ridiculous."[49] This sweeping generalization then leads Kant to belittle examples of individual Black people who, by dint of what they accomplished, challenged this reductive and prejudiced framework.

Kant had presumably adopted this strategy directly from David Hume. Ten years earlier, in his "Of National Characters," Hume had preempted the possibility of the black "counterexample" by dismissing the literary and intellectual accomplishments of the Jamaican poet and scholar Francis Williams as little more than the squawking of a parrot who had learned to imitate its master.

Kant, too, had felt obliged to refute a possible exception to his own race-based view of Black people while reading Jean-Baptiste Labat's famous travelogue about plantation life in Martinique. The Dominican priest, who actually told several stories about thoughtful and industrious Black people in his memoirs, related how an enslaved carpenter had made a devilishly clever observation about the "White" husbands living on the island. These foolish men, joked the man, allow their women to enjoy far too much freedom — before complaining bitterly when these same women "drive them mad."[50] Labat clearly found this little bit of misogyny as droll as it was insightful.

Kant, however, reacted to the possibility of even a hint of "wit" coming from this same carpenter in an entirely different way: "There might be something here worth considering, except for the fact that this scoundrel was completely black from head to foot, a distinct proof that what he said was stupid."[51] Although Kant had yet to put Black Africans into a formal racial classification at this point in time, he had already established what he believed was a seemingly unbridgeable divide between "white" and "black," mapping pigmentation directly onto capacity of mind.

Looking back at the *Observations on the Feeling of the Beautiful and Sublime*, one cannot help but shake one's head at Kant — a man who never ventured farther than the outskirts of Königsberg — for his belittling comments about non-European peoples. Yet as prejudicial as some of these early remarks from the 1760s were, they were only the beginning of Kant's "anthropology." In the years that followed, he would strip away much of the prevailing ambiguity surrounding the concept of race and, in the process, offer its first rigorous definition.[52]

1775: KANT AND THE FIRST DEFINITION OF RACE

Life improved remarkably for Kant in the years after he published his essay on the sublime. Having applied on several occasions for a professorship at the university, he was finally admitted to the ranks of Königsberg's *ordinary* faculty in June of 1770 as chair of logic and metaphysics.[53] His ascension to this lofty rank—it ultimately took fifteen years—had myriad benefits: fewer teaching hours, a more stable financial situation, and a social status that the philosopher had coveted for decades.

By 1770, the forty-six-year-old academic now had a reputation for many of the somewhat unusual routines for which he is now famous. Relying on his watch to regiment virtually every aspect of his life, Kant woke at five in the morning, quickly sat down to tea, and then read for precisely twenty minutes while smoking a pipe. On days when he was lecturing at the university, the so-called Königsberg Clock opened his door to head off at exactly eight a.m. Other scheduled routines were also strictly controlled, including his never-missed afternoon walk, which he generally took alone so that he could concentrate on what he believed to be the best way of breathing: uniquely through the nose.[54]

Now that Kant finally had enough money to organize proper dinner parties, he also established specific rules about how people were to "comport" themselves at table. According to various sources, the first part of the evening was always dedicated to swapping stories. The second phase was a period of intense and thoughtful discussion on an important subject. The final portion of the evening was dedicated to good cheer, jokes, and jocularity, an intellectual dessert of sorts. Such habits reflected Kant's deep-seated desire to rationalize and control his existence, especially his body. This last goal, however, was becoming increasingly harder to achieve. In addition to often having the feeling that he could not catch his breath, Kant was tortured by palpitations and extra heartbeats. These jolting sensations generated adrenaline-fueled panic attacks and sometimes made him feel like he was dying.[55]

Whatever Kant's exact mindset, his anxiety may explain why he remained safely within Königsberg's city limits throughout most of his life. Living in this isolated Baltic city, a city that European academics sometimes referred to as "scholars' Siberia," clearly suited him just fine.[56] While Königsberg was far removed from the epicenters of enlightened thought at the time—Paris, Göttingen, Berlin, Edinburgh, and London among them—this remoteness did not prevent him from engaging in global anthropology. This was certainly the case during the early 1770s, when Kant increased his consumption of travel literature in order to revise the Physical Geography lectures that he had been teaching for nearly twenty years.[57]

As professors customarily did when offering a new class at the university, Kant distributed something of a teaser essay that announced the main ideas he would treat in his seminar. This bit of "marketing," which appeared first in 1775 and was widely published in 1777 in a slightly altered version, is entitled "On the Different Human Races."[58] Few texts are as important in the history of race.[59]

Kant had clearly been disconcerted by the contradictory terms and methods used to refer to different types of humans. Some naturalists used the word *nation*, others *variety*, others *race*. Voltaire had even claimed that Africans, Chinese, and Europeans were entirely separate *species*. Some of this taxonomical confusion, he realized, was the fault of the two most prominent thinkers who had taken up the question, Linnaeus and Buffon. Linnaeus's *Systema* had categorized humankind as *varieties* without providing a corresponding explanation or justification for such a conclusion other than simply declaring it as so. The Swede's so-called *system of nature*, in short, not only lacked clarity and philosophical rigor when it came to the human species; it sidestepped the obvious question of *how* humankind's so-called *varieties* came into being. Without such an explanation the categories seemed perfectly arbitrary.

Buffon's *Natural History* had also spawned uncertainty. Compared to Linnaeus's *Systema*, the thrust of Buffon's "anthropology" had obviously been non-definitional and anti-classificatory in nature. At numerous points in his *Natural History*, he had claimed that separating an enormous number of human *varieties* into a small number of categories was as arbitrary as it was nonsensical. And yet, Buffon had also sprinkled in the more *zoological* word *race* in his *Natural History* from time to time, especially when he wanted to convey the idea of a group of people who passed down specific traits to their descendants.[60] One finds, in his writing, references to a *race* of Tartars, a *race* of *Negroes*, or the idea that the Chinese were of the same *race* as the Japanese. This presumably left Kant perplexed. If Buffon believed that he could identify a certain *group* of humans as a *race* because they passed on distinctive characteristics over time, what was the real conceptual difference between a *variety* and a *race*?

To resolve some of these questions, Kant told his own version of the story of *degeneration* — one where the human species had degenerated first into a small number of identifiable *races*, not dozens or hundreds of *varieties*. Beginning his chronicle, like Buffon, with the incontrovertible fact that all humans, regardless of color, were able to reproduce, Kant declares that humankind had a common ancestor group that he identified as the *stamm*, or the *stem*, of the species. Kant then speculated that this primeval category, which he identified as a race of Europeans living somewhere between Portugal and Germany in ancient times, was bestowed with *seeds* or *germs* (*keime*) that contained a latent ability to produce new kinds (*Arten*) of people under certain conditions.[61]

It was this theory of *seeds* that set Kant's white-originating degeneration apart from Buffon's.[62] In Kant's view, humankind had an innate ability to *adapt* to different climates throughout the world via the power of *generation* or, as we would put it, reproduction. According to this theory, when the original group of Whites split up and migrated to markedly different climates, their *germs* slowly revealed a "predetermined capacity or natural predisposition" to generate features or corporeal changes that better allowed these migrant populations to survive. This is best summarized in two memorable remarks:

> It is the care of Nature to equip her creature through hidden inner provisions for all future circumstances.[63]

And . . .

> The human being was destined for all climates and for every soil.[64]

Heat or cold, sun or darkness, in Kant's view, produced *predictable* changes within the populations that moved away from Europe's temperate climes. "Glacial zones," he explains, "suppress" hair growth, "flatten" the face, and create "half-closed" eyes.[65] In "hot and humid" zones, such as sub-Saharan Africa, he claims that changes take place on both the morphological and *chemical* level.

The "spongy parts of the [African's] body" such as the nose and lips grow in size, while the percentage of iron increases in the blood.[66] This warm-climate transformation, in his mistaken estimation, is accompanied by an important adaptation: the appearance of oily black skin that helps prevent "evaporation" in the heat.[67]

Not all of the supposed changes brought about by extreme climates were benign or useful in Kant's view. When discussing the African climate, he specifies that the extreme heat and humidity of the region, while beneficial to plants and "to the robust growth of animals," creates a natural environment of *plenty* that has made Africans "lazy, soft, and trifling."[68] His view of how the American environment affected its original inhabitants is equally pessimistic. In a marked departure from what he had written about Native Americans in his essay on the sublime, Kant here claims that all Amerindians are the descendants of a Kalmuckian or Hunnish group that made its way across the land bridge between Russia and Alaska. The problem, however, is that this group split into two main branches. Those who remained in the north adapted to the cold and, over time, reached the highest expression or "perfection" of the Kalmuckian race (e.g., "Eskimos" or Inuit). Those who went south, and settled throughout the rest of the continent, however, changed into the lesser "American" race.

Kant characterizes these Amerindians as an *incipient* race (*angehende Race*), suggesting they have not yet "resided long enough in the warmer climate to assume the respective character" that their race will eventually acquire in such an environment.[69] In his view, they are unfinished, adjusting, incomplete. Although he concedes that their faces are becoming "more open and more elevated" in these warmer regions, he maintains that they retain the ancestral markers of their ancestors' "coldness and insensitivity." As a result, the Indian race remains impassive from "the extreme north of [the

American continent] all the way to Staten Island."[70] Ultimately, Kant concludes that Amerindians are "incompletely adapted" and suffer from "a half-extinguished life power."[71] Gone was the idea that the Amerindian had a unique access to the sublime.

THE DEFINITION OF *RASSE*

Kant's novel understanding of degeneration set up his definition of race. Degeneration, he believed, was far more than a simple mechanical transformation of facial features, hair, skin, chemistry, or temperament. It was a *quantifiable* deterioration of the prototype—a measurable divergence from the "original formation of the stem."[72] Expressed slightly differently, Kant claimed that once a given group of degenerated humans (e.g., Black Africans) are no longer able to replicate the features of the stem race—e.g., whiteness—while simultaneously reproducing their own specific features over several generations (e.g., elevated iron in the blood), then they constitute a distinct *race*.

Yet Kant did not rely solely on morphological or chemical changes to determine racial difference. He also employed a more formal, almost equation-like mode of reasoning to define what makes a race distinct.[73] The logic of this theory, which hinges on the observable outcome of racial mixing, is best understood as a deductive formula:

> Since race A + race B = C, with C being a new hybrid human entity, then A and B are necessarily separate conceptual and biological categories.[74]

The example he provides to substantiate this idea, not surprisingly, conjures up "race mixing" between White and Black: "*Negroes* and *Whites* . . . are . . . *two different races* because each of the two perpetuates itself in all regions and both beget half-free children or *blends* (mulattoes) with one another."[75]

It is with all this in mind that Kant identifies the four major races to come from the stem: White, Negro, Hunnish, and Hindu. All four categories, he states, are *real*, not arbitrary designations. They are not only the main offshoots of the original prototype; they are the source of a dizzying number of new subspecies that are being produced due to the influence of the climate or via race mixing.[76]

This explanation of how the human species morphed into four conceptually different races accomplished something that no other eighteenth-century naturalist or philosopher had done before: Kant had reconciled the muddy aspects of climate theory (and monogenism) with the possibility of a real classification scheme that seemed both fixed and real. Such an achievement, he presumably thought, had not only resolved the contradictions inherent in Linnaeus's *Systema* and Buffon's *Natural History*; it had surpassed both of these texts, making his own essay the century's newest and most important intervention on the subject. Little did Kant know, however, that he was far from the only person in 1775 who was grappling with the question of humankind and its races. Indeed, within months of the appearance of his 1775 "On the Different Human Races," several new theories and classification schemes related to the idea of *race* appeared in print.

BLUMENBACH AND THE RACE TO THEORIZE RACE

A staggering range of books and theories related to race appeared in 1774 and 1775. In Switzerland, Johann Kaspar Lavater invented the "science" of physiognomy or "face reading," a practice that included sweeping statements about the moral and intellectual qualities of the world's different races based on their perceived facial features.[77] Across the border, in France, the Jesuit writer François Para du Phanjas provided his own classification of the species by dividing humankind into the *race blanche*, *race nègre*, and *race tartare* in his 1774 *Principles of Healthy Philosophy Reconciled with Those of Religion*.[78] English and Scottish writers also generated taxonomies during the same two-year period. In 1774, the London-based novelist Oliver Goldsmith identified six different human races according to their geographical location and dominant psychology. "Europeans," Goldsmith explains to his readers, can be identified by "the beauty of their complexions . . . and the vigor of their understandings." The five other races, he continues, were less blessed by nature. These included the superstitious Polar race (e.g., Laplanders); the dishonest Tartar race (Asian); the cowardly and "effeminate" South Asian race (Indians); the race of unthinking Amerindians; and the "gloomy race" of Black Africans that, Goldsmith claims, is altogether "stupid, indolent, and mischievous."[79] A similar breakdown was proposed by the Edinburgh surgeon John Hunter. He divided the world's peoples into what he called a "table of colors": Black (Africans), sub-Black (Moors, Hottentot), copper (East Indians), Red (Americans), Brown (Tartars, Persians, Arabs, Africans on the Mediterranean, Chinese), Light Brown (Southern Europeans, etc.), White (all remaining Europeans).[80]

Most of the era's classifiers, including Goldsmith and Hunter, believed that the world's varied climate had produced such marked differences in morphology and pigmentation. There were, however, several notable exceptions. Following in the footsteps of Voltaire, the Edinburgh writer and philosopher Lord Kames (aka Henry Home) claimed, also in 1774, that God had created individual types or "Adams" that were *designed* for each particular region of the world. There are, as he puts it, "different races of men fitted for different climates."[81] Kames's breakdown of humans into different species was seconded that same year in a far more brutal fashion by the ex-planter turned historian Edward Long in his *History of Jamaica*.

Unlike many of his contemporaries, Long became involved in the era's anthropological debates in order to support the proslavery agenda. This was a turning point in the history of race. While most of the virulent racism in the *History of Jamaica* had been "available" for decades, proslavery thinkers and writers such as himself had not really needed to draw from it because the opposition to the institution of slavery had been so negligible. There was simply no need to fight for the right to enslave. Once abolitionists such as Anthony Benezet began *humanizing* the "slaves" who were working in Caribbean plantations, however, the era's racial science began being utilized in a far more insidious fashion. Long, for example, reduced what he called the African "species" to a machinelike automaton who could not think, could not feel, and was so different from Europeans (and Europeans' "biology") that, he maintained, they had specific insects living on their bodies, including black lice. This was not the worst thing that he published about enslaved Africans. In addition to asserting that Africans were an entirely different type of human, he claimed that "Negroes" were directly related to and had sexual relations with the great apes.[82] This, too, would become an increasingly common idea as the debate on slavery raged into the nineteenth century.

The type of pro-slavery classification put forward by Long had not yet taken root in the Kingdom of Prussia or in other German-speaking lands in the 1770s. And yet, the racialized thinking that emerged in German thought during the last thirty years of the eighteenth century is among the most influential *and* the most virulent of the Enlightenment era.[83] Some of this trend began when a now-forgotten Dutch naturalist named Cornelius de Pauw, who was residing at Frederick the Great's summer palace of Sanssouci in Potsdam, published his hugely influential 1768 *Recherches philosophiques sur les Américains* (Philosophical research on the Americans). A bestseller that was republished and translated several times in the 1770s, de Pauw's book effectively rewrote Buffon's climate-based chronicle of human migration and mutation. In stark contrast to the Frenchman's comparatively gentle tale of degeneration, de Pauw described the irreparable damage that Europeans supposedly underwent after leaving Europe. Degenerate Amerindians, he writes caustically, are only "superior to animals because they have use of their hands and tongue" and are "inferior to the most inferior of Europeans."[84] What de Pauw asserted regarding the Black African is even worse. In his view, the equatorial climate has shrunk the Black African mind: "[H]e is unable to govern himself. . . . In one word, he becomes a Negro, and this Negro becomes the slave of slaves."[85]

The most significant and influential German racial thinker to come on the scene in the 1770s, however, was a twenty-three-year-old doctor and naturalist named Johann Frederich Blumenbach (1752–1840). In contrast to many of the better-known eighteenth-century intellectuals fascinated by the budding science of *race*—Voltaire, Hume, Kames, Goldsmith, de Pauw, and Kant—Blumenbach's interest in the riddle of human races stemmed from his obsession with comparative anatomy.[86]

Blumenbach's interest in dissection and physiology began at an unusually early age. When he was ten years old, the young Johann met a medical doctor who owned the only human skeleton available for study in the city of Gotha. This encounter apparently led Blumenbach to scour Gotha's streets in search of animal carcasses from which he assembled his own little natural history cabinet.[87] According to family lore, when Blumenbach's father discovered the noisome collection, which was hidden under the boy's bed, he was not alarmed. As the headmaster of the local Gymnasium with the same passion for natural history as his son, he merely asked his son to move it to the house's attic.[88]

BLUMENBACH AS A YOUNG MAN, ENGRAVING

By the age of seventeen, Blumenbach was given his parents' blessing to leave home to study anatomy and physiology at the University of Jena in the Duchy of Saxe-Weimar.[89] Three years later, he moved to the University of Göttingen, which had become Germany's preeminent academic institution.[90] A relatively new university that had only come into existence forty years before, Göttingen had been able to break free from many of the hidebound academic practices found in other such German institutions. In addition to prioritizing "avant-garde learning," the university actively recruited "innovative, often controversial thinkers from across the German Lands" who might even develop "controversial research."[91] It was perhaps not a surprise that Göttingen became a cutting-edge center for race theory over the next few decades.

UNIVERSITY OF GÖTTINGEN, LITHOGRAPH, C. 1830

Soon after arriving in Göttingen, Blumenbach sought out a retired professor named Christian Wilhelm Büttner, who would shape the trajectory of his early intellectual life.[92] Buttner was well known for his natural history cabinet as well as for his library, which was rich in works of philology, travel literature, and geography.[93] During Blumenbach's first six months in Göttingen, he met with Büttner nearly on a daily basis. One of the primary subjects of conversation, as it turned out, was the twelfth edition of Linnaeus's *Systema Naturae*, especially his classification of the human species into different *varieties*.

Given what Blumenbach ultimately wrote about human classification, one can imagine that several questions came up during these private seminars: 1) What is the difference, if any, between humans and animals? 2) Should humans be "classified and visually represented along the same lines as flora, according to similar assumptions about visible features"? And 3) To what extent can morphology and anatomy tell us about the human species as a whole?[94]

Blumenbach took up each of these questions in the doctoral dissertation that he defended in September of 1775. Published several months later, his *De generis humani varietate nativa* or *On the Different Varieties of Mankind* might seem to be a response to Kant's "On the Different Human Races," which was also circulating the same year.[95] Yet neither Kant nor Blumenbach was aware of the other's work in 1775. This was not a surprise: Blumenbach's Göttingen was 375 miles to the west of Königsberg.[96]

Yet even though the twenty-three-year-old Blumenbach and the fifty-one-year-old Kant did not know the other's work on race, they shared a common outlook: They were both vehemently opposed to the increasing popularity of polygenist theory being disseminated by thinkers including Voltaire, Kames, and Long. Blumenbach combatted this idea directly in his *On the Varieties of Mankind*. As he put it, denying a *biological* relationship among different human groups was a cynical attempt to throw "doubt on the accuracy of Scripture" stemming from "ill-feeling, negligence, or the love of novelty."[97] He also felt it was bad science.

Drawing on anatomical evidence, Blumenbach stated that all humans, be they Asian, European, Amerindian, or African, share a set of defining characteristics (such as reason, speech, hands, erect posture, bipedalism, and hymen) that distinguish them as members of a single, unified species that is biologically distinct from other animals. He also specifically rejected the claim — advanced by figures like Edward Long — that Black Africans constituted a separate species that was somehow closer to apes.[98] For Blumenbach, the only possible explanation for human variation, given the species' universal ability to interbreed, was Buffon's: Differences in pigmentation and morphology among human groups are the result of environmental factors, diet, and way of life.[99] To ignore this basic and obvious fact, he contended, was to produce bad science, not to mention human taxonomies that were "very arbitrary indeed."[100]

Despite the many salvos that Blumenbach launched against both polygenesis and human classification in the first edition of his *Varieties*, several strands of thought in the work undercut his generally anti-classificatory stance.[101] Most notably, he followed in Linnaeus's footsteps by dividing humankind into four "classes of inhabitants," allegedly because such a scheme was "serviceable to the memory."[102] Freely admitting that his criteria were little more than a rough *geographical* approximation, Blumenbach aligned these four groups with what he considered the "four quarters of the globe." The first group were found in "Europe writ large," including not only Europe proper, but North Africa, northern Asia (north of the Ganges River and the Amoor [Amur] River in Siberia), and the northernmost parts of North America.) The second group was located in southern Asia (south of the Ganges), Polynesia, and Australia. The third group, whose inhabitants he described in essentializing terms as "men of dark color, snub noses, with winking eyelids drawn outwards at the corners, scanty, and stiff hair," were found in Africa.[103] The final group included the remaining native inhabitants of the Americas.

Another indication of a properly racializing tendency in the first edition the *Varieties* stems from Blumenbach's anatomical orientation. Although he was committed to refuting the spurious idea that the "Ethiopian, the White, and the Red American" constituted "different species of mankind," he nonetheless cited contemporary "data" that appeared to suggest otherwise. In particular,

Blumenbach acknowledged dissection studies conducted on African cadavers by anatomists Pierre Barrère and Johann Friedrich Meckel, which allegedly demonstrated that Blacks had black blood and darkened brains."[104] This concession clearly undermined the central claim of his book: that the differences among human varieties were superficial or, quite literally, only skin deep.

TOWARD A WIDER DEBATE ON ANATOMY

The publication of the 1775 *Varieties* cemented Blumenbach's place at the university. Unlike Kant, who spent years cobbling together a livelihood as the equivalent of an adjunct professor, the twenty-three-year-old naturalist quickly ascended the academic ladder. In the same year that he defended his thesis, he was appointed associate professor of medicine and *prosector* of anatomy. Months later, in 1776, he was also named sub-curator of the Academic Museum's natural history collections.[105] And only two years later, in 1778, he attained the rank of full professor.[106]

Blumenbach's increasing fame in these early years of his career put him in contact with travelers and naturalists from across the globe. By 1780, he had heard so much about the "new" human types being identified in the relatively unknown South Pacific that he decided that it was time to rethink his initial four-part geographical breakdown of humankind. The following year, in 1781, he published a new edition of his *On the Natural Varieties of Mankind* that introduced a fifth category of human: the *Malaicae* or *Malay*, which he classified as a *brown* race.

Around the same time that Blumenbach identified this new type of human, he began to believe that the all-important field of comparative anatomy could provide an enhanced understanding of humankind's diversity. This discipline, which had been his most important weapon against polygenists and classifiers alike was now becoming the means to reflect more seriously on the *differences* in the human species.[107]

Blumenbach's increasing belief in the power of morphological study and measurement is best illustrated by a clever joke he used to play on his students. Sometime in the 1780s or 1790s, Blumenbach would tell the men in his anatomy classes that he had attended a traveling show of "natural rarities" during which he saw sitting in a chair a strange man with a broad face, pointy snout, sharp teeth, and an uncanny, almost ghostly white complexion. Dressed in the uniform of a Hussar—a cavalryman in the Prussian army—this bizarre creature seemed to defy classification. As part of Blumenbach's teasing, he always added that the great French naturalist Buffon had examined this same figure and had concluded that it was some sort of "human being, because it was reluctant to have its trousers taken off."[108]

Blumenbach's description of this creature was reportedly so vivid that his audience sometimes went "mad." On one occasion, the hair of one of his students "stood up with fright, like spikes."[109] It was presumably at such a critical point in his story that Blumenbach would finally reveal the creature's true identity. This was a trained, shaved bear who only sat upright because the uniform it was wearing had been nailed to a chair. This elaborate prank presumably set up a powerful lesson. When it came to studying the human species, the smart naturalist should not be deceived by outward appearances.[110] To understand the specificity of human beings, one should rely solely on comparative anatomy: the only discipline that can distinguish among humans, not to mention humans and bears dressed in military uniform.[111]

As part of his increased interest in comparative anatomy in the mid-1780s, Blumenbach assembled what he called his "apparatus anthropologicus." This collection of human remains, which included fetuses, hair, and skulls, was not to be confused with a *kunstkammer*, or cabinet of curiosities, meant to provoke shock or wonder.[112] On the contrary, these specimens—especially his collection of skulls—were the means of identifying the measurable differences among the different varieties of the human species.

Blumenbach was far from the only German to turn his attention to racial physiology in the mid-1780s. Less than a mile from his house in Göttingen, a philosophy professor (and longtime thorn in Blumenbach's side) named Christoph Meiners was completing the manuscript version of his *Outline of the History of Mankind*.[113] Ultimately published in 1785, Meiners's book targeted the unified vision of humankind that Blumenbach had disseminated in the two editions of his *On the Natural Varieties of Mankind*. In stark contrast to Blumenbach's assertion that the notion of race was, for all intents and purposes, arbitrary and meaningless, Meiners claimed that the world's peoples could be split into two primary races.[114] He called the first and supposedly inferior group the *Mongolian* race, a branch that included Blacks and Asians. As for the "superior" second and white group, he invented a new category, the *Caucasian* race, which he subdivided into *Celts* and *Slavs*.[115]

Meiners's raciology went far beyond this simple division of the species. He offered three political opinions that hinted at the future of race. The first was an unambiguous endorsement of racial slavery, the second a warning that a liberal treatment of the Jewish people in Europe would lead to disaster, the third that Europeans had a biological birthright to dominate the world.[116] It is hardly a surprise that, in the 1940s, the Nazis identified Meiners as a brilliant and insightful precursor to their own worldview.[117]

New race-based publications grounded in anatomical study were emerging beyond Göttingen as well. In the city of Mainz, approximately 160 miles southwest of Göttingen, Blumenbach's longtime friend Samuel Thomas Sömmerring published his controversial and influential *On the Physical Difference of the Moor from the European*.[118] In this brief work, which appeared in 1784, Sömmerring detailed his dissections of several Black soldiers who had been resettled in Germany after serving as mercenaries for the British during the American Revolution.[119] Following in the footsteps of previous anatomists who had dissected black bodies, Sömmerring identified corporeal structures that had no basis in anatomical reality. In his case, he announced that Black Africans had "thicker cranial nerves," a feature that not only explained their supposedly impaired cognition and primal sensations, but also suggested a similarity (if not a direct biological link) with the great apes.[120]

Blumenbach's own anatomical orientation and findings differed significantly from those of Meiners and Sömmerring. Yet when one considers the broader impact of all three men, it becomes clear that German anatomists were collectively helping to transform race into something that could ostensibly be measured through the internal structures of the body.

KANT, RACE, AND THE CONTRADICTIONS OF THE "CRITICAL PERIOD"

Much like Blumenbach, Meiners, and Sömmerring, Kant, too, turned his attention to the question of race in the mid-1780s. This is actually quite surprising, given how busy the now sixty-one-year-old philosopher was at the time. Having recently moved to a sixteenth-century house near Königsberg's castle, the philosopher had found himself bogged down by the splendor and the misery of home ownership.[121] In addition to suffering through the chaos of renovation, he was also terribly distracted by the neighborhood's (hateful) children who screamed loudly in the street and threw stones over his fence. Even more bothersome for the fastidious philosopher was the strident, out-of-tune singing coming from the inmates in at the nearby prison. Although he could do very little about the children, he did write a letter to the prison's warden, complaining that these prisoners were hypocrites who only sang at the top of their lungs so that the authorities would hear and take mercy upon them.[122]

There were also other far more important things keeping him occupied. Beginning in 1781, Kant had entered into his so-called critical period, the "astonishing decade" (1781–1791) of philosophical production during which he published the master works with which his name is now generally associated.[123] Among these books are several interventions that seemingly clash with his less-than-generous ideas about non-White races. The most important of these is the *Groundwork of the Metaphysics of Morals*, which appeared in 1785.[124]

In the *Groundwork*, Kant examined the question of the human condition from a far more universal point of view than he did when writing about specific races. Having admitted that there is no such thing as a universal moral system that all humans can agree upon, he recommends that every last person, regardless of who they are, should, instead, rely on human reason and embrace what he called a "categorical imperative." This imperative, he goes on to explain, is the idea that all beings on the planet should act according to principles that they could imagine holding true for everybody. This was a powerful and prescriptive philosophy: The philosopher was asking humankind to choose a course of behavior if and only if these actions were noble enough or good enough to become law. One of the more famous insights from the *Groundwork* is the dictum that we should treat people if they were "ends in themselves, never as mere means."[125]

Kant might have easily remained absorbed by such properly moral questions in 1785 had it not been for his former star student, Johann Gottfried Herder (1744–1803).[126] Herder had raised Kant's hackles by publishing his *Ideas for a Philosophy of History of Humanity* earlier that year.[127] Among other things, Herder rejected his former teacher's belief in moral absolutes, one of the most important parts of the Kantian philosophical project. Far more culturally relativistic than Kant, Herder asserted that the identities of both individuals and larger groups of people result from what he called a series of "unspecified organic forces" that span "all creation."[128] He also ridiculed the notion that there was a specific number of races when it was obvious that there was a continuum of pigmentation on the planet.[129] Kant could not stomach this wishy-washy and unempirical understanding of the human species. Summing up the anthropological implication of such a view, he lamented the fact that his former student was asserting that the concept of race "is not distinctly enough *determined*."[130]

When Kant responded to this provocation several months later, he deliberately included the word *determination* in the title of his response.[131] At first glance, the "Determination of the Concept of a Human Race" does not seem to break new ground, simply reiterating as it does his earlier breakdown of the species into four conceptually coherent races according to color: *whites*, *yellow* Indians, *black Negroes*, and *copper-red* Americans. What is new in the "Determination," however, are two far more rigorous definitions of race. The first explains *how* to identify race, namely, by identifying the characteristics that have become hereditary deviations within a subspecies:

> Race is determined by "hereditary qualities [within a certain group] that do not belong to the character of the species."[132]

The second restates this in taxonomical terms:

> Race is "the classificatory difference of the animals of one and the same *phylum* in so far as this difference is unfailingly hereditary."[133]

To underscore the "reality" of race, Kant also identified what he believed were specific inheritable traits (e.g., eye shape, skin color, or, in the case of Africans, the supposed presence of *phlogiston* in the blood).[134]

Kant did not restate some of the truly pejorative things he had been saying about Africans and Amerindians for decades in his "Determination" of race essay. Perhaps he found it *unseemly* to do so in the same year that he was composing the more universalist *Groundwork of the Metaphysics of Morals*? In any case, just three years later, when he returned to the question of race in his *On the Use of Teleological Principles in Philosophy*, Kant revived some of the more virulent race-based ideas he had first articulated in 1775.[135] His most biting remarks in this 1788 essay were directed at Amerindians. Echoing the increasingly negative views of Native Americans that were emerging in the late eighteenth century, Kant described this "race" as weak, cultureless, and nomadic — occupying the lowest rung of humankind. Indeed, he claimed that the Amerindian could be classed "far below the Negro, who undoubtedly holds the lowest of all remaining levels."[136]

1795: KANT AND BLUMENBACH, KÖNIGSBERG AND GÖTTINGEN

By the mid-1790s, Kant had been teaching his students about race at the University of Königsberg for exactly forty years. The much younger Blumenbach had been engaged in a similar endeavor in Göttingen for two decades. Though the naturalist and the philosopher had never met, both concluded in 1794 that further intervention in the debate over the human species was urgently needed. Each responded within the framework of his own discipline: Blumenbach through natural history, Kant in philosophy.

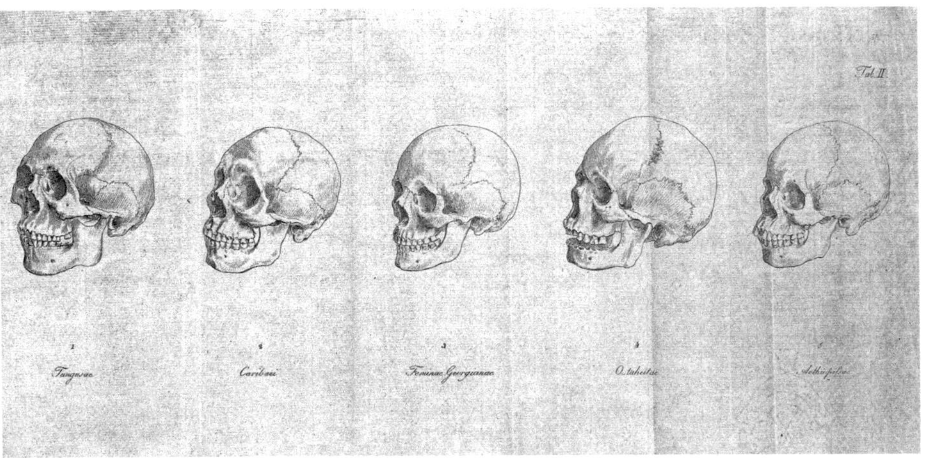

BLUMENBACH'S ARRANGEMENT OF SKULLS, ILLUSTRATION, 1795

Sometime in late 1794, while Blumenbach was writing the third and final version of his *On the Natural Varieties of Mankind*, he began organizing the crania that he had displayed in his office's cabinets. Placing the specimens on his desk, he picked each one up in succession, rotating it in order to appreciate the contours of the bones. He then arranged all five skulls in a line. On the far left was his Mongolian or Asian skull. Just to the right, an Amerindian skull (from the Caribbean). In the center position was the most beautiful skull in his estimation, the cranium from a Georgian woman. To the right of this cranium, he placed a Malay skull (from Tahiti) and, finally, on the other extreme, a so-called *Aethiopissae*, or African, skull.[137] Each of these specimens represented one of the primary human archetypes that he was now calling *races*.

By now, Blumenbach had concluded that comparative craniometry was the best tool for sorting humankind into different varieties or races. Yet unlike some of the other naturalists or anatomists who had also become interested in skulls, among them Petrus Camper and the French naturalist Jean-Louis Daubenton, he had no desire to measure facial angles or reduce specific groups to some sort of geometrical formula.[138] In fact, to prevent his readers from getting the impression that he believed in some sort of a racial hierarchy, he commissioned an illustration that, exactly like the skulls lying in front of him, situated the "white" skull in the middle. This way his readers could not infer some sort of "great chain of being" that moved "up" from ape, to African, to Amerindian, to Asian, to European for example.

But there was also another reason why Blumenbach put the Georgian skull in the center of this illustration: He was identifying the original human form from which two other offshoots had supposedly come. To the left of the central Georgian prototype, one sees a branch of humankind whose main racial categories are the Amerindian and the Asian. To the right is another branch, which splits into the Malay and the African races.

When naming this original stem, Blumenbach did not simply call it the *Georgian* race. Instead, he adopted the relatively new term previously coined by Meiners, *Caucasici* or *Caucasian*. This was more than a simple geographical marker. For Blumenbach the term hinted at a biblical certainty: the fact that all humans could trace their origins to the Caucasus mountains where Noah's Ark was thought to have come to rest, and from where his three sons had set off after the Great Flood.

This fusion of biblical geography and natural history was yet another way for Blumenbach to reinforce his monogenism. In an era where the influence of polygenism was on the upswing, he not only remained committed to asserting the fundamental unity of humankind, but to the idea that the only thing that truly separated humankind's races was "opportunity," not innate ability.[139] In fact, in one of the few instances where he wrote of some sort of inherent potential, he claimed that the "Negro" race had an "original capacity for scientific culture" and was therefore closest in nature "to the most civilized nations of the earth."[140]

BLUMENBACH IN 1823, ETCHING BY L. E. GRIMM

Over the next half century, many of Blumenbach's more progressive ideas found favor among humanitarians and abolitionists.[141] Yet it was his breakdown of the species into *five* races—based on skull measurements—and the notion of the Caucasian race that proved most enduring.[142] One of the ironies of Blumenbach's legacy is that he had hoped that the very term *Caucasian* would evoke a shared human heritage and potential. The reality turned out to be quite different. Quickly translated into multiple languages, the notion of the *Caucasien*, *Kaukasisch*, *Kaukaski*, *Kavkazskiy*, and *Caucásico*, soon became an internationally accepted marker emphasizing racial primacy and superiority. Indeed, over the course of the nineteenth century naturalists began restricting the meaning of the term *Caucasian*. If the original definition comprised North Africans and some Asians, including the Indians of the subcontinent, by the 1850s, the term *Caucasian* had become synonymous with the supposedly highest expression of humankind, White Europeans.[143]

During the same months that Blumenbach was working on the final edition of *On the Natural Varieties of Mankind*, Immanuel Kant, too, was composing a work that also featured a universalist and progressive view of humankind. Kant titled this remarkable piece, which appeared in 1795, "Toward Perpetual Peace: A Philosophical Project." It is in this essay that we see Kant at his most republican and most liberal — entirely unfettered by what he believed in his heart of hearts was the empirical and nasty reality of race.

As had been the case for all his writing since 1784, Kant composed "Perpetual Peace" in the study in his Königsberg house, now blackened by fireplace soot, pipe smoke, and the oily vapors given off by the room's gas lamps.[144] In stark contrast to Blumenbach's office in Göttingen, there were no skulls to remind him of the different morphologies of the human species. Indeed, the sole "mounted head" in his entire house was a small portrait — the one piece of framed art in the whole house — that hung above his desk. This was an engraving of Kant's hero, Jean-Jacques Rousseau, a thinker whose belief that society should be entirely rethought in order to promote its welfare had had a significant impact on the essay that he was composing.[145]

KANT IN 1804, LITHOGRAPH

"Perpetual Peace" is a reflection of a revolutionary era, written as it was against the backdrop of the birth of the new United States, the fall of the French monarchy, and the bloody slave revolt in Saint-Domingue.[146] As Kant cast his eye on these and other world events, worrying as he did about the possibility of a widespread European war, he believed that the only way to achieve a truly peaceful global order was through the adoption of *Weltbürgerrecht*, or cosmopolitan law.[147] By signing on to a pact of peace, he suggested, the world's countries would agree to no longer produce armaments; they would no longer seek to acquire territory; they would no longer maintain standing armies; they would neither hold nor impose national debt; they would not interfere in other countries' affairs; and they would take no extreme actions if and when war broke out.[148] This proposal was far more than a simple interdiction of gun powder and empire building, however. Kant was asking his readers to endorse principles that apply to all of humankind, to accept the idea that "violations of right at any *one* place on the earth is felt in *all places*," and to endorse a republican form of government guaranteeing the freedom and equality of all its citizens.[149] To a large degree, "Perpetual Peace" puts forward an international version of his categorical imperative.[150]

It is this same belief in a new form of global morality that generates one of the most memorable moments in the essay, a Rousseau-like accusation of European colonialism:

> [T]he injustice that [the civilized states in our part of the world, especially the commercial nations] show when *visiting* foreign lands and peoples (which to them is one and the same as *conquering* them) takes on terrifying proportions. America, the Negro countries, the Spice Islands, the Cape, etc., were at the time of their discovery lands that [Europeans] regarded as belonging to no one, for the native inhabitants counted as nothing to them.[151]

Such liberal positions—given Kant's views on race—have perplexed historians of philosophy. Was "Perpetual Peace" a philosophical thought experiment? Was it a deeply felt protest against the increasingly violent and unjust world in which Kant believed he was living? Or does this capstone moment in the philosopher's career actually signal some form of regret about his racist views? And if this is truly the case, did he really believe that these universalist principles could apply to everybody?

Rather than debate such questions, there is perhaps a straightforward answer that may have nothing to do with Kant's actual beliefs. Like many of his contemporaries, the philosopher may simply have been following the conventions of the genre in which he was writing. In his anthropologically minded essays, he employed hierarchical language, particularistic history, and reductionist anthropological classifications. In philosophical and humanistic works such as "Perpetual Peace," where he conjured up a human species unified in a common cause, he adopted a universalist tone that soared above anthropological considerations. Indeed, in such moments, Kant was perhaps envisioning an idealized humanity that did not exist in the real world. Or, perhaps as likely, he believed these ideals were only achievable for a select few — the elite men of the White race.[152]

Kant's legacy, much like those of Voltaire, David Hume, and Thomas Jefferson, remains fraught because his very name is seen as synonymous with the Enlightenment itself. Indeed, it was actually he who famously defined the "Enlightenment" (in a newspaper article) as "man's emergence from his self-imposed immaturity."[153] *Enlightenment* for Kant was not a specific era in human history; it was a process. To become enlightened during the eighteenth century, in his view, was to free oneself from the strictures of religion and other received authorities — to accept the far more demanding responsibility of reasoning independently and critically in order to promote the betterment of the species as a whole. "*Sapere aude* (dare to know!)," he proclaimed, is the ethos of Enlightenment.

The problem, when one considers Kant's career as a whole, is that he also believed that there was an unequal distribution of human reason among the different races.[154] Indeed, how does one reconcile the goal of humankind's universal intellectual emancipation with his 1802 claim that:

> humanity has its highest degree of perfection in the White race. The yellow Indians have a somewhat lesser talent. The Negroes are much lower, and the lowest of all is part of the American races.[155]

Kant may or may not have realized it, but he had effectively excluded most of the world from participating in the intellectual movement that he had defined.[156]

Kant's racial theories undoubtedly undermine the inclusiveness of his Enlightenment ideals. Yet it is important to note that the intellectual origins of his racism, though derived from "colonial ethnography," lay in a broader set of speculative concerns that differed from the explicitly exploitative racism used to justify slavery in the New World. In Kant's geography, which he first developed for students at the University of Königsberg, non-European peoples were less *real people* than conceptual cases used to debate emerging theories of human origins, heredity, and ultimately category.

Racial theory tended to function far less abstractly in other lands, especially in the New World. By the late eighteenth century, various forms of European raciology had thoroughly infused every aspect of colonial life from the southern tip of South America to the northern settlements of Canada. The most profound clash between Enlightenment universalism and race, however, was taking place in the newly founded United States of America. Here, in a land where approximately eighteen percent of the population was enslaved (c. 700,000 versus 3,800,000), European race thinking was at the heart of debates on slavery, citizenship, the status of Native Americans, and the universal values that were ostensibly the foundation of the new country. If the debates on race were written "on paper" in Europe, they were written "on skin" in the United States. And among the Americans to grapple with the question of race during this era, no one engaged more fully — or more ambiguously — than the slaveholder, legislator, and future president of the United States, Thomas Jefferson.

IX

THOMAS JEFFERSON, PAINTING BY MATHER BROWN, 1786

THOMAS JEFFERSON: NATION BUILDER, RACE BUILDER

Why is it that we hear the loudest yelps for liberty among the drivers of Negroes?

—SAMUEL JOHNSON, *Taxation No Tyranny*, 1775

On Tuesday, June 1, 1779, three delegates from Virginia's General Assembly arrived at Thomas Jefferson's house to inform him that he had been elected governor of the Commonwealth of Virginia, effective immediately. The next morning, shortly before the legislature reconvened at ten a.m., Jefferson arrived at the Williamsburg state house, where he was greeted with applause by the members of the Virginia House of Delegates and Senate. Several minutes into the joint session, the Speaker of the House invited the perennially ruddy-faced Jefferson to address the assembly. Reluctantly rising from his seat—he detested public speaking—Jefferson expressed his gratitude: "In a virtuous and free State no rewards can be so pleasing to sensible minds, as those which include the approbation of our fellow citizens." He concluded by expressing the hope that he would live up to "the expectations of [his] country."[1]

This was not mere rhetoric on Jefferson's part. Everyone in the room knew that the Revolutionary War against the British was not going well, especially in the southern states. The year before, in late 1778, the British had actually re-established colonial rule over the neighboring state of Georgia. And only a few weeks before the election, the British rear admiral George Collier had attacked the Virginia coast, burning six million pounds of tobacco and sinking 130 American ships at Gosport.[2]

Jefferson, however, had not been elected for his military experience.[3] Nor did he possess the ability to inspire the militia with the kind of rousing speeches that the previous governor, the bombastic Patrick Henry, could seemingly conjure up out of thin air. In truth, this plantation owner and enslaver of 135 men, women, and children had won this election for being the country's most farsighted theoretician of liberty.

Jefferson had begun establishing his reputation as what would later be called a "Founding Father" in 1774, when he circulated a hugely influential pamphlet on the illegitimacy of British sovereignty in North America. Two years later, he composed the American Declaration of Independence.[4] But it was while serving as a member of the Virginia House of Delegates that he had earned his colleagues' respect by proposing a number of progressive Enlightenment reforms: public schools, the freedom of religious expression, extending voting rights to "lower" classes of people, abolishing the practice of primogeniture, and eliminating the death penalty. He had even brought up the possibility of banning slavery in Virginia.[5] Jefferson's greatest feats did not burst forth from the end of a musket; they generally flowed from his quill.

During the two years he would serve as governor, Jefferson had few opportunities to produce the kind of visionary document that ultimately made him famous. As wartime leader of the Commonwealth, Jefferson faced a series of intractable issues, most of which stemmed from the fact that the English blockade was strangling the state's economy.[6] Yet the worst part of being governor, as it turned out, were two stunning military fiascos. Six months after he was elected, in early January 1781, Benedict Arnold and a flotilla of twenty-seven ships carrying 1,600 British troops sailed ninety miles inland on the James River, burning farms and raiding warehouses on their way to Richmond. After easily taking possession of the state capital, Arnold contacted Jefferson with a proposition: He would leave the city unscathed if allowed to confiscate all the valuable tobacco in the area.[7] Jefferson sent back a note rejecting the deal, and Arnold immediately ordered his soldiers to set every building in Richmond on fire. Jefferson, who had taken up a position on the other side of the James River, watched helplessly as the capital of his beloved commonwealth went up in flames.[8]

The destruction of Richmond was not Jefferson's worst humiliation. On June 4, 1781, a messenger arrived at Monticello to warn him that a squadron of 250 British troops was en route to arrest him.[9] Jefferson immediately sent his wife, children, and several enslaved domestic servants to Poplar Forest, one of his properties near Lynchburg. After hesitating over what to do, he too fled on horseback and joined the exodus.

His enemies — and even some of his former friends — accused him of being spineless.[10] Two weeks after Jefferson's hasty departure, the same General Assembly to which he had dedicated so much of his time, opened a six-month investigation into his conduct. Though he was eventually cleared of all wrongdoing, for the next twenty years his political opponents took great joy in resurrecting old stories about his lily-livered departure from Monticello.

Such accusations, as he put it, could only be "cured by the all-healing grave."[11]

Jefferson's two years presiding over Virginia nearly ruined his career as a politician, not to mention his mental health. Yet there was one task that he had accepted as governor that became his salvation and, ironically, has now muddied his reputation. In 1779, a French diplomat named François Marquis de Barbé-Marbois asked Jefferson to respond to a series of probing questions about Virginia.[12] Barbé-Marbois's queries were not simple: He sought detailed information about topography, history, major cities, population, religions, educational facilities, the justice system, military readiness, customs, weights and measures, and trade, along with several other topics related to natural history.

Jefferson, who was far more suited to this intellectual task than he was to the more mundane aspects of the governorship, threw himself into the research necessary to respond to the questions. Shortly after concluding his term as governor—still reeling from accusations of being gutless—he completed a first draft of what he began calling *Notes on the State of Virginia*. He made further progress on the project in the summer of 1780 while bedridden after falling from a horse. By late 1781, Jefferson had sent Barbé-Marbois an early version of his responses to the questionnaire.

In the early 1780s, Jefferson decided to revise the first version of this manuscript and publish it at some point. During the next three years, while traveling between Philadelphia, Annapolis, Princeton, and Monticello, he refined the *Notes*. Within these unpublished pages were some of his most eloquent expressions of Enlightenment ideology: pleas for religious freedom, indictments of hereditary privilege, and an explanation of how scientific inquiry should be encouraged to produce an enlightened citizenship. Yet there was also something else that Jefferson developed in this text: a fierce rebuttal of European anthropology, especially what naturalists had said about the inhabitants of North America.

No other United States citizen was, during the 1780s, as well suited as Jefferson to undertake this latter task. Already, as a young man, he had begun amassing an enormous collection of books related to "ethnography" that included Lafitau, Charlevoix, and Condamine on North America; Vertot on Spain; Schefferus on "Lapland"; Labat on the Caribbean; Bernier on India; Chardin on Persia; Du Halde on China; Bougainville on Tahiti; Kaempfer on Japan; and Adanson and Abbé de Manet on Africa.[13] Alongside these and many more primary sources he also collected the era's most avant-garde theories of race. Within a few feet of his small desk at Monticello, he had or would come to have books written by Linnaeus, Montesquieu, Buffon, Hume, Voltaire, Kant, Blumenbach, Robertson, de Pauw, Raynal, Goldsmith, and Edward Long. It was, in short, Jefferson's resources, erudition, and disposition that led him to develop a properly American and, in certain instances, a particularly brutal understanding of race. Several years would pass, however, before these views would make it into print.

PUBLISHING THE *NOTES* (FROM FRANCE)

Working on the *Notes* project had offered Jefferson a welcome escape from some of the most distressing and painful years of his life. The same manuscript was even more vital to his well-being after the death of his wife in 1782. During their ten years together, Martha had been the center of Jefferson's existence, the most "cherished companion of [his] life."[14] After she died, Jefferson often hinted that Monticello seemed haunted by the spaces she had occupied, especially the house's sun-filled parlor where they had played harpsichord and violin duets or read their favorite book, Laurence Sterne's *Tristram Shandy*.[15]

Martha Wayles Jefferson had been both bright and stalwart, and arguably more psychologically resilient than her husband. Over the years, she had braved chronic illnesses, numerous family tragedies, and the demands of running an enormous household while her husband was away. She had also provided moral support and advice to Jefferson during the dark days of the governorship. Her greatest sacrifice, as it turned out, was trying to provide Jefferson with a male heir.

During the first nine years of her marriage, Martha gave birth to five children.[16] Only two of these babies, both daughters, were alive in May of 1782 when she delivered her final child, Lucy Elizabeth.[17] Contemporary accounts suggest that Martha remained bedridden for four months following the birth. During this time, Jefferson reportedly moved a writing desk to an adjoining room, where he kept up with his correspondence and worked on the *Notes*, all the while keeping a watchful eye on her. Legend has it that when Martha realized that she was nearing death, she called Jefferson to her bedside and made him promise never to marry again. He is said to have agreed.[18]

On the day that Martha finally succumbed, on September 6, 1782, Jefferson was devastated. For several weeks after the funeral, he claimed that he experienced "a stupor of mind" that "rendered [him] as dead to the world as she whose loss occasioned it."[19] Ironically, after all that he had been through as governor, it would be a return to political life that helped him recover.

In June 1783, after first turning down an invitation to travel to France to help negotiate peace terms with England, Jefferson was elected to represent Virginia in the United States Congress.[20] The following year, Congress once again asked Jefferson to travel to France, this time as Minister Plenipotentiary to the court of Louis XVI at Versailles. His mission, which was described to him in a long missive, was to coordinate with the current ambassador working in Paris, Benjamin Franklin, and help negotiate treaties of "friendship" and "commerce" now that the war was over. Congress was counting on him, along with John Adams (in England) and Franklin in France, to open up markets for American whale oil, salted fish, salted meat, rice, and, of special interest to Jefferson, Virginia tobacco.[21]

If, in the past, Jefferson had hesitated about moving to Paris, he was now eager to make the voyage. Arguably the United States's greatest Francophile, Jefferson wanted to discover the country where so much of his aesthetic and political sensibility had originated. Though he certainly appreciated English writers and Italian chamber music, he was especially drawn to French neocolonial architecture, French anticlericalism, French deism, French political theory, and French anthropological thought. Many of his aspirations for the United States—especially those related to freedom *from* religion—had come from French books, including an edition of Diderot's twenty-eight volume *Encyclopédie* that he had purchased while governor in 1781.[22]

In May 1784, Jefferson said an emotional goodbye to his two youngest daughters, Mary and Lucy, before setting off on a voyage that would take him away from Monticello for five years. His oldest daughter, the twelve-year-old Martha, aka "Patsy," went with him.[23] The longest part of the trip to France was not spent at sea. Before leaving Virginia, Jefferson had decided to tour parts of the northeastern United States in preparation for his mission as trade envoy.[24] The result was that he and Patsy spent two months being jolted up and down in his phaeton through New York, Connecticut, Rhode Island, and Massachusetts. Traveling behind them on horseback during this whole time was Jefferson's enslaved valet, the nineteen-year-old James Hemings. He, too, had left family behind—his mother, Elizabeth Hemings, and five siblings, including his ten-year-old sister, Sally.

In early July 1784, Jefferson, Patsy, and James (and the disassembled carriage) were finally under sail from Boston harbor in an American ship named the *Ceres*. After changing ships at Portsmouth, England, the group finally landed at Le Havre on July 31, 1784. The arrival on French soil came with a major surprise for Jefferson. Despite his ability to read French, he was dismayed to discover that he could neither understand nor really make himself understood when speaking with actual French people.[25] Five days after their arrival, he and his entourage nonetheless managed to reach their first stop in Paris, the Hôtel d'Orléans, on the rue de Richelieu. Jefferson's hosts very likely informed him that the famous (and infamous) encyclopedist Denis Diderot, one of the American's heroes, had died across the street exactly one week earlier.[26]

Like most foreigners who made it to the French capital during the eighteenth century, Jefferson was overwhelmed by the city's cultural and culinary wonders.[27] Writing to his friend Charles Bellini in 1785, Jefferson enthused about the French arts: "Were I to proceed to tell you how much I enjoy [French] architecture, sculpture, painting, music, I should want words."[28] His five years in Paris nonetheless had its challenges. Not long after arriving in the capital, when the long days of the summer had given way to Paris's increasingly dark and rainy skies, he came down with a terrible case of bronchitis that kept him in bed for weeks. Winter weather in this northern city—Paris is the same latitude as Newfoundland—was profoundly depressing for the Virginian.[29]

Even more challenging was the fact that he was initially being measured against Benjamin Franklin. Despite Jefferson's astonishing ability to master virtually any subject—from architectural drawing to natural history—he was ill-equipped to participate in the type of rapid-fire conversation and diplomacy that was de rigueur in Paris or at Versailles. In some ways, it was almost as if his most meaningful "interactions" with the French had already taken place before he left the United States, in his study at Monticello. It was here that he had come to know and often "debate" with Montesquieu, Voltaire, Diderot, and Rousseau, all of whom had died by the time that he had arrived in Paris.

Franklin had had a very different relationship with the greatest generation of French philosophes, having personally met many of them before they died, including both Diderot and Voltaire.[30] This famous "inventor of electricity," who had been speaking French *in France* for nearly a decade by the time that Jefferson arrived, had also managed to ingratiate himself in virtually all social circles, both liberal and conservative. Some of Franklin's diplomatic successes (especially during the Revolution) had also come from being the type of person that Jefferson was most emphatically not. Whereas the soft-spoken Virginian often came across as cool and remote, Franklin was friendly, quick-witted, and entertaining, not to mention generally recognized as the first New World genius—a useful example of what one might achieve in a country unburdened by aristocracy and monarchy.

Despite some of the challenges that Jefferson confronted during his five-year posting in France, he did achieve several significant diplomatic victories. In addition to nurturing the all-important Franco-American alliance—this included securing favorable treatment of American merchants in French ports—he negotiated a sweeping "Treaty of Amity and Commerce" with Prussia.[31] But none of his diplomatic feats had made him famous in France; it was ultimately his *Notes on the State of Virginia* that earned him that recognition.

The impact of the *Notes* came in waves. In 1785, shortly after arriving in Paris, Jefferson commissioned a small print run of 200 copies (in English), as if to test the waters. Though he claimed that the contents of the book amounted to little more than a series of unworthy scribbles, he sent copies to Williamsburg so that every student at the College of William and Mary might have access to the book. He also made sure to dispatch the *Notes* to thirty or so European notables, including statesmen and natural historians.[32]

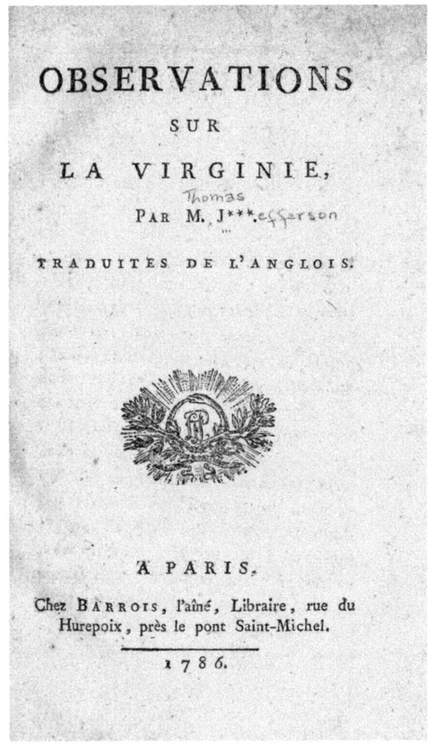

OBSERVATIONS
SUR
LA VIRGINIE,
PAR M. J***.
TRADUITES DE L'ANGLOIS.

A PARIS,
Chez BARROIS, l'aîné, Libraire, rue du Hurepoix, près le pont Saint-Michel.
1786.

OBSERVATIONS SUR LA VIRGINIE

The following year Jefferson also worked with the former French encyclopedist Abbé André Morellet to produce a French translation of the *Notes*, which was published as the *Observations sur la Virginie*. This edition, which appeared in 1787, has a slightly more synthetic structure than the original *Notes*. In particular, Morellet fused Jefferson's scattered observations on race and slavery into a coherent section that gave the impression that Jefferson had been far more actively engaged in the antislavery movement than he really was.[33]

The real impact of the *Notes* came later that same year when a London publisher named John Stockdale brought out a very popular and slightly updated version of the English-language edition. Its success in the English market did not go unnoticed in the United States. The Philadelphia printers Robert Pritchard and John Hall quickly produced a pirated edition in which they identified the book's anonymous author as Jefferson for the first time. By 1788, the American ambassador to France had become the foremost interpreter of North America—including its White citizens, its Amerindians, and its 650,000 enslaved men, women, and children—on both sides of the Atlantic.

THE *NOTES*

Regardless of which edition of the *Notes on the State of Virginia* one reads, it is crucial to recognize the multiple audiences that Jefferson had in mind when writing. These included his friends in the Virginia legislature and the United States Congress, his fellow plantation owners, his antislavery-minded colleagues in Paris and Philadelphia, and the European natural historians who were defining the notion of race for the rest of the globe. The book presented Jefferson with an opportunity to reconcile, ultimately unsuccessfully, his liberalism, his thinking on the institution of slavery, and his biological views of the human race.

The tension between Jefferson's ideals and his practices began when he was still a young man. In 1769, at age twenty-six, this slaveholding member of the Virginia House of Delegates proposed a bill (through his cousin Richard Bland) permitting "owners" to emancipate their slaves for "meritorious services" without the required consent of the legislature.[34] (The proposal provoked outrage and was promptly withdrawn.) A year later, in his capacity as lawyer, Jefferson took on the case of a "mulatto" youth who claimed that he should be free because his grandmother had been the "daughter of a white woman and a slave father."[35] Unsurprisingly, this case was summarily dismissed. Had the judge found in favor of the plaintiff, it would have meant entertaining the possibility that a White woman would willingly consent to have sex with an enslaved Black man.[36]

Some of Jefferson's views and even actions during these early years were, by the standards of the era, broad-minded to say the least. Yet they never interfered with his responsibilities as owner of thirty-five or forty individuals at his Shadwell plantation. Indeed, the same year that he was advocating for the right to emancipate certain enslaved individuals, Jefferson became enraged after one of his slaves, a thirty-five-year-old shoemaker named Sandy, stole a horse and escaped from Shadwell. As was customary in the Tidewater region, Jefferson placed an advertisement in the *Virginia Gazette* offering a forty-shilling reward for the man's capture and return.[37] The announcement proved effective, and Sandy was taken back to Shadwell.

Until the 1970s, most Jefferson scholars tended to pass over stories such as Sandy's, preferring instead to underscore the Founding Father's stirring condemnations of slavery.[38] By isolating these memorable outbursts from the broader context of Jefferson's life—especially the lived experience of the enslaved workers at

Monticello — they painted a selective portrait of Jefferson as a principled critic of slavery who was tormented by the ongoing reality of human bondage.[39]

Many of Jefferson's most famous indictments of slavery can be found in the *Notes*. Here, he accuses slavery as a "great political and moral evil" and a terrible "blot" on the new republic. Even more perceptibly (and speaking from personal experience), he condemns the cancerous effect that human bondage has on both the enslaved *and* the slave holder:

> The whole commerce between master and slave is a perpetual exercise of the most boisterous passions, the most unremitting despotism on the one part, and degrading submissions on the other.[40]

In addition to diagnosing the stunning social pathology of enslavement, Jefferson also declared in the *Notes* that the institution had put the United States on an untenable and dangerous path. As a slave owner himself, he also admitted that when the enslaved population of America finally wreaks vengeance on their White masters, God himself will be on the side of the oppressed:

> I tremble for my country when I reflect that God is just: that his justice cannot sleep forever.[41]

Jefferson's memorable aphorisms on the malevolence of slavery, however, must be seen as coexisting with a litany of other considerations. One of these is his long-standing belief that it was a political impossibility to do anything *immediately* about slavery in the plantation-oriented southern United States without ripping the country apart.

Early in his career, Jefferson and his antislavery-minded colleagues in Virginia looked on with admiration while the New

England states managed to either end or at least restrict the institution of slavery. The most complete and unambiguous act of abolition had occurred in Vermont. Within months of the signing of the 1776 American Declaration of Independence, the small northern state not only officially banned slavery; it extended voting rights to free Black men.

Extending suffrage for a population of free Blacks, however, would have been unthinkable for Jefferson. All of his early antislavery initiatives (and musings) from the 1770s and 1780s reflect the fact that he was a so-called *gradualist*, a proponent of an unrushed and careful abolition. His most complete thinking on how this might be done is found in the fourteenth chapter of the *Notes*.[42]

Similar to the gradualist policy that the State of Connecticut enacted in 1784, Jefferson stipulates that Virginia's enslaved children would live "with their parents to a certain age."[43] At that point, he imagines that these same individuals would be separated from their families and "brought up, at the public expense, to tillage, arts, or sciences, according to their geniuses, till the females should be eighteen, and the males twenty-one years."[44] Once this vocational training program was completed, these educated Blacks would be "colonized," put on carriages and sent deep into the Western Territories to set up their own settlement with Virginia's "protection" until their colony "acquired strength."[45] The ostensibly high-minded goal of this scenario would be allowing transplanted Blacks to become "a free and independent people."[46] And yet, bigotry remained the primary motive behind the creation of this new Black colony. By removing a large and fertile population of young Blacks from the state (leaving behind older generations who would eventually die out), he was envisioning a white Virginia that could fully and finally embody its "democratic" values.

Taken as a whole, Jefferson's fantasy reveals several of his deep-seated preoccupations. First is the fear of slaves and a slave uprising; second, his aversion to miscegenation; and third, his general pessimism vis-à-vis the capabilities of the African "race." The comprehensive proposal that he included in the *Notes*, in his view, would have solved all of these "problems" by eliminating both slavery and the entirety of Virginia's Black population.

Jefferson's many proposals to bring slavery to an end were quite unlike those of the abolitionist militants he either frequented or had read. In contrast to the most influential American abolitionist, Anthony Benezet, or Jefferson's good friend Benjamin Rush, Jefferson never called for the unconditional end to human bondage.[47] He would have been even more hostile to the article on the "Negro Trade" found in Diderot's thirty-five-volume *Encyclopédie* (which had sat on his bookshelf in Monticello).

In this remarkable essay, the prolific Chevalier de Jaucourt—he contributed 17,000 articles to Diderot's *Encyclopédie*—presents one of the most forceful abolitionist perspectives of his time.[48] Far from proposing a gradualist, "pragmatic," "progressive," or "physiocratic" solution to the problem of slavery, the encyclopedist draws a line in the sand between enslavers like Jefferson and those who demand an immediate end to the practice. As Jaucourt famously puts it: "The European colonies should be destroyed rather than create so many unhappy people!"[49]

This, of course, would have been Jefferson's worst nightmare: the annihilation of the genteel Virginian way of life. In stark contrast to such radical measures and rhetoric, Jefferson repeatedly affirmed that any solution to the problem of bondage needed to come about in collaboration with the people most affected by the institution in his view: namely, the planters and White citizens living in each state of the union. Although we now remember Jefferson for asserting that some truths are "self-evident"—or "sacred and undeniable" as he originally put it in his draft of the Declaration of Independence — he was far more of a "realist," relativist, and legal-minded legislator when it came to the specifics of ending human bondage. In the *Notes*' section on manners, for example, Jefferson states that he hopes that "total emancipation" will come, but he stipulates that it should only occur "with the consent of the masters, rather than by their extirpation."[50] Much of this had to do with what he believed to be true about the "Negro" race.

THE DEGENERATION DEBATE

Jefferson's motivations for developing his own understanding of race differed from those of his contemporaries. Unlike Kant or Blumenbach, he had little interest in either defining the concept of race or debating the number of human subspecies believed to inhabit the planet.[51] Nor did he attempt to answer the persistent questions posed by European naturalists: Which race came first? From where did this race originate? And how was this first race related — if at all — to the others? Indeed, Jefferson's primary reason for engaging with the subject in the *Notes* was to refute a prevalent belief held by European thinkers: that the physical and intellectual capabilities of America's inhabitants had degenerated because of the continent's inferior soil, "cold" climate, and humid air.

Some of Europe's most famous authors and naturalists — including Buffon, Blumenbach, de Pauw, Kant, and Raynal — had argued or implied that there were essentially three "degenerated" races in what was now the United States. The first of these degenerate groups was the continent's indigenous Amerindians, who were typically characterized as nomadic, unthinking savages, stunted both physically and intellectually by the climate. The second group consisted of Black Africans, who, according to degeneration theory, had already been adversely affected by the Torrid Zone's climate before being forcibly relocated to another harsh environment in America. Finally, there were the descendants of Europeans, the "Creole Whites," who were supposedly becoming weaker and less intelligent over time.

Jefferson entered the race debate to defend the first and last of these groups — Amerindians and Whites — from what he perceived as European slander. The task, he knew, would be difficult. Belief in the climate's ability to change both humans and animals over time had begun circulating in antiquity, had subsisted in various forms through the medieval and Renaissance eras, and had finally been "substantiated" by travelers during the seventeenth and eighteenth centuries. One of the most cited examples of degeneration was the supposed transformation of Portuguese sailors who had settled in the Cape Verde islands, Sierra Leone, or in the Congo (Kongo). According to numerous naturalists, travel writers, and compilers, these White populations had eventually turned *black*.[52]

The core of degeneration theory as it took shape during the eighteenth century was racial primacy. Its supporters claimed that the original race of humans on the planet was *white* and had suffered a global collapse after they migrated to less advantageous environments. Such thinking understandably appealed to Europeans more than it did to non-Europeans for a simple reason: It allowed the continent's Whites to position themselves as an archetype group of comparatively uncorrupted humans who remained physically and intellectually superior to the rest of humanity.

The degeneration premise had also melded with new and compelling ways of distinguishing among human groups. Classification-oriented thinkers such as Kant used the idea of degeneration to create a vertical hierarchy of human races based on the perceived extent of deviation from an (original) white stem.

Naturalists interested in skulls, including Blumenbach, claimed that the supposed esthetic superiority of the Caucasian skull reflected Europeans' status as closest to an "undegenerated" prototype. Partisans of stage theory also drew on the theory of human degeneration. William Robertson, for example, claimed that the most degenerated groups suffered from a stunted development.[53]

Jefferson had access to virtually every existing version of degeneration theory in his library. The most influential of these works was Buffon's *Natural History*, the book that had first popularized the idea of degeneration throughout the western world in 1749.

Jefferson was actually a great admirer of Buffon. He celebrated the Frenchman's vast erudition, magisterial prose, and encyclopedic knowledge of nature. But he (along with George Washington and many other Founding Fathers) was also vexed by how the Frenchman's theory of degeneration had been used to "explain" North America. This had begun with the continent's animals. Throughout several volumes of the *Natural History*, Buffon had given credence to the idea that American animals were the smaller and weaker offshoots of superior European prototypes. As Jefferson writes in the *Notes*, Buffon had made the preposterous claim that:

> "Nature" [itself] is less active, less energetic on one side of the globe than she is on the other. As if both sides were not warmed by the same genial sun; as if a soil of the same chemical composition was less capable of elaboration into animal nutriment.[54]

Jefferson composed many pages designed to refute this idea. How could it be, he writes, that American animals are smaller due to the cold and humidity if, as Buffon had stated elsewhere, "cattle thrive in the cold and humid environments of Denmark and Ukraine"?[55] To drive home his argument, Jefferson also compiled a list of the largest domestic and wild animals found in North America, bragging that there were enormous "bullocks" weighing "2,500, 2,200, and 2,100" pounds in Connecticut that far outweighed their European counterparts.[56] According to the painstaking charts and figures that he included alongside such statements in the *Notes*, American bears, elks, otters, weasels, and beavers were all far larger and heavier than their European equivalents.

[77]

A comparative View of the Quadrupeds of Europe and of America.

I. *Aboriginals of both.*

	Europe.	America.
	lb.	lb.
Mammoth		
Buffalo. Bifon		*1800
White bear. Ours blanc		
Caribou. Renne		
Bear. Ours	153.7	*410
Elk. Elan. Orignal, palmated		
Red deer. Cerf	288.8	*273
Fallow deer. Daim	167.8	
Wolf. Loup	69.8	
Roe. Chevreuil	56.7	
Glutton. Glouton. Carcajou		
Wild cat. Chat fauvage		†30
Lynx. Loup cervier	25.	
Beaver. Caftor	18.5	*45
Badger. Blaireau	13.6	
Red Fox. Renard	13.5	
Grey Fox. Ifatis		
Otter. Loutre	8.9	†12
Monax. Marmotte	6.5	
Vifon. Fouine	2.8	
Hedgehog. Heriffon	2.2	
Martin. Marte	1.9	†6
	oz.	
Water rat. Rat d'eau	7.5	
Wefel. Belette	2.2	oz.
Flying fquirrel. Polatouche	2.2	†4
Shrew moufe. Mufaraigne	1.	

II. *Abori-*

COMPARISON OF ANIMALS,
FROM *NOTES ON THE STATE OF VIRGINIA*

Jefferson knew that presenting *tangible* proof of the size of America's animals was critical for his argument.[57] He had hoped, in fact, that some American explorer moving into the new Western Territories would stumble upon the carcass of what he believed to be the largest North American animal, a 15,000-pound mastodon, or *Mammut americanum*. Having heard reports that these massive herbivores still roamed the plains "in the northern parts of America," Jefferson fantasized that he would one day present the remains of such a beast—perhaps an enormous head and eight-foot tusks—to Buffon at the Royal Academy of Sciences or the King's Garden.[58]

Jefferson was never able to find the hoped-for mastodon remains. But before leaving for France, he purchased an enormous panther skin that he sent to Buffon when he arrived in Paris.[59] Although Jefferson knew that this feline pelt did not provide a refutation of degeneration, he had nonetheless hoped that it would demonstrate that this particular animal was far from the small and comparatively meek cat that Buffon had attributed to the United States. The Frenchman, however, was not convinced that the fur proved anything.

Jefferson had another opportunity to plead his case two years later when he visited the seventy-nine-year-old Buffon at his estate at Montbard, in January 1786.[60] Though the two men once again disagreed about degeneracy, there was one important fact that Jefferson learned while dining with the famous naturalist: Buffon had never heard of the American animal called the "moose," a beast that Jefferson knew could reach a height of ten feet.

Jefferson had already considered procuring a moose cadaver to shock his European colleagues as early as 1784, but now he was hell-bent on showing Buffon a creature so large that a "reindeer" could walk under its "belly."[61] Reaching out to several contacts in New Hampshire while still living in France, Jefferson let it be known that he was seeking to procure a "good-sized moose."[62]

After several months and an equal number of setbacks, a friend in New Hampshire finally sourced an American moose that was seven feet tall. By early spring, the cadaver of the animal was packed in an enormous wooden crate, loaded on a ship in Durham, New Hampshire, and sent on its way to Paris. When Buffon finally laid his eyes on the moose, he was apparently very impressed. This was well worth the enormous sum of forty-seven pounds sterling (c. $12,000) that Jefferson was billed.[63]

Jefferson's entry into what had been the European-dominated discussion of animal degeneration turned out to be one of his greatest intellectual victories. By the end of the century, no less than the *Encyclopedia Britannica* concluded that Jefferson had proven Buffon wrong about North American animals. As the article's author put it, the American had done so convincingly, "both by argument and by facts."[64]

Jefferson's rebuttal of the theory of *human* degeneration is a more complicated story. Much to his chagrin, Buffon had more than hinted that what was true for (degenerated) American animals held for the continent's humans as well. This was especially the case, he suggested, for Amerindians, whom he portrayed as effeminate, cowardly, hairless, unintelligent, and lacking in sexual desire.[65] In the *Notes*, Jefferson methodically refutes each of these points, often with anecdotes that underscore indigenous peoples' courage, insight, moral fortitude, and oratory abilities. Regarding the one supposedly distinctive physical characteristic found among Amerindian men — a lack of facial hair — Jefferson mockingly explains that the only reason that they are seemingly beardless is that they diligently pluck their whiskers.[66] In Jefferson's view, there was actually no real measurable *racial* distinction between red and white. Indeed, to prove his point, he referenced Linnaeus's 1758 racial taxonomy. In a rare instance of racial classification being used to refute racializing ideas, Jefferson proclaims: "[W]e shall probably find that [Indians] are formed in mind as well as in body, on the same module with the 'Homo sapiens Europaeus.'"[67]

If Jefferson had been vexed by Buffon's denigrating portrait of Amerindians, he was even more mortified by the common European claim that America's "Whites" had also degenerated. The book that most inflamed his indignation was Abbé Raynal's bestselling *History of the Two Indies*. In its first (1770) edition, Raynal had gone so far as to assert that North America had produced no geniuses — a "fact," he claimed, demonstrated by the sad reality that the region had not yet given rise to a single great poet.[68]

To rectify the problem of white degeneracy, which Raynal believed stemmed from excess humidity, the Frenchman recommended that North America's engineers drain the continent's many swamps immediately.[69] He also allowed that a better education of the population might help "improve the insurmountable obstacle of the climate." "Maybe, maybe, one day," he admits, "America will favor the [birth of intelligent men]. Maybe one day will be born another Newton in New England?"[70]

In responding to such comments, Jefferson asked his European readers to remember that centuries passed before Greece had its Homer, France its Racine, and England its Shakespeare and Milton.[71] He also provided specific examples of American prodigies, including the military genius George Washington, the physics genius Benjamin Franklin, and the brilliant Philadelphia astronomer, David Rittenhouse. "As a child of yesterday," Jefferson proclaims proudly, America has already "given hopeful proofs of genius."[72] Indeed, in his view, the ratio of American geniuses already compared quite favorably to that in France and perhaps exceeded the same ratio in England.[73]

THE UNFORTUNATE BUSINESS OF COLOR

To defend the White and "Red" inhabitants of North America from European slander, Jefferson challenged the belief that climate could deform or diminish the human species. Part of this argument was insisting that White Americans were equal to Europeans in intellect and accomplishment, while Amerindians possessed the potential to reach that same level. This line of reasoning took a very different turn when it came to the "Black" race. Rather than contest the prevailing stereotypes related to Africans, Jefferson made use of them as part of his argument. To maintain consistency—and deny that climate had altered Black people—he claimed that their "inferiority" must instead stem from something innate, essential, and unchangeable.[74]

In stark contrast to his most famous dictum—"All men are created equal"—Jefferson states in the *Notes* that nature itself had made "real distinctions" between Blacks and other human races, beginning with their skin.[75] Demonstrating a remarkable familiarity with two hundred years of spurious racial anatomy, he then cites a long list of possible explanations related to the cause of blackness: that it resides in the *reticulum mucosum*, that it is actually found in the scarf skin (second layer), that it originates in the blood, and that it comes perhaps from the bile. He even refers to an unnamed source, claiming that it might stem from a specific "organ," presumably the brain.[76] Interestingly enough, Jefferson's reaction to this contradictory "data" was both skeptical and dogmatic. Although careful not to side with any one of the possible explanations he mentions, he asserts defensively that color is not only "fixed in nature," but is "as real as if its seat [location] and cause were better known to us."[77]

Much of what Jefferson then wrote is even more difficult to stomach. He criticizes Africans' textured hair, their supposedly asymmetrical heads and faces, and the fact that black skin, in his estimation, is little more than an "immoveable veil" covering "all the emotions."[78] Race, however, was not only skin-deep for Jefferson. He declares that Blacks secrete less by the kidneys; that they have a stronger odor than Whites; that their bodies are more tolerant of heat; that they require less sleep; and that they have less "forethought" and seem to understand the outside world more with "sensation" than with "reflection."[79] Several of his observations also highlighted Africans' supposed hypersexuality. In addition to asserting that African males are more "ardent" than European Whites, he maintains that Blacks are constitutionally drawn to Whites in a sexual way—in the same way that the male "Oranootan" is more attracted to Black women than he is to "those of his own species."[80] That Jefferson evokes the orangutan in this context is more than an analogy. The implication is that there is a primal, animal lust among male Africans that is ingrained and race- or species-specific.[81]

Jefferson concludes this section by asserting that Blacks' liabilities cannot simply be "the effect merely of their condition of life."[82] To prove his point, he claims that, while some enslaved individuals have benefitted from the "experience of their masters," their minds nonetheless remain "dull, tasteless, and anomalous."[83] Unlike the Amerindian race, which he ardently defends throughout the *Notes*, Jefferson laments the fact that he has supposedly never met "a Black [who] had uttered a thought above the level of plain narration."[84] He concludes this dismal section by denigrating one of the era's great counterexamples to a racialized view of the "Black race," the former slave and poet "Phyllis Whately" (sic). Reminiscent of what David Hume wrote about Francis Williams in 1748, and what Kant said about Labat's Black carpenter in 1764, Jefferson states flatly that Wheatley's poetry is "below the dignity of criticism."[85]

Jefferson's final words on Black Africans in the *Notes* nonetheless reveal a measure of skepticism. He concedes that his "general conclusions" about Africans "must be hazarded with great diffidence," acknowledging that an error in judgment could "degrade a whole race of man."[86] Yet despite these cautionary remarks, Jefferson proceeds to make two final—and troubling—assertions. First, he speculates that Black Africans might constitute a "distinct race," a group of humans that is biologically separate from other human groups. This taxonomic claim is followed by a bio-political one: that the "unfortunate difference of color, and perhaps of faculty, is a powerful obstacle to the emancipation of these people."[87]

SALLY HEMINGS AND THE MISCEGENATION TABOO

Among the many race-based prejudices found in the *Notes on the State of Virginia*, few haunted Jefferson as much as what was called an "abominable mixture," the mingling of "black" and "white" blood.[88] Four years after publishing his condemnation of interracial mixing in the *Notes*, however, Jefferson violated this taboo by engaging in a long sexual relationship with Sally Hemings. The connection between Jefferson and Sally Hemings has become the subject of tremendous scrutiny and debate in the United States over the past few decades.[89]

This book is not the venue to retrace the "*history* of the history" of Sally Hemings and the other "Monticello Hemings."[90] Yet it is crucial to remember that her relationship with Jefferson—once widely rejected—has shifted from a "dubious" possibility, dismissed by historians for more than a century, to a DNA-substantiated certainty. Tours at Monticello now (appropriately) spend as much time evoking the lives of the Hemings family as they do, for example, explaining the kinship diagram of Jefferson's "real" family.

Jefferson's ongoing relationship with Sally Hemings first became known on a national level in 1802, when a muckraking journalist named James Thomson Callender published an article in a Richmond newspaper asserting that the then-president had not only been sleeping with an "African Venus," but that this same "wench" had borne him five children.[91] For the next seven years, broadsides, cartoons, and allusions to the "couple" appeared from time to time in the press. Jefferson did not respond, either officially or unofficially.[92]

Nearly fifty years after Jefferson died, a far more accurate account of his relationship with Sally Hemings was published in the March 13, 1873, edition of the *Pike County Republican*.[93] Appearing under the title "Life Among the Lowly," this version of events was provided by none other than Sally Hemings's third (surviving) child, Madison Hemings (b. 1805).

Madison Hemings's story, along with that of his mother, Sally, is one of multigenerational miscegenation. He begins with his great-grandmother, a "full-blooded African." Sometime around 1735, this unnamed woman, who was living on a plantation on the James River, became pregnant by a ship captain named Hemings. A decade later, this same woman (Madison's great-grandmother) and her mixed-race daughter Elizabeth (Madison's grandmother) were given to the slave trader and plantation owner John Wayles as part of a wedding dowry.[94]

The ten- or eleven-year-old Elizabeth Hemings (Madison's grandmother) would presumably have been lighter skinned than most of the enslaved workers on Wayles's plantation. As was often the case on southern plantations, this may have led John Wayles to choose Elizabeth Hemings as his "concubine" once she had grown "to womanhood," as Madison delicately puts it.[95] Regardless of the actual circumstances, for well over a decade, Madison Hemings's grandmother remained subject to this *concubinage*, and ultimately gave birth to six of Wayles's children, all of whom took the Hemings name.

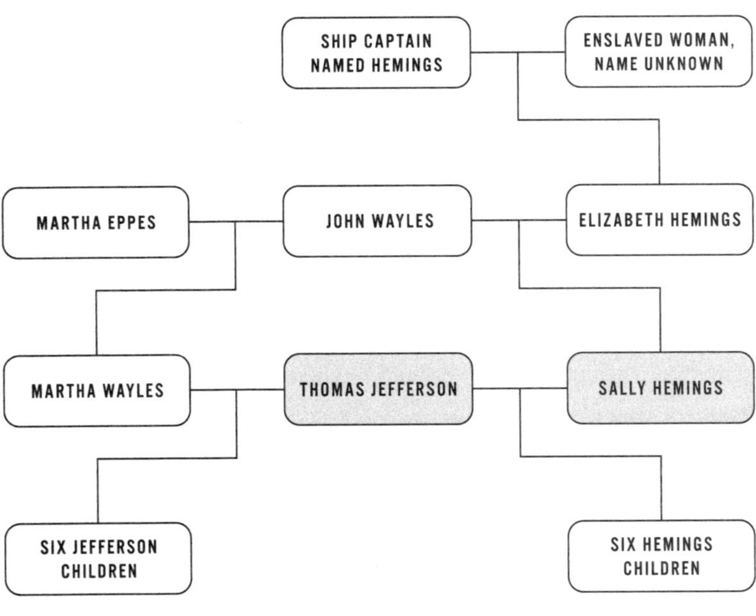

HEMINGS GENEALOGY

A year after Wayles died, in 1773, Elizabeth Hemings and her children were inherited by Wayles's son-in-law, Thomas Jefferson. Among the family members who were transported from Wayles's plantation in Charles City County to Monticello was Madison Hemings's future mother, the then-infant Sally Hemings. Jefferson, who was very much aware that each and every Hemings child had been "sired" by his father-in-law, assigned those of his wife's half siblings who were old enough to a series of domestic tasks and trades in and around Monticello.

Madison relates the rest of his mother's story according to the norms of the era, which is to say with more resignation than outrage. At age fourteen, the enslaved Sally Hemings was chosen to accompany Jefferson's sole surviving daughter in the United States, Maria, on the long voyage from Virginia to Paris.[96] The two girls finally arrived at Jefferson's townhouse — the Hôtel de Langeac on the Champs Elysées — on July 14, 1787. It is worth noting that, one day before Sally became part of the household, Jefferson sent a letter to a friend stating that the "abomination [of slavery] must have an end, and there is a superior bench reserved in heaven for those who hasten it."[97]

Madison Hemings did not elaborate on his mother's experience in Paris. Yet one can readily imagine her initial excitement at seeing the city, especially in the company of her twenty-two-year-old brother, James, who had been studying French cuisine in Paris for years.[98] One incontrovertible fact that Madison did share about this era is that, during Sally Hemings's eighteenth months in France, she like her own mother, became her master's "concubine." One possible clue related to when this began shows up in Jefferson's punctilious account book. Under April and May 1789, we see the following entries: April 6. "Pd for clothes for Sally 96 livres"; April 16. "Paid for clothes for Sally 72 livres"; May 25. "Paid for clothes for Sally 25 livres."[99] In today's dollars, this comes to approximately $1,150.[100]

Other than the DNA link between Jefferson and the Hemings, very little is known about Sally as a person. Scholars who have pored over the archives have had to content themselves with several (eighteenth-century) descriptions of her physical appearance that give us an idea of how she might have been seen by Jefferson.[101] Technically "three-quarters White," Sally apparently had lightish skin, long straight hair, and was generally seen as quite beautiful.[102] To Jefferson, she might also have looked very much like his deceased wife, who was, it is once again worth recalling, Sally Hemings's half sister.

One clue related to Sally's intelligence and negotiating skills can nonetheless be inferred from a story that Madison shared in this same article. Sometime after her arrival in France, Sally understood that, legally speaking, she was no longer a slave in France thanks to the country's Free Soil principle. Sally apparently used this as a bargaining chip when Jefferson announced that their household would soon be sailing back to the United States.[103] Refusing to return until the future terms of their relationship had been established, she convinced the Virginia lawyer and future president of the United States to agree to a series of "extraordinary privileges," the most important of which was his "solemn pledge that her children should be free at the age of twenty-one years."[104]

With this deal in place, Jefferson, his two daughters, Sally, James, and the family sheepdog sailed from Le Havre to Virginia on a ship named the *Clermont* in September 1789. In the short account of this return trip, Madison relates that his mother was "enceinte," or pregnant, with Jefferson's child during the voyage but lost the baby shortly after arriving in Virginia.

So many questions linger about this relationship. Just who was Sally for Jefferson over the years? Did Jefferson record anything about her at all in his writing? Were these writings, assuming that they existed, destroyed by his family? Did Jefferson ultimately allow or encourage Sally to become literate, in the same way that her brother the chef had been able to do?[105] Another set of questions concerns Sally herself. What did she think of Jefferson after "becoming his concubine"? Did she resent him, have affection for him, or vacillate between both emotions as she bore six of his children? Whatever the nature of her bond with Jefferson, for thirty-five years, Sally Hemings's life remained perversely intertwined with her "master's" in a way that was strikingly ordinary in the South.

HAITI, LOUISIANA, AND THE FRENCH LINK TO AMERICAN SLAVERY

Before sailing for the United States, Jefferson fully expected to resume his ambassadorship once the French Revolution had run its course. But much to his surprise, upon arriving in America he learned that he had been appointed Secretary of State by the newly elected president, George Washington. Recognizing that his life in France had come to a close, he wrote to his assistant in Paris, instructing him to dismiss the household staff and ship most of his belongings — including two carriages, books, furniture, works of art, cookware, an extensive stock of foodstuffs, and 700 bottles of wine — to a house he was renting in Philadelphia, the new capital of the United States. By the fall of 1790, eighty crates arrived at his Market Street residence.[106]

As Secretary of State, Jefferson was charged with overseeing the young nation's "foreign" affairs, among them negotiations with France's new revolutionary government. Yet during the three and a half years that he served as Secretary of State in Washington's cabinet, he spent much of his time arguing about the future of the country with the then-Secretary of the Treasury, Alexander Hamilton, and the Federalists.

From Jefferson's point of view, the term "United States" was supposed to mean what it implied — a united nation perhaps, but one whose political sovereignty lay primarily with its respective *states*. His corollary hope was that the country would remain largely agrarian, a large network of country farms where democracy, virtue, and liberty would flourish, far from the twin vices of urban life and unwanted government mandates. These dreams clashed dramatically with Hamilton's belief that the United States needed more manufacturing and international trade, more urban growth, a national banking system, and, above all, a strong and far more efficient centralized government akin to what he admired in England.

Jefferson and Hamilton's squabbles were not limited to domestic issues. The two men often disagreed on international matters as well, including how the fledgling United States should respond to the massive slave rebellion that had broken out in Saint-Domingue in 1791. As Secretary of State, planter, and Francophile, Jefferson reacted with horror to reports that Black "insurrectionaries" were burning French plantations and putting their White "masters" to death. Fearing the rise of a nation of "cannibals" whose fury might spur similar revolts in the United States, Jefferson counseled George Washington to throw the country's weight behind the beleaguered French colonists.[107] The president agreed. Over the next few years, the United States provided over $700,000 to Saint-Domingue's planters to suppress what Washington described as "the alarming insurrection of the Negroes in Hispaniola."[108]

Up to a certain point, Alexander Hamilton had supported this initiative. Yet, as Secretary of the Treasury, he also insisted that American merchants be allowed to trade with Black revolutionaries as well as with French planters. This stance had little to do with sympathy for the revolution; it was simply an economic imperative. During the early 1790s, the French colony accounted for fully eleven percent of the United States' overseas trade.[109] Nearly 500 French and American cargo ships were sailing back and forth between Cap-François and a number of American cities including Philadelphia, New York, Charleston, and Boston. Ships leaving Saint-Domingue transported sugar, molasses, and coffee beans. When these same vessels returned to the French colony, they carried American livestock, smoked meat, smoked fish, lumber, and two of the biggest and uninterrupted exports to the island regardless of who was in power: guns and ammunition.[110]

The United States' inconsistent stance on Saint-Domingue—ostensibly supporting the French but trading with the rebels—actually had minimal impact on the course of the rebellion. Far more decisive in these early years was the execution of Louis XVI, the same king with whom Jefferson had dined at Versailles. In the aftermath of the king's beheading—at 10:22 a.m. on January 21, 1793—both England and Spain concluded that France had become so embroiled in revolutionary politics that it could no longer defend the most profitable colony in the world. By September 1793, both countries had launched major military operations against the French in Saint-Domingue. The Spanish, who already possessed one side of the island of Hispaniola, sought to extend their territory while simultaneously curbing French expansionism. England had a far more ambitious objective: taking over the entire French side of the island and reinstating slavery.

During the fall of 1793, French forces in Saint-Domingue were simultaneously waging war against tens of thousands of Black revolutionaries, Spanish and English invaders, and, ironically, a sizable number of (French) royalist planters who had aligned themselves with foreign powers against the French Republic. Who would ultimately seize control of the colony was unclear to Washington's cabinet members. What had become apparent, however, was the fact that Saint-Domingue had descended into a period of increasingly violent chaos.[111] By October, the situation had become so dire for French government forces that France's Civil Commissioner in Saint-Domingue, Léger-Félicité Sonthonax, took the unexpected step of abolishing slavery in the northern portion of the island. This was a strategic move. Although Sonthonax was an abolitionist, he had declared emancipation primarily to gain favor with the Black population. His true goal, in short, was to prevent the French colony from falling into the hands of Royalists or the British.[112]

Jefferson stepped down as Secretary of State several months after this occurred, in December 1793. When he returned to politics four years later as vice president under the Federalist president John Adams, the situation in Saint-Domingue had shifted dramatically. A brilliant revolutionary leader named Toussaint Louverture had become the de facto ruler of the French colony, having beaten back the Spanish invasion and crushed the Royalists. The United States' position on the war had changed as well. The profoundly antislavery (and increasingly anti-French) John Adams had implemented what was called the "Toussaint Clause," an enormous about-face in foreign policy that meant that the United States would not only increase trade with the rebels, but actively promote "the separation of the island from France."[113] The United States, in short, had effectively sided with the rebellion, in large measure to weaken France's position in the Americas.

Jefferson, who looked on at this shift in foreign policy from his comparatively powerless position as vice president, lamented the fact that the United States had turned its back on its greatest ally.[114] By the end of Adam's term, this swing in foreign policy had nearly dragged the United States into a full-scale military conflict with France. During what was referred to as the Quasi-War (1798–1800), both France and the United States seized each other's vessels and sometimes participated in direct naval engagements in the Caribbean.

The United States' relationship with both France and Saint-Domingue changed yet again in 1801, when Jefferson succeeded the one-term John Adams in the office of the president of the United States. In addition to de-escalating tensions with France, Jefferson decreed that the United States was adopting a policy of neutrality.[115] In reality, Jefferson told the French minister in Washington that Adams's "collaboration with Toussaint had violated neutral relations with France" and that henceforth the United States would respect France's sovereign right to Saint-Domingue.[116] Not only was Jefferson cutting off trade with Louverture, he was communicating an unmistakable message to Napoleon Bonaparte. France's First Consul now had tacit permission to crush the revolution on Saint-Domingue by any means possible and without any American interference.[117]

Napoleon ultimately seized this opportunity when Louverture announced a new constitution for the colony on July 8, 1801. Furious that the rebel leader had not only permanently abolished slavery in the French colony, but also designated himself "Governor-General" of the colony for life, Napoleon ordered his brother-in-law, General Charles Victor-Emmanuel Leclerc, to prepare to invade the island with an expeditionary force of 20,000 troops. This enormous army, carried by almost 800 ships, arrived in Saint-Domingue in December of 1801.[118] The ostensible purpose of this military intervention was bringing peace to the colony. The real objective, however, was to arrest the Black leaders, disarm the rebel army, and reinstate slavery on plantations where men, women, and children were now working as paid, yet bonded, laborers.

In the early months of what was effectively a conquest of their "own" colony, the French army had a certain amount of success. Leclerc had even managed to (duplicitously) arrest Louverture in June of 1802 and send him to France.[119] Yet later that same summer, after the Haitian population discovered that Napoleon had reestablished slavery in Guadeloupe and Martinique, a much broader and more unified revolt broke out across the colony.[120] In a telltale letter that Leclerc wrote to Napoleon on October 7, the increasingly besieged general gave the impression that he was fighting the entire island. Indeed, his desperation was such that he now advocated more genocidal tactics, among them killing "all the male and female Negroes who live in the mountains and only keeping children under twelve years of age."[121]

It is difficult to imagine the scale of the carnage that took place in Saint-Domingue during this era. Before the Leclerc campaign had even started, at least 100,000 formerly enslaved Africans (of c. 500,000 total) and 25,000 White colonists and free people of color had already been killed.[122] Tens of thousands of English and Spanish soldiers had also died in the fighting. By 1803, 50,000 more French soldiers including Leclerc would perish as well, most of them from the ravages of yellow fever. How many more Haitians died during the last months of the fighting is unknown. What historians emphasize, however, is that Leclerc's successor, the bloodthirsty General Donatien-Marie-Joseph de Rochambeau, was partial to mass executions and drownings.[123]

The final stage of what is now called the Haitian Revolution began in November 1803, when rebel leader Jean-Jacques Dessalines won a decisive victory over Rochambeau's army at the Battle of Vertières. Surrounded and facing certain death if captured, the French general negotiated terms of surrender that required French troops to evacuate the island not as free men, but as prisoners of the British navy—which had been strategically blockading the port of Cap-François throughout the conflict. By late November, between 3,000 and 5,000 French soldiers were transported to the British colony of Jamaica, where they were held as prisoners of war.[124] Weeks later, on January 1, 1804, Dessalines declared Haiti's independence.

The campaign to subdue Saint-Domingue was a catastrophic debacle for Napoleon. For Jefferson, however, this extended and costly military fiasco paved the way for what he believed to be the greatest accomplishment of his two presidencies: the purchase of France's Louisiana Territory. Although he had been a (wary) supporter of the French against the "insurgent" Blacks as far back as 1791, he finally admitted that he was now indebted, as he put it, to "the deadly climate of St. Domingo, and to the courage and obstinate resistance made by its Black inhabitants."[125]

Even before the Battle of Vertières, Jefferson had sensed that Napoleon, who was girding his loins for an inevitable and larger conflict with Great Britain, might be willing to sell two French territories strategically located on the United States' borders. The first was a large swath of "Florida," including sections of what is now Alabama and Mississippi. The real prize, however, was the French city of New Orleans. Over the course of several decades, New Orleans had become increasingly critical to American commerce. Positioned at the mouth of the 2,300-mile-long Mississippi River, the city effectively controlled access to a waterway that linked America's southern plantations, frontier settlements, and international markets. Grains, pork, lumber, furs, whisky, and tobacco flowed out; critical tools, textiles, sugar, and guns flowed in. For Jefferson, the possibility that some other foreign power would oversee a port through which "three-eighths of our territory must pass to market," was simply unacceptable.[126]

To secure the purchase of both New Orleans and parts of Florida, Jefferson charged his longtime friend James Monroe and Robert Livingston, the U.S. Ambassador to France, with negotiating with Napoleon. The offer they were instructed to tender for both regions was ten million dollars. Napoleon's famous counter proposition — ceding the entirety of the far larger Louisiana Territory for an extra five million dollars — stunned the American diplomats.[127] The French emperor was offering to relinquish an expanse of 828,000 square miles that began with New Orleans (and a large portion of the Gulf of Mexico) and extended as far as Canada and the Rocky Mountains.[128] Though the two American emissaries were not authorized to do so, they signed on behalf of the United States. France's signatory during the negotiations was none other than Barbé-Marbois, the same man who had prompted Jefferson to begin writing what later became the *Notes on the State of Virginia*.

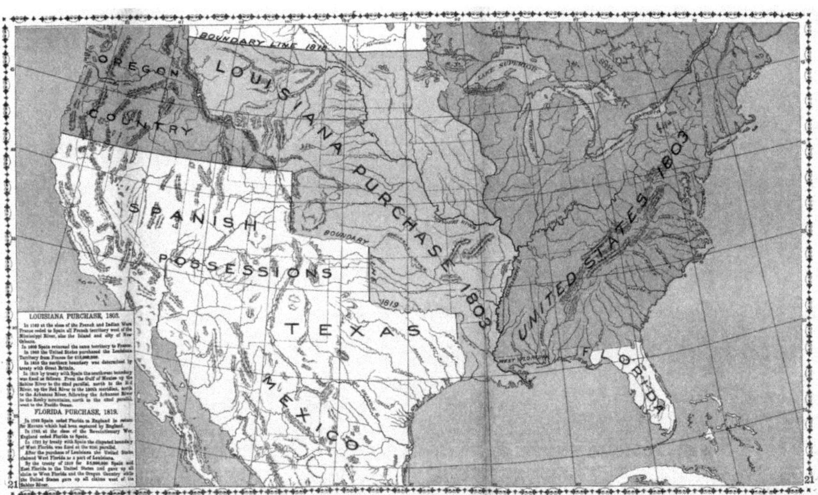

THE LOUISIANA PURCHASE

Several months after Congress approved the treaty, the Jefferson administration was obliged to confront an enormously important question: what to do about slavery in this new territory. At the time of the purchase, in 1803, Spanish and French settlers in the region already held somewhere between 30,000 to 50,000 enslaved laborers, most of whom worked on sugar, tobacco, or rice plantations near the Mississippi Delta.[129] The status of the *currently* enslaved population was the first of two thorny issues. The second, far more contentious matter, was deciding if slavery would be allowed to expand in a region that was as large as the current United States.

Jefferson had already taken up a similar question in 1784 when, as a member of Congress, he was tasked with creating a path to statehood for the so-called Western Territories (Ohio, Indiana, Illinois, Michigan, Wisconsin, and part of Minnesota). This was perhaps the last moment when he lived up to his abolitionist rhetoric. In one provision of his proposed ordinance, he stipulated that any enslaved person living in one of these new states should be freed in 1800. This important antislavery clause was ultimately struck down by a single vote. Several years later, when Jefferson reflected on this lost opportunity, he lamented that "the fate of millions unborn [had hung] on the tongue of one man, and Heaven was silent in that awful moment."[130]

What President Jefferson envisioned for the country's expansion into the Louisiana Territory in 1804 could not have been more different from how he had reacted during the 1780s. Although abolitionists including Thomas Paine pleaded with him to prevent "the curse of slavery" from infecting the newly acquired region, his perceived responsibilities as president eclipsed his earlier misgivings.[131] From Jefferson's point of view, enslaved labor was already the foundation of the economy in much of the region and he had no intention of running afoul of the southern states by banning the practice. Indeed, when Congress passed legislation in 1804 that effectively prohibited both the interstate and international slave trade in the Louisiana Territory, Jefferson requested that this decree be revised to allow for the transfer of "domestically produced slaves" into the region. The House and the Senate promptly complied, effectively opening the floodgates to the era's burgeoning domestic slave trade.[132] The demographic consequences were immediate: By 1820, fully ten percent (c. 150,000) of the country's

1,500,000 enslaved individuals were living in the state of Louisiana and the territory of Missouri.[133]

THE LEGACY

After two terms as president in Washington, Jefferson was eager to be done with what he often called the anxiety of "public life."[134] On Saturday, March 4, 1809, exactly eight years after he had walked to his own inauguration, he rode in a carriage to the House of Representatives to watch his closest political protégé, James Madison, be sworn in. The city of Washington, DC, had come alive on this cold and rainy day to welcome the new president. As one witness described it, Pennsylvania Avenue was "overspread" with 10,000 "persons of every description."[135]

A week later, after settling his affairs in the capital, Jefferson climbed on his horse and set off on a solo ride for Charlottesville. On March 15, after finishing the last leg of the 120-mile trip in a blinding snowstorm, he was finally back at Monticello.[136] This was not the first time he had returned home during his two terms as president. During the summer recess, he typically spent five or six weeks at Monticello. Some of these visits had coincided with Sally's pregnancies.[137]

In the early months of his retirement, the ex-president gradually reimmersed himself in the rhythms of plantation life, especially the lives of the 130 or so enslaved individuals at Monticello. Although Jefferson occasionally interacted with the plantation's field hands, he spent most of his time with the "privileged" members of the enslaved community — those with artisanal skills or domestic roles that brought them into daily contact with the main house. In 1808, the enslaved people he saw most often — apart from Sally Hemings and her children — included his valet Burwell

Colbert; the blacksmiths James Fosset and Isaac Jefferson Granger; the carpenter John Hemings and his brother Peter, who had become a master brewer; and the chefs Fanny Hern and Edith Fossett, both of whom had learned the techniques of French cuisine passed down from James Hemings.[138] As on most plantations, the enslaved individuals in the "master's" immediate circle were generally of mixed race. In a world where slavery distorted every human relationship, proximity to power followed the logic of skin tone.

To oversee such a vast enterprise—largely through the delegated authority of overseers—was not unusual in a state where nearly 400,000 people were enslaved in 1808. And yet Jefferson was hardly a typical Virginia planter. As a young lawyer, he had defended Black men in court, drafted a bill to legalize manumission, and even entertained the idea of ending slavery altogether. It was he, too, who in 1808 signed the federal law banning the international slave trade.[139]

But it was primarily as both intellectual *and* plantation owner that Jefferson had truly set himself apart. As a scholar, he had drawn from his knowledge of law, history, geography, natural history, anatomy, and travelogues to advance a uniquely American understanding of race and human enslavement. His pessimistic view on both subjects had made him a curious figure in plantation society: a slave-holding ex-politician who claimed that the best way to rid the country of slavery was by *expatriating* the "racially inferior" members of the nation's labor force.[140]

There was also another way that Jefferson himself believed to differ from many of his fellow slave owners: He repeatedly portrayed himself as an "enlightened" planter, an owner of humans who reacted with outrage if he heard about a sadistic overseer torturing somebody to death on a neighboring property. In a letter he sent to Angelica Schuyler Church in November of 1793, he famously asserted that it was his duty to tend to "the happiness of those who labor for mine."[141] Some of his reputation for being a comparatively kind "master" came from a Frenchman named François-Alexandre-Frédéric de La Rochefoucauld-Liancourt. When this exiled aristocrat passed through the Tidewater in 1796, he spent a few days at Monticello. In the published account of life at the Virginia plantation that appeared two years later, Rochefoucauld-Liancourt marveled at how Jefferson's "Negroes [were] nourished, clothed, and treated as well as White servants could be." He also lauded the vocational education that Jefferson had provided for some of his workers, the result being that the "master" had a competent staff of "cabinetmakers, carpenters, masons, bricklayers, [and] smiths" who could accomplish all the tasks on the plantation without outside help. What had impressed him the most was Jefferson's nail factory, where enslaved children beginning at age ten or eleven tirelessly produced tiny spikes all day long—one of the few activities on the heavily indebted plantation yielding "a considerable profit."[142]

There is certainly enough written evidence to conclude that Jefferson sought to avoid the most barbaric methods of torture employed by some of his fellow planters. And yet, how much credit should one receive for reserving the lash for only the most extreme offenses? As was the case for all plantation owners, Jefferson reigned over a population of humans whose lives were structured by meager rewards and enormous punishments. When a blacksmith named James Hubbard ran off from the plantation in the spring of 1812, Jefferson hired a slave hunter to track him down. Once Hubbard had been captured and taken back to Monticello, Jefferson ordered that he be flogged in front of his friends, imprisoned, and then sold "out of the state."[143]

It is important to note that the brutal reality of plantation life spared none of Jefferson's enslaved workers, not even the comparatively privileged Hemings family. Consider the fate of Sally Hemings's nephew, the seventeen-year-old James Hemings (not the same James Hemings who had accompanied Jefferson to Paris). In 1804, after being stricken by a debilitating illness, Hemings was unable to report to his workstation at Jefferson's nailery. For this "infraction," the plantation's overseer, Gabriel Lilly, subjected him to three whippings in the span of one day. When Hemings was well enough to walk, he fled, never to return. In this particular case, Jefferson did not dispatch a slave hunter.[144]

It is sometimes said that Jefferson's decisions as plantation owner (as well as his concomitant racism) reflect the broader cultural norms of his era. This can be argued *up to a point*. It is certainly true that the future president was born into a world where subservient blackness was the norm and racial inferiority was assumed. It is also a fact that he came of age at a time when an increasingly trenchant form of racialized thinking was crystalizing under his feet.

When Jefferson had first begun being interested in "anthropology" in the 1770s — an era when he expressed his strongest antislavery opinions — a great deal of nascent race theory remained anecdote-based and, at times, downright anti-classificatory. Over the course of the next few decades, however, the vagueness of race was giving way to a more brutal, dogmatic, determinist, and even polygenetic classification of humankind. While virtually every racialized idea that Jefferson adopted by the mid-1780s had been asserted decades if not a century before, *how* these concepts were being expressed had also changed dramatically. The lyrical prose and overall skeptical tone of the high Enlightenment, which was evident in the writings of older naturalists such as Buffon, had given way to a far more clinical and scientific form of race.[145]

It is nonetheless important to underscore the fact that Thomas Jefferson was not the unwitting dupe of his era's thinking. He was neither an illiterate sailor working on a slave ship nor a member of a colonial militia on a remote plantation in Jamaica where the Black–White ratio was 12:1. He was, in fact, the most important proponent of the Enlightenment project of liberty, equality, and human progress in the United States. To the extent that historians can second-guess the dead — or play historical tricks on them as Voltaire famously said — one can confidently affirm that Jefferson had the intellectual tools, opportunity, and contacts to interrogate his race-based thinking.

Numerous people throughout Jefferson's life, in fact, had attempted to convince Jefferson that he was mistaken about Black people's biological potential. The most concerted effort to set Jefferson straight was orchestrated by at least two members of the "Société des amis des Noirs" (The Society of Friends of Blacks), the French abolitionist organization founded in 1788 by Jacques-Pierre Brissot de Warville. The campaign to convert Jefferson had begun in February of 1788, when Brissot asked the American to become a member of the Société. Jefferson demurred. In turning this invitation down, Jefferson claimed that it would be inappropriate for him to join for the most noble of reasons. To become a "Friend of the Blacks," he explained, might compromise his ability to speak out effectively against slavery upon his return to the United States.[146]

A far more likely reason that he declined this honor was that he had a fundamental disagreement with one of the Société's founding principles: that Africans possessed the same innate capacities as Europeans or Whites. Jefferson made himself quite clear about this later that same year when he got into a heated argument on this very subject with another member of the Société, the Marquis de Condorcet. According to Jefferson's secretary, who witnessed and recorded highlights of this conversation, his master would not budge from the position he had expressed in the *Notes*: namely, that Black Africans and people of African descent suffered from a series of innate moral, physical, and intellectual liabilities.[147]

Benjamin Bannaker's
PENNSYLVANIA, DELAWARE, MARY-
LAND, AND VIRGINIA
ALMANAC,
FOR THE
YEAR of our LORD 1795;
Being the Third after Leap-Year.

BANNAKER.

—PRINTED FOR—
And Sold by JOHN FISHER, *Stationer*.
BALTIMORE.

FRONTISPIECE OF BENJAMIN BANNEKER'S *ALMANAC*, 1795

Three years later, Jefferson's racism was challenged yet again. This time, however, it was not a French philosopher who confronted him. It was a sixty-year-old free Black man named Benjamin Banneker who, very much like Jefferson himself, was both a prodigy and a polymath. A self-taught mathematician, astronomer, surveyor, and inventor, Banneker had first gained fame for crafting a highly accurate clock made only of wood. His notoriety grew further in the late 1780s when he was hired to survey a large stretch of land along the Potomac River in preparation for the relocation of the future U.S. capital. But it was only after he began publishing an annual *Almanac* (or *Ephemeris*) that combined predictions of the weather, medical advice, calculations related to eclipses and tides, that this member of the "African race," as he called himself, became quite famous.

In the letter he sent to the then–Secretary of State in August 1791, Banneker "cheerfully" presented himself to Jefferson as a living counterexample to the "narrow prejudices" found in the *Notes on the State of Virginia*.[148] He then called upon the author of the Declaration of Independence to abandon his racism and live up to the noble principles of liberty and equality that Jefferson had so eloquently outlined in this same document. It was, as Banneker put it, the sacred "duty" of those who had professed the "rights of human nature" to "extend their power and influence to the relief of every part of the human race."[149] This, however, was not the most forceful moment in the letter. Toward the end of this missive, Banneker laid bare the contradiction between Jefferson's supposed abhorrence of slavery and his own continued involvement in the institution. "[H]ow pitiable is it to reflect . . . that you should at the same time be found guilty of that most criminal act, which you professedly detested in others."[150]

Jefferson sent back a fascinatingly ambiguous response. He began by expressing his profound desire that, one day, it would become obvious that the Black race is, in fact, equal to the White—that Blacks' current "imbecility" would be shown to be the result of the "degraded condition of their existence in both Africa and America."[151] "[N]obody wishes more than I do," he proclaims, "that nature has given to our black brethren, talents equal to those of the other colors of men."[152] Before concluding his letter, in what he clearly hoped would be interpreted as a further gesture of support, Jefferson also informed Banneker that he would be forwarding his almanac to the Marquis de Condorcet, the Secretary of the Paris Royal Academy of Sciences.[153] He then went on to sign his letter with the closing salutation that he would have used with any other "savant": "I am with great esteem, Sir, your most obedient humble servant."[154]

Although this response might seem commendable by eighteenth-century standards, Jefferson conspicuously avoided addressing the charges of hypocrisy leveled against him. Nor did he actually admit that Blacks were the equal of Whites. What the lawyer and statesman had affirmed — very carefully — was that he wished that this would be true.[155]

Perhaps the most telling aspect of Jefferson's letter to Banneker is that he had conveniently outsourced the chore of antiracist advocacy to his French counterpart. This decision may have had ironic consequences. Upon receiving the "Black Astronomer's" almanac from Jefferson, Condorcet doubtless discussed Banneker's abilities (and perhaps shared Banneker's book) with his fellow member of the "Society of Friends of Blacks," Abbé Grégoire. Some years later, when Grégoire compiled a series of short biographies of notable Black authors, scientists, and intellectuals for his influential antiracist work, *De la littérature des nègres* (On the literature of Negroes), he dedicated several paragraphs to Banneker's extraordinary life.[156] This alone would not have bothered Jefferson. But as part of Grégoire's overall indictment of racism, the Frenchman decided to lambast the man who had provided the information on Banneker in the first place: Thomas Jefferson — a writer whom he describes as denying "Negroes the ability of deep reflection, genius, and reason."[157]

Jefferson learned about this rebuke a year later, when Grégoire decided to send a copy of his book to the former American president at Monticello. Jefferson was incensed, although he responded with a cordial note thanking Grégoire for providing him with a chance to observe "the respectable intelligence in that race of men, which cannot fail to have effect in hastening the day of their relief."[158] Several months later, however, Jefferson revealed what he really thought about Grégoire and Banneker in a far more honest letter. Here, Jefferson not only mocked the French abbot for his idiotic "credulity" regarding the supposed intelligence of Africans, but for "gather[ing] up every [positive] story he could of men of color."[159] Jefferson also remarked sardonically that, if Grégoire had been able to identify examples of several intelligent Blacks, it was presumably because these same men and women were of mixed race. It is at this precise point that Jefferson suddenly circled back to his 1791 exchange with Banneker, the only Black man who had challenged his racist views in writing. In retrospect, Jefferson writes, the eloquent letter he had received from Banneker proved nothing; it had clearly come from a "mind of a very common stature."[160]

MONTICELLO, ENGRAVING, 1820

Jefferson's varied pronouncements on race and slavery can often be understood in light of the person to whom he was writing or speaking. Perhaps the most forthright paragraphs that he wrote about race, slavery, and the future of the United States came toward the end of his life, in a letter he sent to the feminist poet and Indian rights activist Lydia Huntley Sigourney.

Sigourney had written Jefferson to congratulate the "sage of Monticello" for providing a "lucid and forcible delineation of the genius of our Aborigines" in his *Notes on the State of Virginia*.[161] In his reply to Sigourney, the eighty-year-old Jefferson laments the fact that the same American Indians that he had hoped to "civilize" in the South had now been displaced and "destroyed" during a recent war. He then adds that the country's treatment of Native Americans is not "the only blot in our moral history."[162] Alluding obliquely to the treatment of the country's Blacks, he sighs that they have even "higher charges to bring against us [Whites]," especially as it related to the ongoing existence of the horrors of chattel slavery. The problem, he explains to Sigourney, is that there is now no way of doing away with the institution. It is a "deplorable entanglement" akin to holding a "wolf by the ears."[163] This telling metaphor perfectly encapsulated Jefferson's thoughts on slavery in the 1820s. As sickening as the institution clearly was to him, he had concluded that the only possible course of action in the current situation was to hold on to it ever tighter.[164]

The following year, in 1825, when yet another woman activist named Frances Wright asked Jefferson to use his considerable influence to help end slavery in the United States, Jefferson sent back yet another pessimistic response about abolition's prospects:

> [W]ith one foot in the grave, and the other uplifted to follow it, I do not permit myself to take part in any new enterprises, even

> for bettering the condition of man, not even in the great one which is the subject of your letter. . . . The march of events has not been such as to render its completion practicable within the limits of time allotted to me; and I leave its accomplishment as the work of another generation.[165]

In his view, if resolving the horror of slavery was even possible, it was a task for the country's children or grandchildren, not its forefathers.

JEFFERSON, PAINTING BY THOMAS SULLY, 1821

Less than a year after writing this letter, Jefferson died quietly at Monticello, surrounded by family and the closest of his enslaved valets. As was the case for John Adams, he expired on July 4, 1826, fifty years to the day after the United States had declared itself into existence. Per his wishes, he was buried the next day in a wooden coffin, presumably made by the carpenter John Hemings.[166] He had instructed that his tombstone list only three accomplishments: that he was the author of the Declaration of American Independence, that he had composed the "Statute of religious freedom for the state of Virginia," and that he had founded the University of Virginia.

Few legacies are as hotly debated as that of this architect, surveyor, inventor, political theorist, partisan of public education, free speech advocate, defender of religious tolerance, diplomat, politician, race theorist, and enslaver. Regarding this last facet of Jefferson's life, the complex set of issues related to his role as an owner of slaves, it is important to recall that the debt that he left behind at his death had an enormous impact on the lives of the enslaved at Monticello. According to Virginia law, insolvent landowners could not free their workers in their will. Indeed, several years after his death, Jefferson's descendants were ultimately obliged to sell his beloved Monticello and its bonded workforce as well (often breaking up families). Some of these enslaved people were taken to auction in Richmond; many more were transported to Louisiana. The only "slaves" to be manumitted during Jefferson's own lifetime were the children or relatives of Sally Hemings, per their 1789 agreement. Sally herself technically remained enslaved, although Martha aka "Patsy" Jefferson allowed her to leave the plantation with two of her sons. By 1830, Sally had declared herself a free White woman on the national census.[167]

Jefferson's many contradictions are difficult to reconcile. Perhaps it is best to conclude that the divergent set of ideas that this inspired wordsmith left behind — in 19,000 letters, in his political writing, and in the *Notes on the State of Virginia* — helped shape the

United States both for the better and for the worse. The best of Jefferson's written legacy incontestably did tremendous good after his death, providing powerful rhetorical fodder for both Abraham Lincoln's antislavery crusade and, in the twentieth century, Martin Luther King's "I Have a Dream" speech. Whatever Jefferson's own views may have been about Blacks themselves, the United States *needed* to have a Founding Father to have said what Jefferson said about universal principles.[168]

The so-called worst of Jefferson — his race-based views — have an equally long legacy.[169] Indeed, in the same decade that Abraham Lincoln was praising Jefferson as a champion of liberty, proslavery advocates eagerly quoted his virulent racist beliefs to justify the notion of Blacks' biological inferiority and, by extension, their supposed suitability for enslavement.

Scrutiny of Jefferson's acts and ideas has reached a new level in recent years. Yet twenty-first-century scholars and activists are not the first to confront the contradictions of his legacy. Nineteenth-century abolitionist Frederick Douglass, who battled both slavery and the race-based thinking that saturated American life, recognized that Jefferson's influence cut both ways. While Douglass acknowledged that Jefferson had labeled "slavery an evil," he also reminded the public that the third president of the United States "entertained a rather low estimate of the Negro's mental ability."[170] Jefferson, alas, would not have disagreed. Like many of his peers, he had accepted the racialization of humanity — particularly the degradation of Black Africans — as fact. Worse yet, Jefferson had woven this dangerous idea into the fabric of a new nation.

EPILOGUE

ENTER THE ANTIRACISTS

Judging from the enthusiasm that often shined through their prose, the race theorists in this book thought themselves on a thrilling adventure. The nineteenth-century French writer, Arthur de Gobineau, understood the power of this endeavor better than most. Race, he believed, had the seductive power to explain *everything*. It could divide unequivocally, dehumanize politically, degrade aesthetically, and it could also label colonized peoples as suitable for enslavement or civilization.[1] By the twentieth century, many of the same ideas praised by Gobineau reached their inevitable conclusion: policies of segregation, sterilization, and genocide.

Most people's first reaction to this long history is understandably moral condemnation. The undergraduates I have had in my History of Race classes are particularly keen on separating themselves intellectually and psychologically from these earlier "unenlightened" eras. One of my students, who was eager to distance herself from the horrors of Enlightenment-era racism, asked the following question: "How hard would it have been for me, as an average literate European living in London, Paris, Madrid, or Stockholm in 1800, to reject the increasingly widespread concept of race?" Before I could answer, another member of the class calmly announced that she would have been *antiracist* from birth, even if she had been born in Liverpool at the height of the slave trade. Both wanted other members of the seminar to know that, had they been alive during the eighteenth or early nineteenth century, they would not have been one of the "villains" described in this book.

"Would I have been a racist or an antiracist in Jefferson's era?" might seem like a futile debate topic. Nonetheless, each year I encourage students to try to answer this same question by looking at the most commonly accepted "anthropological" theories of the eighteenth century. It inevitably becomes a sobering exercise. Students are generally distressed to conclude that for many or perhaps even most Europeans living in 1820, denying the notion of race was probably as unthinkable as rejecting another invisible early modern truth: the theory of *gravity*. Yet, as I always try to reassure them, *history certainly demonstrates that combatting such ideas was possible*. In fact, antiracism, like race itself, began in the eighteenth century.

A complete history of antiracist writing, which would include the contributions of both religious and secular thinkers, is beyond the scope of this already lengthy book. Suffice it to say that such efforts emerged within the broader currents of antislavery activism.[2] This was particularly true after the 1770s, when writers such as Anthony Benezet in North America, Denis Diderot and the Marquis de Condorcet in France, and Thomas Clarkson and Granville Sharp in Britain recognized that to effectively oppose slavery, they needed to challenge the race-based ideas being used to justify it. The most compelling arguments directed against the new idea of race during this time, however, were not put forward by well-intentioned White activists. They were published by Black writers who had forced themselves into the public sphere.

Black Africans and Black people of African descent had been the first to be racialized. They were also the first "non-European" group that, on a large scale, responded to the new construction of race in writing. To be a Black author was to challenge the very foundation of racist ideology by way of *counterexample*. The proslavery lobby was only too aware of this "threat" to their worldview. Accordingly, virtually every time a Black writer published a book, the bigoted proponents of slavery quickly claimed that the author in question was simply imitating (or had been helped by) a White person, thereby undermining the validity of the work.

This was precisely why the title of the most explicitly antiracist book of the era was titled *De la littérature des nègres*.[3] Across the book's 285 pages, Abbé Grégoire emphasized the literary capabilities of a number of the era's best-known Black authors, among them Anton Wilhelm Amo (c. 1703–1759), a philosophy professor who taught in several Prussian universities; Ignatius Sancho (1729–1780), a composer and author of biting abolitionist letters that circulated throughout Europe; Phillis Wheatley (1753–1784), a formerly enslaved domestic in Boston who became a sensation after she published the first book of "African-American" poetry; Ottobah Cugoano (1751–1791), the Ghana-born moral philosopher and abolitionist who was the first formerly enslaved writer to publish a short account of his life; and Francis Williams (c. 1690 – c. 1770), the Cambridge University graduate whose prodigious talents as a mathematician and astronomer would presumably have earned him a place within the Royal Society, had he not been voted down on account of his complexion.[4]

The most influential and famous writer activist cited by Grégoire, however, was the formerly enslaved sailor, London-based abolitionist, and self-published autobiographer Gustavus Vassa, also known as Olaudah Equiano (c. 1745–1797). Equiano's astonishing autobiography—a personal account of a man whose entire life had been determined by the theories of race circulating at the time—was the most effective rebuttal of race and slavery written during the eighteenth century. It is no exaggeration to say that the book marked the beginning of a new era of antiracism.[5]

OLAUDAH EQUIANO, FRONTISPIECE FOR
THE INTERESTING NARRATIVE, ENGRAVING, 1789

For several years before publishing his book, Equiano had been sparring in the press with the racist proponents of slavery. Knowing full well that these same people would claim that he was not the author of his book, Equiano chose the following title:

> *The Interesting Narrative of the Life of Olaudah Equiano, Or Gustavus Vassa, the African*. Written by himself

Much to the proslavery lobby's chagrin, Equiano's autobiography turned out to be a resounding success. By May of 1789, he was distributing hundreds of copies to prepaid subscribers in London, while also selling additional books at seven shillings apiece from his apartment at number 10 Union Street.[6] Within five years, he had commissioned eight more press runs from his printers to keep up with demand. He also became extremely well-known — the first Black man to embark on a book tour, traveling across England, and to Scotland, Wales, and Ireland.

Whether speaking to audiences in public or through the pages of his book, Equiano demanded engagement from his White audiences. To listen to or read Equiano was to confront the unspeakable scenes of horror that were common in Caribbean slave colonies: the rape of children, bloodthirsty overseers cutting off human ears, or slaves beaten until their "bones were broken," as he put it, "for even letting a pot boil over."[7]

Equiano's first-person account transformed slavery from an abstract concept into a lived reality. It was with this in mind that he related his own story, which begins in a remote village in the Kingdom of Benin (Nigeria), roughly 200 miles north of the Bight of Biafra. The Africa he describes here is anything but the backward and impious terra incognita often conjured up in the era's sensationalist travelogues. Writing at times like an ethnographer, Equiano captures the complexities of life in an Igbo community — the strict moral codes, the significance of *scarification*, the practice of polygamy, and the political structure. On a more personal note, he recalls being his mother's favorite child (of seven) and the son of a prominent elder, or chief, within a small community of craftspeople, musicians, poets, dancers, farmers, and medicine men. Most of his days, he remembers, were spent training to be a warrior by playing with javelins.[8]

The only true source of West Africa's "liabilities," Equiano makes clear, lies in the insatiable demand for human cargo created by European traders. At around eleven years old, he himself was swept up into this transatlantic economy when two "kidnappers" scaled the walls of his village and overpowered him and his sister. Bound, gagged, and sold to a succession of local "merchants and travelers," the two children were eventually separated on their journey to the coast. On what he knew to be his last day in Africa, Equiano was rowed through the surf to a slave ship anchored in Bonny Bay. There, as both witness and victim, he confronted the full brutality of the Middle Passage: the stench, the screams, the iron clamps, the floggings—the horror of hundreds of chained people confined below deck.

If the early part of his story allowed Equiano to advocate for those captives who suffered "under the lash of tyranny" in the New World, much of his narrative also takes aim at the racialized justification for enslavement.[9] The most effective part of this counterargument is how his own life unfolded. When the ship carrying Equiano arrived in Barbados, Equiano was theoretically destined to spend the rest of his (presumably short) life working on a sugar plantation somewhere on the island. Yet in a strange twist of fate, he remained unsold at auction and was ultimately "trans-shipped" on a small sloop to be sold in England's colony in Virginia.

Arriving in port somewhere along the Potomac River, perhaps

100 miles or so from where the fourteen-year-old Thomas Jefferson was growing up, Equiano was purchased by a British naval officer named Michael Henry Pascal. It is at this point that the now-twelve-year-old boy began a long life at sea working alternatively as valet, "deck slave," "powder monkey," clerk, and, eventually, business agent.

Equiano was far from the only enslaved African serving on British ships in the 1750s and 1760s. Yet his status and his trajectory were highly unusual. For one, in an era where the baptism of English slaves was very much discouraged—the status of Christian conferred upon Blacks certain legal rights—Equiano was allowed to take this sacrament in 1759. Even more uncommon, when shipping dropped off during the Seven Years War, he was sent to school in London to learn how to read and write.

Equiano's ability to express himself in writing—a skill that he clearly cultivated—later allowed him to negotiate and refute the supposed racial divide between White and Black. By the time that he published his book in the 1780s, he knew that many people in Europe were saying that Africans had black blood and bile; that they were members of a separate "apelike" human species unrelated to Whites; that they, like the Sámi and Amerindians, were "stuck" in a primitive stage of being, occupying the lowest rung in a racial hierarchy. The worst and most threatening racist ideas that Equiano confronted in London had been disseminated by Edward Long in his 1774 *History of Jamaica*. From Long's point of view, Blacks were members of an entirely separate, lice-infested, unthinking, unfeeling species of humans. Not even the most loathsome of Equiano's former enslavers had thought or said such a thing.

Combating this and all such race-based ideas became a necessary but often overlooked part of Equiano's autobiography. On several occasions, he was obliged, incredibly enough, to assert that he and all other members of his "sable race" were also members of the human species. Drawing on both the universalism of the Bible and environmentalist notions advanced by Buffon and Blumenbach, this proud and pious Christian contends that there is but one human race, and that human pigmentation is merely a surface effect of the environment.[10] Elsewhere, he mocks the widely held notion that Europe's technological superiority stems from some sort of innate intellectual advantage. Putting forward his own version of "stage theory," he declares: "Let the polished and haughty European recollect that his ancestors were once, like the Africans, uncivilized, and even barbarous."[11] Indeed, Equiano's very existence challenged the logic of racial determinism — especially the spurious belief that Black people were somehow trapped in a primitive and pre-civilized phase of being. How credible could such a theory be when he himself "jumped" from a "rude state" to a theoretically "higher" stage after a few months in school?[12]

The success of Equiano's narrative was not only groundbreaking in its own right; it served as a precursor to the powerful wave of antiracist "slave narratives" that emerged throughout the late eighteenth and into the nineteenth century. Writers such as the formerly enslaved Frederick Douglass, Mary Prince, and Solomon Northup followed in Equiano's footsteps, demonstrating conclusively that the intellectual and emotional depth of Black individuals was far beyond what figures such as Thomas Jefferson had been willing to acknowledge.

The ability of these Black writers to define themselves within the constraints of a race-based society — what Henry Louis Gates Jr. has recently called "the black box" — underscores one of the great ironies of the Enlightenment.[13] Although philosophers such as David Hume, Immanuel Kant, and Voltaire remain synonymous with the era, it was actually marginalized figures such as Equiano who truly embodied the era's ideals of progress, human rights, and universal equality. These men and women, rather than the intellectual giants of the Enlightenment, are perhaps the true heirs of the era's aspirations. Unsurprisingly, they are also the thinkers with whom many people now tend to identify.

ACKNOWLEDGMENTS

I am profoundly grateful to a group of remarkable scholars, colleagues, and friends whose insights and expertise helped shape this project. The people who have peered most deeply into the book, and to whom I am the most indebted, include Jennifer Mayo Curran, Anne Duthoit, John Eigenauer, Daniel Glickman, Thierry Hoquet, Meredith Martin, and Adrian Peoples. As has been the case for virtually every project I have undertaken, I also want to extend special thanks to Patrick Lebicé-Graille.

Other generous souls who advised or helped me in various ways include Mary Allen, Linda Andersson Burnett, Debby Applegate, Sophie Audidière, Robert Bernasconi, Elizabeth Bobrick, Wolfgang Böker, Beatrix Briggs, Marisol Calderon Gonzalez, Robert Cheetham, Andrew Clark, Nicholas Cronk, Bill Curran, Carolyn Curran, Surekha Davies, Madeleine Dobie, Hamilton dos Santos, Jane Edwards, Fadi Elsaid, Jeffrey Freedman, Amity Gaige, Henry Louis Gates Jr., Antonio González, Paul Halliday, Hanna Hodacs, Rana Hogarth, Katja Kolcio, Anne Lafont, Typhaine Leservot, Hua-ping Lu-Adler, Walter and Anne Mayo, Michael Meere, Jennifer Mensch, William Max Nelson, Erick Noël, Christy Pichichero,

Dennis Rasmussen, Carolyn Roberts, Meghan Roberts, Charles Salas, Silvia Sebastiani, Joanna Stalnaker, Ying Jia Tan, Kate Tunstall, and Courtney Weiss-Smith.

I am also deeply grateful to a group of individuals who generously answered my questions, provided valuable bibliographical references, or were willing to point out where I was moving in the wrong direction. Thank you, Michael Armstrong-Roche, Jean-Baptiste Aurran, Bruce Bachan, Meredeth Belden, Karine Bénac, Chantal and Jean-Philippe Bernasconi, Jacqueline Charles, John Charles, Robert Conn, Liana DeMarco, Alex Dupuy, Peter Gottschalk, Julia Landwebber, Liza McAllister, Alison Muir, Sue Peabody, Vijay Pinch, Michael Roth, Nicholas Rupke, Kari Weil, and the late great Louis Lapham.

I would also like to express my gratitude to the librarians at Wesleyan University, especially Tess Goodman and Amanda Nelson. Over the past few years, I have also been helped by the excellent research librarians at numerous institutions, among them Yale University, Brown University, the Bibliothèque nationale de France, the Wellcome Collection, the Library of Congress, the Château de Versailles, and the Archives Municipales de Bordeaux. Additionally, I would like to extend special thanks to the incredibly knowledgeable guides and curators who welcomed me into some of the "spaces" once occupied by some of the "characters" in this book: especially Alicia Leclercq at Buffon's house in Montbard; Dinah Nicholas at Jean-Baptiste Labat's *habitation*, the Fonds Saint-Jacques in Martinique, and Anna Backman at Linnaeus's respective houses in Stockholm and at Hammarby. The kindness and knowledge provided by these people added a rich layer to my research.

In addition, I would like to recognize the individuals and institutions whose generous financial support made this extensive project possible, among them Nicole Stanton and Roger Grant of Academic Affairs at Wesleyan University; the Catharine and Thomas McMahon Memorial Fund, the School for Advanced Research in Santa Fe, the Instructing Natural History Research Group of Uppsala, the Fondazione 1563 per l'Arte e la Cultura of Turin, Wesleyan's College of the Environment, and the Valmont de Bomare Research Consortium. Their belief in the importance of this work and their commitment to supporting scholarly pursuits have been vital to its completion.

Finally, I am once again deeply indebted to the wonderful team at Other Press for their steadfast support of this project from its inception. My heartfelt thanks go to Judith Gurewich, as well as to Yvonne Cárdenas, Alex Poreda, Lauren Shekari, Brianna Caszatt, and Julie Fry. I am equally grateful to my agent, Simon Lipskar at Writers House, for his guidance and encouragement during this process.

NOTES

PROLOGUE

1. See Marie-Ève Thérenty and Adeline Wrona, eds., *Objets insignes, objets infâmes de la littérature* (Paris: EAC, 2018), 66–61. Wrona writes that while the criteria for selection often seemed haphazard, "the philosophers of the Enlightenment disappeared massively."

2. For an excellent survey of the various debates related to race and slavery in the early modern era (including those related to natural slavery), see Julia Jorati, *Slavery and Race: Philosophical Debates in the Sixteenth and Seventeenth Centuries* (Oxford: Oxford University Press, 2024), 203.

3. In England, for example, it is estimated that 30 percent of the women were literate in 1700 and 40 percent of the men. This rose to approximately 65 percent by 1825. See D. F. McKenzie et al., *The Cambridge History of the Book in Britain* (Cambridge: Cambridge University Press, 1999), 4:17–18.

4. The eighteenth-century scholar Lynn Festa came up with this concept.

5. Other European figures could also have represented the legal and judicial aspects of race construction during this era, among them King Charles of Spain or Humphrey Walrond, the governor of Barbados.

6. Voltaire, *Complete Works of Voltaire*, Nicholas Cronk et al., eds. (Oxford: Liverpool University Press, Voltaire Foundation, 2001), 1a:383.

1. LOUIS XIV: KING OF THE SLAVES

1. For an excellent survey of daily life at Versailles, see Guy Walton, *Louis XIV's Versailles* (Chicago: Chicago University Press, 1986).

2. The music of Jean-Baptiste Lully was favored in the court of Versailles and left a monumental impression on the French Baroque style for the rest of *le Grand Siècle*. See John Hadju Heyer, *The Lure and Legacy of Music at Versailles: Louis XIV and the Aix School* (Cambridge: Cambridge University Press, 2014), 7.

3. James Eugene Farmer, *Versailles and the Court Under Louis XIV* (New York: The Century Company, 1906), 170.

4. Norman Davies, *Europe: A History* (Oxford: Oxford University Press, 1996), 618.

5. See Guillaume Lelièvre, *Les Précurseurs de la Compagnie française des Indes orientales* (Caen: Presses universitaires de Caen, 2021), 16. Louis XIII had also delegated the task of managing the colonies to Richelieu who, in turn, created trading companies to which he deputized the headaches of managing a colony. See Helen Dewar, "Government by Trading Company?: The Corporate Legal Status of the Company of New France and Colonial Governance," *Nuevo Mundo, Mundos Nuevos* (2018): 11.

6. René Plissonneau-Duquêne, *Un Essai de contingentement d'importation au XVII*e *siècle* (Paris: Recueil Sirey, 1935), 15. Theoretically, the taxable proceeds that the crown would levy on French tobacco and sugar as it came into French ports would provide the income necessary to finance a significant expansion of colonization of the enormous territory of New France. See also Paul Butel, *Histoire des Antilles françaises* (Paris: Perrin, 2007), 35.

7. Long an important crop for Amerindians, tobacco became a profitable and habit-forming European commodity (whether chewed, smoked, or inhaled as snuff) by the 1540s, when the Spanish began exporting it throughout the world. Eighty or so years later, this monopoly had disappeared. The Dutch were producing tobacco in Brazil; the English were planting large crops in Virginia and in Barbados; and the French were also harvesting relatively large quantities of the crop in Guadeloupe and Martinique. See Butel, *Histoire des Antilles françaises*, 27.

8. In the mid-1670s, when the comparable British colony of Barbados was at the peak of its sugar-based prosperity, it boasted a population of approximately 21,500 White people, free and indentured. See Jerome S. Handler and Matthew C. Reilly, "Contesting 'White Slavery' in the Caribbean: Enslaved Africans and European Indentured Servants in Seventeenth Century Barbados," *New West Indian Guide* 91, no. 1/2 (2017): 33.

9. Some of these *engagés* also came from cities linked to these same cities by river. For a discussion of the relative cost of *engagés* versus that of African

captives, see Frédéric Régent, *La France et ses esclaves de la colonisation aux abolitions, 1620–1848* (Paris: Grasset, 2007), 26.

10. Creating order out of a chaotic situation had fallen to Richelieu. In 1626, the famous Cardinal formed the trading company, the Compagnie de Saint-Christophe, with the specific mission of undermining and assailing Spanish holdings and shipping in the region. See Butel, *Histoire des Antilles françaises*, 27 and 36. See also Brian Brazeau, *Writing a New France, 1604–1632: Empire and Early Modern French Identity* (Oxfordshire, UK: Taylor and Francis, 2016), 15.

11. It is said that the smell of tobacco repelled these same vipers. See Henry de Lalung, *Le Serpent de la Martinique* (Paris: Corbière, 1934), 55.

12. It was not just the dangers associated with sugar that had driven off the indentured servants, however. Colbert and the king had inadvertently contributed to this trend by granting huge tracts of land to well-capitalized investors and aristocrats. They had also pushed island administrators to facilitate the consolidation of small tobacco properties into much more extensive *sucreries*, the result being that land prices shot up to such an extent by the 1670s that newer *engagés* felt shut out from the prospect of acquiring their own small farms. See Philip P. Boucher, *France and the American Tropics to 1700: Tropics of Discontent?* (Baltimore: Johns Hopkins University Press, 2008), 212.

13. Jacques Petitjean Roget, "Les Femmes des colons à la Martinique au XVIe et XVIIe siècles," *Revue d'histoire de l'Amérique française* 9, no. 2 (1955): 204. See also Françoise Vergés, *Le Ventre des femmes. Capitalisme, racialisation, féminisme* (Paris: Albin Michel, 2017).

14. Unlike earlier French trading companies, this successor to the French West India Company allowed independent ship owners to participate in the trade — a departure from typical mercantilist policies that favored state-controlled monopolies. During this time, the crown also provided a cash bonus for each "Negro" delivered to the islands alive. For a complete history of incentives, e.g., tax exemptions, bonuses, see Régent, *La France et ses esclaves*, 42.

15. Anne Pérotin-Dumon, *La Ville aux îles, la ville dans l'île. Basse-Terre et Pointe-à-Pitre, Guadeloupe, 1650–1820* (Paris: Éditions Karthala, 2000), 15. See also Jean-Pierre Sainton, *Histoire et civilisation de la Caraïbe: Guadeloupe, Martinique, Petites Antilles. Le Temps des matrices: Économie et cadres sociaux du long XVIIIe siècle* (Paris: Éditions Karthala, 2012), 2:287.

16. Richard S. Dunn, "The Barbados of 1680: Profile of the Richest Colony in English America," *The William and Mary Quarterly* 26, no. 1 (1969): 7, 18.

17. See James A. Rawley and Stephen D. Behrendt for an assessment of the economics of the slave trade, including the "costs of goods, shipping fees, commissions insurance, crew, and losses by mortality." *The Transatlantic Slave Trade: A History* (Lincoln: University of Nebraska Press, 2007), 227.

18. Letter to M. D'Argouges, premier président à Rennes. November 6, 1670, in *Lettres, instructions et mémoires de Colbert, publiés par Pierre Clément. Industrie, commerce* (Paris: Imprimerie impériale, 1863), 2:577.

19. Centre des Archives d'Outre-Mer, C8A 1, November 20, 1672. Cited in Boucher, *France and the American Tropics*, 281.

20. Sue Peabody, *There Are No Slaves in France* (Oxford: Oxford University Press, 1996), 12.

21. Cited in Keila Grinberg and Sue Peabody, eds., *Free Soil in the Atlantic World* (Oxfordshire, UK: Taylor & Francis, 2016), 26.

22. Meredith Martin and Gillian Weiss, *The Sun King at Sea: Maritime Art and Galley Slavery in Louis XIV's France* (Los Angeles: J. Paul Getty Trust, 2022), 1–3, 174.

23. André Zysberg, *Les Galériens: Vies et destins de 60.000 forçats sur les galères de France 1680–1748* (Paris: Seuil, 1991), 66. The minister at the time was Louis II Phélypeaux de Pontchartrain.

24. Laurent Busseau, "Sur les traces du galérien iroquois Ouréhouaré: Nouvelle analyse des archives du XVIIe siècle," *Histoire Québec* 22, no. 3 (2017): 11–14.

25. Pierre Duval, *Le Monde, ou La Géographie Universelle* (Paris: n.p. 1676), 137.

26. See Henry Louis Gates Jr. and Andrew S. Curran, *Who's Black and Why? A Hidden Chapter from the Eighteenth-Century Invention of Race* (Cambridge: Harvard University Press, 2022), x–xi, for a discussion of the etymology of this and other words associated both with blackness and Africa.

27. Allada was a coastal kingdom that is today part of Benin.

28. See Christina Brauner, "To Be the Key for Two Coffers: A West African Embassy to France (1670/1)," *IFRA-Nigeria E-Papers Series* 30 (2013): 13.

29. Louis and Lopes ultimately came to agreement on a short-lived trade agreement that, from the French point of view at least, gave France sovereignty over the region. This desire to exert French influence in Africa gave rise to several other visits from West African dignitaries as well. Ibid., 20.

30. Other foreign visitors to Versailles, while uncommon, generated much attention among nobles, indulging the French taste for the exotic. Among these were ambassadors from Siam, Persia, and the Ottoman Empire. See Meredith Martin, "Special Embassies and Overseas Visitors" in *Visitors to Versailles: From Louis XIV to the French Revolution*, eds. Daniëlle Kisluk-Grosheide and Bertrand Rondot (New York: Metropolitan Museum of Art, 2018), 108, 110.

31. Ibid., 114.

32. Phillipe Halbert, "An African Prince at the Court of the Sun King," *The Monitor: Journal of International Studies* 16, no. 2 (Summer 2011): 14.

33. Ibid., 12.

34. Stefan Goodwin, *Africa in Europe: Volume Two: Interdependencies, Relocations, and Globalization* (Lanham: Lexington Books, 2009), 2:22.

35. See Anne Lafont, *L'Art et la race: L'Africain (tout) contre l'oeil des Lumières* (Dijon: Les Presses du réel, 2019), 45–53, for a discussion of how these enslaved children were represented in seventeenth- and eighteenth-century European painting.

36. Serge Aroles, "L'Énigme de la fille noire de Louis XIV résolue par les archives? La 'Mauresse de Moret', ca. 1675–1731" (n.p., 2007), 1.

37. According to Saint-Simon, the nun supposedly said that the dauphin was "my brother." Other than this anecdote, there are no documents that might clearly confirm her high birth. See Henri Louis Duclos, *Madame de La Vallière et Marie-Thérèse d'Autriche, femme de Louis XIV, avec pièces et documents inédits* (Paris: Didier, 1869), 2:978.

38. Ibid., 5.

39. The slave-based colonies of the Lesser Antilles were not the first settlements to experience the demographic boom that led to slave laws. As early as the sixteenth century, African slaves in the Spanish empire and in Brazil far outnumbered their so-called masters. See *General History of the Caribbean: The Slave Societies of The Caribbean*, ed. Franklin W. Knight (London: Unesco, 1997), 3:86.

40. Blénac to Colbert, September 5, 1678. See Etienne Taillemite, *Inventaire analytique de la correspondance générale avec les colonies*, 1959. Départ. Série B, déposée aux Archives nationales: Registres 1 à 37, 1654–1715.

41. Giuseppe Patisso and Fausto Ermete Carbone, "Slavery and Slave Codes in Overseas Empires," in *Modern Slavery and Human Trafficking*, ed. Jane Reeves (London: Intechopen, 2021), 44.

42. *Memoires of the First Settlement of Barbados* (1743), reproduced in P. F. Campbell, *Some Early Barbadian History* (St. Michael, Barbados, 1993), 208. See also Edward B. Rugemer, "The Development of Mastery and Race in the Comprehensive Slave Codes of the Greater Caribbean during the Seventeenth Century," *The William and Mary Quarterly* 70, no. 3 (July 2013): 433.

43. Patisso and Carbone, "Slavery and Slave Codes in Overseas Empires," 45–48.

44. Vernon Valentine Palmer, "The Origins and Authors of the Code Noir," *Louisiana Law Review* 56 no. 2 (Winter 1996): 367. My translation.

45. For a summary of Patoulet's career, see Céline Melisson, "Jean-Baptiste Patoulet, un administrateur au service de l'empire français," *Nuevo Mundo, Mundos Nuevos* (2018), https://doi.org/10.4000/nuevomundo.74810.

46. Butel, *Histoire des Antilles françaises*, 62.

47. Ibid., 59, 61–62.

48. Palmer, "The Origins and Authors of the Code Noir," 374.

49. Ibid.

50. Ibid., 378.

51. Ibid.

52. Jacob Soll, *The Information Master: Jean-Baptiste Colbert's Secret State Intelligence System* (Ann Arbor: University of Michigan Press, 2009), 153. Louis had become "irritated with this harbinger of bad news, and his all-too-clear information updates on the state of French politics, finance, and industry."

53. Her real name was Françoise d'Aubigné.

54. This was a so-called morganatic marriage: one where the king's and Maintenon's respective ranks precluded any possibility of her becoming queen.

55. See Mark Bryant, "'Romancing the Throne': Madame de Maintenon's Journey from Secret Royal Governess to Louis XIV's Clandestine Consort, 1652–84," *Court Historian* 22, no. 2 (2017): 2–4.

56. Philip F. Riley, "Louis XIV: Watchdog of Parisian Morality," *The Historian* 36, no. 1 (1973): 19–33, 21.

57. R. Père Mongin: Lettre du 20 décembre 1678, ms. no. 2459, Bibliothèque municipale de Carcassone. Cited in Gérard Lafleur, "Les Juifs aux îles françaises du vent (XVIIe–XVIIIe siècles)," *Bulletin de la Société d'Histoire de la Guadeloupe* no. 65–66 (3rd–4th trimester, 1985): 77.

58. In all, c. 1,600 Jews had been expelled from Brazil before the Inquisition's priests arrived. The Jewish community was allowed to take their money and, in some cases, their slaves with them. Most of these refugees simply returned to Holland; a handful even settled in New Amsterdam (New York City). See Mordehay Arbell, *The Jewish Nation of the Caribbean: The Spanish-Portuguese Jewish Settlements in the Caribbean and the Guianas* (Jerusalem: Gefen Publishing House, 2002), 130.

59. This population, Colbert knew, had had a tremendously positive effect on the island's economy; in addition to passing on many of the technological secrets related to sugarcane production that had been perfected in Brazil, they and the other Dutch colonists who had also come from Brazil invested heavily

in both sugar plantations and warehouses. One of these Jewish settlers, Benjamin d'Acosta de Andrade, had created two of the larger sugar plantations on Martinique and had even established the first cacao-processing facility in the entire French Caribbean. See Celia D. Shapiro, "Nation of Nowhere: Jewish Role in Colonial American Chocolate History," in *Chocolate History, Culture, and Heritage* (Hoboken, NJ: Wiley, 2009), 54. See also Gérard Lafleur, "Les Juifs aux îles françaises du vent," 114–155.

60. Jacques Savary, *Le Parfait négociant, ou Instruction générale pour ce qui regarde le commerce* (Paris: chez Jean Guignard, 1675), 139–140.

61. Jean-François Melon, David Bindon, trans., *A Political Essay upon Commerce Written in French by Monsieur M**** (Dublin: printed for Philip Crampton, 1738), 81.

62. The most telling example of this phenomenon is related to race mixing. Expressly forbidden in later versions of the *Code*, *métissage* became the hallmark of the French Caribbean. See Doris L. Garraway, *The Libertine Colony: Creolization in the Early French Caribbean* (Durham, NC: Duke University Press, 2005), 263–266.

63. This was known as *Partus sequitur ventrem*, which means "offspring follows the womb."

64. By 1704, officials in the small colony of Cayenne (French Guiana) also voted to accept the slave guidelines.

65. Palmer, "The Origins and Authors of the Code Noir," 389.

66. James Falkner, *The War of Spanish Succession* (South Yorkshire, UK: Pen and Sword Military, 2015), 212.

67. See https://www.slavevoyages.org/voyage/database#tables, accessed June 12, 2024.

68. Sara E. Melzer and Kathryn Norberg, *From the Royal to the Republican Body: Incorporating the Political in Seventeenth- and Eighteenth-Century France* (Berkeley: University of California Press, 1998), 113.

II. JEAN-BAPTISTE LABAT: THE PRIESTLY ETHNOGRAPHER

1. Labat's memoir of his experience was first published in 1722 as the *Nouveau voyage aux îsles de l'Amérique* (Paris: chez Guillaume Cavelier, 1722). In this chapter, I will be citing the (shorter but still very complete) modern edition edited by Michel Le Bris, which is based on the 1732 edition: *Voyage aux Isles* (Lonrai: Phébus libretto, 2001).

2. *Papers of the New Haven Colony History Society* (New Haven: Printed for the Society, 1900), 6:241. The infestation of yellow-fever-infected mosquitos became so prevalent on Martinique in 1693 that an invasion by the English ship captain Sir Francis Wheeler was beaten back, in part, when the majority of his men died from the virus.

3. The Dominicans did not have monks in their order; hence their residences were called *convents* not *monasteries*.

4. Labat, *Voyage*, 21.

5. Ibid., 22–23.

6. Ibid., 34.

7. Ibid., 34–38.

8. Alwyn Scarth, *La Catastrophe: The Eruption of Mount Pelée, the Worst Volcanic Disaster of the 20th Century* (Oxford: Oxford University Press, 2002), 184. There were several other survivors, many of whom died soon after the eruption.

9. Ibid., 34.

10. Ibid.

11. Ibid., 65.

12. This was very much like the Jesuits, who founded their first plantation just north of Saint-Pierre for this purpose in the 1640s. See Steve Lenik, "Mission Plantations, Space, and Social Control: Jesuits as Planters in French Caribbean Colonies and Frontiers," *Journal of Social Archaeology* 12, no. 1 (2012): 57.

13. The governor was Jacques Dyel du Parquet; his widow was Marie Bonnard du Parquet. The land grant took place in 1658. See Jean-Bapiste Du Tertre, *Histoire générale des Antilles habitées par les François* (Paris: chez Thomas Jolly, 1667), 2:435.

14. Labat, *Voyage*, 48.

15. Ibid., 49.

16. Ibid.

17. Bertie Mandelblatt, "Atlantic Consumption of French Rum and Brandy and Economic Growth in the Seventeenth- and Eighteenth-Century Caribbean," *French History* 25, no. 1 (2011): 15–17. The expulsion of Dutch sugar planters from Brazil in 1654 resulted in a boom of sugar refinery and a new understanding of distillation in the Caribbean.

18. On the eve of the French Revolution, sugar production at the Fond Saint-Jacques had risen to the point that the *habitation* had more than 500 enslaved workers living on the property. This information comes from the director of the Fonds Saint-Jacques, Dinah Nicolas, during a visit in 2021. See also Jean

Benoist, *Chronique d'un lieu de pensée. Fonds Saint-Jacques, Martinique* (Motoury: Ibis Rouge Éditions, 2015).

19. See Bris's preface, "Un Sacré bonhomme," in Labat, *Voyage*, 11.

20. Marcel Chatillon, "Le Père Labat à travers ses manuscrits," *Bulletin de la Société d'Histoire de la Guadeloupe* no. 40–42 (1979): 172.

21. Ibid., 35.

22. Jean-Baptiste Labat, *Nouvelle relation de l'Afrique occidentale* (Paris: chez Guillaume Cavelier, 1729), 1:i.

23. It was hardly a surprise that, fatigued from the two-month voyage, and now stuck in Cadiz for what would turn out to be several months, from the first moment he set foot in Europe, he sought to return to the Caribbean. Jean-Baptiste Labat, *Voyages du P. Labat de l'ordre des FF. Prêcheurs, en Espagne et en Italie* (Paris: Jean-Baptiste et Charles Delespine, 1730), 1:2.

24. Jean-Baptiste Labat, *Voyages du P. Labat de l'ordre des FF. Prêcheurs, en Espagne et en Italie* (Paris: Jean-Baptiste et Charles Delespine, 1730), 2:1.

25. For the history of this ministerial family, see Sara E. Chapman, *Private Ambitions and Political Alliances: The Phélypeaux de Pontchartrain Family and Louis XIV's Government 1650–1715* (Rochester: University of Rochester Press, 2004), 22–25.

26. Letter from Michon, November 10, 1706, *Archives nationales des Colonies* C8 A16. Cited in *Revue d'histoire des missions* (Paris: Les Amis des missions, 1926), 3:226.

27. "Extraits de lettres reçues des Îles d'Amérique," Vaucresson and the Governor M. De Machault, *Archives nationales d'Outre-Mer*, COL C8 B No. 89, February 8, 1708.

28. Volume des ordres du Roi de 1708. Cited in *Revue d'histoire des missions*, 3:147.

29. This was due to the intervention of the Maître Antonin Cloche, the head of the Dominican order in Bologna, who esteemed the disgraced priest and obtained permission for him to come to Italy. Jules Rennard, *Le P. Labat O.P. aux Antilles* (Paris: Editions Spes, 1927), 27.

30. This is where the so-called Jacobins, including Robespierre, met during the French Revolution.

31. Labat, *Voyage*, xxxiii. The *New Voyage* would presumably have appeared in English as well — the British readership loved travelogues as much as anybody — but Labat's book was not only filled with anti-English sentiment; it described English slave colonies as little more than murder prisons.

32. *The Present State of the Republick of Letters for July, 1729* (London: William Innys, 1729), 402.

33. Labat drew heavily from Jean-Baptiste Du Tertre, *Histoire générale des Antilles habitées par les François*. See Christina Kullberg, *Lire l'Histoire générale des Antilles de J.-B. Du Tertre* (Leiden and Boston: Brill Rodopi, 2021), 41, for a discussion of the differences between the two "Caribbeanists."

34. Hilary McDonald Beckles, "Kalinago (Carib) Resistance to European Colonization of the Caribbean," *Caribbean Quarterly* 54, no. 4 (2008): 81, no. 14.

35. Labat, *Voyage*, 121.

36. Ibid., 132.

37. Du Tertre had said that widespread cannibalism had taken place during this era. Labat also downplays some of the mythology associated with the Kalinago, contradicting rumors that they were ferocious cannibals: "I know that it is true that in the beginning [of colonization], when the French and the English established themselves in the islands, several people from [these two European] nations were killed, cooked, and eaten . . . but it was an unusual act. Such extreme actions, he asserts with a certain amount of sympathy, were entirely understandable given the Kalinagos' frustration with the Europeans: "It was rage that made the Indians commit this excess, because they could not fully avenge the injustice that the Europeans had inflicted upon them by chasing them from their lands." See *Nouveau voyage*, 264.

38. Ibid., 261.

39. Ibid.

40. Ibid.

41. Ibid., 267.

42. Nathaniel Millet and Charles H. Parker, eds., "Introduction" in *Jesuits and Race: A Global History of Continuity and Change, 1530–2020* (Albuquerque: University of New Mexico, 2022), 4. Although the most famous Dominican, Bartolomé de las Casas, had fought tirelessly to prevent Native Americans from being enslaved in Spanish colonies, few members of the order saw anything wrong with the enslavement of Black Africans. See Sue Peabody, "'A Nation Born into Slavery': Missionaries and Racial Discourse in Seventeenth-Century French Antilles," *Journal of Social History* 38, no. 1 (2004): 117. See also Lawrence A. Clayton, *Bartolomé de las Casas* (Cambridge: Cambridge University Press, 2012), 428.

43. Nicholas Hudson, "From 'Nation' to 'Race': The Origin of Classification in Eighteenth Century Thought," *Eighteenth-Century Studies* 29, no. 3 (Spring 1996): 251.

44. Labat, *Voyage*, 221.

45. Ibid., 223.

46. Ibid., 221–222.

47. Ibid., 228–229.

48. For further information on Labat's employment of language and the linguistics of the French Caribbean, see Morgan Dalphinis, *History and Language in St. Lucia 1654–1915* (Morrisville, NC: Lulu.com, 2019), 47–51.

49. Labat, *Voyage*, 106–107.

50. Ibid., 229.

51. Ibid., 232.

52. Ibid., 230.

53. Ibid., 230–231.

54. Ibid., 230.

55. Ibid., 117.

56. Ibid., 118. The whipping of slaves was a protected right in Article 42 of the *Code Noir*. What was prohibited, however, was unruly abuse or torture of slaves. Labat's *pimentade*, however, would have likely been seen by a judicial court as benefitting the slave, again, preventing their potential gangrene and "nourishment" for the slave's soul. See Bernard Moitt, *Women and Slavery in the French Antilles, 1635–1848* (Bloomington: Indiana University Press, 2001), 101–111.

57. Due to the Treaty of Utrecht (1713), which ended the long and costly War of the Spanish Succession, peripherally involved nations, such as France and England, found a prime economic opportunity to seize the slave market from a damaged Spain. After the war, Caribbean slave commerce increased dramatically. See Dan Hicks, "'Material Improvements': The Archaeology of Estate Landscapes in the British Leeward Islands, 1713–1838," in *Estate Landscapes: Design, Improvement, and Power in the Post-Medeival Landscape*, eds. Jonathan Finch and Katherine Giles (Suffolk: Boydell and Brewer, 2007), 210.

58. Great Britain, a country whose population was only six million, had been responsible for carrying 700,000 of these captives; Portugal 286,000; and Holland 182,000. And although France was the last major power to participate in the trade, it had already carried 110,000 Africans to the Caribbean by the 1720s. See www.slavevoyages.org, accessed June 17, 2024.

59. These marriages were described as "mésalliances" and "later viewed in purely racial terms." On this and all matters related to miscegenation and French law, see Doris L. Garraway, *The Libertine Colony: Creolization in the Early French Caribbean* (Durham: Duke University Press, 2005), 207.

60. Chatillon, "Labat à travers ses manuscrits," 16.

61. Nicholas Hudson, "From 'Nation' to 'Race,'" 251.

62. Jean-Baptiste Labat, *Nouvelle relation de l'Afrique occidentale* (Paris: Guillaume Cavelier, 1728). It is now generally assumed that Labat borrowed from André Brue and Michel Jajolet de la Courbe to produce this work.

63. Jean-Baptiste Labat, *Voyage du Chevalier Des Marchais en Guinée, Isles voisines, et à Cayenne* (Amsterdam: Ordre des frères prêcheurs, 1730).

64. Andrew S. Curran, *The Anatomy of Blackness: Science and Slavery in an Age of Enlightenment* (Baltimore: Johns Hopkins University Press, 2011), 63.

65. Ibid., 63.

66. The most famous person to draw from Labat's account of the Kongo was none other than the Marquis de Sade, who read about the Jaga while imprisoned in the Bastille and wrote a short novel called *Aline et Valcourt* (1795) that featured numerous scenes of African cannibalism directly inspired by the novelist and philosopher Jean-Louis Castilhon's novel, *Reine d'Angola, histoire africaine*, which had been inspired by Labat's version of Cavazzi's stories. See Geoffrey Gorer, *The Life and Ideas of Marquis de Sade* (Redditch, UK: Read Books Limited, 2013), 139–141. See also the introduction to the only modern critical edition of this book: Jean-Louis Castilhon, *Zingha, Reine d'Angola, histoire africaine, suivie de recherches et d'observations sur la férocité naturelle des Giagues, et d'une relation exacte de leurs mœurs, de leurs coutumes et de la barbarie de leurs usages*, eds. Patrick Graille et Laurent Quillerié (Bourges: Éditions Ganymède, 1993).

III. FRANÇOIS BERNIER: THE FIRST CLASSIFIER

1. The English mathematician, physician, and one of the founders of the Royal Society, William Petty, was also thinking in this direction in the 1670s, albeit within a profoundly religious context. See Rhodri Lewis, "William Petty's Anthropology: Religion, Colonialism, and the Problem of Human Diversity," *Huntington Library Quarterly* 74, no. 2 (June 2011): 261–288.

2. In La Fontaine's "Ulysses et les Sirènes," the poet writes about Madame de La Sablière: "Quand je devais cent fois manquer à ma parole, Je n'irai point chez vous, mardi, manger de sole." Jean de La Fontaine, *Suite des Œuvres posthumes de La Fontaine* (Paris: n.p., 1797), 30. La Fontaine was not only a regular at the salon; he was Sablière's lodger.

3. Samuel Menjot d'Elbenne, *Madame de La Sablière: ses pensées chrétiennes et ses lettres à l'abbé de Rancé* (Paris: Plon-Nourrit et Cie, 1923), 72–73.

4. Charles Giraud, *Œuvres mêlées de Saint-Evremond* (Paris: J. Leon Techener Fils, Libraire, 1865), 3:402.

5. József Böröcz, *The European Union and Social Change: A Critical Geopolitical-Economic Analysis* (Oxfordshire, UK: Taylor and Francis, 2009), 19–22.

6. See Boris Noguès, "L'Encadrement pédagogique et disciplinaire dans les collèges d'humanités en France du XVIe au XVIIIe siècle," *Paedagogica Historica* 47, no. 3 (2011): 243–262.

7. Ibid.

8. Nicholas Dew, *Orientalism in Louis XIV's France* (Oxford: Oxford University Press, 2009), 147. See also A. Martin, *Histoire de la vie et des écrits de Pierre Gassendi* (Paris: Librarie philosophique de Ladrange, 1854), 24.

9. Saul Fisher, "Refutations of Aristotelians and Descartes" under "Pierre Gassendi" in *The Stanford Encyclopedia of Philosophy*, Spring 2014 edition, ed. Edward N. Zalta (Stanford, CA: Stanford University, 2014), https://plato.stanford.edu/entries/gassendi/.

10. Ibid., 4. To a large degree, Gassendi's nature-based worldview flowed from an *atomist* understanding of the world. First proposed by the ancient philosopher Epicurus, this highly controversial theory maintained that all matter is composed of invisible atoms and that the universe itself is endless. In his classes and in his writings, Gassendi envisioned the universe as an enormous nexus of atomic-level particles forming the larger structures that appear before our eyes. See also, Dew, *Orientalism*, 9.

11. Fisher, "Pierre Gassendi," in *The Stanford Encyclopedia of Philosophy*.

12. Dew, *Orientalism*, 146.

13. *Un Libertin dans l'Inde Moghole. Les Voyages de François Bernier (1656–1669)*, Frédéric Tinguely, ed. (Paris: Chandeigne, 2008), 146.

14. Ibid., 149.

15. Ibid., 451–452.

16. Ibid., 12.

17. Dew, *Orientalism*, 163.

18. George Bruce Malleson, *History of the French in India: From the Founding of Pondichery in 1674 to the Capture of that Place in 1761* (Cambridge: Cambridge University Press, 2010), 1–15. Of the five largest colonial European empires, France was the fourth to formally enter trade with India. Colbert and the court of Versailles, however, were not blind to the spoils that relations with India promised, though their accomplishments were minor. Starting around 1616, the French East India Company launched a slew of failed voyages to India,

thwarted by lost ships and defensive attacks from the Dutch navy. By the time that Bernier returned, however, the French had already begun setting up their first trading "factory" in Surat in 1668.

19. There are various spellings of the Arabic word "Mughal" over time. The word ultimately became Mogul in English and French.

20. Cited in Siep Stuurman, "François Bernier and the Invention of Race Classification," *History Journal Workshop* 50 (Autumn, 2000): 8. See also Thierry Hoquet, "Biologisation de la race et racialisation de l'humain: Bernier, Buffon, Linné," in *L'Invention de la race. Des Représentations scientifiques aux exhibitions populaires* (Paris: La Découverte, 2014), 25–29; Mathilde Bedel, "La Pigmentation, un outil pour une première description hiérarchisée des *races* humaines," in *Mirabilia Indiae. Voyageurs français et représentations de l'Inde au XVIIe siècle* (Paris: Garnier, 2021), 66–72; and Faith E. Beasley, "Bernier à l'origine du racisme?" in *Versailles à la rencontre du Taj Mahal. Conversations éclairées sur l'Inde au temps du Roi-Soleil*, trans. Patrick Graille (Paris, Les Belles Lettres, 2024), 188–195.

21. Malleson, *History of the French in India*, 11.

22. Robert Alan Hatch, "Between Astrology and Copernicanism: Morin-Gassendi-Bouilliau," *Early Science and Medicine* 22 (2017): 495.

23. Dew, *Orientalism*, 163.

24. The first title of the book is *Histoire de la dernière révolution des États du grand Mogol, dédiée au Roy, par le Sieur F. Bernier médecin de la Faculté de Montpellier* (1670). The following year, he published the sequel: the so-called *Suite des Mémoires du Sieur Bernier sur l'Empire du Grand Mogol*. The first volume of this work contains letters to François La Mothe Le Vayer, Jean Chapelain, and Chapelle [Claude-Emmanuel Lhuillier], and the second contains his trip to Kashmir, his *Relation du voyage fait en 1664 . . . au royaume de Cachemire composée de neuf lettres à M. de Merveilles*. In addition to many international editions, in 1699, eleven years after Bernier's death, the Amsterdam editor Paul Marret published the four volumes together with illustrations with the title, *Voyages de François Bernier*. The English title was *François Bernier, Travels in the Mogul Empire*, trans. Irving Brock (Paris: n.p., 1670–1671).

25. François Bernier, *Abregé de la Philosophie de Gassendi* (Lyon: Anisson, Posuel & Rigaud, 1684). The book had seven volumes.

26. Barbarian (from the Greek *bárbaros*) not only describes perceived cultural inferiorities, but linguistic ones as well. Julius Pokorny notes similarities between *bárbaros* and Indo-European words for "meaningless" or "inarticulate." This likely refers to what the Greeks perceived as poor locution from

neighboring polities, their languages sounding like gibberish (i.e., "bar bar bar").

27. "Barbare," in *Le Dictionnaire de l'académie Françoise* (Paris: chez Jean Baptiste Coignard et sa veuve, 1694), 1:82. See Maria Boletsi, *Barbarism and Its Discontents* (Palo Alto: Stanford University Press, 2013), 69–72. See also Françoise Le Borgne, Odile Parsis-Barubé, and Nathalie Vuillemin, eds., *Les Savoirs des barbares, des primitifs et des sauvages. Lectures de l'Autre aux XVIII*[e] *et XIX*[e] *siècles* (Paris, Classiques Garnier, 2018).

28. For a summary of Aristotelian classification, see Pierre Pellegrin, *Aristotle's Classification of Animals: Biology and the Conceptual Unity of the Aristotelian Corpus* (Berkeley: University of California Press, 2021).

29. Aristotle, *Aristotle's Politics: Writings from the Complete Works: Politics, Economics, Constitution of Athens* (Princeton, Princeton University Press, 2016), 7.

30. For more on the Great Chain (and its great pitfalls), see Robert J. Sternberg, "It's Time to Move beyond the 'Great Chain of Being,'" *The Behavioral and Brain Sciences* 40 (2017).

31. Bernier, *Abregé de la Philosophie de Gassendi*, 5:24–25.

32. Joseph L. Graves, *The Emperor's New Clothes: Biological Theories of Race at the Millennium* (New Brunswick, NJ: Rutgers University Press, 2003), 25.

33. See Gates and Curran, *Who's Black and Why?*, 30–31, 251.

34. Richard Henry Popkin, *Isaac La Peyrère (1596–1676): His Life, His Work, and Influence* (Leiden: E. J. Brill, 1987), 74.

35. Bernier, *Abregé de la Philosophie de Gassendi*, 5:25. See Stuurman, "François Bernier and the Invention of Race Classification," 10, for an excellent summary of this history.

36. Ibid.

37. François Bernier, "A New Division of the Earth," trans. Janet L. Nelson, *History Workshop Journal* no. 51 (Spring, 2001): 247. The original title is: "Nouvelle division de la Terre, par les différentes Espèces ou Races d'hommes qui l'habitent, envoyée par un fameux voyageur à M. l'abbé de la *** à peu près en ces termes," *Le Journal des Sçavants* [sic], Paris, Jean Cusson, lundi 24 avril 1684.

38. Ibid.

39. Ibid.

40. Johannes Schefferus, *Histoire de la Laponie* (Paris: Varennes, 1678), 19–33. The full title of Schefferus's book is *Lapponia, id est Religionis Lapponum et gentis nova et verissima description*. Schefferus suggested that Laplanders had migrated from Asia into the northern part of Europe. See Robert T. Anderson, "Lapp

Racial Classifications as Scientific Myths," *Anthropological Papers of the University of Alaska* 11, no. 1 (1964): 16–17.

41. Johannes Schefferus, *Histoire de la Laponie*, 22.

42. Bernier, "A New Division of the Earth," 248.

43. While the number of East Africans forcibly removed from the continent is contested (the highest estimates suggest that seventeen million slaves were taken from the region), the reality of the East African slave trade is one that is often neglected by the Eurocentric gaze. For more information on the subject, see Gwyn Campbell, *Structure of Slavery in Indian Ocean Africa and Asia* (Oxfordshire, UK: Taylor and Francis, 2004).

44. Bernier, "A New Division," 249.

45. Ibid.

46. Ibid., 248.

47. Ibid.

48. Ibid.

49. Ibid. Many of these ideas come from a conversation with Patrick Graille.

50. My translation.

51. Pierre Boule points out that Henri de Boulainvilliers (1658–1722) made a contribution to the idea of race by tying the notion of hierarchy to biology (in his case ancestry). See "François Bernier and the Origins of the Modern Concept of Race," in *The Color of Liberty: Histories of Race in France*, eds. Sue Peabody and Tyler Stovall (Durham and London: Duke University Press, 2003), 11–13.

52. Menjot d'Elbenne, *Madame de La Sablière*, 73, no. 3. This book cites the letter that was published in the *Mercure de France* in 1722.

53. *Copie des étrennes envoyées à Madame de La Sablière par Mr Bernier* (Montpellier: n.p., 1688), 5.

54. Ibid.

55. Sylvia Murr, "Bernier et Gassendi: Filiation déviationniste?" in *Gassendi et l'Europe, 1592–1792: Actes du colloque international de Paris* (Paris: Vrin, 1997), 75.

56. François Bernier, "Nouvelle division de la terre, par les différentes espèces ou races d'hommes qui l'habitent," *Mercure de France* (December 1722): 62–70. Voltaire, for one, was undoubtedly very influenced by it.

57. Leibniz cited Bernier's article (though he forgot Bernier's name) in a wider discussion on race, where he concluded that the only way to divide humans was linguistically. See Justin E. H. Smith, *Nature, Human Nature, and Human Difference: Race in Early Modern Philosophy* (Princeton: Princeton University Press, 2015), 162–163.

IV. CARL LINNAEUS: THE BOTANIST WHO TRANSFORMED MAN INTO AN ANIMAL

1. Gunnar Broberg, *The Man Who Organized Nature: The Life of Linnaeus*, trans. Ann Patterson (Princeton: Princeton University Press, 2023), 2.

2. Richard Pulteney, *A General View of the Writings of Linnaeus* (London: Mawman, 1805), 558, 565.

3. Andrea Wulf, *The Brother Gardeners* (New York: Random House, 2008), 121.

4. Pulteney, *A General View of the Writings of Linnaeus*, 563–563.

5. Broberg, *The Life of Linnaeus*, 18–20.

6. Pulteney, *A General View of the Writings of Linnaeus*, 512.

7. Ibid.

8. Wilfrid Blunt, *Linnaeus: The Compleat Naturalist* (London: Cox and Wyman Ltd, 2004), 15.

9. Broberg, *The Life of Linnaeus*, 30.

10. Pulteney, *A General View of the Writings of Linnaeus*, 513.

11. Ibid.

12. Rothman not only volunteered to provide Carl with room and board during his last year of Gymnasium, but to give him lessons in physiology and botany in preparation for further study. Pulteney, *A General View of the Writings of Linnaeus*, 515.

13. Linnaeus was also tutored by Kilian Stobaeus, a natural scientist, who not only lodged him for a time but also provided the student with access to his library. Blunt, *Linnaeus: The Compleat Naturalist*, 21.

14. Ibid., 21–24.

15. Ibid., 517.

16. William Carr, *Travels Through Flanders, Holland, Germany, Sweden, and Denmark* (Amsterdam: Jacob ter Beek, 1733), 129.

17. Blunt, *Linnaeus: The Compleat Naturalist*, 25.

18. Ibid., 29. Linnaeus ultimately attended six dissections of the same woman during January and February of 1729. See also Broberg, *The Life of Linnaeus*, 46.

19. He was the uncle of Anders Celsius, who created the Celsius temperature scale, according to which 100 was freezing and 0 was boiling. Linnaeus later reversed this.

20. Broberg, *The Life of Linnaeus*, 34. After Linnaeus's work was presented to Prof. Rudbeck at Uppsala, Rudbeck "honored it with the highest approbation,

and expressed a wish to be better acquainted with the author of so masculine a composition." Pulteney, *A General View of the Writings of Linnaeus*, 519.

21. Philip R. Sloan, "The Buffon-Linnaeus Controversy," *Isis* 67, no. 3 (September 1976): 358.

22. Ibid., 360.

23. Broberg, *The Life of Linnaeus*, 337. Linnaeus used his own collection of 600 or so botanical specimens to evaluate the three major competing ways of dividing up the flower world. The first and most famous of these classifications was Joseph Pitton de Tournefort's enormous breakdown of 7,000 species of plants into 700 genera and twenty-two classes according to the morphology of flower itself. The second was Augustus Quirinus Rivinus's classification of the morphology of the flower petals. The final was the Englishman John Ray's taxonomy, which divided the plant world according to a complicated matrix that took seeds, flowers, fruits, and roots into consideration. Among these three, Linnaeus concluded that Ray's system generated the most "natural" of the classification schemes, although he believed that the many variables in Ray's system made it cumbersome and too complicated for most people. See also Karen Magnuson Beil, *What Linnaeus Saw: A Scientist's Quest to Name Every Living Thing* (New York: Norton, 2019), 53.

24. Like Linnaeus, Artedi had begun his studies with the intention (or at least his family's intention) of becoming a priest. Blunt, *Linnaeus: The Compleat Naturalist*, 30.

25. Ibid., 7.

26. Pulteney, *A General View of the Writings of Linnaeus*, 518.

27. Blunt, *Linnaeus: The Compleat Naturalist*, 40.

28. Theodor Magnus Fries, *Linnaeus* (Cambridge: Cambridge University Press, 2011), 62.

29. Ibid.

30. Carl Linnaeus, *Lachesis Lapponica or a Tour in Lapland* (London: Richard Taylor & Co., 1811), 1:1–2.

31. Ibid.,1:283.

32. Ibid., 1:36; 1:89.

33. Ibid., 1:126.

34. Ibid., 1:102; 1:167; 1:169, 1:326–333; 1:334. When Linnaeus later wrote about Lapland, his *Flora Lapponica*, in 1737, he also praised the way in which the Sámi had developed innovative medicines.

35. Linnaeus, *Lachesis Lapponica*, 2:132.

36. Blunt, *Linnaeus: The Compleat Naturalist*, 41.

37. Linnaeus, *Lachesis Lapponica*, 1:191.

38. Ibid.

39. Koerner, *Linnaeus: Nature and Nation*, 65–76. The object in question had been confiscated from a Sámi who had been arrested by the Swedish military for non-Christian practices. This spoliation of Sámi material culture, while not necessarily beginning with Linnaeus, endures today. For a description of the legacy of tourists in Lapland, see also Stein R. Mathisen, "Souvenirs and the Commodification of Sámi Spirituality in Tourism," *Religions* 11, no. 9 (2020).

40. Blunt, *Linnaeus: The Compleat Naturalist*, 72.

41. Pulteney, *A General View of the Writings of Linnaeus*, 560.

42. This article, written by the Chevalier de Jaucourt, actually criticized Linnaeus's method. Denis Diderot and Jean le Rond D'Alembert, eds., *Encyclopédie, ou Dictionnaire raisonné des sciences, des arts et des métiers, par une société de gens de lettres* (Paris: Le Breton et al., 1751–1772), 6:392.

43. The word *manatee* came, originally, from a curious combination of the Caribbean word *manatí* and the Latin verb *lamentari*, to *mourn* or emit sad sounds. "Manatee," Merriam-Webster, https://www.merriam-webster.com/dictionary/manatee.

44. Georg Wilhelm Steller, *Journal of a Voyage with Bering, 1741–1742* (Palo Alto: Stanford University Press, 1988), 158.

45. Labat, *Nouveau voyage*, 2:200.

46. Twenty years later, after getting rid of the category of paradoxa itself, he understood that these siren "sightings" were manatees or dolphins. On the larger debates related to mammal taxonomy, see Rebecca Giggs, *Fathoms: The World in the Whale* (New York: Simon & Schuster, 2020), 237–266.

47. Theophrastus (c. 371–287 BCE), one of Aristotle's students, actually coined the expression *classification*. See Sergio Pennazio, "Elements of Plant Physiology in Theophrastus' Botany," *Theoretical Biology Forum* 107 (2014): 97–108.

48. Thierry Hoquet, *Buffon / Linné: Éternels rivaux de la biologie?* (Paris: Dunod, 2007), 13.

49. Carl Linnaeus, *Systema Naturae 1735, Facsimile of the First Edition* (Nieuwkoop: B. De Graaf, 1974), 26.

50. See Koerner for an interesting discussion of how "Linnaeus never grasped the outlines of this natural order." *Linnaeus: Nature and Nation*, 29.

51. Linnaeus's "scientific" justification for stability of the animal world came from his belief that one could detect no apparent changes in a given species from generation to generation. In his later years, however, Linnaeus confronted the reality of plant hybrids and questioned the supposed constancy of each species. See Peter J. Bowlers, *Evolution: The History of an Idea, 25th Anniversary Edition with a New Preface* (Berkeley and Los Angeles: University of California Press, 2009), 70.

52. Heinz Goerke, *Linnaeus* (New York: Scribner, 1973), 24.

53. Broberg, *The Life of Linnaeus*, 110.

54. A. M. van der Woude, "Population Developments in the Northern Netherlands (1500–1800) and the Validity of the 'Urban Graveyard' Effect," *Annals de démographie historique* (1982): 56. See also R. Paping, "General Dutch Population Development 1400–1850: Cities and Countryside," paper presented at 1st European Society of Historical Demography Conference, Alghero, Italy (2014): 13. Lennart Andersson Palm, "Estimating Sweden's Population in the Early Modern Period," *Bebyggelsehistorisk tidskrift, Nordic Journal of Settlement History and Built Heritage* 81 (2021): 79.

55. In Leyden, he also attended lectures by the Dutch botanist, chemist, and physician, Herman Boerhaave. See Broberg, *The Life of Linnaeus*, 111.

56. Blunt, *Linnaeus: The Compleat Naturalist*, 101.

57. For a description of early greenhouses, see Esther Helena Arens, "Flowerbeds and Hothouses: Botany, Gardens, and the Circulation of Knowledge in Things," *Historical Social Research / Historische Sozialforschung* 40, no. 1 (2015): 265–283.

58. Broberg, *The Life of Linnaeus*, 112.

59. Though Linnaeus had originally contracted to work with Burman, Clifford made a deal with Burman to "release" Linnaeus in exchange for a precious book. Soon thereafter Linnaeus took a paid position at Hartekamp as Clifford's personal physician and cataloger of the garden. Blunt, *Linnaeus: The Compleat Naturalist*, 101.

60. "The Ariadne thread of botany is classification, without which there is chaos." Goerke, *Linnaeus*, 99.

61. See William Thomas Stearn, "The Background of Linnaeus's Contributions to the Nomenclature and Methods of Systematic Biology," *Systematic Zoology* 8 (1959): 4–22.

62. Christopher Cumo, ed., *The Encyclopedia of Cultivated Plants* (New York: Bloomsbury, 2013). 72. At the time, the banana's fruit was so prized, so mythically exotic, that some believed it had been the *banana* (and not the *apple*) that

was the true fruit bringing about Adam's fall. Indeed, the banana was often called "Adam's fig."

63. Pulteney, *A General View of the Writings of Linnaeus*, 532.

64. Karel Davids, "The Scholarly Atlantic: Circuits of Knowledge Between Britain, the Dutch Republic, and the Americas in the Eighteenth Century" in *Dutch Atlantic Connections, 1680–1800: Linking Empires, Bridging Borders*, eds. Gert Oostindie and Jessica V. Roitman (Leiden: Brill, 2014), 224. One of his more important contacts during this time was the Dutch naturalist Johan Frederik Gronovius, who provided Linnaeus with duplicate samples from his herbarium, particularly those from North America.

65. Pulteney, *A General View of the Writings of Linnaeus*, 530.

66. Ann-Mari Jönsson, "Linnaeus's International Correspondence. The Spread of a Revolution," in *Languages of Science in the Eighteenth Century*, ed. Britt-Louise Gunnarsson (Berlin & Boston: De Gruyter, 2011), 178.

67. Johannes Georgius Siegesbeck,"*Epicrisis in clar. Linnaei nuperrime evulgatum systema plantarum sexuale, et huic superstructam methodum botanicam*" (1737), cited in Ann-Mari Jönsson, "The Reception of Linnaeus's Works in Germany with Particular Reference to His Conflict with Siegesbeck," in *Germania Latina*, eds. E. Kessler and H.C. Kuhn (München: Wilhelm Fink Verlag, 2003), 2:724.

68. Jonas Gerlings, "Linnaean Science in Kant's Königsberg," in *Linnaeus, Natural History, and the Circulation of Knowledge*, eds. Hanna Hodacs, Kenneth Nyberg, and Stéphane Van Damme (Oxford: Voltaire Foundation, 2018), 143.

69. Corinthians 15:39 (NIV).

70. Corinthians 15:45 (NIV).

71. Linnaeus, *Systema Naturae*, 14–15.

72. James S. Slotkin, *Readings in Early Anthropology* (Taylor and Francis, 2012), 179. Linnaeus's quote comes from *Fauna Suecica* (1746).

73. See Londa Schiebender, "Why Mammals Are Called Mammals: Gender Politics in Eighteenth-Century Natural History," *The American Historical Review* 98, no. 2 (April 1993): 382–411, for a discussion of the wider implications of these terms, including the gendered origins of the term *Mammalia* in the 1758 edition of the *Systema Naturae*.

74. Carl Peter Thunberg, *Travels at the Cape of Good Hope, 1772–1775*, ed. Vernon Siegfried Forbes (Cape Town: Van Riebeeck Society, 1986), 1. Thunberg, a student of Linnaeus's and patron of Blue John's (Blauuwe Jean), likewise notes in his journals the exotic animals on display at the tavern.

75. But by putting apes and humans under the same category in his *Systema*, Linnaeus was breaking with earlier naturalists, particularly the greatest classifier of the previous generation, John Ray. In many ways, Ray had effectively paved the way for Linnaeus by creating his own systematic arrangements of virtually all of nature — insects, fish, birds, plants, and mammals. But he had also carefully separated humankind from the rest of creation in his most important work, the *Synopsis methodica animalium quadrupedum* (1693). For more on Ray's foresight in the field of taxonomy, see Ethan S. Rogers and Stephanie L. Canington, "Lemurs before Lemur: Depictions of Captive Lemurs Prior to Linnaeus," *Notes and Records of the Royal Society of London* 77, no. 1 (2023): 19–48.

76. Carl Linnaeus, *Critica Botanica* (Lugduni Batavorum: Apud Conradum Wishoff, 1737), quoted in Staffan Müller-Wille, "Linnaeus and the Four Corners of the World" in *The Cultural Politics of Blood, 1500–1900*, eds. Kimberly Anne Coles et al. (Basingstoke: Palgrave Macmillan, 2015), 199.

77. See David Bindman, *Ape to Apollo: Aesthetics and the Idea of Race in the 18th Century* (Ithaca: Cornell University Press, 2002), 61. See also Linda Anderson Burnett and Bruce Buchan, *Race and the Scottish Enlightenment: A Colonial History, 1750–1820* (New Haven: Yale University Press, 2025), 31.

78. Linda Andersson Burnett and Bruce Buchan, "The Edinburgh Connection" in *Linnaeus, Natural History, and the Circulation of Knowledge*, eds. Hodacs et al. (Berkeley: Voltaire Press, 2018), 166. See also James Delbourgo, *Collecting the World: Hans Sloane and the Origins of the British Museum* (Cambridge: Harvard University Press, 2017), 296.

79. Pulteney, *A General View of the Writings of Linnaeus*, 535.

80. Charles T. Ambrose, "Carolus Linnaeus (Carl von Linné), 1707–1778: The Swede Who Named Almost Everything," *The Pharos of Alpha Omega Alpha Honor Medical Society* 73, no. 2 (2010): 4.

81. Broberg, *The Life of Linnaeus*, 276.

82. Koerner, *Linnaeus: Nature and Nation*, 42. See also Hanna Hodacs, "In the Field: Exploring Nature with Carolus Linnaeus," *Endeavour* 34, no. 2 (2010): 46. See also Hanna Hodacs and Kenneth Nyberg, *Naturalhistoria på resande fot. Om att forska, undervisa och göra karriär i 1700-talets Sverige* (Lund: Nordic Academic Press, 2007) for a discussion of the teaching of science in Uppsala.

83. Koerner, *Linnaeus: Nature and Nation*, 42.

84. Ibid., and Pulteney, *A General View of the Writings of Linnaeus*, 542.

85. Quoted in Linnaeus, *Miscellaneous Tracts Relating to Natural History*, ed.

Benjamin Stillingfleet (London: J. Dodsley, Baker and Leigh, and T. Payne, 1775), from his 1736 speech at Uppsala University's annual conferment of doctoral degrees, 125. Quoted in Koerner, *Linnaeus: Nature and Nation*, 45.

86. Linnaeus, *Miscellaneous Tracts*, 223. Quoted in Koerner, *Linnaeus: Nature and Nation*, 44–45.

87. No one really knows exactly of course. See Norman Maclean, ed., *The Living Planet: The State of the World's Wildlife* (Cambridge: Cambridge University Press, 2023), 5.

88. For an excellent data-driven study of the impact of Linnaeus's classificatory system, see Staffan Müller-Wille and Isabell Charmantier, "Natural History and Information Overload: The Case of Linnaeus," *Studies in History and Philosophy of Science. Part C, Studies in History and Philosophy of Biological and Biomedical Sciences* 43, no. 1 (2012): 4–15.

89. Koerner, *Linnaeus: Nature and Nation*, 44–49.

90. Hodacs et al., *Linnaeus, Natural History, and the Circulation of Knowledge*, 21. Carl Peter Thunberg, Linnaeus's student, traveled for nine years on Dutch ships, exploring South and Southeast Asia, making it all the way to Japan. See also, Lars Hansen, ed., *The Linnaeus Apostles: Global Science and Adventure* (London: IK Foundation, 2007). This is an eleven-volume work containing the travelogues of Linnaeus's students between the years of 1745 and 1799. For a discussion of the effect of Linnaeus's writings on racial discourse, see Linda Andersson Burnett, "Selling the Sami: Nordic Stereotypes and Participatory Media in Georgian Britain," in *Communicating the North: Media Structures and Images in the Making of the Nordic Region*, ed. Peter Stradius (Oxfordshire, UK: Taylor and Francis, 2016).

91. There were also some really insightful relocations from one kingdom to another, especially for the world's largest animals, whales. See Aldemaro Romero, "When Whales Became Mammals: The Scientific Journey of Cetaceans from Fish to Mammals in the History of Science," *New Approaches to the Study of Marine Mammals* (2012): 24.

92. Before ultimately deciding to describe all of humankind by the word *sapiens* or *sagacity*, Linnaeus had initially considered dividing the genus *Homo* into two separate binomial categories: *Homo diurnus* and *Homo nocturnus*. *Homo diurnus* — daylight dwelling humans — corresponded to the normal geographical categories that had been previously established: Africans, Europeans, Amerindians, Laplanders, nearly everybody. *Homo nocturnus* was a separate taxon reserved solely for albinos, whom he believed to be strange

White humans living in Africa who dwelled in caves or only came out at night because they fled the sun. In the final classification of 1758, albinos became *Homo troglodytes*. Kalpana Sheshadri, *HumAnimal: Race, Law, Language* (Saint Paul: University of Minnesota Press, 2012), 149, 182. See also Koerner, *Linnaeus: Nature and Nation*, 87.

93. Linnaeus's treatment of the Sámi is one of the greatest inconsistencies of his career. They were classed as Europeans, Asians, and also *monstrous*. Monica Libell, "Universal Aspirations and Racial Asymmetries in Linnaeus's Descriptions of *Homo Sapiens*," in *Beyond "Hellenes" and "Barbarians": Asymmetrical Concepts of European Discourse*, ed. Kirill Postoutenko (Oxford & New York: Bergen Books, 2022), 76.

94. Linnaeus, *Critica Botanica*, 153.

95. Some of the humoral notions may have come from Linnaeus's contact with Hans Sloane, the great collector, colonial physician, and founder of the British Museum of Natural History. Sloane described his Negro patients in Jamaica as naturally "much given to Venery," arguing that they had an innate inclination toward hypersexual behavior that resulted from natural as opposed to environmentally generated elevated levels of black bile. See Hans Sloane, *A Voyage to the Islands Madera, Barbados, Nieves, S. Christophers and Jamaica* (London: Printed by B.M. for the author, 1707), 1:xlviii.

96. Pulteney, *A General View of the Writings of Linnaeus*, 176. See also François-Xavier Fauvelle-Aymar, *L'Invention du Hottentot, histoire du regard occidental sur les Khoisan (15e–19e siècles)* (Paris: Publications de la Sorbonne, 2002).

97. Hair was also an important criterion for Linnaeus. *Americanus* had thick, straight, very black hair; Asiaticus had abundant black hair (virtually no difference); and Africans or the Afer had "frizzled" or textured black hair, a marked difference from the light, flowing, long, and seemingly pure hair of the European. See Angela Rosenthal, "Raising Hair," in *Eighteenth-Century Studies* 38, no.1 (Fall 2004): 4. Linnaeus never modified the section related to *Homo sapiens* after the 1758 edition. Indeed, one of the few times he wrote about anything related to "Africans" after 1758, interestingly enough, was when a Swede living in Dutch Surinam informed him that a "new root with medical properties" had been discovered by a formerly enslaved man named Kwasímukámba of Tjedúa. Unlike many eighteenth-century naturalists, who would have given the credit to the former owner of the slave, Linnaeus promptly named the plant — *Quassia Amara* — to honor the Black man. See Burnett and Buchan, "The Edinburgh Connection," 165–166.

98. Broberg, *The Life of Linnaeus*, 384.

99. Ibid., 391.

100. Ibid.

101. Ibid.

V. BUFFON: THE MAN WHO PUT HUMANS IN TIME

1. Georges-Louis Leclerc, Comte de Buffon, *Histoire naturelle, générale et particulière, avec la description du cabinet du roi* (Paris: Imprimerie royale, 1749–1788), 1:10.

2. Linnaeus did not associate humans with horses, but rather with sloths and apes. Wilfrid Blunt, *Linnaeus: The Compleat Naturalist* (London: Cox and Wyman Ltd, 2004), 8.

3. There are several versions of this story. According to another version, Voltaire, Buffon, and the doctor La Mettrie had begun a conversation (probably by mail) about Linnaeus's new *Systema Naturae*. See Thierry Hoquet, *Buffon/Linné: Éternels rivaux de la biologie* (Paris: Dunod, 2007), 85. See also Antoine Laurent Apollinaire Fée, *Vie de Linné, rédigée sur les documents autographes, et suivie de l'analyse de sa correspondance avec les principaux naturalistes de son époque* (Paris: F.G. Levrault, 1832), 293.

4. Buffon, *Histoire naturelle*, 1:40.

5. This comment is found in the first paragraphs of the 1749 "Variétés dans l'espèce humaine" section of the *Histoire naturelle*. Later in the *Histoire naturelle*, however, Buffon seemingly contradicts this point.

6. Lisbet Koerner, "Purposes of Linnaean Travel: A Preliminary Research Report," in *Visions of Empire: Voyages, Botany, and Representations of Nature*, eds. David Phillip Miller and Peter Hans Reill (Cambridge: Cambridge University Press, 2011), 119, no. 5.

7. See Joanna Stalnaker, *The Unfinished Enlightenment: Description in the Age of the Encyclopedia* (Ithaca: Cornell University Press, 2010), 32–35.

8. See Anna Svenbro, "Linné et la France: Entre botanique et politique," *La Revue de la BNU* 8 (2013): 29. Svenbro provides an excellent chart that summarizes some of the major differences between the two thinkers.

9. Jean-Aymar Piganiol de La Force, *Nouvelle description de la France* (Amsterdam: Du Villard & Changuion, 1719), 3:210.

10. Ibid.

11. Jacques Roger, *Buffon: Un philosophe au Jardin du Roi* (Paris: Fayard, 1989), 22.

12. Théodule Ribot, *Heredity* (New York: D. Appleton and Company, 1875), 159–160.

13. His siblings, on the other hand, were destined for ecclesiastical careers. His two younger brothers, Jean-Marc and Claude-Benjamin, gravitated toward the priesthood, and both ultimately joined the Cistercian order south of Dijon. His one surviving sister, Jeanne, also chose a religious vocation, and took her vows at the Ursulines convent in Montbard, where she eventually rose to the ranks of mother superior. See Henri Nadault de Buffon, *Buffon, sa famille, ses collaborateurs et ses familiers: Mémoires par M. Humbert-Bazile son secrétaire* (Paris: Jules Renouard, 1863), 297. See also Paul-Marie Grinevald, *Buffon 1788–1988* (Paris: Imprimerie nationale 1988), 121.

14. Jacques Roger, *Buffon: A Life in Natural History*, ed. L. Pearce William (Ithaca: Cornell University Press, 1997), 7. Roger, *Buffon: Un philosophe au Jardin du Roi*, 25. It is also quite likely that Bouhier, who had a solid base in mathematics, exposed Buffon to the possibilities of Leibniz's probability theory, as well as differential and integral calculus. See also Lee Alan Dugatkin, *Mr. Jefferson and the Giant Moose: Natural History in Early America* (Chicago: University of Chicago Press, 2019), 13.

15. In a display of his future aspirations, the young man even managed to enter into fruitful correspondence with Gabriel Cramer, one of Europe's leading mathematicians. Virginia P. Dawson, "The Disciplines of Science: The Limits of Observation and the Hypotheses of Georges Louis Buffon and Charles Bonnet," in Elizabeth Garber, *Beyond History of Science: Essays in Honor of Robert E. Schofield* (Lehigh, Lehigh University Press, 1990), 112. His time in Angers drew to a close the following year, however, when he got into some sort of scrap with another young man that ultimately led to an illegal dual—with either sword or pistols. Though the archive is silent on what transpired, Buffon seems to have prevailed in the affair, but having either injured or even killed his opponent, he was forced to flee back to Dijon.

16. The bequest came in 1714. Buffon's father, who controlled the money for years, had used the inheritance, in part, to buy the village of Buffon. Years later, after his father sold the town of Buffon, the young man would buy it back. Roger, *Buffon: Un philosophe au Jardin du Roi*, 43. See also *Correspondance inédite de Buffon*, ed. M. Henry Nadault de Buffon (Paris: Libraire de L. Hachette et Co., 1860), 1:15.

17. Roger, *Buffon: Un philosophe au Jardin du Roi*, 28.

18. It was an insightful paper on the possibility of calculating probabilities in a game called the *franc carreau*, or fair square, that had assured his election

to the Academy in 1734. *Correspondance inédite de Buffon*, ed. M. Henry Nadault de Buffon (Paris: Libraire de L. Hachette et Co., 1860), 1:15.

19. See Jean Pierre Drox,"Experiments and Observations on the Strength of Timber, by Mr. Buffon," *Literary Journal* 3 (1745): 121–132, for a contemporary description of Buffon's experiments.

20. Ibid.

21. Ibid., 73.

22. Dugatkin, *Mr. Jefferson and the Giant Moose*, 15. See also Anita Guerrini, "Perrault, Buffon and the Natural History of Animals," *Notes and Records of the Royal Society of London* 66, no. 4 (2012): 401. See also Roger, *Buffon: A Life in Natural History*, 48–53. Founded in 1635 by Richelieu, the King's Garden served the scholars of the Paris Academy as pleasure-seeking elites.

23. *Encyclopédie*, 2:489.

24. Roger, *Buffon: Un philosophe au Jardin du Roi*, 94.

25. *Encyclopédie*, 2:490.

26. Jean-Frédéric Phélypeaux, the Count of Maurepas, who was also Buffon's advocate.

27. Buffon, *Histoire naturelle*,1:5.

28. Ibid., 1:12.

29. Ibid., 2:443–444. Buffon was of course joining a long line of thinkers including Socrates, Plato, Aristotle, Thomas Aquinas, and Descartes in identifying humankind's rationality as its essence.

30. Thierry Hoquet, *Buffon illustré: Les Gravures de l'Histoire naturelle (1749–1767)* (Paris: Publications scientifiques du Muséum national d'Histoire naturelle, 2007), 71, 150. See also Hoquet, *Buffon/Linné*, 91.

31. Buffon, *Histoire naturelle*, 2:478. Buffon writes "Everything changes in nature; everything changes [*s'altérer*], everything perishes; the body of man has only arrived at its point of perfection before beginning to perish [*déchoir*]." Ibid., 2:557.

32. Ibid., 2:557.

33. Ibid., 2:571. At several points within this narrative, it is true, Buffon steps back from his universalist story and discusses what we might label specific cases or differences: He discusses women and men's anatomy and sexuality separately and occasionally alludes to the cultures of a particular "variety" of human. This idea led to the most anti-Linnaean view of his *Histoire naturelle*. "It is impossible to provide a general system, a perfect method, not only for all of *Natural History*, but for each one of its branches. . . . Nature works according to unknown gradations and, as a result, it cannot lend itself totally to these divisions" (1:13). To propose a "perfect method," he concluded, "is to propose an impossible task" (1:14). The faulty classificatory systems found in botany, he railed, are less problematic than those used to classify animals because classifiers have "wanted to determine the resemblance and the difference among animals by using only the number of fingers, *ergots*, teeth, or teets" (1:22). The conclusion was clear: The only way to "advance science, is to work toward a description and a history of the different things that are science's objective" (1:24). To classify may be useful, Buffon asserted, but the overall enterprise was "perfectly arbitrary" (1:31).

34. Ibid., 3:372.

35. Ibid.

36. Ibid., 3:520.

37. For an examination of the effect of slavery in terms of institutional repercussions, see Ibram X. Kendi, *Stamped from the Beginning: The Definitive History of Racist Ideas in America* (New York: Public Affairs, 2016).

38. Pierre-François-Xavier de Charlevoix, *Histoire de l'Isle Espagnole ou de S. Domingue* (Paris: chez François l'Honoré, 1733), 1:422.

39. Buffon, *Histoire naturelle*, 3:469.

40. To begin with, Buffon clearly had no intention of calling into question the institution of slavery itself. Instead, like many people during the eighteenth century, he advocated for a gentler, more "decent" or "humane" form of enslavement in the Caribbean.

41. Buffon and Needham even collaborated on experiments pertaining to "spontaneous generation." See Jacques Roger, *The Life Sciences in Eighteenth Century French Thought*, ed. Keith R. Benson (Palo Alto: Stanford University Press, 1998), 401.

42. Ibid., 203.

43. Roger, *Buffon: A Life in Natural History*, 107–110. See also John H. Eddy, "Buffon, Species and the Forces of Reproduction," *Journal of the History of Biology* 56, no. 3 (2023): 480.

44. Jean-Baptiste Dubos, *Réflexions critiques sur la poésie et la peinture* (Utrecht: Etienne Neaulme, 1719), 2:139–140.

45. See William Max Nelson, *The Time of Enlightenment: Constructing the Future in France, 1750 to Year One* (Toronto: University of Toronto Press, 2021), 26. Nelson writes that "degeneration of animals was one of the central topics animating the first fifteen volumes of the *Histoire naturelle*."

46. Pierre-Louis Moreau de Maupertuis, *Venus physique* (La Haye: Husson, 1746), 203, my translation and emphasis. See also Cristina Malcomson, "*Gulliver's Travels* and Studies of Skin Color in Royal Society," in *Humans and Other Animals in Eighteenth Century British Society*, ed. Frank Palmeri (Oxfordshire, UK: Taylor and Francis, 2020): 139–146. The Irish physicist and chemist Robert Boyle used the same logic to understand Africans with albinism, suggesting them as evidence of a common human origin: whiteness.

47. See Claude-Olivier Doron, *L'Homme altéré. Races et dégénérescence (XVII*[e]*–XIX*[e] *siècles)* (Ceyzérieu: Champ Vallon, 2016), for the best articulation of the evolution of degeneration theory, especially as it was related to Buffon.

48. Though Buffon himself also used the word *race* in order to identify particular biological lineages — including the *Black race* or the *Laplander race* — he only did so to indicate biological lineages, not essential categories.

49. See William Max Nelson, *The Time of Enlightenment: Constructing the Future in France, 1750 to Year One* (Toronto: University of Toronto Press, 2021), 2–4, for a discussion of how French thinkers envisioned a form of eugenics for combatting degeneration in the colonies.

50. Buffon, *Histoire naturelle*, 3:530.

51. Ibid.

52. Buffon was nonetheless very much aware that an enormous amount of information related to sub-Saharan or Black Africans seemingly gave credence to not only the possibility of a separate taxonomic category, but also a separate origin. Ibid., 4:388–389.

53. Buffon, *Correspondance inédite de Buffon; à laquelle ont été réunies les lettres publiées jusqu'à ce jour* (Paris: Hachette, 1860), 1:222.

54. Buffon also worked in a room in the chateau's Tour Saint-Jacques. Herault de Séchelles, *Voyage à Montbard* (Paris: chez Solvet, 1800), 9.

55. Ibid., 15.

56. Buffon undertook this same experiment several times with spheres of various different materials. Ibid. On human origins, see John Reader, *Missing Links: In Search of Human Origins* (Oxford: Oxford University Press, 2011), 14–15.

57. The iron ball experiment allowed Buffon to calculate that it would have taken 42,964 years for the Earth to cool enough so that it was not burning to the touch, and 96,670 years (and 133 days) before it cooled to its actual temperature.

58. See Otis E. Fellows, "Voltaire and Buffon: Clash and Conciliation," *Symposium* 9, no. 2 (1955): 233.

59. Georges-Louis Leclerc, Comte de Buffon, "Époques de la nature," in *Œuvres complètes de Buffon: Matières générales*, I. Théorie de la terre (Paris: chez Furne et ce., 1839), 449.

60. Buffon, *Histoire naturelle*, *Supplément*, 2:370.

61. The editorial note can be found in *Œuvres de Buffon*, ed. Pierre Flourens (Paris: Garnier Frères, 1853), 9:453.

62. As did his young wife, Françoise de Saint-Belin-Malain, whom he had married in 1752, when she was twenty years old.

63. Hérault de Séchelles, *Voyage à Montbard*, 37.

64. Ibid., 42.

65. Roger, *Buffon*, 547.

66. This would be the subject of his *Notes on Virginia*, which he first published in French.

67. See Andrew S. Curran, *Anatomy of Blackness: Science and Slavery in an Age of Enlightenment* (Baltimore: Johns Hopkins University Press, 2011), 127. Cornelius de Pauw, *Recherches philosophiques sur les Américains* (Berlin: G.J. Becker, 1767), 1:30.

VI. VOLTAIRE: THE PHILOSOPHE WHO MADE RACISM *DRÔLE*

1. René Pomeau, *Voltaire en son temps* (Oxford: Fayard and Voltaire Foundation, 1985–1994), 2:408.

2. Ibid., 2:419. He also wrote the *Mémoires pour servir à la vie de M. de Voltaire écrits par lui-même*, but these were not published until 1784, six years after his death.

3. In discussing this tomb with me, Nicholas Cronk has pointed out that the pyramid is actually a half pyramid, which gives the impression that the other half is in the church. This is yet another example of Voltaire's sense of humor: Even in death he would be half in the church and half out of the church.

4. See Roger Pearson, *Voltaire Almighty: A Life in Pursuit of Freedom* (London: Bloomsbury Publishing, 2005), 293.

5. Voltaire, *Commentaire historique sur les œuvres de l'auteur de La Henriade, etc. Avec les pièces originales et les preuves* in Nicholas Cronk et al., *Œuvres complètes de Voltaire* (Oxford: Voltaire Foundation, 1968–2022), 78 B-C:11. Henceforth *OCV*.

6. See Pomeau, *Voltaire*, 2:523–524.

7. Voltaire, *OCV*, 40:237.

8. Ibid.

9. *OCV*, 78C:11.

10. See Pearson, *Voltaire Almighty*, 14.

11. This tax was an investment in a transatlantic trading company, La Compagnie des Indes, for example. This practice of seeking returns from the slave trade is something Voltaire both criticized and contributed to in his later life. Pearson, *Voltaire Almighty*, 14, 56.

12. A. Owen Aldridge, "Problems in Writing the Life of Voltaire: Plural Methods and Conflicting Evidence," *Biography (Honolulu)* 1, no. 1 (1978): 13.

13. Ibid. See also Antony Mckenna, "*La Moïsade*: Un Manuscrit clandestin voltairien," *Revue Voltaire*, 2008, no. 8: 67–97.

14. Barthélemy Gabriel Rolland D'Erceville, *Mémoire sur l'administration du collège de Louis-le-Grand* (Paris: chez Pierre-Guillaume Simon, 1778), 7:31–32. See also Gustave Dupont-Ferrier, *Du Collège de Clermont au Lycée Louis-le-Grand* (Paris: E. De Boccard, 1921), 1:471–472.

15. Dupont-Ferrier, *Du Collège de Clermont au Lycée Louis-le-Grand*, 1:263.

16. Success was not just relegated to the Count d'Argenson (future Minister of War), e.g., Zozo's peers at Louis-le-Grand would go on to boast impressive titles such as Minister of Foreign Affairs (Marquis de d'Argenson, the count's own brother), senior judge presiding over the Dijon Parlement (Fyot de la Marche), and senior official in the Rouen Parlement (Cideville). See Pearson, *Voltaire Almighty*, 22.

17. Voltaire, "Verge," *OCV*, 43:440.

18. The latter quote is apocryphal, a bon mot that Voltaire supposedly shared with Alexander Pope's mother! See Nicholas Cronk, *Voltaire, A Very Short Introduction* (Oxford: Oxford University Press, 2017), 32.

19. For Voltaire's letters to his lover during this debacle, see Jacques Cormier, *Les Amours de Pimpette: Correspondance de Voltaire avec Olympe Du Noyer* (Paris: Éditions L'Harmattan, 2009).

20. See Pomeau, *Voltaire en son temps* (Norwich, UK: Voltaire Foundation, 1995), 1:83–85, for a discussion of his days before, during, and after being in the Bastille.

21. See Ibid., 90–92, for a discussion of the context of the play and its reception.

22. "*Œdipe*" in *OCV*, IA:224.

23. See Pomeau, *Voltaire*, 141–157.

24. See Ibid., 1:158–159 on the two versions of this story, the first by Marais, the second by Montesquieu.

25. Montesquieu claims he went away in a carriage. Ibid., 1:159.

26. Ira Wade, *Intellectual Development of Voltaire* (Princeton: Princeton University Press, 2015), 149.

27. See Pomeau, *Voltaire*, 1:161–163.

28. See the "Voltaire en Angleterre," *Revue d'histoire littéraire de la France* 13, no. 1 (1906): 2. Voltaire was not banned from France, but he was forbidden to step foot within fifty *lieues* of the capital.

29. Cronk, *Voltaire*, 30–31.

30. Wade, *Intellectual Development of Voltaire*, 153.

31. Ibid.

32. See Andrew S. Curran, *Diderot and the Art of Thinking Freely* (New York: Other Press, 2019), 56–58, for more on Voltaire's trip to England.

33. Voltaire would go on to provide a synthesis of Newton's thought in his *Éléments de la philosophie de Newton*, *OCV*, 15:32–37.

34. Wade, *Intellectual Development of Voltaire*, 154.

35. Emeka P. Abanime, "Voltaire et les noirs," PhD dissertation, University Illinois at of Champagne Urbana, 1976, 174.

36. Adam Vartanian, "Voltaire's Quarrel with Maupertuis: Satire and Science," *L'Esprit créateur* 7, no. 4 (1967): 254.

37. See Voltaire, "Dissertation sur les changements arrivés dans notre globe," in *OCV*, 30C:45.

38. See Pomeau, *Voltaire*, 1:250. The poem circulated in manuscript form and was reprinted and supplemented with even more incendiary ideas by anonymous editors. See also "La Pucelle," *OCV*, 7:258–640.

39. After it was finally published in 1752, the Paris Parlement and the King's Council decried that it should be both banned and burned. See Ralph Arthur Nablow, *A Study of Voltaire's Lighter Verse* (Oxford: Voltaire Foundation, 1974), 13. See also Abderhaman Messaoudi, "Voltaire et la censure en France," *PFSCL* 71 (2008): 451.

40. The French edition, which he called the *Lettres philosophiques*, appeared the next year, in 1734.

41. Curran, *Diderot*, 57–59.

42. Pearson, *Voltaire Almighty*, 127–128.

43. Ibid., 120–121.

44. See Ruth Hagengruber, ed., *Émilie du Châtelet between Leibniz and Newton* (Dordrecht: Springer, 2012), for a series of articles that summarize her contributions to mathematics and understanding of Newton, Euler, and Samuel Clark.

45. "Traité de métaphysique," *OCV*, 14:417. My translation.

46. Ibid.

47. The Jesuits were publishing their views on China annually in the *Lettres édifiantes et curieuses*. See Charles Coutel, "Voltaire et la Chine," *L'Enseignement philosophique* 59, no. 4 (2009): 47.

48. "Le Siècle de Louis XIV," *OCV*, 13C:104.

49. "Anthropophage," *Questions sur l'Encyclopédie*, *OCV*, 38:425.

50. "Singularités de la nature," *OCV*, 65B:324.

51. Henry Louis Gates Jr. and Andrew S. Curran, *Who's Black and Why? A Hidden Chapter from the Eighteenth-Century Invention of Race* (Cambridge: Harvard University Press, 2022), 43.

52. "Traité," *OCV*, 14:420.

53. Ibid., 14:421.

54. Ibid.

55. Ibid., 14:422.

56. Ibid.

57. Ibid., 14:423.

58. Ibid., 14:452.

59. John Atkins, a British naval surgeon, had actually suggested that Blacks and Whites were separate species. Atkins writes: "From the whole, I imagine that White and Black must have descended of different protoplasts; and that there is no other way of accounting for it." See *The Appendix to the Navy-Surgeon: or, A Practical System of Surgery* (London: Ward and Chandler, 1734), 23–24.

60. It should be pointed out that the denigrating stereotypes — in contrast to the heretical theory of polygenesis — would not have been controversial. Sébastien G. Longchamp and Jean-Louis Wagnière, *Mémoires sur Voltaire* (Paris: Aimé André, 1826), 1:110.

61. They used this term because they mistakenly believed that the phenomenon of hypopigmentation — a lack of melanin in the skin — was specific to Black Africans.

62. "Diverses observations anatomiques," *Histoire de l'Académie Royale des Sciences* (Paris: Imprimerie royale, 1744), 12. It is in this document that the Academy erroneously claimed that the albino boy came from a city named "Macondé," a strange error resulting from the fact that his name was *Mapondé*.

63. Maupertuis said that he was at a "house," but the book was published anonymously. Revealing that he was at the Academy, where the child was also displayed, would have been a giveaway. *Dissertation physique à l'occasion du nègre blanc* (Leyde: n.p., 1744), i.

64. See Mary Terrall, *The Man Who Flattened the Earth: Maupertuis and the Sciences in the Enlightenment* (Chicago: University of Chicago Press, 2002), 211–215.

65. See Shirley A. Roe, *Matter, Life, Generation: Eighteenth-Century Embryology and the Haller Debate* (Cambridge: Cambridge University Press, 2003), 13. Maupertuis's theory is based on Newtonian principle of *attraction*.

66. See Andrew Curran, "Rethinking Race History: The Role of the Albino in the French Enlightenment Life Sciences," *History and Theory* 48, no. 3 (October 2009): 151–179. See chapter VI, in Maupertuis, *Vénus physique* (n.p., 1746), 188–193.

67. *Relation touchant un Maure blanc amené d'Afrique à Paris en 1744*, *OCV*, 28B:187–200.

68. *De l'esprit des lois*, in *Œuvres complètes de Montesquieu*, ed. Pierre Retat (Paris: Classiques Garnier, 2012). Tome I includes *Livres* I–XIX.

69. During the early 1730s, Buffon and Voltaire (along with Maupertuis and Madame du Châtelet) moved in the same intellectual circles in Paris. They were Newtonians, united in their commitment to empiricism and universal laws, and scornful of Descartes's rearguard rationalism — not to mention his belief that the universe could be understood as a series of enormous swirling vortices. See Stéphane Schmitt, "Voltaire et Buffon: Une 'Brouille pour les coquilles,'" *Revue Voltaire* 8 (2008): 225. See also J. B. Shank, *The Newton Wars and the Beginning of the French Enlightenment* (Chicago: University of Chicago Press, 2008), 409.

70. Schmitt, "Voltaire et Buffon," 236. Buffon had also mocked Voltaire in the first volume of the *Natural History*, for claiming that seashells found on mountains had been dropped by wandering pilgrims. He had done so in his 1746 "Dissertation envoyée par l'auteur, en Italien, à l'Académie de Bologne." See Buffon, *Histoire naturelle*, 1:281.

71. This idea comes from a conversation with Thierry Hoquet.

72. Vartanian, "Voltaire's Quarrel with Maupertuis," 254.

73. Early scholars of Voltaire tended to lament the fact that the French Enlightenment's most famous philosopher somehow missed out on the greatest transformations in the life sciences since Aristotle. See, for example, Roger, *The Life Sciences*, 143. For a discussion of the evolution of the life sciences before Buffon, see Thierry Hoquet, *Buffon: Histoire naturelle et philosophie* (Paris: Champion, 2005), 253–258.

74. Voltaire's career as historian had begun early, in 1723, when the twenty-nine-year-old writer published *The Henriade*, the first version of his epic rendering of the trials and tribulations of Henry IV. Five years later, he composed *The History of Charles XII, King of Sweden* while simultaneously working on (in

English) *An Essay on the Civil Wars of France*. By 1735, he was composing three other historical works: *The Century of Louis XIV*, *The Essay on General History*, and *The Discourse on the Events of 1744*. The same Louis XV who had wanted to throw him in jail in the past now named him the royal historiographer.

75. He had actually engaged in a "war of words" with Maupertuis, which had angered Frederick. This was seen as a "public humiliation." See Cronk, *Voltaire*, 63.

76. Voltaire, "Nouveau plan d'une histoire de l'esprit humain," *Mercure de France* (April 1745): 8.

77. See Vanita Seth for a telling anecdote related to how Voltaire decided (after speaking with Madame du Châtelet about the stupidity of memorizing stupid information) to practice a philosophical sort of history. *Europe's Indians: Producing Racial Difference* (Durham, NC: Duke University Press, 2010), 133.

78. Robert Darnton, "Voltaire, Historian," *Raritan* 35, no. 2 (2015): 20. Not surprisingly, one of Voltaire's other innovations was dethroning Christianity from the lofty position it had traditionally enjoyed in European history.

79. *Essai sur les mœurs et l'esprit des nations*, *OCV*, 22:3.

80. Ibid.

81. Ibid., 26A:196.

82. Ibid.

83. Ibid., 26A:208.

84. John Locke, *Two Treatises of Government* (1689), ed. Peter Laslett (Cambridge: Cambridge University Press, 1967), 319.

85. *Essai*, *OCV*, 22:12.

86. Ibid., 21.

87. Ibid., 26A:147.

88. See Andrew S. Curran, *The Anatomy of Blackness: Science and Slavery in an Age of Enlightenment* (Baltimore: Johns Hopkins University Press, 2011), 1.

89. Had Voltaire read Jean Riolan, he obviously would not have agreed. From Voltaire's point of view, Africans were not only black because they were black; they remained black regardless of the climate.

90. See Stanley Klaus, "A History of the Science of Pigmentation," in *The Pigmentary System: Physiology and Pathophysiology*, ed. James J. Norlund (New York: Oxford University Press, 1998), 5.

91. This "layer" is where melanocytes, or pigmentation-producing cells, produce melanin or skin pigmentation in all humans.

92. See Curran, *Anatomy of Blackness*, 145–146.

93. *Questions sur l'Encyclopédie*, *OCV*, 42A:269.

94. *Essai*, *OCV*, 26A:212–213.

95. Ibid., 26A:200.

96. *Candide*, *OCV*, 48:118.

97. Ibid., 49:194–195. Interestingly enough, the Black man brings up the fact that they are supposed to be "second cousins," an idea inculcated by the Dutch fetishes (priests). Voltaire could not resist a dig at monogenesis.

98. *Essai*, *OCV*, 26A:286. Voltaire had seen a similar idea in Helvétius's 1758 *De l'esprit*, which also affirms that there was not a "cask of sugar arriving in Europe that is not tainted by human blood." See Claude Adrien Helvétius, *De L'Esprit* (Paris: Fayard, 1988), 3:37. See Léon-François Hoffmann, *Le Nègre romantique. Personnage littéraire et obsession collective* (Paris: Payot, 1973), 113–114.

99. Ibid., 285–286.

100. A proslavery writer named Charles Levavasseur cited a false letter (supposedly written by Voltaire) demonstrating that he invested directly in a slave expedition leaving from Nantes. See Charles Levavasseur, *Esclavage de la race noire aux colonies françaises* (Paris: Bajat, 1840), 75–76. See also Jean-François Lopez, "Les Investissements de Voltaire dans le commerce colonial et la traite négrière: Clarifications et malentendus," *Cahiers Voltaire* 7 (2008): 124–139.

101. The term "Compagnie des Indes" is misleading because it is a catch-all phrase that can refer to a series of monopolies. See Patrick Villiers and Jean-Pierre Duteil, "Les Compagnies des Indes au XVIIIe siècle," in *L'Europe, la mer et les colonies (XVIIe–XVIIIe siècle)*, eds. Patrick Villiers et Jean-Pierre Duteil (Vanves: Hachette, 1997), 188–205.

102. Robert Chamboredon, "Des Placements de Voltaire à Cadix," *Cahiers Voltaire* 7 (2008): 66.

103. Where enslaved populations produced the goods that were transported in these ships of course.

104. Ibid. According to Chamboredon, there is no evidence that Voltaire signed off on this in advance.

105. Ibid. It should be noted that apart from this investment in Cadiz, there is no other trace of Voltaire's investment in the slave trade, his commercial correspondence having been burnt.

106. Augustin Cochin, *The Results of Slavery* (Boston: Walker, Wise, and Company, 1863), 351.

107. Silvia Sebastiani and Jean-Frédéric Schaub, *Race et histoire dans les sociétés occidentales (XVe–XVIIIe siècle)* (Paris: Albin Michel, 2021), 366.

108. "Jew," *Philosophical Dictionary*, *OCV*, 45B:138.

109. Ibid.

110. *OCV*, 65B:319.

111. *OCV*, 26A:147.

112. "Défense de mon oncle," *OCV*, 64:234.

113. Jean Louis Armand de Quatrefages de Bréau, "Les Arguments zoologiques du polygénisme," *Revue des cours scientifiques de la France et de l'étranger* 12 (1869): 204. The enduring influence of the French philosophe's racial thinking even reached the United States. In the 1830s, the abolitionist Reverend F. D. Stem lamented that American proslavery thinkers had conveniently adopted some of Voltaire's more memorable (racist) quips about Blacks. See for example, Perceval B. Lord, *Popular Physiology* (London: 1834), 485. See also F. D. Stem, "The Unity of the Human Race," *Mercerburg Review* 3 (1851): 131.

114. Pierson, *Voltaire Almighty*, 372.

115. Curran, *Diderot*, 375–379

116. Ibid.

117. The letter was written to Condorcet. *OCV*, 79B:36.

118. This is actually a loose translation of what Voltaire wrote in *Question sur les miracles*: "Vous croyez des choses incompréhensibles, contradictoires, impossibles, parce que nous vous l'avons ordonné; faites donc des choses injustes parce que nous vous l'ordonnons. Ces gens-là raisonnaient à merveille. *Certainement qui est en droit de vous rendre absurde est en droit de vous rendre injuste*," *OCV*, 139:409. The bad translation of Voltaire's aphorism has actually made its way back into French, and is often attributed to the writer.

119. "Traité sur la tolérance," *OCV*, 56C:247.

VII. THE SCOTS AND STAGE THEORY: DAVID HUME, ADAM SMITH, LORD KAMES, AND WILLIAM ROBERTSON

1. The holdings were specifically related to the "history, laws, and antiquities of Scotland." Gilbert Elliot, *Proposals for Carrying on Certain Public Works in the City of Edinburgh* (Edinburgh: n.p., 1752), 27.

2. Corey E. Andrews, "Drinking and Thinking: Club Life and Convivial Sociability in Mid-Eighteenth-Century Edinburgh," *Social History of Alcohol and Drugs* 22, no. 1 (Autumn, 2007): 67.

3. For information on Scotland's economic revolution, see Richard Saville,

"Scottish Modernisation Prior to the Industrial Revolution, 1688–1763," in *Eighteenth-Century Scotland: New Perspectives*, eds. T. M. Devine and J. R. Young (East Linton: Tuckwell Press, 1999), 6–23.

4. David Hume, *The Letters of David Hume*, ed. J. Y. T. Greig (Oxford: Oxford University Press, 1932), 1:219.

5. Lord Alexander Fraser Tytler Woodhouselee and Henry Home Kames, *Memoirs of the Life and Writings of the Honorable Henry Home of Kames* (Edinburgh: William Creech et al., 1817), 1:177. For a list of topics, see also Rosalind Carr, *Masculinity, Homosexuality, and Intellectual Culture in Eighteenth-Century Scotland* (Edinburgh: Edinburgh University Press, 2014), 46.

6. For information on literacy and universal education in Scotland, see R. A. Houston, *Scottish Literacy and the Scottish Identity: Illiteracy and Society in Scotland and Northern England 1600–1800* (Cambridge: Cambridge University Press, 1985), 1–19.

7. Black was especially known for the concept of "latent heat," the fact that when a substance changes states (from liquid to solid and vice versa) it absorbs or releases heat. This is one of the early principles of thermodynamics.

8. See John Cunningham Wood, *Adam Smith: Critical Assessments* (London and New York: Routledge, 1984), 1:97. In 1755, the Select Society founded a "sister" society, the "Edinburgh Society for Encouraging Arts, Sciences, Manufactures, and Agriculture."

9. Ibid., 38.

10. On the specific evolution of the concepts of nation and race, see Nicholas Hudson, "From 'Nation' to 'Race': The Origin of Classification in Eighteenth-Century Thought," *Eighteenth-Century Studies* 29, no. 3 (Spring 1996): 247–264.

11. Jean Gailhard, *The Compleat Gentleman: or, Directions for the Education of Youth* (London: T. N. for J. Starkey, 1678), 2:178–180.

12. Aaron Garrett and Silvia Sebastiani, "David Hume on Race," in *The Oxford Handbook of Philosophy and Race* (Oxford: Oxford University Press, 2017), 38.

13. He described himself during this time as engaged in the "pursuits of philosophy and general learning." David Hume, "My Own Life," *Delphi Complete Works of David Hume* (Hastings, UK, Delphi Classics, 2016), 1:781.

14. David Hume, *A Treatise on Human Nature*, in *Delphi Complete Works of David Hume*, 490.

15. Ibid., 392.

16. Montesquieu was not a strict climatic determinist, although he was often interpreted as such. He was fascinated by the interplay of climate and

morals, much like Hume. See Dennis C. Rasmussen, *The Pragmatic Enlightenment* (Cambridge: Cambridge University Press, 2014), 256–258.

17. Hume was actually in correspondence with Montesquieu in 1748. On the dates and specifics of this exchange see Emilio Mazza, "'An Irishman Cannot Have Wit': Hume and the Prejudice of National Characters," *Tocqueville Review* 35, no. 1 (2014): 27–54.

18. Voltaire, *Des Singularités de la nature* in *Œuvres complètes de Voltaire* (Paris: Garnier frères, 1879), 6:184.

19. James A. Harris, *Hume: An Intellectual Biography* (Cambridge: Cambridge University Press, 2015), 198.

20. Ibid.

21. It should be noted that the first edition was called *Essays Moral and Political*. See Mazza, "'An Irishman Cannot Have Wit,'" 27–30.

22. David Hume, *Essays: Moral, Political, and Literary* (London: A. Miller, 1748), 276.

23. Hume, "Of National Characters," 267.

24. Ibid.

25. Ibid.

26. Ibid., 270.

27. Hume, *Essays and Treatises on Several Subjects* (London: A. Millar, 1758), 1:125. This is the same text as the 1753 edition. It appears as a footnote.

28. Ibid.

29. Ibid.

30. My emphasis. Ibid.

31. Ibid.

32. Ibid. This section of the footnote, which conjures up the slave societies of the Caribbean, raises the question of Hume's views on human bondage. This has become yet another contested point among Hume scholars. On the one hand it is patently true that Hume "incisively denounced slavery in both moral and economic terms and at length." Kendra Asher, "Was David Hume a Racist? Interpreting Hume's Infamous Footnote (Part I)," *Economic Affairs* 42, no. 2 (June 2022): 228. On the other hand, another detail regarding Hume's relationship to slavery has recently come to light: a letter by Hume in 1766, where he counsels his protector, Lord Hertford, to purchase sugar plantations on Grenada. What exactly this advice means for Hume's legacy is a matter of debate. Was Hume advocating slavery? Was he simply passing on a tip? And does this somehow negate what Hume writes in some of his more philosophical essays, where he categorically rejects the legal and moral basis for enslavement? The question of Hume's views of slavery, and its relationship to race, is fraught. See Danielle Charette, "David Hume and the Politics of Slavery," *Political Studies* 72, no. 3 (2024): 862–882, for an excellent summary of this debate.

33. See Andersson Burnett and Buchan, *Race and the Scottish Enlightenment*, 43.

34. Samuel Estwick, *Considerations on the Negroe Cause Commonly So Called, Addressed to the Right Honorable Lord Mansfield* (London: J. Dodsley, 1773), 79.

35. Ibid.

36. For the 1776 edition.

37. David Hume, *David Hume on Morals, Politics, and Society*, eds. Angela Coventry and Andrew Valls (New Haven: Yale University Press, 2018), 170.

38. Dugald Stewart, *The Works of Dugald Stewart* (Cambridge: Hilliard and Brown, 1829), 7:4.

39. Ibid.

40. John Rae, *Life of Adam Smith* (London: Macmillan, 1895), 5.

41. Ibid., 9.

42. For more on Smith's bitter time at Oxford, see Rae, *Life of Adam Smith*, 18–28.

43. Adam Smith, *The Wealth of Nations* (London: Electric Book Company, 2001), 1016.

44. Nicholas Phillipson, *Adam Smith: An Enlightened Life* (New Haven: Yale University Press, 2012), 60.

45. This was the earlier title.

46. Ibid., 65.

47. Ibid., 68.

48. See John A. Hall, "Adam Smith and Sociology," *European Journal of Sociology* 64, no. 3 (2023): 303–324.

49. Dugald Stewart first used the term *conjectural history* to describe these sweeping accounts of human history in 1793. See the "Account of the Life and Writings of Adam Smith LL." in *The Collected Works of Dugald Stewart, Esq.*, F.R.SS., ed. Sir William Hamilton (Edinburgh: Thomas Constable, 1854), 10:34.

50. Ronald L. Meek, *Social Science and the Ignoble Savage* (Cambridge: Cambridge University Press,1976), 110–112.

51. Thomas Hobbes, Leviathan (Mineola, NY: Dover Publications, 2012). On Hobbes's critics, notably including David Hume, see Bernard H. Baumrin,

Hobbes's Leviathan: Interpretation and Criticism (Belmont, CA: Wadsworth Publishing Co., 1969), 26–34.

52. H.M. Höpfl, "From Savage to Scotsman: Conjectural History in the Scottish Enlightenment," *Journal of British Studies* 17, no. 2 (Spring, 1978): 26.

53. Dennis C. Rasmussen, *The Infidel and the Professor* (Princeton: Princeton University Press, 2019), 50.

54. Smith had succeeded the philosopher Frances Hutcheson as chair of moral philosophy at the University of Glasgow. For more on Smith's professorship, see Rae, *Life of Adam Smith*, 42–65. Hutcheson not only preceded Smith in position, but in ideology as well, influencing much of Smith's writing. See also Erik W. Matson, "Economics and the Moral Theology of Mutual Benefits: Francis Hutcheson, David Hume, and Adam Smith," *The Journal of Markets & Morality* 26, no. 1 (2023): 92–93. See also Erik W. Matson, "Commerce as Cooperation with the Deity: Self-Love, the Common Good, and the Coherence of Francis Hutcheson," *The European Journal of the History of Economic Thought* 30, no. 4 (2023): 507–524.

55. By 1755, Smith had begun refining this narrative of humankind's progress by incorporating some of the brilliant but entirely speculative insights about early humans that Jean-Jacques Rousseau had proposed in his "Essay on the Foundations and Origins of Inequality among Men," which had appeared the same year. Rousseau, too, claimed that humankind's "progress" over time had been anything but a spontaneously occurring mechanism; it had been brought on by pressing needs and accompanying societal forces that, in turn, influenced changes in cognitive development. For more on Rousseau's text, see Charles L. Griswold, "Genealogical Narrative and Self-Knowledge in Rousseau's Discourse on the Origin and Foundation of Inequality among Men," *History of European Ideas* 42, no. 2 (2016): 276–301.

56. Adam Smith, *Lectures on Justice, Police, Revenue and Arms Delivered in the University of Glasgow by Adam Smith, Reported by a Student in 1763* (Oxford: Clarendon Press, 1896), 107. On the significance of these lectures, see Silvia Sebastiani, *The Scottish Enlightenment: Race, Gender, and the Limits of Progress* (Basingstoke: Palgrave Macmillan, 2013), 45.

57. Smith, *Lectures on Justice*, 107.

58. Ibid., 108.

59. Smith ultimately made use of stage theory (with different ends in mind) in the *Theory of Moral Sentiments*, *The Wealth of Nations*, and in the one solo essay he published during his lifetime, the "Considerations on the First Formation

of Languages." In the first of these two works, Smith claimed that morality did not arise from either Scripture or philosophy; it developed organically within the species over time and is now an integral part of our existence as social beings. We are good, Smith argued, because we have become naturally sympathetic or empathetic beings.

60. The expression "rudeness to refinement" was coined by Gilbert Stuart in 1778; it was the title of his book on the "history of law, government, and manners."

61. It should be added, however, that Smith made clear that the division of labor in "Commercial Society" can transform people into unthinking cogs.

62. Adam Smith, *The Theory of Moral Sentiments*, Knud Haakonssen, ed. (Cambridge: Cambridge University Press 2004), 245.

63. Adam Smith, *The Works of Adam Smith* (London: T. Cadell, 1811), 5:84 and 5:85.

64. In fact, Hume used the word *race* to refer to people's professions, most famously the "unprosperous race of men commonly called men of letters." See David M. Levy and Sandra J. Peart, "Group Analytics in Adam Smith's Work," *Eastern Economic Journal* 42 (2016): 514–527.

65. There were also other high-minded ideas embedded in Smith's writings. Indeed, Smith went as far as to compare the greedy White merchant to Africans in general. "There is not a negro from the coast of Africa who does not possess a degree of magnanimity which the soul of his sordid master is too often scarce capable of conceiving." Eric Schliesser, *Adam Smith: Systematic Philosopher and Public Thinker* (Oxford: Oxford University Press, 2017), 166.

66. *The Edinburgh Literary Journal*, July 1830–December 1830 (Edinburgh: Ballantyne and Co., 1830), 160.

67. Höpfl, "From Savage to Scotsman," 24.

68. Hume had changed the spelling of his given surname, "Home," to "Hume" when he was in England in order to indicate the proper (Scottish) pronunciation of the family name. He also used his considerable influence to convince some of the more conservative members of the Kirk from excommunicating his younger cousin, David.

69. Andreas Rahmatian, *Lord Kames: Legal and Social Theorist* (Edinburgh: Edinburgh University Press, 2015), 2.

70. William C. Lehmann, *Henry Home, Lord Kames, and the Scottish Enlightenment: a Study in National Character in the History of Ideas* (Dordrecht: Springer

Science and Business Media, 1971), xvii. See also T. C. Smout, "A New Look at the Scottish Improvers," *The Scottish Historical Review* 91, no. 231 (April 2012): 138.

71. Henry Home, Lord Kames, *Historical Law-Tracts* (Edinburgh: A. Kincaid, 1761), v. See also Silvia Sebastiani, *The Scottish Enlightenment: Race, Gender, and the Limits of Progress*, 73.

72. Henry Home, Lord Kames, *Sketches of the History of Man* (Edinburgh: W. Creech, 1774), 1:v.

73. Ibid., 1:13.

74. Ibid., 1:20.

75. Ibid.

76. Ibid., 1:32.

77. The idea of separate "Adams," which was one of Isaac de La Peyrère's ideas, was also taken up to great effect by the American polygenists associated with the so-called American School of Ethnography, among them Samuel G. Morton, Josiah C. Nott, and Louis Agassiz. See Walter H. Conser, *God and the Natural World: Religion and Science in Antebellum America* (Columbia: The University of South Carolina Press, 1993), 22–23.

78. Henry Home, Lord Kames, *Sketches of the History of Man*, 1:10. Kames's separation of humans into distinct biological categories was shocking. By the mid-1770s, he had come to be known, alongside Voltaire, as one of the two most famous men to put forward a polygenist explanation for the human species. This perhaps explains why he seemingly recanted later in the book by saying that, despite all the evidence pointing to different "species" of men, "we are not permitted to adopt" such a view because of the revelation. Ibid., 1:39.

79. This was not an entirely triumphalist narrative. Kames was also worried that selfishness during this new era would undermine civic values. See Rahmatian, *Lord Kames*, 3.

80. See Jeffrey R. Smitten, *Life of William Robertson: Minister, Historian, and Principal* (Edinburgh: Edinburgh University Press, 2016), 38. Robertson began his career as a theology and arts student at the University of Edinburgh in the late 1730s. Studying under Charles Mackie, the university's first chair of universal history, he supplemented his career path toward the ministry with classes on history, law, rhetoric, and literature. In 1743, after receiving his degree, the twenty-two-year-old Robertson was named minister in the neighboring village of Gladsmuir.

81. Dugald Stewart, "An Account of the Life and Writings of William Robertson," in *The Works of William Robertson D.D.* (London: T. Cadell, 1840), 1:vii.

As a member of the Moderate Party of clerics within the Church of Scotland, Robertson saw absolutely no contradiction between his spiritual calling and his participation in some of the most important debates of the Scottish Enlightenment. Well before he had officially returned to Edinburgh as minister of the city's Lady Yester's Church in 1758, Robertson had been deeply involved with the Edinburgh literati and had even been one of the founders of the Select Society. On Robertson and the Moderates, see Smitten, *Life of William Robertson*, 129–130.

82. William Robertson, *The History of America* (London: Strahan, et al., 1800), 2:25.

83. William Robertson, *The History of the Reign of Charles the Fifth* (Philadelphia: J. B. Lippincott, 1899), 95. First printed in 1770–1771.

84. Smitten, *Life of William Robertson*, 172.

85. William Robertson, *An Historical Disquisition Concerning the Knowledge Which the Ancients Had of India* (Utrecht and Rotterdam: for B. Wild and Altheer, 1792).

86. Robertson, *The History of America*, 2:51. While speaking about the Spanish in America, Robertson had had occasion to speak about the "advanced peoples of the Americas," e.g., the Aztecs and the Inca, the "two nations in this vast continent which had emerged from this rude state." Ibid., 1:283. For an assessment of the overall "Amerindian ethnography," see Stewart J. Brown, "An Eighteenth-Century Historian on the Amerindians: Culture, Colonialism, and Christianity in William Robertson's History of America," *Studies in World Christianity* 2, no. 2 (1996): 204.

87. Robertson, *The History of America*, Ibid.

88. Ibid., 2:65.

89. Ibid., 2:66.

90. Ibid., 2:65. The screaming paradox of this presentation of Amerindians was the fact that, in an era when European women had few real rights, many eighteenth-century naturalists congratulated themselves that "their" women were able to participate far more fully in society. See Sylvia Sebastiani, "Race, Women, and Progress in the Late Scottish Enlightenment," in *Women, Gender and Enlightenment*, eds. Sarah Knott and Barbara Taylor (London: Palgrave Macmillan UK, 2005) for an exceptional consideration of the role of women in Enlightenment Scotland.

91. Robertson, *The History of America*, 2:96.

92. After Robertson's death, his son published the final two volumes of the

History in 1796. See Florence Petroff, "William Robertson's Unfinished History of America. The Foundation of the British Empire in North America and the Scottish Enlightenment," *Transatlantica* 2 (2017): 1.

93. There were certainly Americans who rejected his views — in 1785, Thomas Jefferson took Robertson to task for his views of America's "aboriginal" men. Jefferson writes: "He relates nothing on his own knowledge, he is a compiler only of the relations of others, and a mere translator of the [negative] opinions of Monsieur de Buffon." See Joyce Appleby and Terence Ball, eds., *Jefferson: Political Writings* (Cambridge: Cambridge University Press, 1999), 516.

94. Bernard Aspinwall, "William Robertson and America," in *Eighteenth Century Scotland: New Perspectives*, eds. T. M. Devine and J. R. Young (East Linton: Tuckwell Press, 1999), 155. Aspinwall's thesis that Robertson was part of a "transatlantic network" is a real contribution to our understanding of the influence of conjectural history.

95. Ibid., 152.

96. William Robertson, *The History of America Including the United States* (New York: Blakeman and Mason, 1859), 2:1110.

97. Lehmann, Henry Home, xvi. See also Silvia Sebastiani, *The Scottish Enlightenment: Race, Gender, and the Limits of Progress*, 77. At the old judge's funeral in 1782, Smith sadly proclaimed that Kames had been "the master of us all."

98. Rasmussen, *The Infidel and the Professor*, 12. I am grateful to Rasmussen for this keen insight.

99. Joe Blosser, "Relational History: Adam Smith's Types of Human History," *Erasmus Journal for Philosophy and Economics* 12, no. 2 (2019): 24–48.

100. Hume, "Of the Study of History," *Delphi Complete Works of David Hume*, 1280.

101. Sir James Prior, *Memoir of the Life and Character of the Right Honorable Edmund Burke* (n.p., printed for Baldwick, Cradock, and Joy, 1826), 333.

102. Hume, "The Natural History of Religion," *Delphi Complete Works of David Hume*, 1721.

103. Rasmussen, *The Infidel and the Professor*, 215.

104. Contemporary critics to highlight Hume's racism include: Bentham, Garrett, Sebastiani, Popkin, Gates, and Eze. During his lifetime, Hume was understandably unpopular with his religious contemporaries, yet he continued to make posthumous ripples in the philosophical community. See Danielle Charette, "David Hume's Balancing Act: The Political Discourses and the

Sinews of War," *The American Political Science Review* 115, no. 1 (2021): 69–81, for one such example of Hume's confounding ideological legacy.

105. Hume, *Enquiry Concerning Human Understanding*, *Delphi Complete Works of David Hume*, 1280.

106. Hume, "Of the Populousness of Ancient Nations," *Delphi Complete Works of David Hume*, 1131.

107. Other "facts" that have occasionally been put forward in the philosopher's "favor" or "defense" include his stance on slavery. In an era where "virtually every nook and cranny of Hume's Scotland . . . benefited from the plantation slave-based across the Atlantic," the philosopher "rejected the legality and logic of human slavery each time he examined it critically." Philip Morgan, "Forward," in *Recovering Scotland's Slavery Past: The Caribbean Connection*, ed. T. M. Devine (Edinburgh; Edinburgh University Press, 2015), xiv, cited in Peter Hutton and David Ashton, "David Hume—An Apologia," *Scottish Affairs* 32, no. 3 (2023): 349. Though he did not get actively involved in the very nascent abolitionist movement, his arguments against slavery, which he generally transposed to ancient Rome, were eagerly deployed by more active participants in the antislavery movement decades later. Hume's supposed condemnation of slavery has been most forcefully countered by Felix Waldman, who discovered a letter from Hume advising Lord Hertford that he might want to consider purchasing plantations in Grenada. See Charette, "David Hume and the Politics of Slavery," 1–21.

108. James Beattie, *An Essay on the Nature and Immutability of Truth, in Opposition to Skepticism* (London: Mawman, 1812), 8. Beattie also organized a debate at the Aberdeen Philosophical Society that clearly targeted the idea that Europeans were biologically superior. See Andersson Burnett and Buchan, *Race and the Scottish Enlightenment*, 76.

VIII. KANT AND BLUMENBACH AND THE GERMAN DEFINITION OF RACE

1. Like many other privatdozents, Kant saved money by renting a room in the *Neustadt*, in his case from a full professor named Kypke. See Martin Schönfeld, *The Philosophy of the Young Kant: The Precritical Project* (Oxford: Oxford University Press, 2000), 185.

2. Manfred Kuehn, *Kant: A Biography* (Cambridge: Cambridge University Press, 2001), 108.

3. The first surviving notebooks date from the 1770s.

4. Amazingly enough, Kant taught a version of this course an astonishing forty-eight times. After 1772, he also offered an annual course on anthropology until he retired in 1796. See Jennifer Mensch, *Kant's Organicism: Epigenesis and the Development of Critical Philosophy* (Chicago: University of Chicago Press, 2015), 197.

5. Huaping Lu-Adler, "Know Your Place, Know Your Calling: Geography, Race, and Kant's 'World Citizen,'" *Studia Kantiana* 21, no. 2 (2023): 82.

6. Namsoon Kang, *Cosmopolitan Theology: Reconstituting Planetary Hospitality, Neighbor-Love and Solidarity in an Uneven World* (Des Peres, MO: Chalice Press, 2013), 75. See also Huaping Lu-Adler, "Know Your Place," 82–85.

7. Kuehn, *Kant*, 26.

8. John Wall, "Human Rights in Light of Childhood," *International Journal of Children's Rights* 16, no. 4 (2008): 530.

9. Kuehn, *Kant*, 35–37. For more on Kant's later interactions with and thoughts on the Prussian theology, see Jonathan Head, "Scripture and Moral Examples in Pietism and Kant's Religion," *Irish Theological Quarterly* 83, no. 3 (2018): 217–234.

10. Kant's mother, née Anne Regina Reuter, had achieved a level of literacy seldom seen among the daughters of tradesmen. The children in his neighborhood — all of Kant's friends were the children of tradesmen — also had access to free schooling, if their parents were inclined to send them. See Kuehn, *Kant*, 58. Later in life Kant credited his mother for having "a continual and beneficial influence in [his] life." Ibid., 31.

11. See Manchester University's useful website on the college's curriculum: https://users.manchester.edu/facstaff/ssnaragon/kant/students/studentCollFrid.htm.

12. Ernst Cassirer, *Kant's Life and Thought* (New Haven and London: Yale University Press, 1981), 16.

13. Kuehn, *Kant*, 26. See also Graham Bird, ed., *A Companion to Kant* (New York: Wiley-Blackwell, 2015), 35.

14. Kuehn, *Kant*, 61.

15. Ibid., 63.

16. Kuehn, *Kant*, 64.

17. Ibid. Kant not only made money on the parlor game, but often cited it to discuss the notion of causation. See also Benjamin S. Llamzon, *A Humane Case for Moral Intuition* (Boston: Brill, 2022), 139–140.

18. During his last two years before coming back to university, Kant had

actually served as tutor to Heinrich Christian von Keyserling, the richest man in Königsberg. Cassirer, *Kant's Life and Thought*, 32–33.

19. Kant had already written a short treatise entitled the "True Estimation of Living Forces" in German during 1746 and 1747 and finally published it in 1749. Given that it was written in German, it did not count as a master's thesis, one of the reasons he was unable to secure his diploma before leaving. See "Introduction," Immanuel Kant, *Universal Natural History*, in *The Cambridge Edition of the Works of Immanuel Kant, Natural Science*, ed. Eric Watkins (Cambridge: Cambridge University Press, 2012), 1–4.

20. The articles in question include: "Examination of the question whether the rotation of the Earth on its axis by which it brings about the alternation of day and night has undergone any change since its origin and how one can be certain of this," which was submitted to a prize puzzle contest organized by the Royal Academy of Sciences in Berlin (1754), and "The question, whether the Earth is aging, considered from a physical point of view" (1754). See Kant, *Natural Science*.

21. Kant, *Natural Science*, 193.

22. These included Voltaire and the notorious atheist Julien Offray de La Mettrie. He also invited Maupertuis to run the Berlin Academy of Sciences. See Mary Terrall, *The Man Who Flattened the Earth: Maupertuis and the Sciences in the Enlightenment* (Chicago: University of Chicago Press, 2002), 182. See also Ina Goy, "Kant's Theory of Biology and the Argument from Design" in Ina Goy, Eric Watkins, eds., *Kant's Theory of Biology* (Berlin and Boston: De Kruyter, 2014).

23. Kant, *Universal Natural History*, 263.

24. Ibid., 266.

25. Ibid.

26. Ibid., 267.

27. Ibid., 200.

28. Ibid., 267.

29. Ibid., 298, 301.

30. Ibid.

31. Bird, *A Companion to Kant*, 59.

32. Eric Watkins, "Editor's Introduction," *Universal Natural History*, 186.

33. John H. Zammito, *Kant, Herder, and the Birth of Anthropology* (Chicago: Chicago University Press, 2002), 102.

34. See "Introduction" to Kant, *Universal Natural History*, 18. See also Zammito, *Kant, Herder, and the Birth of Anthropology*, 83. Kant ultimately achieved a

certain amount of fame in 1763 by publishing a work entitled "The Only Possible Argument in Support of a Demonstration of the Existence of God" and another essay on natural theology and morality that he submitted to a contest organized by the Berlin Academy.

35. Zammito, *Kant, Herder, and the Birth of Anthropology*, 83. Readers who were aware of recent *aesthetic* debates presumably expected Kant to build on what Johann Joachim Winckelmann, David Hume, and Edmund Burke had recently written on *the beautiful*, *the sublime*, *the grotesque*, and even *the ridiculous*.

36. Immanuel Kant, *Observations on the Feeling of the Beautiful and Sublime*, in *Anthropology, History, and Education: The Cambridge Edition of the Works of Immanuel Kant*, eds. Robert B. Louden and Günter Zöller (Cambridge: Cambridge University Press, 2007), 23.

37. Ibid., 24.

38. Ibid. Kant divides *sublimity* into the terrifying, noble, and magnificent. See Rachel Zuckert, "The Momentary Inhibition and Outpouring of the Vital Powers: Kant on the Dynamic Sublime," in *Kant and the Feeling of Life: Beauty and Nature in the Critique of Judgment*, ed. Jennifer Mensch (Albany: State University of New York Press, 2024), 129–152.

39. Kant, *Observations on the Feeling of the Beautiful and Sublime*, 24–26.

40. Ibid., 33, 35. See also Anthony Halliday, *The Temperamental Nude: Class, Medicine, and Representation in Eighteenth-century France*. Studies on Voltaire and the Eighteenth Century (Oxford: Voltaire Foundation, 2010), 78.

41. Halliday, *The Temperamental Nude*, 40. Explicitly contrasting this "female" orientation with that of the male, Kant claims that if woman has "just as much understanding as the male," it is a beautiful understanding, while [the male's] understanding . . . should be a deeper understanding . . . the same thing as the sublime" (ibid., 41).

42. Ibid., 41.

43. Ibid.

44. Referring specifically to men in this case.

45. Ibid., 51.

46. Ibid., 56.

47. Ibid., 58–59. In assessing the aesthetic orientation of China and India, Kant is unexpectedly harsh. The Indians, he claims, "have a dominant taste for grotesqueries of the kind that comes down to the adventurous. Their religion consists of grotesqueries." Similar comments are made regarding the Chinese: "What ridiculous grotesqueries do the verbose and studied compliments of the Chinese not contain: even their paintings are grotesque and represent marvelous and unnatural shapes" (Ibid., 59).

48. Ibid., 60. "[The savages] have a strong feeling for honor, and as hunt of it they will seek wild adventures hundreds of miles away, they are also extremely careful to avoid the least injury to it [honor] where their ever so harsh enemy, after he has captured them, tries to force a cowardly sigh from them by dreadful tortures."

49. Ibid., 59.

50. Ibid., 61.

51. Ibid. Here he is borrowing from Montesquieu.

52. "Translator's Introduction" in Kant, *Observations on the Feeling of the Beautiful and Sublime*, 19.

53. Stuckenberg, *The Life of Immanuel Kant*, 86. In 1769, he had turned down a different chair at Erlangen, some 50 miles south of his beloved Königsberg.

54. Arsenji Gulyga, *Immanuel Kant: His Life and Thought* (New York: Springer, 2012), 153.

55. Kuehn, *Kant*, 238–239.

56. Ibid., 6.

57. He had also begun offering a new class on anthropology. Immanuel Kant, *Lectures on Anthropology*, eds. Allen W. Wood and Robert B. Louden (Cambridge: Cambridge University Press, 2012), "General Introduction," 2.

58. It was in the 1777 version that Kant stipulated that the original stem was white. See Robert Bernasconi, "Who Invented the Concept of Race? Kant's Role in the Enlightenment Construction of Race," in *Race*, ed. Robert Bernsconi (Oxford: Blackwell, 2000), 21.

59. "Editor's Introduction," in Kant, "Of the Different Races of Human Beings" (1775) in Louden et al., *Anthropology, History, and Education*, 82.

60. Kant had very much agreed with the definition of species based on *interfertility*. This was not the only way of identifying "a natural species," as he puts it, it also proves that "all human beings on earth belong to one and the same natural species because they consistently beget fertile children with one another, no matter what great differences may otherwise be encountered in their shape." Kant, "Of the Different Races of Human Beings," 84–85.

61. Kant, "Of the Different Races of Human Beings," 85.

62. This "turn" is explained very well by Huaping Lu-Adler, *Kant, Race, and Racism* (Oxford: Oxford University Press, 2023), 129.

63. Ibid., 89.

64. Ibid., 90.

65. Ibid., 91.

66. Ibid., 92. See also Jimmy Yab, *Kant and the Politics of Racism: Toward Kant's Racialised Form of Cosmopolitan Right* (New York: Springer International Publishing, 2021), 109, no. 32.

67. Kant, "Of the Different Races of Human Beings," 92–93.

68. Ibid., 93.

69. Ibid., 87.

70. Ibid., 88. Later on he says that one can infer that Indians came from the North since they have "suppressed hair growth on all parts of the body except the head" and an "extinguished life power." Ibid., 92.

71. Ibid.

72. Ibid., 85.

73. Ibid.

74. Ibid.

75. Ibid., 86. See also Robert Bernasconi, "Who Invented the Concept of Race?" in *Race*, 95.

76. To demonstrate this, Kant supplies several examples of how preexisting categories can create new categories, including: "[T]he mixing of the Tartaric with the Hunnish blood has produced *half-races* in the Karakulpacks, the Nagajens." Bernasconi, "Who Invented the Concept of Race?" in *Race*, 87.

77. The practice of "face reading" has been around since the times of Aristotle. See Ran Hassin and Yaacov Trope, "Facing Faces: Studies on the Cognitive Aspects of Physiognomy," *Journal of Personality and Social Psychology* 78, no. 5 (2000): 837–852. Physiognomy as a "science," however, only took shape with Lavater. See also Graeme Tytler and Melissa Percival, eds., *Physiognomy in Profile: Lavater's Impact on European Culture* (Newark: University of Delaware Press, 2005), 25–26.

78. François Para du Phanjas, *Les Principes de la saine philosophie conciliés avec ceux de la religion ou la philosophie de la religion* (Paris: Charles-Antoine Joubert, 1774), 144.

79. Oliver Goldsmith, *A History of the Earth and Animated Nature* (London: J. Nourse, 1774), 2:219.

80. John Hunter, *Disputation Inauguralis*, in Johann Friedrich Blumenbach, *The Anthropological Treatises of Johann Friedrich Blumenbach*, ed. Thomas Bendyshe (London: Longman, Green, et al., 1865), 366–367.

81. Henry Home, Lord Kames, *Sketches of the History of Man* (Edinburgh: W. Creech, 1774), 1:10.

82. See Markman Ellis, Catherine Hall, Miles Ogborn, and Silvia Sebastiani, "Edward Long and Other Animals: The Orangutan and Race-Making in the Late Eighteenth Century," *Modern Intellectual History* (2024): 1–30.

83. Robert Bernasconi has made an interesting point about this: The "fact that the scientific concept of race was developed initially in Germany rather than in Britain or America suggests that it was not specifically the interests of the slaveowners that led to its introduction," it was a defense of "monogenism." See "Who Invented the Concept of Race?" 21.

84. Cornelius de Pauw, *Recherches philosophiques sur les Américains, ou Mémoires intéressants pour servir à l'histoire de l'espèce humaine* (Berlin: George Jacques Decker, imprimeur du roi, 1769), 2:155.

85. Ibid.

86. Born into a family of distinguished professors and civil servants, Blumenbach was particularly influenced by his father, a professor and *prorector* at the prestigious Gotha grammar school and, as one contemporary put it, a "zealous admirer of geography and natural history." M. Flourens, "Memoir of Blumenbach," in *The Anthropological Treaties of Johann Friedrich Blumenbach*, 49.

87. Ibid., 50. Gotha was part of the Duchy of Saxe-Gotha-Altenburg, one of the many small German principalities.

88. Ibid., 51.

89. While at Jena, Blumenbach often worked closely with a fellow student who would become a close colleague and lifelong friend, Samuel Thomas Sömmerring. The two men belonged to a new and profoundly empirical generation of naturalists that was increasingly preoccupied with the relationship between human variation, human origins, and the extent to which comparative anatomy might illuminate such mysteries. In later years, Blumenbach and Sömmerring would disagree about the significance of some of their respective findings. See Han F. Vermeulen, *Before Boas: The Genesis of Ethnography and Ethnology in the German Enlightenment* (Lincoln: University of Nebraska Press, 2015), 371. See also Claudio Pogliano, *Brain and Race: A History of Cerebral Anthropology* (Leiden: Brill, 2020), 39–40. Sömmerring came to Gottïngen as well.

90. Morgan Golf-French, "Teaching Race in the German Enlightenment: Christoph Meiners' History of Humanity in Institutional Context," in *History of Universities: Volume XXXVI/2*, edited by Mordechai Feingold (Oxford: Oxford University Press, 2023), 244.

91. Ibid., 244.

92. Büttner's stance that humans "should be a primary topic in natural history" inspired Blumenbach's dissertation topic ("the natural variety of mankind") and his eventual directorial position in the Academic Museum's natural history collections. See Mark Larrimore and Sara Eigen, eds., *The German Invention of Race* (Albany: State University of New York Press, 2012), 44.

93. M. Flourens, "Memoir of J. F. Blumenbach," 51.

94. Snait B. Gissis, "Visualizing Race in the Eighteenth Century," *Historical Studies in the Natural Sciences* 41, no. 1 (Winter 2011): 42.

95. Blumenbach's *De generis humani varietate nativa* became one of the best-selling and most influential works of natural history ever published.

96. Larrimore and Eigan, *The German Invention of Race*, 43–44. Larrimore and Eigan point out that Blumenbach only became "aware" of Kant in 1777 and only took an interest in his racial writing "in the late 1780s."

97. Johann Friedrich Blumenbach, *De generis humani varietate nativa* in *The Anthropological Treatises of Johann Friedrich Blumenbach*, 98. Comparing the brain of a mandrill to that of a human, he noted that the mandrill's brain weighed "three ounces and one drachm, while the rest of the body of the ape weighed eight common pounds and a half." Ibid., 92.

98. The Scottish judge and member of the Select Society, Lord Monboddo, had also claimed that apes had a common ancestor with man. Monboddo began hinting at this idea in his 1773 *Antiquities of Man*. This idea solidified in his multivolume *The Origin and Progress of Language* (1773–1792). See Rurmer Bijlsma, "Of Savages and Stoics: Converging moral and political ideals in the conjectural histories of Rousseau and Ferguson," *Philosophy & Social Criticism* 48, no. 2 (2022): 209–244.

99. Blumenbach, *De generis humani varietate nativa*, in *The Anthropological Treatises of Johann Friedrich Blumenbach*, 67.

100. Ibid., 99.

101. Blumenbach's views on the particular physiognomy of Jews, for example, are far from enlightened. "The Jewish race presents the most notorious and least deceptive, which can easily be recognized everywhere by their eyes alone, which breathe of the East." Ibid., 122.

102. Ibid., 100.

103. Ibid., 99.

104. Ibid., 106.

105. Larrimore and Eigen, *The German Invention of Race*, 44. Blumenbach held (and advanced) his position in the museum until his death. Ibid., 136. In 1784, while still a young man, he was inducted into the Göttingen Academy of Sciences.

106. Nicolaas Rupke and Gerhard Lauer, eds., *Blumenbach and Natural History* (Oxfordshire: Routledge, 2019), 252.

107. See Aaron Garrett, "Human Nature," in *The Cambridge History of Eighteenth-Century Philosophy*, Knud Haakonssen, ed. (Cambridge: Cambridge University Press, 2006), 1:192.

108. Johann Christian Wilhelm Marx, "Memoir of J. F. Blumenbach," 25.

109. Ibid.

110. Carl Niekerk, "Man and Orangutan in Eighteenth-Century Thinking: Retracing the Early History of Dutch and German Anthropology," *The Eighteenth Century* 27, no. 4 (Winter 2004): 488.

111. I am deeply indebted to the great Kant scholar Wolfgang Böker for his analysis of this anecdote. In his words, "The source of this anecdote is not Blumenbach himself, but his obituarist/biographer, the Göttingen physician and historian of medicine Karl Friedrich Heinrich Marx (1796–1877). Marx did not study at Göttingen university; he came to Göttingen in 1820, after he had gained his PhD in medicine at Jena. Still, he may have attended Blumenbach's lectures himself. Marx's text was published in 1840." The earliest trace of the anecdote is a letter by Blumenbach's father-in-law, the Hanoverian politician Georg Friedrich Brandes (1719–1791), to Blumenbach. Brandes writes: "The natural rarities on display at your fair [in Göttingen] have also been presented here [i.e., in Hanover], and our zoologist, LeibChirurgus Lampe, also suspected the fraud with the pseudo-monstro, whereupon they [i.e., the showmen who presented the bear] were ordered to leave Hanover" (G. F. Brandes to Blumenbach, March 19, 1791). See Norbert Klatt, ed., *The Correspondence of Johann Friedrich Blumenbach: 1791–1795* (Göttingen: Klatt, 2012), 4:36–37. It seems that Blumenbach formed from the original incident a little story which became part of the standard repertoire of anecdotes he used in his natural history lectures.

112. Wolfgang Böker, "Blumenbach's Collection of Human Skulls," in *Johann Friedrich Blumenbach: Race and Natural History, 1750–1850*, eds. Nicolaas Rupke and Gerhardt Lauer (London and New York: Routledge, 2020), 81. See Paul Wolff Mitchell, "Origins of Races, Organs of Intellect: Polygenism, Political Order, and the Enlightenment Construction of Cranial Race Science," in *Ordering the Human: The Global Spread of Racial Science*, eds. Eram Alam, Dorothy

Roberts, and Natalie Shibley (New York: Columbia University Press, 2024), 44, 81–82.

113. See John H. Zammito, "Policing Polygeneticism in Germany," in *The German Invention of Race*, eds. Mark Larrimore and Sara Eigen (Albany: State University of New York Press, 2006), 44–45.

114. Ibid.

115. Caucasians included Arabs, the Habesha peoples of Ethiopia, and some Indian groups.

116. Morgan Golf-French, "Teaching Race in the German Enlightenment," 245.

117. Tuska Benes, *The Rebirth of Revelation: German Theology in an Age of Reason and History, 1750–1850* (Toronto: University of Toronto Press, 2022), 56, 58–59. See also Jon M. Mikkelson, trans. and ed., *Kant and the Concept of Race: Late Eighteenth-Century Writings* (Albany: State University of New York Press, 2013), 197.

118. Walter Demel, "How the Mongoloid Race Came into Being: Late Eighteenth-Century Constructions of East Asians in Europe," in *Race and Racism in Modern East Asia*, eds. Rotem Kowner and Walter Demel (Leiden and Boston: Brill, 2013), 79.

119. See Londa Schiebinger, "The Anatomy of Difference: Race and Sex in Eighteenth-Century Science," *Eighteenth-Century Studies* 23, no. 4 (1990): 387.

120. Unlike Blumenbach, whose use of anatomy served to *separate* man from beast, Sömmerring drew from anatomy to put forward a natural hierarchy that descended "by degrees from the *white man* to the *Negro*, and from the *Negro* to the *Hottentot*: from the *Hottentot* to the *Orang-Outang*." This "anatomically" justified link to a simian lineage would become a leitmotif within nineteenth-century scientific racism. Interestingly enough, in the second edition of the book, Sömmerring claimed that there is a fundamental divide between humans (including Africans) and apes. I'm grateful to Morgan Golf-French for pointing this out to me.

121. Kuehn, *Kant*, 271.

122. Ibid., 270.

123. Bernard Boxill, "Kantian Racism and Kantian Teleology," in *The Oxford Handbook of Race and Philosophy*, ed. Naomi Zack (New York: Oxford University Press, 2017), see 44–48.

124. The critical period includes *The Critique of Pure Reason* (1781, 1787), the *Prolegomena to Any Future Metaphysics* (1883), *Critique of Practical Reason* (1788),

and *Critique of the Power of Judgment* (1790). One can also include his *Religion within the Bounds of Pure Reason* (1793).

125. Immanuel Kant, *Groundwork for the Metaphysics of Morals*, ed. Allen W. Wood (New Haven: Yale University Press, 2008), 41.

126. Kant had, however, been contemplating this question for years, prompted by E. A. W. Zimmermann's *Geographical History of Man* (1778–1783). See Mikkelsen, *Kant and the Concept of Race: Late Eighteenth-Century Writings*, 90.

127. This was the first of two volumes.

128. Jennifer Mensch, "Kant and the Skull Collectors: German Anthropology from Blumenbach to Kant," in *Kant and His German Contemporaries: Logic, Mind, Epistemology, Science and Ethics*, vol. 1, eds. Corey Dyck and Falk Wunderlich (Cambridge: Cambridge University Press, 2018), 1:194.

129. See Bernasconi, "Who Invented the Concept of Race?" 28.

130. Immanuel Kant, "Review of Herder's *Ideas*" in Louden et al., *Anthropology, History, and Education*, 139. This appeared in the periodical *Allgemeine Literaturzeitung*. Herder knew immediately who had written this assessment.

131. Immanuel Kant, "Determination of the Concept of a Human Race," 148.

132. Ibid., 148.

133. Ibid., 154.

134. Georg Ernst Stahl, a German chemist and physician, put forward the theory that phlogiston might be present in the human body. See Martin Carrier, "Kant's Theory of Matter and His View of Chemistry," in *Kant and the Sciences*, ed. Eric Watkins (Oxford: Oxford University Press, 2001), 216–217. To demonstrate how this definition works, Kant asks his reader to imagine the following scenario: Relocate a Black African to comparatively sunless France, where you will see over time just what amount of his blackness is *hereditary* and, thus, what constitutes a "classificatory difference." Kant, "Determination of the Concept of a Human Race," 146. On this, see also Bernasconi, "Who Invented the Concept of Race?" 94.

135. This ponderous title essentially means that Kant is distinguishing between a "mechanical" use of philosophy — the disinterested explanation of natural phenomena as the product of various physical or deterministic variables — and one that explains natural phenomena in terms of a *telos*, or a built-in purpose, the most famous example being the notion that nature has created *germs* or *races* with specific intent.

136. Immanuel Kant, *On the Use of Teleological Principles in Philosophy*, in Louden et al., *Anthropology, History, and Education*, 186–187.

137. The 1781 breakdown can be found in Blumenbach, *De generis humani varietate nativa*, in *The Anthropological Treatises of Johann Friedrich Blumenbach*, 99–100.

138. Wolfgang Böker, "Blumenbach's Collection of Human Skulls," in *Johann Friedrich Blumenbach: Race and Natural History*, 89.

139. Blumenbach had even translated and published letters from the formally enslaved writer Ignatius Sancho — Blumenbach writes that, among the supposedly "savage" nations around the globe, the one that has "distinguished itself by such examples of perfectibility and original capacity for scientific culture, and thereby attached itself so closely to the most civilized nations of the earth" was that of "*the Negro*." Blumenbach, "Contributions to Natural History," in *The Anthropological Treatises of Johann Friedrich Blumenbach*, 312.

140. Ibid.

141. Roger Downey, *Riddle of the Bones: Politics, Science, Race, and the Story of the Kennewick Man* (New York: Springer New York, 2000), 52–53. See also Nicolaas Rupke and Gerhard Lauer, "Introduction," in *Johann Friedrich Blumenbach: Race and Natural History, 1750–1850* (London: Routledge, 2018), 5–6.

142. Justin E. H. Smith, *Nature, Human Nature, and Human Difference*, 156.

143. Rambachan Aksharananda, "Overcoming the Racial Hierarchy: The History and Medical Consequences of 'Caucasian,'" *Journal of Racial and Ethnic Health Disparities* 5, no. 5 (2018): 907–912.

144. Kuehn, *Kant*, 272.

145. See Lu-Adler for a discussion of the "turn" toward a Rousseau's way of thinking. *Kant, Race, and Racism*, 125.

146. Kant, *Perpetual Peace: A Philosophical Essay* (Frankfurt: Outlook Verlag, 2020), "Introduction," 25.

147. Ibid., 383. See also James Bohman and Matthias Lutz-Bachmann, eds., *Perpetual Peace: Essays on Kant's Cosmopolitan Ideal* (Cambridge: MIT Press, 1997), 1–8.

148. Keuhn, *Kant*, 383. See Inés Valdez, *Transnational Cosmopolitanism: Kant, DuBois, and Justice as Political Craft* (Cambridge: Cambridge University Press, 2019), for a discussion of Kant, colonialism, and the challenges of a neo-Kantian cosmopolitanism that theoretically expands past Europe, especially 1–11.

149. Immanuel Kant, "Toward Perpetual Peace: A Philosophical Sketch," in *Toward Perpetual Peace and Other Writings on Politics, Peace, and History*, ed. Pauline Kleingeld (New Haven: Yale University Press, 2006), 84.

150. See Pauline Kleingeld's essay "Kant's Second Thoughts on Colonialism," in *Kant and Colonialism: Historical and Critical Perspectives*, eds. K. Flikschuh

and L. Ypi (Oxford: Oxford University Press, 2014), 43–76. Kleingeld argues that Kant actually recanted his racial beliefs.

151. Ibid., 82–83.

152. There is no absolute answer to such questions of course. Indeed, there is also another possible explanation regarding this monumental tension. Like many writers, Kant makes use of a different *register* — meaning specialized vocabulary and worldview — when writing in different genres. When Kant changes genres, from anthropology to philosophy for example, he often modifies his ideas to suit the structure and the conventions of the type of writing and arguments he is making. When writing on anthropology, for example, he writes as an anthropologist. When writing a philosophical treatise such as "Perpetual Peace," he trucks in universals.

153. Immanuel Kant, "An Answer to the Question: What is Enlightenment?" in *Princeton Readings in Political Thought: Essential Texts since Plato* (Princeton: Princeton University Press, 2018), 356. This was written in response to an essay contest organized by the *Berlinische Monatsschrift*.

154. Kant argued that different races had inherent and fixed cognitive abilities, maintaining that the peoples of the Indian subcontinent were incapable of reasoning at the same level as Europeans. Take, for example, what one of his students recorded during one of Kant's lectures: "[T]he Hindus all like philosophers. Despite this, they are nevertheless very much inclined toward anger and love. As a result, they acquire culture in the highest degree, but only in the arts and not in the sciences. They never raise it up to abstract concepts." See Jennifer Mensch and Michael J. Olsen, eds., *Key Texts in the History and Philosophy of the German Life Sciences, 1745–1845: Generation, Heredity, and Race* (London: Bloomsbury Academic, 2025), 1187.

155. He had said this as well in 1777–1778. Kant, "Physical Geography," *Natural Science*, 576.

156. During his career, Kant not only revolutionized epistemology, ethics, and aesthetics, he was also instrumental in putting into practice a new philosophical method characterized by a single-minded and rigorous treatment of basic questions having to do with the human condition. To a large degree, Kantian thinking helped define what the discipline of philosophy became in the Western world. This was certainly not racist in and of itself, of course. Yet when coupled with the idea that Africans, Amerindians, and Asians lacked the same ability to reason and thus ability to participate in the discipline, Western philosophy arguably became the most exclusionary of intellectual

fields. See Peter Park, *Africa, Asia, and the History of Philosophy: Racism in the Formation of the Philosophical Canon, 1780–1830* (Albany: State University of New York Press, 2013), 4.

IX. THOMAS JEFFERSON: NATION BUILDER, RACE BUILDER

1. *Journal of the House of Delegates* (Richmond: Thomas White, 1827), 32. By country, he meant Virginia.

2. "Norfolk Naval Shipyard," *Bureau of Ships Journal* 2, no. 1 (May 1953): 16–17. For the fullest account, see John Ferling, *Jefferson and Hamilton: The Rivalry That Forged a Nation* (New York: Bloomsbury Publishing, 2013), 91. South Carolina had become a target as well.

3. Jon Meacham, *Thomas Jefferson: The Art of Power* (New York: Random House Publishing Group, 2013), 80. Though he had served on committees where such matters were discussed in the Continental Congress, between 1775 and 1776, Jefferson was by no means a military mind.

4. John L. Cotter, Daniel G. Roberts, and Michael Parrington, *The Buried Past, An Archaeological History of Philadelphia* (Philadelphia: University of Pennsylvania Press, 1992), 129.

5. Richard B. Bernstein, *Thomas Jefferson* (Oxford: Oxford University Press, 2005), 38. The text reads: "No person hereafter coming into this country shall be held . . . in slavery under any pretext whatever." This obviously did not make it into the Constitution. Jefferson's notes can be found in Thomas Jefferson, *The Writings of Thomas Jefferson*, ed. Paul Leicester Ford (New York: Putnam, 1893), 2:26. Note: When Jefferson says "this country" in this citation, he means Virginia. Virginia had actually voted to abolish the trade in 1772, but Parliament vetoed it.

6. The challenges were overwhelming. The tobacco-dependent economy was in shambles. See Anne Bezanson, *Prices and Inflation During the American Revolution* (Philadelphia: University of Pennsylvania Press, 1951), 247–269. There was widespread disagreement among his advisors regarding what to do, and the Continental Congress was pressuring Jefferson to meet the state's quota of soldiers. Francis D. Cogliano, *Emperor of Liberty, Thomas Jefferson's Foreign Policy* (New Haven: Yale University Press, 2014), 17. See also John Ferling, *Apostles of Revolution: Jefferson, Paine, Monroe, and the Struggle Against the Old Order in America and Europe* (New York: Bloomsbury Publishing, 2018), 98. Jefferson had despised being governor to such an extent that he had implored a friend to replace him,

to no avail. See John R. Maass, *The Road to Yorktown: Jefferson, Lafayette and the British Invasion of Virginia* (Cheltenham, UK: History Press, 2015), 157–159.

7. Ibid., 212. Benedict Arnold's investment in the spoils of Virginia was not just financial, but seemingly personal too. Before Arnold retreated to the coast, he seized a number of Jefferson's slaves (notably including Isaac Granger Jefferson). Meacham, *Jefferson: The Art of Power*, 135. James A. Bear, *Jefferson at Monticello* (Charlottesville: University Press of Virginia, 1967), 8–9.

8. See Joseph J. Ellis, *American Sphinx: The Character of Thomas Jefferson* (New York: Knopf, 1997), 66.

9. Michael Kranish, *Flight from Monticello: Jefferson at War* (New York: Oxford University Press, 2010), 278–279.

10. For a nineteenth-century account see, George Tucker, *The Life of Thomas Jefferson, Third President of the United States* (Philadelphia: Carey, Lea & Blanchard, 1837), 1:165. See also Meacham, *Jefferson: The Art of Power*, 300.

11. "Letter from Thomas Jefferson to James Monroe," May 20, 1782, *Founders Online*, National Archives, https://founders.archives.gov/documents/Jefferson/01-06-02-0174.

12. He asked the governors or representatives of the other states to do the same. François Marquis de Barbé-Marbois, *Our Revolutionary Forefathers: The Letters of François, Marquis de Barbé-Marbois, During His Residence in the United States as Secretary for the French Legation, 1779–1785* (Ann Arbor: University of Michigan, 2006), 21.

13. One can get a sense of his enormous knowledge as well from a note he sends regarding his nephew's education: "From Thomas Jefferson to Walker Maury, with a List of Books, 19 August 1785," *Founders Online*, National Archives, https://founders.archives.gov/documents/Jefferson/01-08-02-0321 [PTJ: 409–412].

14. Thomas Jefferson, "Autobiography" in *Jefferson's Writings*, PTJ: 6:210.

15. Cynthia A. Kierner, *Martha Jefferson Randolph, Daughter of Monticello: Her Life and Times* (Chapel Hill: University of North Carolina Press, 2012), 16. See also William G. Hyland Jr., *Martha Jefferson: An Intimate Life with Thomas Jefferson* (Lanham, MD: Rowman and Littlefield, 2015), 74, 82. See also the traces of how important the Sterne novel was to them: "Lines Copied from Tristram Shandy by Martha and Thomas Jefferson, [before 6 September 1782]," *Founders Online*, National Archives, https://founders.archives.gov/documents/Jefferson/01-06-02-0185 [PTJ: 6:196–197].

16. Martha had given birth to one child during a previous marriage; that child had died.

17. Lucy died at age two, in October, 1784, when Jefferson was in Paris.

18. Jefferson's daughter later recalled that her father acted as her mother's "nurse," displaying as much "tenderness" as any female member of the profession. Kierner, *Martha Jefferson Randolph*, 36.

19. "From Thomas Jefferson to Chastellux, 26 November 1782," *Founders Online*, National Archives, https://founders.archives.gov/documents/Jefferson/01-06-02-0192 [PTJ: 6:21].

20. In November 1782, only a month after the final exchange of gunfire between American and English troops had taken place in Georgia, the United States Congress asked Jefferson to travel to Paris to help John Adams and Benjamin Franklin negotiate peace terms with Great Britain.

21. See *Thomas Jefferson, Autobiography Draft Fragment, January 6 through July 27*. 1821. Library of Congress, Washington, DC, https://www.loc.gov/item/mtjbib024000/.

22. The book was purchased for Virginia with state money. See "From Thomas Jefferson to John Fitzgerald, 27 February 1781," *Founders Online*, National Archives, https://founders.archives.gov/documents/Jefferson/01-05-02-0022 [PTJ: 5:25].

23. Patsy's real name was Martha.

24. During this trip, Jefferson consulted a Philadelphia printer about the publication of the latest version of the *Notes*, but decided against it given the expense. See Kevin J. Hayes, *The Road to Monticello: The Life and Mind of Thomas Jefferson* (Oxford: Oxford University Press, 2008), 271.

25. For a fuller assessment of this moment, including the fact that James Hemings was sent off on his own to make arrangements in Paris, see Annette Gordon-Reed, *The Hemingses of Monticello: An American Family* (New York: W. W. Norton, 2008), 161.

26. Hayes, *The Road to Monticello*, 279–280.

27. See Erika Gibson, "'Frenchified': French Food and Salon Culture in Jefferson's White House," *Food Studies* 8, no. 2 (2018): 1–13.

28. In the same letter, however, he spoke of social inequality and various other problems in France. "From Thomas Jefferson to Charles Bellini, 30 September 1785," *Founders Online*, National Archives, https://founders.archives.gov/documents/Jefferson/01-08-02-0448 [PTJ: 8:568–570].

29. See Jeanne E. Abrams, *Revolutionary Medicine: the Founding Fathers and*

Mothers in Sickness and in Health (New York: New York University Press, 2013), 186.

30. Andrew S. Curran, *Diderot and the Art of Thinking Freely* (New York: Other Press, 2019), 375–379.

31. Charles Henry Butler, *The Treaty Making Power of the United States* (New York: The Banks Law Publishing Company, 1902), 1:279.

32. Robert Pierce Forbes, "Introduction," in *Notes on the State of Virginia: An Annotated Edition* (New Haven: Yale University Press, 2022), l–lii. The book was printed by the Parisian printer Phillipe-Denis Pierres.

33. Ibid., liii.

34. Fawn M. Brodie, *Thomas Jefferson: An Intimate History* (New York: W.W. Norton, 1974), 92. See also Eva Sheppard Wolf, *Race and Liberty in the New Nation: Emancipation in Virginia from the Revolution to Nat Turner's Rebellion* (Baton Rouge: LSU Press, 2009), 14.

35. Ibid. Jefferson was arguing that since he had had a White grandmother, and that the status of the child—free or enslaved—passed through the mother, the grandson should technically be free, as should anyone in the lineage.

36. More likely, this problematic possibility would have been attributed to rape. Brodie, *Thomas Jefferson*, 92.

37. "Advertisement for a Runaway Slave, 7 September 1769," *Founders Online*, National Archives, https://founders.archives.gov/documents/Jefferson/01-01-02-0021 [*PTJ*: 1:33]. Sandy, as it turned out, was "recovered," although Jefferson sold him several years later.

38. As early as the early nineteenth century, he was congratulated for being a liberator, a man whose "theory was better than his practice." *The Genius of Universal Emancipation* 12 (no. 12), May 30, 1932: 202.

39. For an assessment of this debate in the 1990s, see Paul Finkelman, "Thomas Jefferson and Antislavery: The Myth Goes On," *The Virginia Magazine of History and Biography* 102, no. 2 (April 1994), 193–228.

40. Jefferson, *Notes*, 249.

41. Ibid., 250.

42. Jefferson claims that the progressive emancipation he describes here was present in an amendment that he had prepared for adoption if the bill for emancipation passed. See *Notes*, 210, no. 46. Forbes here expresses skepticism about this taking place as Jefferson describes it.

43. Abolition came about in different ways in the northern states. Unlike Vermont, Massachusetts did not pass an unambiguous bill abolishing slavery;

in 1783, it rendered it illegal via a series of judicial decisions. Connecticut also found its own path. According to the state's so-called Act of Gradual Abolition, any enslaved person born after May 1, 1784, would remain a "slave" until the age of twenty-five, at which point he or she would be freed. Joanne Pope Melish, *Disowning Slavery: Gradual Emancipation and "Race" in New England* (Ithaca: Cornell University Press, 1998), 11–49.

44. Jefferson, *Notes*, 210–211.

45. Ibid.

46. Ibid., 211.

47. Anthony Benezet's calls for an end to slavery were as powerful as they were comprehensive: "The evils of this trade, and its consequent slavery, are indeed increased to a degree of enormity that calls aloud for the interpolation of government." See Benezet, *Some Historical Account of Guinea* (London: J. Phillips, 1788 [first pub. 1771]), 131.

48. Jaucourt was a rich aristocrat and medical doctor who dedicated himself, including his financial resources, to helping save the *Encyclopédie* when it came under fire. See Curran, *Diderot and the Art of Thinking Freely*, 166.

49. *Encyclopédie*, 16:532–533.

50. Jefferson, *Notes*, 250.

51. He made this clear in a letter to John Manners in 1814. Having been solicited at the end of his life to talk about the "comparative merits of the different methods of classification adopted by different writers on Natural history," Jefferson replied that he was not able to do so even when "the subject was more familiar" to him when he was younger. "Thomas Jefferson to John Manners, 22 February 1814," *Founders Online*, National Archives, https://founders.archives.gov/documents/Jefferson/03-07-02-0132 [PTJ, Retirement Series: 7:207–211].

52. Antislavery thinkers also made use of this notion to maintain that race, to the extent that it really existed, was only skin deep. See William Dickson, *Letters on Slavery, . . . To Which Are Added, Addresses to the Whites, and to the Free Negroes of Barbados* (London: J. Phillips, 1789), 65. Some of these same books also included reports of "regeneration" or "reversion" to the original white norm. See Henry Louis Gates Jr. and Andrew S. Curran, *Who's Black and Why? A Hidden Chapter from the Eighteenth-Century Invention of Race* (Cambridge: Harvard University Press, 2022), 99–104.

53. Degeneration theorists had not, of course, been able to agree how long it took for this process to occur. Some people asserted that the changes in pigmentation and morphology could begin to happen relatively quickly, over one or two generations. Others imagined the process taking place over several centuries.

54. Jefferson, *Notes*, 77.

55. Ibid., 79.

56. Ibid., 95.

57. Lee Alan Dugatkin, *Mr. Jefferson and the Giant Moose: Natural History in Early America* (Chicago: University of Chicago Press, 2019), 81.

58. The discussion of the mammoth takes place in *Notes*, 72–77.

59. Dugatkin, *Mr. Jefferson and the Giant Moose*, 82.

60. Ibid.

61. Ibid., 95.

62. Ibid., 95.

63. Dugatkin, *Mr. Jefferson and the Giant Moose*, 100. Information related to the cost of shipping the moose can be found in a letter to Thomas Jefferson from John Sullivan, with "Account of Expenses for Obtaining Moose Skeleton, 26 April 1787," *Founders Online*, National Archives, https://founders.archives.gov/documents/Jefferson/01-11-02-0304 [PTJ: 11:320–321].

64. *Encyclopaedia Britannica: or a Dictionary of Arts, Sciences, and Miscellaneous Literature* (Edinburgh: Bell and Maccfarquhar, 1797), 1:559.

65. Compared to some of the other writers who put forward degeneration theory, Buffon was actually more optimistic about the fate of the New World's peoples. He had even allowed the possibility that Amerindians, despite what he maintained about their supposed backwardness, might eventually evolve toward something resembling civilization. See Klaas van Berkel, "'That Miserable Continent': Cultural Pessimism and the Idea of 'America' in Cornelius de Pauw," in *Revolutionary Histories: Transatlantic Cultural Nationalism*, ed. W. M. Verhoeven (New York, Palgrave, 2002), 142.

66. Jefferson, *Notes*, 99.

67. Ibid., 103. When president years later, he claimed that the goal of the United States was "to live in perpetual peace with the Indians, to cultivate an affectionate attachment from them, by everything just and liberal which we can do for them within the bounds of reason, and by giving them effectual protection against wrongs from our own people." "From Thomas Jefferson to William Henry Harrison, 27 February 1803," *Founders Online*, National Archives, https://founders.archives.gov/documents/Jefferson/01-39-02-0500 [PTJ: 39:589–593].

68. *HDI*, 1770, 6:377.

69. "Before anything happens, their climate must improve, the valleys and countryside must be drained/dried more completely, their constitution must harden, and their blood must be purified." Ibid.

70. Ibid.

71. Jefferson, *Notes*, 108.

72. Ibid., 110.

73. Jefferson's discussion of genius now seems somewhat comical. A Francophile to the core, Jefferson acknowledges that France may indeed have "achieved her full quota of genius," given these ratios (*Notes*, 111). In speaking of England, however, Jefferson is not sure that the land of his ancestors is continuing to achieve the same quotient. Although he admits that the recent war prevents a real inventory of British geniuses, he also remarks that the way that Great Britain waged war against its former colony "does not seem [to be] the legitimate offspring either of science or civilization" (Ibid).

74. Like all races, Blacks had supposedly "received from their maker certain laws of extension at the time of their formation" and could neither rise above or fall below these limits. Ibid., 77–78.

75. Ibid.

76. Ibid. See Rana A. Hogarth, *Medicalizing Blackness: Making Racial Difference in the Atlantic World* (Chapel Hill: University of North Carolina Press, 2017), 32.

77. Jefferson, *Notes*, 78.

78. Ibid., 212.

79. Ibid., 213.

80. Ibid., 212.

81. It is fascinating that Jefferson uses this analogy in another context to talk to a woman he may have been sleeping with, Maria Cosway: "Surely it was never so cold before. To me who am an animal of a warm climate, a mere Oranootan, it has been a severe trial." "From Thomas Jefferson to Maria Cosway, 14 January 1789," *Founders Online*, National Archives, https://founders.archives.gov/documents/Jefferson/01-14-02-0216 [*PTJ*: 18:8].

82. Jefferson, *Notes*, 218.

83. Ibid., 214.

84. Ibid., 215. Jefferson had synthesized his century's race thinking. If, according to Diderot's *Encyclopédie*, the human mind could be broken down into Reason, Memory, and Imagination, the African only equaled the White in his ability to memorize.

85. Ibid., 215.

86. Ibid., 222.

87. Such differences, he goes on to assert, are certainly "not against experience" when one considers the fact that "different species of the same genus, or varieties of the same species, may possess different qualifications," meaning abilities (ibid., 222).

88. William W. Henings, ed., *The Statutes at Large; Being a Collection of All the Laws of Virginia, from the First Session of the Legislature, in the Year 1619* (New York: R. & W. & G. Barton, 1823), 3:86.

89. The most vociferous Internet critics have summed up this necessarily coercive arrangement in the following terms: In 1788 or 1789, the future president of the United States began raping the fifteen- or sixteen-year-old Sally Hemings and ultimately enslaved her children. Debate continues to simmer about this topic, as it did in the past, among generations of Jefferson scholars. The best way to come to grips with the complexity of the subject is through two groundbreaking books by Annette Gordon-Reed: *Thomas Jefferson and Sally Hemings: An American Controversy* (Charlottesville: University of Virginia Press, 1997) and *The Hemingses of Monticello: An American Family* (New York: W. W. Norton, 2008).

90. For over a century, Jefferson scholars bent over backward to deny any link between this Founding Father and the Hemings family. Some accused other, less prominent or important, Jefferson ancestors, including Jefferson's nephews Samuel and Peter Carr. The important thing was disassociating the famous president from an act that was considered to be beneath him. Annette Gordon-Reed effectively clinched the argument through historical analysis even before the DNA evidence emerged. See her *Thomas Jefferson and Sally Hemings: An American Controversy*, 94.

91. He mistakenly claimed that one of the resulting offspring was named Tom. See James Thomson Callender, "The President Again," *The Recorder; or Lady's and Gentlemen's Miscellany*, September 1, 1802.

92. The allegation nonetheless stuck. Years after Jefferson's death, his family continually found themselves obliged to refute this "calumny." See Gordon-Reed, *The Hemingses of Monticello*, 608.

93. Madison Hemings, "Life Among the Lowly, No. 1," *Pike County Republican*, March 13, 1873. This is best accessed through: https://encyclopediavirginia.org/6448hpr-21dd90c2c2fa921/.

94. Gordon-Reed, *The Hemingses of Monticello*, 51.

95. Ibid. On concubinage, see Macaira L. Mullen, "Wealth, Desire, and Consequences of the Antebellum Slaveholder," *The Purdue Historian* 10, no. 1 (2022): 2. Mullen points out that enslaved "lighter skinned" girls not only cost more, but were often purchased to "satisfy their sexual desires." Most concubines in the antebellum South were selected due to their light skin tone and straight hair.

96. Lucy Elizabeth Jefferson, who was two years of age, died on October 13, 1784, while Jefferson was already in France. Lucy was the second child to have this name.

97. "From Thomas Jefferson to Edward Rutledge, 14 July 1787," *Founders Online*, National Archives, https://founders.archives.gov/documents/Jefferson/01-11-02-0506 [*PTJ*: 11:1]. This letter was sent to the proslavery Founding Father Edward Rutledge, to applaud the fact that his home state of South Carolina had banned the slave trade.

98. Thomas Kidd, *Thomas Jefferson: A Biography of Spirit and Flesh* (New Haven: Yale University Press, 2022), 104.

99. "Memorandum Books, 1789," *Founders Online*, National Archives, https://founders.archives.gov/documents/Jefferson/02-01-02-0023 [*PTJ*, Second Series: *Jefferson's Memorandum Books*, 1:722–749].

100. Gordon-Reed makes a similar calculation. See *Thomas Jefferson and Sally Hemings*, 160.

101. The most interesting speculation about Sally Hemings's life in Paris comes from Gordon-Reed's sociological explanation of how the servants of the elite lived a life between "two cultures." Hemings was paid for her work in Paris. *The Hemings of Monticello*, 321.

102. Gordon-Reed, *Thomas Jefferson and Sally Hemings*, 324.

103. Hemings, "Life Among the Lowly, No. 1."

104. Ibid. Jefferson largely kept this promise.

105. Kidd, *Thomas Jefferson*, 104.

106. He directed that the remaining six crates be sent directly to Monticello. G. S. Wilson, *Jefferson on Display: Attire, Etiquette, and the Art of Presentation* (Charlottesville: University of Virginia Press, 2018), 142. Wilson makes clear that Jefferson, despite all the sophisticated trappings with which he surrounded himself, often dressed quite casually, indeed often as an unkempt farmer.

107. The "cannibal" citation came later. See "From Thomas Jefferson to Aaron Burr, 11 February 1799," *Founders Online*, National Archives, https://founders

.archives.gov/documents/Jefferson/01-31-02-0015 [*PTJ*: 31:22–23]. Given that France was simultaneously engulfed in its own revolution in 1791, Jefferson brokered a deal according to which the United States Treasury would repay a massive loan provided by France to the United States years before it was due. For information on Washington's position, see Timothy M. Matthewson, "George Washington's Policy Toward the Haitian Revolution," *Diplomatic History* 3 (1979), 325–333.

108. "George Washington to Jean Baptiste de Temant, 24 September 1791," *The Writings of George Washington*, ed. Jarred Sparks (Boston: Russell, Shattuck, and Williams co., 1836), 194. For the aid given to the French planters, see Matthewson, "George Washington's Policy Toward the Haitian Revolution," 325–333.

109. Robert Debs Heinl and Nancy Gordon Heinl, *Written in Blood: The Story of the Haitian People, 1492–1971* (Boston: Houghton Mifflin Co., 1978), 157.

110. Bryan DeLay, "The Arms Trade and American Revolutions," *The American Historical Review* 128, no. 3 (2023): 1161.

111. The first wave of refugees came in 1791. More came after June 1793, when the city of Cap-François was burned beyond recognition. In the aftermath of this disaster, 10,000 or so French colonists had fled to the United States, often with their enslaved workers and valets. See Matthewson, "Jefferson and Haiti," *The Journal of Southern History* 61, no. 2 (May 1995): 216.

112. France's National Convention had followed up on Sonthonax's emancipation and officially abolished slavery in all the French colonies in 1794.

113. For an explanation of the terribly complicated time in history, see James J. Horn, Jan Ellen Lewis, Peter S. Onuf, eds., *The Revolution of 1800: Democracy, Race, and the New Republic* (Charlottesville: University of Virginia Press, 2002), 315.

114. Ibid.

115. Adams had already put an end to the war by signing the Treaty of Mortefontaine (1800).

116. Garry Wills, *Negro President: Jefferson and the Slave Power* (Boston: Houghton Mifflin, 2005), 42–43.

117. Jefferson was, however, nervous about Napoleon's ultimate intentions. See Jeremy D. Popkin, *A Concise History of the Haitian Revolution* (Malden: Wiley-Blackwell, 2012), 119–120.

118. Ibid., 115.

119. He died on April 7, 1803, in a remote prison in Fort-de-Joux.

120. By force in Guadeloupe and by treaty in Martinique (Sainte Lucie and Tobago).

121. Leclerc was even more categorical regarding rebels with military experience: They should not "let a single man live who had worn an epaulette." Victoire Leclerc to Napoléon Bonaparte (October 7, 1802), in *Lettres du Général Leclerc*, ed. Paul Roussier (Paris: Société de l'histoire des colonies françaises, 1937), 254–259.

122. For estimated statistics, see Simon P. Newman, "American Political Culture and the French and Haitian Revolutions: Nathaniel Cutting and the Jeffersonian Republicans," *The Impact of the Haitian Revolution in the Atlantic World*, ed. David P. Geggus (Columbia: University of South Carolina Press, 2002), 78. See also David P. Geggus, *The Haitian Revolution* (Bloomington: Indiana University Press, 2002), 27.

123. See Marlene Daut, *The First and Last King of Haiti* (New York: Knopf, 2025), 219. Daut also provides a bloodcurdling account of Rochambeau's "murder balls," lavish events to which women of color and their husbands were invited. What happened at the ball, however, was that the husbands were executed.

124. Ibid., 234.

125. "Purchase of Louisiana, [5 July 1803]," *Founders Online*, National Archives, https://founders.archives.gov/documents/Hamilton/01-26-02-0001-0101 [PTJ: 26, *Additional Documents 1774–1799, Addenda and Errata*, 129–136].

126. "From Thomas Jefferson to Robert R. Livingston, 18 April 1802," *Founders Online*, National Archives, https://founders.archives.gov/documents/Jefferson/01-37-02-0220 [PTJ: 37:263–267].

127. Jon Kukla, *A Wilderness So Immense: The Louisiana Purchase and the Destiny of America* (New York: Random House, 2003), 335.

128. In 1800, through the Treaty of San Ildefonso, France had reclaimed possession of Louisiana from Spain.

129. Elihu Root et al., ed., *The War of the Rebellion: A Compilation of Official Records of the Union and Confederate Armies* (Washington: Government Printing Office, 1902), 4:322. The exact number is still debated.

130. This came from Jefferson's "Observations on Jean-Nicolas Démeunier's Article on the United States," in *Founders Online*, National Archives, https://founders.archives.gov/documents/Jefferson/01-10-02-0001-0005 [PTJ: 10:58]. At this same basic time, Jefferson was considering advocating for the same thing for Virginia, not merely ending the slave trade but emancipating all slaves in the state: "The General assembly shall not have the power to . . .

permit the introduction of any more slaves to reside in this state, or the continuance of slavery beyond the generation which shall be living on the 31st day of December 1800; all persons born after that day being hereby declared free." See "Jefferson's Draft of a Constitution for Virginia, *Founders Online*, National Archives, https://founders.archives.gov/documents/Jefferson/01-06-02-0255-0004 [*PTJ*: 6:294–308].

131. Henry Wiencek, *Master of the Mountain: Thomas Jefferson and his Slaves* (New York: Farrar, Straus and Giroux, 2012), 256.

132. Jefferson's final word on what he continued to call the "blot" of slavery came twelve years after he had stepped down as president, in 1819. He was seventy-six-years old. Though the former president was long retired, Southern leaders reached out to him for advice regarding the so-called Missouri crisis, which had been brought on when the territory not only applied for statehood, but for the right to allow slavery within its borders. Jefferson, who played no active role in the negotiations, nonetheless suggested that slavery be allowed to exist south of a geographical line to maintain balance between slavery and non-slavery states. While this line, embodied in the Missouri Compromise, temporarily eased tensions, Jefferson privately feared the long-term implications of such a settlement. In his view, the tension that had arisen over the subject of slavery was clearly "a fire bell in the night," a harbinger of national division and North–South antagonism. His actions and words reveal a leader torn between pragmatic politics and moral concerns. "Thomas Jefferson to John Holmes, 22 April 1820," *Founders Online*, National Archives, https://founders.archives.gov/documents/Jefferson/03-15-02-0518 [*PTJ*: 15:550–551].

133. *The Seventh Census of the United States 1850, An Appendix* (Washington: Robert Armstrong, 1853), lxxxvii.

134. "From Thomas Jefferson to John Tyler, 16 February 1809," *Founders Online*, National Archives, https://founders.archives.gov/documents/Jefferson/99-01-02-9814.

135. Schuyler, Sarah Ridg. *Sarah Ridg Schuyler Diary*. Library of Congress, Washington, DC, https://www.loc.gov/item/mm79001273/. Jefferson had noted the weather, as usual.

136. See Ellis, *American Sphinx*, 326. Jefferson's meticulous noting of the weather can be seen at: https://www.jefferson-weather-records.org/weather/40?page=88.

137. Thomas Jefferson was present at Monticello during the estimated conception dates of (her/their) children. Ellis, *American Sphinx*, 429.

138. Gordon-Reed, *The Hemingses of Monticello*, 782.

139. See Justin Gish and Daniel Klinghard, *Thomas Jefferson and the Science of Republican Government: A Political Biography of the Notes on the State of Virginia* (Cambridge: Cambridge University Press, 2017), 172.

140. See Peter S. Onuf and Ari Helo, "Jefferson, Morality, and the Problem of Slavery," *The William and Mary Quarterly* 60, no. 3 (2003): 586.

141. "From Thomas Jefferson to Angelica Schuyler Church, 27 November 1793," *Founders Online*, National Archives, https://founders.archives.gov/documents/Jefferson/01-27-02-0416 [*PTJ*: 27:449–450].

142. François-Alexandre-Frédéric, duc de La Rochefoucauld-Liancourt, *Travels through the United States of North America, the Country of the Iroquois, and Upper Canada, in the Years 1795, 1796, and 1797* (London, R. Phillips, 1800), 3:157–158.

143. "Thomas Jefferson to Reuben Perry, 16 April 1812," *Founders Online*, National Archives, https://founders.archives.gov/documents/Jefferson/03-04-02-0508 [*PTJ*, Retirement Series: 4:620].

144. Wiencek, *Master of the Mountain*, 121.

145. The most significant work of anthropology to reflect this shift—Jefferson ultimately purchased it—was Julien-Joseph Virey's *Histoire naturelle du genre humain* (Natural History of the Human Genus). This tremendously influential two-volume work identified facial angles, skull shape, hair textures, and skin color as the exterior indicators of the mental, moral, esthetic, and physical inferiority of non-Europeans. Most of Virey's book concentrated on the category of humans whom Jefferson "owned" at Monticello, the biologically distinct "African species," a species Virey claimed was related to great apes. See Virey, *Histoire naturelle du genre humain* (Paris: Dufart, 1801).

146. See "From Thomas Jefferson to Brissot de Warville, 11 February 1788," *Founders Online*, National Archives, https://founders.archives.gov/documents/Jefferson/01-12-02-0612 [*PTJ*: 12:577–578]. See also Cara Rogers Stevens, *Thomas Jefferson and the Fight against Slavery* (Lawrence: University of Kansas Press, 2024), 131, and Ellis, *American Sphinx*, 210.

147. The argument had taken place at Jefferson's house. At the time, Jefferson had actually agreed to translate Condorcet's elegant antislavery manifesto, *Réflexions sur l'esclavage des nègres* (Reflections on the Slavery of Negroes). See Peter Thompson, *Heir through Hope: Thomas Jefferson's Lifelong Investment in William Short* (Oxford: Oxford University Press, 2023), 34. One can see the first attempt at a translation in "Jefferson's Notes from Condorcet on Slavery," in Jefferson, *Papers*, 14:494–498 (Princeton: Princeton University Press, 1958). Only four pages were translated.

148. He did not mention the *Notes* specifically, but he certainly asked Jefferson to "wean" himself from these prejudices. "To Thomas Jefferson from Benjamin Banneker, 19 August 1791," *Founders Online*, National Archives. https://founders.archives.gov/documents/Jefferson/01-22-02-0049 [PTJ: 22:49–54].

149. Ibid.

150. Ibid.

151. Ibid.

152. Ibid.

153. This was, of course, the same man whom Jefferson had debated on the subject of black inferiority.

154. "To Thomas Jefferson from Benjamin Banneker, 19 August 1791," *Founders Online*, National Archives. This was abbreviated in the letter.

155. He also said that he hoped that some form of degeneration would explain Africans' liabilities, although he did not believe in degeneration.

156. "From Thomas Jefferson to Condorcet, 30 August 1791," *Founders Online*, National Archives, https://founders.archives.gov/documents/Jefferson/01-22-02-0092 [PTJ: 22:98–99]. See Richard Henry Popkin, *The Third Force in Seventeenth Century Thought* (New York: Brill, 1992), 59.

157. Henri Grégoire, *De la littérature des Nègres, ou Recherches sur leurs facultés intellectuelles, leurs qualités morales et leur littérature* (Paris: chez Maradan, 1808), 36. See Alyssa Goldstein Sepinwall, *The Abbé Grégoire and the French Revolution: The Making of Modern Universalism* (Berkeley: University of California Press, 2021).

158. "From Thomas Jefferson to Henri Grégoire, 25 February 1809," *Founders Online*, National Archives, https://founders.archives.gov/documents/Jefferson/99-01-02-9893.

159. "Thomas Jefferson to Joel Barlow, 8 October 1809," *Founders Online*, National Archives, https://founders.archives.gov/documents/Jefferson/03-01-02-0461 [PTJ, Retirement Series: 1:588–590].

160. Ibid.

161. "To Thomas Jefferson from Lydia Howard Huntley Sigourney, 30 June 1824," *Founders Online*, National Archives, https://founders.archives.gov/documents/Jefferson/98-01-02-4357.

162. Ibid.

163. Ibid.

164. While Jefferson certainly believed that slavery was now the United States' responsibility to solve, he often claimed that this moral horror was the unfortunate vestige of English colonization. As early as 1774, Jefferson

had already begun publicly "blaming" England for the institution of slavery, accusing King George III of perpetuating the institution by repeatedly rebuffing the new colonies' desire to end the slave trade. From Jefferson's point of view, slavery was not the United States' original sin; it was England's.

165. "From Thomas Jefferson to Frances Wright, 7 August 1825," *Founders Online*, National Archives, https://founders.archives.gov/documents/Jefferson/98-01-02-5449.

166. This is a supposition made by the historians at Monticello. See https://www.monticello.org/research-education/thomas-jefferson-encyclopedia/jeffersons-funeral/.

167. Gordon-Reed, *The Hemingses of Monticello*, 521.

168. In 1858, on the 32nd anniversary of Jefferson's death, Lincoln claimed that "all honor" goes to "Jefferson — to the man who, in the concrete pressure of a struggle for national independence by a single people, had the coolness, forecast, and capacity to introduce into a merely revolutionary document, [the] abstract truth [of equality], and so embalm it there, that today in all coming days, it shall be a rebuke and a stumbling block to the very harbingers of reappearing tyranny and oppression." Letter to Henry L. Pierce, April 6, 1859, Abraham Lincoln, *Letters and Telegrams* (New York: The Current Literature Publishing Company, 1907), 39.

169. See Robert Pierce Forbes's eloquent summary of some of these contradictions: "Why would the author of the Declaration of Independence, perhaps the most eloquent spokesman for liberty and equality of the founding generation, if not all of American history, deliberately condemn a portion of the human race to an inferior status? In part, because the contradiction between these founding principles and his own dependence upon slavery threatened his stature as a great man both in his own times and in history." "Secular Damnation: Thomas Jefferson and the Imperative of Race," *Torrington Articles* 3 (May 2012). https://opencommons.uconn.edu/torr_articles/3.

170. John W. Blassingame and John R. McKivigan, eds., *Frederick Douglass Papers: Series One, Speeches, Debates, and Interviews* (New Haven: Yale University Press, 1979–1992), 5:566–567.

EPILOGUE

1. *Essai sur l'inégalité des races humaines* (Paris: Firmin Didot Frères: 1853–1857).

2. In the eighteenth-century context, antiracism concerns the intellectual refutation of race itself. It is to be distinguished from, for example, various acts of rebellion and revolt in Caribbean colonies. See my *Anatomy of Blackness: Science and Slavery in an Age of Enlightenment* (Baltimore: Johns Hopkins University Press, 2011), 186–204.

3. Grégoire's book first appeared in 1808. The 1810 English edition translated Grégoire's title as *An Enquiry Concerning the Intellectual and Moral Faculties, and Literature of Negroes*.

4. See Vincent Carretta, "Who was Francis Williams?" *Early American Literature* 38, no. 2 (2003): 213–237. Caretta provides a short analysis of the painting that Williams may have commissioned himself. It features him in his library in Jamaica. Sitting open on the table next to him is Newton's *Principia*. See also Fara Dabhoiwala's recent discussion of this same portrait, including a digital analysis hinting that Williams may have predicted the arrival of Halley's comet in 1759 using Newtonian physics. "A Man of Parts and Learning," *London Review of Books* 46, no. 22 (November 2024), https:// www.lrb.co.uk/the-paper/v46/n22/fara-dabhoiwala/a-man-of-parts-and-learning.

5. There has been a controversy regarding Equiano's birthplace. Vincent Caretta has suggested that a baptismal record in Saint Margaret's Church in Westminster, which gave "Vassa's" birthplace as South Carolina, raises doubts on the whole African part of his story. He also cites a navy muster roll as further proof. See Vincent Caretta, "Olaudah Equiano or Gustavus Vassa? New Light on an Eighteenth-Century Question of Identity," *Slavery and Abolition* 20, no. 3 (1999): 96–105, and *Equiano, the African: Biography of a Self-Made Man* (Athens: University of Georgia Press, 2005). The argument in favor of Equiano's "African" birth has been made by other authors, including Paul E. Lovejoy, in "Autobiography and Memory: Gustavus Vassa, Alias Olaudah Equiano, the African," *Slavery and Abolition* 27, no. 3 (2006): 317–347. For the purposes of *this* book, I am going to identify Equiano's birthplace as Africa, as would an eighteenth-century reader, as biographical fact.

6. See John Bugg, "The Other Interesting Narrative: Olaudah Equiano's Public Book Tour," *PMLA* 121 no. 5 (2006), 1427. Equiano spread the gospel of abolitionist thought not only to a liberal elite, but to the "minors, glovers, and grocers," the so-called anonymous workers of the industrial north.

7. Olaudah Equiano, *The Interesting Narrative and Other Writings*, ed. Vincent Caretta (New York: Penguin, 2003), 107.

8. Ibid., 39.

9. One of the major racial preconceptions he struggled against was an idea

accepted by virtually every White person he had ever met during his life: namely, that the increasingly racialized notion of "Negro" *and* the political status of the world "slave" were virtually synonyms.

10. Consider, he writes, that the "Spaniards, who have inhabited America, under the torrid zone, for any time, are become as dark colored as our native Indians of Virginia." He also claims that Africans are perhaps yet another example of wandering Jews, since his culture, like the Jews', practiced circumcision. Even more telling, he continues, is the example of the Portuguese in Sierra Leone who have "now become in their complexion, and in the wooly quality of their hair; *perfect negroes*." Ibid., 44–45.

11. Ibid.

12. Europeans, in short, might come closer to the truth about their species by bearing in mind the Bible's own anthropology in the Book of Acts, where it is said that God "hath made of one blood all nations of men for to dwell on the face of the earth" (Acts 17:26). Vincent Caretta, "Introduction," in *Olaudah Equiano, The Interesting Narrative and Other Writings*, xix.

13. Henry Louis Gates Jr., *The Black Box: Writing the Race* (New York: Penguin, 2024).

BIBLIOGRAPHY

PRIMARY SOURCES

"Advertisement for a Runaway Slave, 7 September 1769." *Founders Online*, National Archives. https://founders.archives.gov/documents/Jefferson/01-01-02-0021 [*PTJ*: 1:33].

Archives nationales d'Outre-Mer. Accessed August 4, 2025. http://www.archivesnationales.culture.gouv.fr/anom/fr/.

Aristotle. *Aristotle's Politics: Writings from the Complete Works: Politics, Economics, Constitution of Athens*. Princeton: Princeton University Press, 2016.

Banneker, Benjamin. "To Thomas Jefferson from Benjamin Banneker, 19 August 1791." *Founders Online*, National Archives. https://founders.archives.gov/documents/Jefferson/01-22-02-0049 [PTJ: 22:49–54].

"Barbare." In *Dictionnaire de l'Académie Françoise*. Paris: chez Jean Baptiste Coignard et sa veuve, 1694.

Barbé-Marbois, François, Marquis de. *Our Revolutionary Forefathers, The Letters of François, Marquis de Barbé-Marbois, During His Residence in the United States as Secretary for the French Legation, 1779–1785*. Ann Arbor: University of Michigan Press, 2006.

Beattie, James. *An Essay on the Nature and Immutability of Truth, in Opposition to Skepticism*. London: Mawman, 1812.

Benezet, Anthony. *Some Historical Account of Guinea*. London: J. Phillips, 1788.

Bernier, François. *Abrégé de la philosophie de Gassendi*. Lyon: Anisson, Posuel et Rigaud, 1684.

Bernier, François. "Nouvelle division de la Terre, par les différentes Espèces ou Races d'hommes qui l'habitent, envoyée par un fameux voyageur à M.

l'abbé de la *** à peu près en ces termes." In *Le Journal des sçavants*. Paris: Jean Cusson, 1684.

Bernier, François. *Copie des étrenes envoyées à Madame de La Sablière par Mr Bernier*. Montpellier: n.p., 1688.

Bernier, François. "Nouvelle division de la terre, par les différentes espèces ou races d'hommes qui l'habitent." *Mercure de France*, December 1722, 62–70.

Bernier, François. *Travels in the Mogul Empire*. Translated by Irving Brock. London: W. Pickering, 1826.

Bernier, François. "A New Division of the Earth," translated by Janet L. Nelson. *History Workshop Journal*, no. 51 (Spring 2001): 247–250.

Bernier, François. *Un Libertin dans l'Inde Moghole. Les Voyages de François Bernier (1656–1669)*. Edited by Frédéric Tinguely. Paris: Chandeigne, 2008.

Bible, New International Version. Biblica, 2011. https://www.biblegateway.com/versions/New-International-Version-NIV-Bible/.

Blénac, Charles de Courbon, Comte de. "Blénac à Colbert, le 5 septembre, 1678," Départ. Série B, déposée aux Archives nationales: Registres 1 à 37, 1654–1715. In *Inventaire analytique de la correspondance générale avec les colonies*. Edited by Étienne Taillemite. Paris: Le Ministère, 1959.

Blumenbach, Johann Friedrich. *The Anthropological Treatises of Johann Friedrich Blumenbach*. Edited by Thomas Bendyshe. London: Longman, Green, et al., 1865.

Blumenbach, Johann Friedrich. *The Correspondence of Johann Friedrich Blumenbach: 1791–1795*. Edited by Norbert Klatt. Göttingen: Klatt, 2006–2013.

Buffon, Georges-Louis Leclerc, Comte de. *Histoire naturelle, générale et particulière, avec la description du cabinet du roi*. Paris: Imprimerie royale, 1749–1788.

Buffon, Georges-Louis Leclerc, Comte de. *Œuvres complètes de Buffon*. Paris: chez Furne, 1839–1851.

Buffon, Georges-Louis Leclerc, Comte de. *Œuvres de Buffon*. Edited by Pierre Flourens. Paris: Garnier Frères, 1853–1857.

Buffon, George-Louis Leclerc, Comte de. *Correspondance inédite de Buffon; à laquelle ont été réunies les lettres publiées jusqu'à ce jour*. Edited by Henri Nadault de Buffon. Paris: L. Hachette et Cie., 1860.

Callender, James Thomson. "The President Again." *The Recorder; or Lady's and Gentleman's Miscellany*, September 1, 1802.

Carr, William. *Travels through Flanders, Holland, Germany, Sweden, and Denmark*. Amsterdam: Jacob ter Beek, 1733.

Castilhon, Jean-Louis. *Zingha, Reine d'Angola, histoire africaine, suivie de recherches et d'observations sur la férocité naturelle des Giagues, et d'une relation exacte de leurs mœurs, de leurs coutumes et de la barbarie de leurs usages*. Edited by Patrick Graille et Laurent Quillerié. Bourges: Éditions Ganymède, 1993.

Charlevoix, Pierre-François-Xavier de. *Histoire de l'Isle Espagnole ou de S. Domingue*. Paris: chez François l'Honoré, 1733.

Colbert, Jean-Baptiste. *Lettres, instructions et mémoires de Colbert, publiés par Pierre Clément. Industrie, commerce*. Paris: Imprimerie impériale, 1863.

de Pauw, Cornelius. *Recherches philosophiques sur les Américains, ou Mémoires intéressants pour servir à l'histoire de l'espèce humaine*. Berlin: George Jacques Decker, 1768–1769.

Debow, J. D. B., ed. *The Seventh Census of the United States: 1850, An Appendix*. Washington: Robert Armstrong, 1853.

Dickson, William. *Letters on Slavery, . . . To Which Are Added, Addresses to the Whites, and to the Free Negroes of Barbados*. London: J. Phillips, 1789.

Diderot, Denis, and Jean le Rond D'Alembert, eds. *Encyclopédie, ou Dictionnaire raisonné des sciences, des arts et des métiers, par une société de gens de lettres*. Paris: Le Breton et al., 1751–1772.

"Diverses observations anatomiques." In *Histoire de l'Académie Royale des Sciences*. Paris: Imprimerie royale, 1744.

Dubos, Jean-Baptiste. *Réflexions critiques sur la poésie et la peinture*. Utrecht: Etienne Neaulme, 1719.

Du Tertre, Jean-Baptiste. *Histoire générale des Antilles habitées par les François*. Paris: chez Thomas Jolly, 1667–1671.

Duval, Pierre. *Le Monde, ou La Géographie Universelle*. Paris: n.p., 1676.

The Edinburgh Literary Journal; or Weekly Register of Criticism and Belles Lettres. July–December 1830.

Elliot, Gilbert. *Proposals for Carrying on Certain Public Works in the City of Edinburgh*. Edinburgh: n.p., 1752.

Encyclopaedia Britannica: or a Dictionary of Arts, Sciences, and Miscellaneous Literature. Edinburgh: Bell and Maccfarquhar, 1797.

Equiano, Olaudah. *The Interesting Narrative and Other Writings*. Edited by Vincent Carretta. New York: Penguin, 2003.

Gailhard, Jean. *The Compleat Gentleman: or, Directions for the Education of Youth*. London: Thomas Newcomb, 1678.

Goldsmith, Oliver. *A History of the Earth and Animated Nature*. London: J. Nourse, 1774.

Grégoire, Henri. *De la littérature des Nègres, ou Recherches sur leurs facultés intellectuelles, leurs qualités morales et leur littérature*. Paris: chez Maradan, 1808.

Helvétius, Claude Adrien. *De l'esprit*. Paris: Fayard, 1988.

Hérault de Séchelles, Marie-Jean. *Voyage à Montbard*. Paris: chez Solvet, 1800.

Hobbes, Thomas. *Leviathan*. Mineola, NY: Dover Publications, 2012.

Hume, David. *Essays: Moral, Political, and Literary*. London: Andrew Millar, 1748.

Hume, David. *Essays and Treatises on Several Subjects*. London: Alexander Donaldson, 1758.

Hume, David. *The Letters of David Hume*. Edited by John Young Thomson Greig. Oxford: Oxford University Press, 1932.

Hume, David. *Delphi Complete Works of David Hume*. Hastings, UK: Delphi Classics, 2016. https://www.delphiclassics.com/shop/david-hume/.

Hume, David. *David Hume on Morals, Politics, and Society*. Edited by Angela Coventry and Andrew Valls. New Haven: Yale University Press, 2018.

"An Investigation into the Conduct of Thomas Jefferson." *Journal of the House of Delegates of the Commonwealth of Virginia*, December 12, 1781: 36–38.

Jefferson, Martha, and Thomas Jefferson. "Lines Copied from Tristram Shandy by Martha and Thomas Jefferson, before 6 September 1782." *Founders Online*, National Archives. https://founders.archives.gov/documents/Jefferson/01-06-02-0185 [PTJ: 6:196–197].

Jefferson, Thomas. [Condorcet's *Reflections on the Slavery of Negroes*, 8 October 1788], translation in "Jefferson's Notes from Condorcet on Slavery." *Founders Online*, National Archives. https://founders.archives.gov/documents/Jefferson/01-14-02-0267 [PTJ: 14:494–498].

Jefferson, Thomas. *Thomas Jefferson, Autobiography Draft Fragment, January 6 through July 27, 1821*. Library of Congress, Washington, DC. https://www.loc.gov/item/mtjbib024000/.

Jefferson, Thomas. *The Writings of Thomas Jefferson*. Edited by Paul Leicester Ford. New York: Putnam, 1892–1899.

Jefferson, Thomas. *The Papers of Thomas Jefferson*. Princeton: Princeton University Press, 1950. Accessed in *Founders Online*, National Archives. Last modified July 2025. https://founders.archives.gov/.

Jefferson, Thomas. *Notes on the State of Virginia: An Annotated Edition*. Edited by Robert Pierce Forbes. New Haven: Yale University Press, 2022.

Journal of the House of Delegates. Richmond: Thomas White, 1827.

Kames, Henry Home, Lord. *Historical Law-Tracts*. Edinburgh: A. Kincaid, 1761.

Kames, Henry Home, Lord. *Sketches of the History of Man*. Edinburgh: W. Creech, 1774.

Kant, Immanuel. *The Cambridge Edition of the Works of Immanuel Kant*. Edited by Paul Guyer and Allen W. Wood. Cambridge: Cambridge University Press, 1992.

Kant, Immanuel. "An Answer to the Question: What is Enlightenment?" In *Princeton Readings in Political Thought: Essential Texts since Plato*, edited by Mitchell Cohen. Princeton: Princeton University Press, 2018, 355–359. https://www.jstor.org/stable/j.ctv19fvzzk.

Kant, Immanuel. *Perpetual Peace: A Philosophical Essay*. Frankfurt: Outlook Verlag, 2020.

Kullberg, Christina. *Lire l'histoire générale des Antilles de J. B. Du Tertre*. Leiden and Boston: Brill Rodopi, 2021.

Labat, Jean-Baptiste. *Nouveau voyage aux isles de l'Amérique*. Paris: chez CH. J. B. Delespine, 1722.

Labat, Jean-Baptiste. *Nouvelle relation de l'Afrique occidentale*. Paris: chez Guillaume Cavelier, 1728.

Labat, Jean-Baptiste. *Voyage du Chevalier Des Marchais en Guinée, isles voisines, et à Cayenne, fait en 1725, 1726 et 1727*. Amsterdam: Ordre des frères prêcheurs, 1730.

Labat, Jean-Baptiste. *Voyages du P. Labat de l'ordre des FF. Prêcheurs, en Espagne et en Italie*. Paris: Jean-Baptiste et Charles Delespine, 1730.

Labat, Jean-Baptiste, *Relation historique de l'Éthiopie occidentale*. Paris: Charles-Jean-Baptiste Delespine le fils, 1732.

Labat, Jean-Baptiste. *Voyage aux isles de l'Amérique*. Edited by Michel Le Bris. Lonrai: Phébus libretto, 2001.

La Fontaine, Jean de. *Suite des Œuvres posthumes de La Fontaine*. Paris: n.p., 1797.

Leclerc, Charles Victor-Emmanuel. "Victoire Leclerc à Napoléon Bonaparte (October 7, 1802)." In *Lettres du Général Leclerc*, edited by Paul Roussier. Paris: Société de l'histoire des colonies françaises, 1937, 254–259.

Linnaeus, Carl. *Critica Botanica*. Leiden: Conradum Wishoff, 1737.

Linnaeus, Carl. *Flora Lapponica*. Amsterdam: Salomonem Schouten, 1737.

Linnaeus, Carl. *Miscellaneous Tracts Relating to Natural History*. Edited by Benjamin Stillingfleet. London: J. Dodsley, Baker and Leigh, and T. Payne, 1775.

Linnaeus, Carl. *Lachesis Lapponica or a Tour in Lapland*. London: Richard Taylor & Co., 1811.

Linnaeus, Carl. *Systema Naturae 1735, Facsimile of the First Edition*. Nieuwkoop: B. De Graaf, 1974.

Locke, John. *Two Treatises of Government*. Edited by Peter Laslett. Cambridge: Cambridge University Press, 1967.

Manchester University. "Kant's Classes at the *Collegium Fridericianum*." Kant in the Classroom. Last updated December 4, 2016. https://users.manchester.edu/facstaff/ssnaragon/kant/students/studentCollFrid.htm.

Maupertuis, Pierre-Louis Moreau de. *Dissertation physique à l'occasion du nègre blanc*. Leiden: n.p., 1744.

Maupertuis, Pierre-Louis Moreau de. *Vénus physique*. The Hague: Husson, 1746.

Melon, Jean-François. *A Political Essay upon Commerce Written in French by Monsieur M****. Translated by David Bindon. Dublin: printed for Philip Crampton, 1738.

Michon. "Lettre, 10 novembre 1706," *Archives nationales des Colonies* C8 A16. Cited in *Revue d'histoire des missions*. Paris: Les Amis des missions, 1926, 3:226.

Mongin, Père Edme. "Lettre du 20 décembre 1678," Bibliothèque municipale de Carcassonne, Manuscript no. 2459. Cited in Gérard Lafleur, "Les Juifs aux îles françaises du vent (XVIIe–XVIIIe siècles)." *Bulletin de la Société d'Histoire de la Guadeloupe*, no. 65–66 (1985): 77. https://doi.org/10.7202/1043818ar.

Montesquieu. *De l'esprit des lois*. In *Œuvres complètes de Montesquieu*. Edited by Pierre Rétat. Paris: Classiques Garnier, 2012.

"Norfolk Naval Shipyard." *Bureau of Ships Journal* 2, no. 1 (May 1953): 16–17.

Para du Phanjas, François. *Les Principes de la saine philosophie conciliés avec ceux de la religion ou la philosophie de la religion*. Paris: Charles-Antoine Joubert, 1774.

Piganiol de La Force, Jean-Aymar. *Nouvelle description de la France*. Amsterdam: Du Villard & Changuion, 1719.

The Present State of the Republick of Letters for July, 1729. London: William Innys, 1729.

"Purchase of Louisiana, 5 July 1803." *Founders Online*, National Archives. https://founders.archives.gov/documents/Hamilton/01-26-02-0001-0101 [PTJ: 26:129–136].

Raynal, Guillaume Thomas François. *Histoire philosophique et politique des établissemens et du commerce des Européens dans les deux Indes*. Amsterdam: n.p., 1770.

Robertson, William. *An Historical Disquisition Concerning the Knowledge Which the Ancients Had of India*. Utrecht and Rotterdam: for B. Wild and Altheer, 1792.

Robertson, William. *The History of America*. London: Strahan et al., 1800.

Robertson, William. *The History of America Including the United States*. New York: Blakeman and Mason, 1859.

Robertson, William. *The History of the Reign of Charles the Fifth*. Philadelphia: J. B. Lippincott, 1899.

Rochefoucauld-Liancourt, François-Alexandre-Frédéric de La. *Travels through the United States of North America, the Country of the Iroquois, and Upper Canada, in the Years 1795, 1796, and 1797*. London: R. Phillips, 1800. Library of Congress, Washington, DC. https://www.loc.gov/item/01024772/.

Saint-Évremond, Charles de Marguetel de Saint-Denis, seigneur de. *Œuvres mêlées de Saint-Évremond*. Edited by Charles Giraud. Paris: J. Léon Techener Fils, 1865.

Savary, Jacques. *Le Parfait négociant, ou Instruction générale pour ce qui regarde le commerce*. Paris: chez Jean Guignard, 1675.

Schefferus, Johannes. *Histoire de la Laponie*. Paris: Varennes, 1678.

Schuyler, Sarah Ridg. *Sarah Ridg Schuyler Diary*. 1809. Library of Congress, Washington, DC. https://www.loc.gov/item/mm79001273/.

Siegesbeck, Johannes Georgius. *Botanosophiae verioris brevis sciagraphia in usum discentium ornamentata: accedit ob argumenti analogiam epicrisis in clar. Linnaei nuperrime evulgatum systema plantarum sexuale et huic superstructam methodum botanicam*. Saint Petersburg: Typis Academiae, 1737.

Sigourney, Lydia Howard Huntley. "To Thomas Jefferson from Lydia Howard Huntley Sigourney, 30 June 1824." *Founders Online*, National Archives. https://founders.archives.gov/documents/Jefferson/98-01-02-4357.

Slave Voyages. Accessed July 5, 2025. https://www.slavevoyages.org/.

Sloane, Hans. *A Voyage to the Islands Madera, Barbados, Nieves, S. Christophers and Jamaica*. London: B.M., 1707.

Smith, Adam. *The Works of Adam Smith*. London: T. Cadell, 1811–1812.

Smith, Adam. *Lectures on Justice, Police, Revenue and Arms Delivered in the University of Glasgow by Adam Smith, Reported by a Student in 1763*. Oxford: Clarendon Press, 1896.

Smith, Adam. *The Wealth of Nations*. London: Electric Book Company, 2001.

Smith, Adam. *The Theory of Moral Sentiments*. Edited by Knud Haakonssen. Cambridge: Cambridge University Press, 2004.

Steller, Georg Wilhelm. *Journal of a Voyage with Bering, 1741–1742*. Palo Alto: Stanford University Press, 1988.

Sullivan, John. "Letter to Thomas Jefferson from John Sullivan, with Account of Expenses for Obtaining Moose Skeleton, 26 April 1787." *Founders Online*, National Archives. https://founders.archives.gov/documents/Jefferson/01-11-02-0304 [*PTJ*: 11:320–321].

Thunberg, Carl Peter. *Travels at the Cape of Good Hope, 1772–1775*. Edited by Vernon Siegfried Forbes. Cape Town: Van Riebeeck Society, 1986.

Vaucresson, Arnoul de, et Charles-François de Machault de Belmont. "Extraits de lettres reçues des Îles d'Amérique." *Archives nationales d'Outre-Mer* COL C8 B, no. 89 (8 February 1708).

Virey, Julien-Joseph. *Histoire naturelle du genre humain*. Paris: Dufart, 1801.

Voltaire. "Nouveau plan d'une histoire de l'esprit humain." *Mercure de France*, April 1745, 3–37.

Voltaire. *Œuvres complètes de Voltaire*. Paris: Garnier, 1877–1885.

Voltaire. *Œuvres complètes de Voltaire*. Edited by Nicholas Cronk et al. Oxford: Voltaire Foundation, 1968–2022.

Washington, George. "George Washington to Jean Baptiste de Temant, 24 September 1791." In *The Writings of George Washington*, edited by Jarred Sparks. Boston: Russell, Shattuck, and Williams co., 1836, 194.

Wood, John Cunningham. *Adam Smith: Critical Assessments*. London and New York: Routledge, 1984.

SECONDARY SOURCES

Abanime, Emeka P. "Voltaire et les noirs," PhD diss., University of Illinois at Urbana-Champaign, 1976.

Abrams, Jeanne E. *Revolutionary Medicine: The Founding Fathers and Mothers in Sickness and in Health*. New York: New York University Press, 2013.

Aksharananda, Rambachan. "Overcoming the Racial Hierarchy: The History and Medical Consequences of 'Caucasian.'" *Journal of Racial and Ethnic Health Disparities* 5, no. 5 (2018): 907–912.

Aldridge, A. Owen. "Problems in Writing the Life of Voltaire: Plural Methods and Conflicting Evidence." *Biography (Honolulu)* 1, no. 1 (Winter 1978): 5–22. https://www.jstor.org/stable/23539163.

Ambrose, Charles T. "Carolus Linnaeus (Carl von Linné), 1707–1778: The Swede Who Named Almost Everything." *The Pharos of Alpha Omega Alpha Honor Medical Society* 73, no. 2 (2010): 4–10.

Anderson, Robert T. "Lapp Racial Classifications as Scientific Myths." *Anthropological Papers of the University of Alaska* 11, no. 1 (1964): 15–31.

Andersson Burnett, Linda. "Selling the Sami: Nordic Stereotypes and Participatory Media in Georgian Britain." In *Communicating the North: Media Structures and Images in the Making of the Nordic Region*, edited by Peter Stradius. Oxfordshire, UK: Taylor and Francis, 2013, 171–196.

Andersson Burnett, Linda, and Bruce Buchan. *Race and the Scottish Enlightenment. A Colonial History, 1750–1820*. New Haven: Yale University Press, 2025.

Andrews, Corey E. "Drinking and Thinking: Club Life and Convivial Sociability in Mid-Eighteenth-Century Edinburgh." *The Social History of Alcohol and Drugs* 22, no. 1 (Autumn 2007): 65–82. https://doi.org/10.1086/SHAD 22010065.

Appleby, Joyce, and Terence Ball, eds. *Jefferson: Political Writings*. Cambridge: Cambridge University Press, 1999.

Arbell, Mordehay. *The Jewish Nation of the Caribbean: The Spanish-Portuguese Jewish Settlements in the Caribbean and the Guianas*. Jerusalem: Gefen Publishing House, 2002.

Arens, Esther Helena. "Flowerbeds and Hothouses: Botany, Gardens, and the Circulation of Knowledge in Things." *Historical Social Research/Historische Sozialforschung* 40, no. 1 (2015): 265–283.

Aroles, Serge. "L'Énigme de la fille noire de Louis XIV résolue par les archives? La 'Mauresse de Moret', ca. 1675–1731." n.p., 2007.

Asher, Kendra. "Was David Hume a Racist? Interpreting Hume's Infamous Footnote (Part I)." *Economic Affairs* 42, no. 2 (June 2022): 225–239. https://doi.org/10.1111/ecaf.12519.

Aspinwall, Bernard. "William Robertson and America." In *Eighteenth Century Scotland: New Perspectives.*, edited by T. M. Devine and J. R. Young. East Linton: Tuckwell Press, 1999, 152–176.

Atkins, John. *The Appendix to The Navy-Surgeon: or, A Practical System of Surgery*. London: Ward and Chandler, 1734.

Barnard, John, and D. F. McKenzie, eds. *The Cambridge History of the Book in Britain, Volume IV, 1557–1695*. Cambridge: Cambridge University Press, 1999.

Baumrin, Bernard H. *Hobbes's Leviathan: Interpretation and Criticism*. Belmont, CA: Wadsworth Publishing Co., 1969.

Bayly, Christopher Alan. *The Birth of the Modern World 1780–1914*. New York: Malden, 2004.

Bear, James A. *Jefferson at Monticello*. Charlottesville: University of Virginia Press, 1967.

Beasley, Faith E. "Bernier à l'origine du racisme?" In *Versailles à la rencontre du Taj Mahal. Conversations éclairées sur l'Inde au temps du Roi-Soleil*, translated by Patrick Graille. Paris: Les Belles Lettres, 202, 188–195.

Beckles, Hilary McDonald. "Kalinago (Carib) Resistance to European Colonization of the Caribbean." *Caribbean Quarterly* 52, no. 4 (2008): 77–94.

Bedel, Mathilde. "La Pigmentation, un outil pour une première description hiérarchisée des *races* humaines." In *Mirabilia Indiae. Voyageurs français et représentations de l'Inde au XVIIe siècle*. Paris: Garnier, 2021, 66–72.

Beil, Karen Magnuson. *What Linnaeus Saw: A Scientist's Quest to Name Every Living Thing*. New York: Norton, 2019.

Benes, Tuska. *The Rebirth of Revelation: German Theology in an Age of Reason and History, 1750–1850*. Toronto: University of Toronto Press, 2022.

Benoist, Jean. *Chronique d'un lieu de pensée. Fonds Saint-Jacques, Martinique*. Matoury: Ibis Rouge Editions, 2015.

Berkel, Klaas van. "'That Miserable Continent': Cultural Pessimism and the Idea of 'America' in Cornelius de Pauw." In *Revolutionary Histories: Transatlantic Cultural Nationalism*, edited by W. M. Verhoeven. New York: Palgrave, 2002, 135–151.

Bernasconi, Robert. "Who Invented the Concept of Race? Kant's Role in the Enlightenment Construction of Race." In *Race*, edited by Robert Bernasconi. Oxford: Blackwell, 2000, 11–36.

Bernstein, Richard B. *Thomas Jefferson*. Oxford: Oxford University Press, 2005.

Bezanson, Anne. *Prices and Inflation during the American Revolution*. Philadelphia: University of Pennsylvania Press, 1951.

Bijlsma, Rurmer. "Of Savages and Stoics: Converging Moral and Political Ideals in the Conjectural Histories of Rousseau and Ferguson." *Philosophy & Social Criticism* 48, no. 2 (2022): 209–244.

Bindman, David. *Ape to Apollo: Aesthetics and the Idea of Race in the 18th Century*. Ithaca: Cornell University Press, 2002.

Bird, Graham, ed. *A Companion to Kant*. New York: Wiley-Blackwell, 2015.

Blassingame, John W., and John R. McKivigan, eds. *Frederick Douglass Papers: Series One, Speeches, Debates, and Interviews*. New Haven: Yale University Press, 1979–1992.

Blosser, Joe. "Relational History: Adam Smith's Types of Human History." *Erasmus Journal for Philosophy and Economics* 12, no. 2 (2019): 24–48.

Blunt, Wilfrid. *Linnaeus: The Compleat Naturalist*. London: Cox and Wyman Ltd, 2004.

Bohman, James, and Matthias Lutz-Bachmann, eds. *Perpetual Peace: Essays on Kant's Cosmopolitan Ideal*. Cambridge: MIT Press, 1997.

Böker, Wolfgang. "Blumenbach's Collection of Human Skulls." In *Johann Friedrich Blumenbach: Race and Natural History, 1750–1850*, edited by Nicolaas Rupke and Gerhardt Lauer. London and New York: Routledge, 2019: 80–95.

Boletsi, Maria. *Barbarism and Its Discontents*. Palo Alto: Stanford University Press, 2013.

Böröcz, József. *The European Union and Social Change: A Critical Geopolitical-Economic Analysis*. Oxfordshire, UK: Taylor and Francis, 2009.

Boucher, Philip P. *France and the American Tropics to 1700: Tropics of Discontent?* Baltimore: Johns Hopkins University Press, 2008.

Boule, Pierre. "François Bernier and the Origins of the Modern Concept of Race." In *The Color of Liberty: Histories of Race in France*, edited by Sue Peabody and Tyler Stovall. Durham and London: Duke University Press, 2003, 11–13.

Bowlers, Peter J. *Evolution: The History of an Idea, 25th Anniversary Edition with a New Preface*. Berkeley and Los Angeles: University of California Press, 2009.

Boxill, Bernard. "Kantian Racism and Kantian Teleology." In *The Oxford Handbook of Race and Philosophy*, edited by Naomi Zack. New York: Oxford University Press, 2017, 44–53.

Brauner, Christina. "To Be the Key for Two Coffers: A West African Embassy to France (1670/1)." *IFRA-Nigeria E-Papers Series* 30 (2013): 1–26.

Brazeau, Brian. *Writing a New France, 1604–1632: Empire and Early Modern French Identity*. Oxfordshire, UK: Taylor and Francis, 2016.

Broberg, Gunnar. *The Man Who Organized Nature: The Life of Linnaeus*. Translated by Ann Patterson. Princeton: Princeton University Press, 2023.

Brodie, Fawn M. *Thomas Jefferson: An Intimate History*. New York: W.W. Norton, 1974.

Brown, Stewart J. "An Eighteenth-Century Historian on the Amerindians: Culture, Colonialism, and Christianity in William Robertson's History of America." *Studies in World Christianity* 2, no. 2 (1996): 204–222.

Bryant, Mark. "'Romancing the Throne': Madame de Maintenon's Journey from Secret Royal Governess to Louis XIV's Clandestine Consort, 1652–84." *Court Historian* 22, no. 2 (2017): 123–150.

Bugg, John. "The Other Interesting Narrative: Olaudah Equiano's Public Book Tour." *PMLA* 121, no. 5 (October 2006): 1424–1442.

Buffon, Henri Nadault de. *Buffon, sa famille, ses collaborateurs et ses familiers: Mémoires par M. Humbert-Bazile son secrétaire*. Paris: Jules Renouard, 1863.

Busseau, Laurent. "Sur les traces du galérien iroquois Ouréhouaré: Nouvelle analyse des archives du XVIIe siècle." *Histoire Québec* 22, no. 3 (2017): 11–14.

Butel, Paul. *Histoire des Antilles françaises*. Paris: Perrin, 2007.

Butler, Charles Henry. *The Treaty-Making Power of the United States*. New York: The Banks Law Publishing Company, 1902.

Campbell, Gwyn. *Structure of Slavery in Indian Ocean Africa and Asia*. Oxfordshire, UK: Taylor and Francis, 2004.

Campbell, P. F. *Some Early Barbadian History*. St. Michael, Barbados: n.p., 1993.

Carr, Rosalind. *Masculinity, Homosexuality, and Intellectual Culture in Eighteenth-Century Scotland*. Edinburgh: Edinburgh University Press, 2014.

Carretta, Vincent. "Olaudah Equiano or Gustavus Vassa? New Light on an Eighteenth-Century Question of Identity." *Slavery and Abolition* 20, no. 3 (1999): 96–105.

Carretta, Vincent. "Who was Francis Williams?" *Early American Literature* 38, no. 2 (2003): 213–237.

Carretta, Vincent. *Equiano, the African: Biography of a Self-Made Man*. Athens: University of Georgia Press, 2005.

Carrier, Martin. "Kant's Theory of Matter and His View of Chemistry." In *Kant and the Sciences*, edited by Eric Watkins. Oxford: Oxford University Press, 2001, 205–230.

Cassirer, Ernst. *Kant's Life and Thought*. New Haven and London: Yale University Press, 1981.

Chamboredon, Robert. "Des Placements de Voltaire à Cadix." *Cahiers Voltaire* 7 (2008): 41–72.

Chapman, Sara E. *Private Ambitions and Political Alliances: The Phélypeaux de Pontchartrain Family and Louis XIV's Government 1650–1715*. Rochester: University of Rochester Press, 2004.

Charette, Danielle. "David Hume's Balancing Act: The Political Discourses and the Sinews of War." *The American Political Science Review* 115, no. 1 (2021): 69–81.

Charette, Danielle. "David Hume and the Politics of Slavery." *Political Studies* 72, no. 3 (2024): 862–882. https://doi.org/10.1177/00323217231157516.

Chartrand, René. *French Fortresses in North America 1535–1763: Québec, Montréal, Louisbourg and New Orleans*. London: Bloomsbury Publishing and Osprey Publishing, 2013.

Chatillon, Marcel. "Le Père Labat à travers ses manuscrits." *Bulletin de la Société d'Histoire de la Guadeloupe*, no. 40–42 (1979): 13–178. https://doi.org/10.7202/1043900ar.

Clayton, Lawrence A. *Bartolomé de las Casas*. Cambridge: Cambridge University Press, 2012.

Cochin, Augustin. *The Results of Slavery*. Boston: Walker, Wise, and Company, 1863.

Cogliano, Francis D. *Emperor of Liberty: Thomas Jefferson's Foreign Policy*. New Haven: Yale University Press, 2014.

Conser, Walter H. *God and the Natural World: Religion and Science in Antebellum America*. Columbia: The University of South Carolina Press, 1993.

Cormier, Jacques. *Les Amours de Pimpette: Correspondance de Voltaire avec Olympe Du Noyer*. Paris: Éditions L'Harmattan, 2009.

Cotter, John L., Daniel G. Roberts, and Michael Parrington. *The Buried Past: An Archaeological History of Philadelphia*. Philadelphia: University of Pennsylvania Press, 1992.

Coutel, Charles. "Voltaire et la Chine." *L'Enseignement philosophique* 59, no. 4 (2009): 47–54.

Cronk, Nicholas. *Voltaire: A Very Short Introduction*. Oxford: Oxford University Press, 2017.

Cumo, Christopher, ed. *The Encyclopedia of Cultivated Plants*. New York: Bloomsbury, 2013.

Curran, Andrew S. "Rethinking Race History: The Role of the Albino in the French Enlightenment Life Sciences." *History and Theory* 48, no. 3 (October 2009): 151–179.

Curran, Andrew S. *The Anatomy of Blackness: Science and Slavery in an Age of Enlightenment*. Baltimore: Johns Hopkins University Press, 2011.

Curran, Andrew S. *Diderot and the Art of Thinking Freely*. New York: Other Press, 2019.

Curran, Andrew S., and Henry Louis Gates Jr. *Who's Black and Why? A Hidden Chapter from the Eighteenth-Century Invention of Race*. Cambridge: Harvard, 2022.

Dabhoiwala, Fara. "A Man of Parts and Learning." *London Review of Books* 46, no. 22 (November 2024). https://www.lrb.co.uk/the-paper/v46/n22/fara-dabhoiwala/a-man-of-parts-and-learning.

Dalphinis, Morgan. *History and Language in St. Lucia 1654–1915*. Morrisville, NC: Lulu.com, 2019.

Darnton, Robert. "Voltaire, Historian." *Raritan* 35, no. 2 (2015): 20–28.

Daut, Marlene. *The First and Last King of Haiti*. New York: Knopf, 2025.

Davids, Karel. "The Scholarly Atlantic: Circuits of Knowledge Between Britain, the Dutch Republic, and the Americas in the Eighteenth Century." In *Dutch Atlantic Connections, 1680–1800: Linking Empires, Bridging Borders*, edited by Gert Oostindie and Jessica V. Roitman. Leiden: Brill, 2014, 224–248.

Davies, Norman. *Europe: A History*. Oxford: Oxford University Press, 1996.

Dawson, Virginia P. "The Disciplines of Science: The Limits of Observation and the Hypotheses of Georges Louis Buffon and Charles Bonnet." In *Beyond History of Science: Essays in Honor of Robert E. Schofield*, edited by Elizabeth Garber. Lehigh: Lehigh University Press, 1990, 107–125.

DeLay, Bryan. "The Arms Trade and American Revolutions." *The American Historical Review* 128, no. 3 (2023): 1144–1181.

Delbourgo, James. *Collecting the World: Hans Sloane and the Origins of the British Museum*. Cambridge: Harvard University Press, 2017.

Demel, Walter. "How the Mongoloid Race Came into Being: Late Eighteenth-Century Constructions of East Asians in Europe." In *Race and Racism in Modern East Asia*, edited by Rotem Kowner and Walter Demel. Leiden and Boston: Brill, 2013, 59–85.

Dew, Nicholas. *Orientalism in Louis XIV's France*. Oxford: Oxford University Press, 2009.

Dewar, Helen. "Government by Trading Company?: The Corporate Legal Status of the Company of New France and Colonial Governance." *Nuevo Mundo, Mundos Nuevos* 14, no. 88 (June 2018). https://doi.org/10.4000/nuevomundo.72105.

Doron, Claude-Olivier. *L'Homme altéré. Races et dégénérescence (XVIIe–XIXe siècles)*. Ceyzérieu: Champ Vallon, 2016.

Downey, Roger. *Riddle of the Bones: Politics, Science, Race, and the Story of the Kennewick Man*. New York: Springer New York, 2000.

Drox, Jean Pierre. "Experiments and Observations on the Strength of Timber, by Mr. Buffon." *Literary Journal* 3 (1745): 121–132.

Dubois, Laurent. *Avengers of the New World: The Story of the Haitian Revolution*. Cambridge: Harvard University Press, 2004.

Duclos, Henri Louis. *Madame de La Vallière et Marie-Thérèse d'Autriche, femme de Louis XIV, avec pièces et documents inédits*. Paris: Didier, 1869.

Dugatkin, Alan. *Mr. Jefferson and the Giant Moose: Natural History in Early America*. Chicago: University of Chicago Press, 2009.

Dunn, Richard S. "The Barbados of 1680: Profile of the Richest Colony in English America." *The William and Mary Quarterly* 26, no. 1 (1969): 3–30.

Dupont-Ferrier, Gustave. *Du Collège de Clermont au Lycée Louis-le-Grand*. Paris: E. De Boccard, 1921–1925.

Eddy, John H. "Buffon, Species and the Forces of Reproduction." *Journal of the History of Biology* 56, no. 3 (October 2023): 479–493. https://doi.org/10.1007/s10739-023-09722-y.

Ellis, Joseph J. *American Sphinx: The Character of Thomas Jefferson*. New York: Knopf, 1997.

Ellis, Markman, Catherine Hall, Miles Ogborn, and Silvia Sebastiani. "Edward Long and Other Animals: The Orangutan and Race-Making in the Late Eighteenth Century." *Modern Intellectual History* (2024): 1–30.

Estwick, Samuel. *Considerations on the Negroe Cause Commonly So Called, Addressed to the Right Honorable Lord Mansfield*. London: J. Dodsley, 1773.

Falkner, James. *The War of Spanish Succession*. South Yorkshire, UK: Pen and Sword Military, 2015.

Farmer, James Eugene. *Versailles and the Court Under Louis XIV*. New York: The Century Company, 1906.

Fauvelle-Aymar, François-Xavier. *L'Invention du Hottentot, histoire du regard occidental sur les Khoisan (15e–19e siècles)*. Paris: Publications de la Sorbonne, 2002.

Fée, Antoine Laurent Apollinaire. *Vie de Linné, rédigée sur les documents autographes, et suivie de l'analyse de sa correspondance avec les principaux naturalistes de son époque*. Paris: F. G. Levrault, 1832.

Fellows, Otis E. "Voltaire and Buffon: Clash and Conciliation." *Symposium* 9, no. 2 (1955): 222–235.

Ferling, John. *Jefferson and Hamilton: The Rivalry that Forged a Nation*. New York: Bloomsbury Publishing, 2013.

Ferling, John. *Apostles of Revolution: Jefferson, Paine, Monroe, and the Struggle Against the Old Order in America and Europe*. New York: Bloomsbury Publishing, 2018.

Finkelman, Paul. "Thomas Jefferson and Antislavery: The Myth Goes On." *The Virginia Magazine of History and Biology* 102, no. 2 (April 1994): 193–228.

Fisher, Saul. "Gassendi." In *The Stanford Encyclopedia of Philosophy, Spring 2014 edition*, edited by Edward N. Zalta. Stanford, CA: Stanford University Press, 2014. https://plato.stanford.edu/entries/gassendi/#3.

Forbes, Robert Pierce. "Secular Damnation: Thomas Jefferson and the Imperative of Race." *Torrington Articles* 3 (May 2012). https://opencommons.uconn.edu/torr_articles/3.

Foulet, Lucien. "Voltaire en Angleterre." *Revue d'histoire littéraire de la France* 13, no. 1 (1906): 119–125.

Fries, Theodor Magnus. *Linnaeus*. Cambridge: Cambridge University Press, 2011.

Garraway, Doris L. *The Libertine Colony: Creolization in the Early French Caribbean*. Durham, NC: Duke University Press, 2005.

Garrett, Aaron. "Human Nature." In *The Cambridge History of Eighteenth-Century Philosophy*, edited by Knud Haakonssen. Cambridge: Cambridge University Press, 2006, 1:160–233.

Garrett, Aaron, and Silvia Sebastiani. "David Hume on Race." In *The Oxford Handbook of Philosophy and Race*. Oxford: Oxford University Press, 2017, 31–43.

Gates, Henry Louis, Jr. *The Black Box: Writing the Race*. New York: Penguin, 2024.

Geggus, David P. *The Haitian Revolution*. Bloomington: Indiana University Press, 2002.

Guerrini, Anita. "Perrault, Buffon and the Natural History of Animals." *Notes and Records of the Royal Society of London* 66, no. 4 (2012): 393–409. https://doi.org/10.1098/rsnr.2012.0044.

Gibson, Erika. "'Frenchified': French Food and Salon Culture in Jefferson's White House." *Food Studies* 8, no. 2 (2018): 1–13.

Giggs, Rebecca. *Fathoms: The World in the Whale*. New York: Simon & Schuster, 2020.

Gish, Justin, and Daniel Klinghard. *Thomas Jefferson and the Science of Republican*

Government: A Political Biography of the Notes on the State of Virginia. Cambridge: Cambridge University Press, 2017.

Gissis, Snait B. "Visualizing Race in the Eighteenth Century." *Historical Studies in the Natural Sciences* 41, no. 1 (Winter 2011): 41–103.

Gobineau, Arthur de. *Essai sur l'inégalité des races humaines*. Paris: Firmin Didot Frères, 1853–1855.

Goerke, Heinz. *Linnaeus*. New York: Scribner, 1973.

Golf-French, Morgan. "Teaching Race in the German Enlightenment: Christoph Meiners' History of Humanity in Institutional Context." In *History of Universities: Volume XXXVI/2*, edited by Mordechai Feingold. Oxford: Oxford University Press, 2023, 243–260.

Goodwin, Stefan. *Africa in Europe, Volume Two: Interdependencies, Relocations, and Globalization*. Lanham: Lexington Books, 2009.

Gordon-Reed, Annette. *Thomas Jefferson and Sally Hemings: An American Controversy*. Charlottesville: University of Virginia Press, 1997.

Gordon-Reed, Annette. *The Hemingses of Monticello: An American Family*. New York: W. W. Norton, 2008.

Gorer, Geoffrey. *The Life and Ideas of Marquis de Sade*. Redditch, UK: Read Books Limited, 2013.

Goy, Ina. "Kant's Theory of Biology and the Argument from Design." In *Kant's Theory of Biology*, edited by Ina Goy and Eric Watkins. Berlin and Boston: De Kruyter, 2014, 203–220.

Graves, Joseph L. *The Emperor's New Clothes: Biological Theories of Race at the Millennium*. New Brunswick, NJ: Rutgers University Press, 2003.

Gribbin, John, and Mary Gribbin. *On the Origin of Evolution: Tracing 'Darwin's Dangerous Idea' from Aristotle to DNA*. Amherst, NY: Prometheus, 2022.

Grinberg, Keila, and Sue Peabody, eds. *Free Soil in the Atlantic World*. Oxfordshire, UK: Taylor and Francis, 2016.

Grinevald, Paul-Marie. *Buffon 1788–1988*. Paris: Imprimerie nationale, 1988.

Griswold, Charles L. "Genealogical Narrative and Self-Knowledge in Rousseau's Discourse on the Origin and Foundation of Inequality among Men." *History of European Ideas* 42, no. 2 (2016): 276–301.

Gulyga, Arsenji. *Immanuel Kant: His Life and Thought*. New York: Springer, 2012.

Hagengruber, Ruth, ed. *Émilie du Châtelet between Leibniz and Newton*. Dordrecht: Springer, 2012.

Halbert, Phillipe. "An African Prince at the Court of the Sun King." *The Monitor: Journal of International Studies* 16, no. 2 (Summer 2011): 7–17. https://www.academia.edu/12235938An_African_Prince_at_the_Court_of_the_Sun_King.

Hall, John A. "Adam Smith and Sociology." *European Journal of Sociology* 64, no. 3 (2023): 303–324.

Halliday, Anthony. *The Temperamental Nude: Class, Medicine, and Representation in Eighteenth-century France — Issue 5*. Oxford: Voltaire Foundation, 2010.

Handler, Jerome S. and Matthew C. Reilly. "Contesting 'White Slavery' in the Caribbean: Enslaved Africans and European Indentured Servants in Seventeenth-Century Barbados." *New West Indian Guide* 91, no. 1–2 (2017): 30–55. https://doi.org/10.1163/22134360-09101056.

Hansen, Lars, ed. *The Linnaeus Apostles: Global Science and Adventure*. London: IK Foundation, 2007.

Harris, James A. *Hume: An Intellectual Biography*. Cambridge: Cambridge University Press, 2015.

Hassin, Ran, and Yaacov Trope. "Facing Faces: Studies on the Cognitive Aspects of Physiognomy." *Journal of Personality and Social Psychology* 78, no. 5 (2000): 837–852.

Hatch, Robert Alan. "Between Astrology and Copernicanism: Morin-Gassendi-Bouilliau." *Early Science and Medicine* 22 (2017): 487–516.

Hayes, Kevin J. *The Road to Monticello: The Life and Mind of Thomas Jefferson*. Oxford: Oxford University Press, 2008.

Head, Jonathan. "Scripture and Moral Examples in Pietism and Kant's Religion." *Irish Theological Quarterly* 83, no. 3 (2018): 217–234.

Heinl, Robert Debs, and Nancy Gordon Heinl. *Written in Blood: The Story of the Haitian People, 1492–1971*. Boston: Houghton Mifflin Co., 1978.

Hemings, Madison. "Life Among the Lowly, No. 1." *Pike County Republican*, March 13, 1873. https://encyclopediavirginia.org/6448hpr-21dd90c2c2fa921.

Henings, William W., ed. *The Statutes at Large; Being a Collection of All the Laws of Virginia, from the First Session of the Legislature, in the Year 1619*. New York: R. & W. & G. Bartow, 1823.

Heyer, John Hadju. *The Lure and Legacy of Music at Versailles: Louis XIV and the Aix School*. Cambridge: Cambridge University Press, 2014.

Hicks, Dan. "'Material Improvements': The Archaeology of Estate Landscapes in the British Leeward Islands, 1713–1838." In *Estate Landscapes: Design, Improvement, and Power in the Post-Medieval Landscape*, edited by Jonathan Finch and Katherine Gilese. Suffolk: Boydell and Brewer, 2007, 205–227.

Hodacs, Hanna. "In the Field: Exploring Nature with Carolus Linnaeus." In *Endeavour* 34, no. 2 (2010): 45–49.

Hodacs, Hanna, and Kenneth Nyberg. *Naturalhistoria på resande fot. Om att forska, undervisa och göra karriär i 1700-talets Sverige*. Lund: Nordic Academic Press, 2007.

Hodacs, Hanna, Kenneth Nyberg, and Stéphane Van Damme, eds. *Linnaeus, Natural History, and the Circulation of Knowledge*. Oxford: Voltaire Foundation, 2018.

Hoffmann, Léon-François. *Le Nègre romantique. Personnage littéraire et obsession collective*. Paris: Payot, 1973.

Hogarth, Rana A., *Medicalizing Blackness: Making Racial Difference in the Atlantic World*. Chapel Hill: University of North Carolina Press, 2017.

Hoquet, Thierry. *Buffon: Histoire naturelle et philosophie*. Paris: Champion, 2005.

Hoquet, Thierry. *Buffon illustré: les gravures de l'Histoire naturelle (1749–1767)*. Paris: Publications Scientifiques du Muséum national d'Histoire naturelle, 2007.

Hoquet, Thierry. *Buffon / Linné: éternels rivaux de la biologie?* Paris: Dunod, 2007.

Hoquet, Thierry. "Biologisation de la race et racialisation de l'humain: Bernier, Buffon, Linné." In *L'Invention de la race. Des Représentations scientifiques aux exhibitions populaires*. Paris: La Découverte, 2014.

Höpfl, H. M. "From Savage to Scotsman: Conjectural History in the Scottish Enlightenment." *Journal of British Studies* 17, no. 2 (Spring 1978): 19–40. https://doi.org/10.1086/385720.

Horn, James J., Jan Ellen Lewis, and Peter S. Onuf, eds. *The Revolution of 1800: Democracy, Race, and the New Republic*. Charlottesville: University of Virginia Press, 2002.

Houston, Robert Allan. *Scottish Literacy and the Scottish Identity: Illiteracy and Society in Scotland and Northern England 1600–1800*. Cambridge: Cambridge University Press, 1985.

Hudson, Nicholas. "From 'Nation' to 'Race': The Origin of Classification in Eighteenth-Century Thought." *Eighteenth-Century Studies* 29, no. 3 (Spring 1996): 247–264. https://www.jstor.org/stable/30053821.

Hutton, Peter, and David Ashton. "David Hume — An Apologia." *Scottish Affairs* 32, no. 3 (2023): 347–364.

Hyland, William G., Jr. *Martha Jefferson: An Intimate Life with Thomas Jefferson*. Lanham, MD: Rowman and Littlefield, 2015.

Jönsson, Ann-Mari. "The Reception of Linnaeus's Works in Germany with Particular Reference to His Conflict with Siegesbeck." In *Germania Latina*, edited by E. Kessler and H. C. Kuhn. München: Wilhelm Fink Verlag, 2003, 2:721–739.

Jönsson, Ann-Mari. "Linnaeus's International Correspondence. The Spread of a Revolution." In *Languages of Science in the Eighteenth Century*, edited by Britt-

Louise Gunnarsson. Berlin & Boston: De Gruyter, 2011, 171–191. https://doi.org/10.1515/9783110255065.171.

Jorati, Julia. *Slavery and Race: Philosophical Debates in the Sixteenth and Seventeenth Centuries*. Oxford: Oxford University Press, 2024.

Kang, Namsoon. *Cosmopolitan Theology: Reconstituting Planetary Hospitality, Neighbor-Love and Solidarity in an Uneven World*. Des Peres, MO: Chalice Press, 2013.

Kendi, Ibram X. *Stamped from the Beginning: The Definitive History of Racist Ideas in America*. New York: Public Affairs, 2016.

Kidd, Thomas. *Thomas Jefferson: A Biography of Spirit and Flesh*. New Haven: Yale University Press, 2022.

Kierner, Cynthia A. *Martha Jefferson Randolph, Daughter of Monticello: Her Life and Times*. Chapel Hill: University of North Carolina Press, 2012.

Klaus, Sidney. "A History of the Science of Pigmentation." In *The Pigmentary System: Physiology and Pathophysiology*, edited by James J. Norlund. New York: Oxford University Press, 1998, 1–10.

Kleingeld, Pauline, ed. *Toward Perpetual Peace and Other Writings on Politics, Peace, and History*. New Haven: Yale University Press, 2006.

Kleingeld, Pauline. "Kant's Second Thoughts on Colonialism." In *Kant and Colonialism: Historical and Critical Perspectives*, edited by K. Flikschuh and L. Ypi. Oxford: Oxford University Press, 2014, 43–76.

Knight, Franklin W., ed. *General History of the Caribbean: The Slave Societies of the Caribbean*. London: Unesco, 1997.

Koerner, Lisbet. *Linnaeus: Nature and Nation*. Cambridge: Harvard University Press, 1999.

Koerner, Lisbet. "Purposes of Linnaean Travel: A Preliminary Research Report." In *Visions of Empire: Voyages, Botany, and Representations of Nature*, edited by David Phillip Miller and Peter Hans Reill. Cambridge: Cambridge University Press, 2011, no. 5, 117–140.

Kranish, Michael. *Flight from Monticello: Jefferson at War*. New York: Oxford University Press, 2010.

Kuehn, Manfred. *Kant: A Biography*. Cambridge: Cambridge University Press, 2001.

Kukla, Jon. *A Wilderness So Immense: The Louisiana Purchase and the Destiny of America*. New York: Random House, 2003.

Lafleur, Gérard. "Les Juifs aux îles françaises du vent (XVIIe–XVIIIe siècles)." *Bulletin de la Société d'Histoire de la Guadeloupe*, no. 65–66 (1985): 77–128.

Lafont, Anne. *L'Art et la race: L'Africain (tout) contre l'oeil des Lumières*. Dijon: Les Presses du réel, 2019.

Lalung, Henry de. *Le Serpent de la Martinique*. Paris: Corbière, 1934.

Larrimore, Mark, and Sara Eigen, eds. *The German Invention of Race*. Albany: State University of New York Press, 2006.

Le Borgne, Françoise, Odile Parsis-Barubé, and Nathalie Vuillemin, eds. *Les Savoirs des barbares, des primitifs et des sauvages. Lectures de l'Autre aux XVIIIe et XIXe siècles*. Paris: Classiques Garnier, 2018.

Lehmann, William C. *Henry Home, Lord Kames, and the Scottish Enlightenment: A Study in National Character in the History of Ideas*. Dordrecht: Springer Science and Business Media, 1971.

Lelièvre, Guillaume. *Les Précurseurs de la Compagnie française des Indes orientales*. Caen: Presses universitaires de Caen, 2021.

Lenik, Steve. "Mission Plantations, Space, and Social Control: Jesuits as Planters in French Caribbean Colonies and Frontiers." *Journal of Social Archaeology* 12, no. 1 (2012): 51–71.

Levavasseur, Charles. *Esclavage de la race noire aux colonies françaises*. Paris: Bajat, 1840.

Levy, David M., and Sandra J. Peart. "Group Analytics in Adam Smith's Work." *Eastern Economic Journal* 42 (2016): 514–527.

Lewis, Rhodri. "William Petty's Anthropology: Religion, Colonialism, and the Problem of Human Diversity." *Huntington Library Quarterly* 74, no. 2 (June 2011): 261–288.

Libell, Monica. "Universal Aspirations and Racial Asymmetries in Linnaeus's Descriptions of *Homo sapiens*." In *Beyond 'Hellenes' and 'Barbarians': Asymmetrical Concepts of European Discourse*, edited by Kirill Postoutenko. Oxford and New York: Bergen Books, 2022, 56–84.

Lincoln, Abraham. *Letters and Telegrams*. New York: The Current Literature Publishing Company, 1907.

Llamzon, Benjamin S. *A Humane Case for Moral Intuition*. Boston: Brill, 2022.

Longchamp, Sébastien G., and Jean-Louis Wagnière. *Mémoires sur Voltaire*. Paris: Aimé André, 1826.

Lopez, Jean-François. "Les Investissements de Voltaire dans le commerce colonial et la traite négrière: Clarifications et malentendus." *Cahiers Voltaire* 7 (2008): 124–139.

Lord, Perceval B. *Popular Physiology; Being a Familiar Explanation of the Most Interesting Facts Connected with the Structure and Functions of Animals, and Particularly of Man*. London: John W. Parker, 1834.

Lovejoy, Paul E. "Autobiography and Memory: Gustavus Vassa, alias Olaudah Equiano, the African." *Slavery and Abolition* 27, no. 3 (2006): 317–347.

Lu-Adler, Huaping. *Kant, Race, and Racism*. Oxford: Oxford University Press, 2023.

Lu-Adler, Huaping. "Know Your Place, Know Your Calling: Geography, Race, and Kant's 'World Citizen.'" *Studia Kantiana* 21, no. 2 (2023): 81–96. https://doi.org/10.5380/sk.v21i2.92101.

Maass, John R. *The Road to Yorktown: Jefferson, Lafayette and the British Invasion of Virginia*. Cheltenham, UK: History Press, 2015.

Maclean, Norman, ed. *The Living Planet: The State of the World's Wildlife*. Cambridge: Cambridge University Press, 2023.

Malcomson, Cristina. "Gulliver's Travels and Studies of Skin Color in Royal Society." In *Humans and Other Animals in Eighteenth Century British Society*, edited by Frank Palmeri. Oxfordshire, UK: Taylor and Francis, 2020.

Malleson, George Bruce. *History of the French in India: From the Founding of Pondichery in 1674 to the Capture of That Place in 1761*. Cambridge: Cambridge University Press, 2010.

"Manatee." Merriam-Webster Dictionary. https://www.merriam-webster.com/dictionary/manatee.

Mandelblatt, Bertie. "Atlantic Consumption of French Rum and Brandy and Economic Growth in the Seventeenth- and Eighteenth-Century Caribbean." *French History* 25, no. 1 (March 2011): 9–27.

Martin, Abbé A. *Histoire de la vie et des écrits de Pierre Gassendi*. Paris: Librairie philosophique de Ladrange, 1853.

Martin, Meredith. "Special Embassies and Overseas Visitors." In *Visitors to Versailles: From Louis XIV to the French Revolution*, edited by Daniëlle Kisluk-Grosheide and Bertrand Rondot. New York: Metropolitan Museum of Art, 2018, 108–121.

Martin, Meredith, and Gillian Weiss. *The Sun King at Sea: Maritime Art and Galley Slavery in Louis XIV's France*. Los Angeles: J. Paul Getty Trust, 2022.

Mathisen, Stein R. "Souvenirs and the Commodification of Sámi Spirituality in Tourism." *Religions* 11, no. 9 (August 2020). https://doi.org/10.3390/rel11090429.

Matson, Erik W. "Commerce as Cooperation with the Deity: Self-Love, the Common Good, and the Coherence of Francis Hutcheson." *The European Journal of the History of Economic Thought* 30, no. 4 (2023): 507–524.

Matson, Erik W. "Economics and the Moral Theology of Mutual Benefits: Francis Hutcheson, David Hume, and Adam Smith." *The Journal of Markets & Morality* 26, no. 1 (2023): 85–103.

Matthewson, Tim. "George Washington's Policy Toward the Haitian Revolution." *Diplomatic History* 3 (1979): 325–333.

Matthewson, Tim. "Jefferson and Haiti." *The Journal of Southern History* 61, no. 2 (May 1995): 209–248.

Mazza, Emilio. "'An Irishman Cannot Have Wit': Hume and the Prejudice of National Characters." *Tocqueville Review* 35, no. 1 (2014): 27–54.

Mckenna, Antony. "*La Moïsade*: Un Manuscrit clandestin voltairien." *Revue Voltaire*, no. 8 (2008): 67–97.

Meacham, Jon. *Thomas Jefferson: The Art of Power*. New York: Random House Publishing Group, 2013.

Meek, Ronald L. *Social Science and the Ignoble Savage*. Cambridge: Cambridge University Press, 1976.

Melish, Joanne Pope. *Disowning Slavery: Gradual Emancipation and "Race" in New England*. Ithaca: Cornell University Press, 1998.

Melisson, Céline. "Jean-Baptiste Patoulet, un administrateur au service de l'empire français." *Nuevo Mundo, Mundos Nuevos* (2018). https://doi.org/10.4000/nuevomundo.74810.

Melzer, Sara E., and Kathryn Norberg. *From the Royal to the Republican Body: Incorporating the Political in Seventeenth- and Eighteenth-Century France*. Berkeley: University of California Press, 1998.

Menjot d'Elbenne, Samuel. *Madame de La Sablière: Ses pensées chrétiennes et ses lettres à l'abbé de Rancé*. Paris: Plon-Nourrit et Cie, 1923.

Mensch, Jennifer. *Kant's Organicism: Epigenesis and the Development of Critical Philosophy*. Chicago: University of Chicago Press, 2015.

Mensch, Jennifer. "Kant and the Skull Collectors: German Anthropology from Blumenbach to Kant." In *Kant and His German Contemporaries: Logic, Mind, Epistemology, Science and Ethics*, edited by Corey Dyck and Falk Wunderlich. Cambridge: Cambridge University Press, 2017, 1:192–210.

Mensch, Jennifer, and Michael J. Olsen, eds. *Key Texts in the History and Philosophy of the German Life Sciences, 1745–1845: Generation, Heredity, and Race*. London: Bloomsbury Academic, 2025.

Messaoudi, Abderhaman. "Voltaire et la censure en France." *Papers on French Seventeenth-Century Literature* 36, no. 71 (2009): 445–457.

Mikkelsen, Jon M., trans. and ed. *Kant and the Concept of Race: Late Eighteenth-century Writings*. Albany: State University of New York Press, 2013.

Millet, Nathaniel, and Charles H. Parker, eds. "Introduction." In *Jesuits and Race: A Global History of Continuity and Change, 1530–2020*. Albuquerque: University of New Mexico, 2022.

Mitchell, Paul Wolff. "Origins of Races, Organs of Intellect: Polygenism, Political Order, and the Enlightenment Construction of Cranial Race Science."

In *Ordering the Human: The Global Spread of Racial Science*, edited by Eram Alam, Dorothy Roberts, and Natalie Shibley. New York: Columbia University Press, 2024, 21–47.

Moitt, Bernard. *Women and Slavery in the French Antilles, 1635–1848*. Bloomington: Indiana University Press, 2001.

Morgan, Philip D. "Forward." In *Recovering Scotland's Slavery Past: The Caribbean Connection*, edited by T. M. Devine. Edinburgh: Edinburgh University Press, 2015, xiii–xv.

Mossner, Ernest Campbell. "Hume at La Flèche, 1735: An Unpublished Letter." *Texas Studies in English* 37 (1958): 30–33.

Mullen, Macaira L. "Wealth, Desire, and Consequences of the Antebellum Slaveholder." *The Purdue Historian* 10, no. 1 (2022): 1–20. https://docs.lib.purdue.edu/puhistorian/vol10/iss1/3/.

Müller-Wille, Staffan. "Linnaeus and the Four Corners of the World." In *The Cultural Politics of Blood, 1500–1900*, edited by Kimberly Anne Coles et al. Basingstoke: Palgrave Macmillan, 2015, 191–209.

Müller-Wille, Staffan, and Isabelle Charmantier. "Natural History and Information Overload: The Case of Linnaeus." *Studies in History and Philosophy of Science. Part C, Studies in History and Philosophy of Biological and Biomedical Sciences* 43, no. 1 (2012): 4–15.

Murr, Sylvia. "Bernier et Gassendi: Filiation déviationniste?" In *Gassendi et l'Europe (1592–1792): Actes du colloque international de Paris.* Paris: Vrin, 1997, 71–114.

Nablow, Ralph Arthur. *A Study of Voltaire's Lighter Verse*. Oxford: Voltaire Foundation, 1974.

Nelson, William Max. *The Time of Enlightenment: Constructing the Future in France, 1750 to Year One*. Toronto: University of Toronto Press, 2021.

Nelson, William Max. *Enlightenment Biopolitics: A History of Race, Eugenics, and the Making of Citizens*. Chicago: Chicago University Press, 2024.

Newman, Simon P. "American Political Culture and the French and Haitian Revolutions: Nathaniel Cutting and the Jeffersonian Republicans." In *The Impact of the Haitian Revolution in the Atlantic World*, edited by David P. Geggus. Columbia: University of South Carolina Press, 2002.

Niekerk, Carl. "Man and Orangutan in Eighteenth-Century Thinking: Retracing the Early History of Dutch and German Anthropology." *The Eighteenth Century* 96, no. 4 (Winter 2004): 477–502.

Noguès, Boris. "L'Encadrement pédagogique et disciplinaire dans les collèges d'humanités en France du XVIe au XVIIIe siècle." *Paedagogica Historica* 47, no. 3 (2011): 243–262.

Onuf, Peter S., and Helo, Ari. "Jefferson, Morality, and the Problem of Slavery." *The William and Mary Quarterly* 60, no. 3 (2003): 583–614.

Palm, Lennart Andersson. "Estimating Sweden's Population in the Early Modern Period." *Bebyggelsehistorisk tidskrift, Nordic Journal of Settlement History and Built Heritage* 81 (2021): 67–99.

Palmer, Vernon Valentine. "The Origins and Authors of the Code Noir." *Louisiana Law Review* 56, no. 2 (Winter 1996): 363–407.

Papers of the New Haven Colony History Society. New Haven: Printed for the Society, 1900.

Paping, R. "General Dutch Population Development 1400–1850: Cities and Countryside." Paper presentation, 1st European Society of Historical Demography Conference, Alghero, Italy, September 25–27, 2014.

Park, Peter. *Africa, Asia, and the History of Philosophy: Racism in the Formation of the Philosophical Canon, 1780–1830*. Albany: State University of New York Press, 2013.

Patisso, Giuseppe, and Fausto Ermete Carbone. "Slavery and Slave Codes in Overseas Empires." In *Modern Slavery and Human Trafficking*, edited by Jane Reeves. London: Intechopen, 2020. https://doi.org/10.5772/intechopen.91411.

Peabody, Sue. *There Are No Slaves in France*. Oxford: Oxford University Press, 1996.

Peabody, Sue. "'A Nation Born into Slavery': Missionaries and Racial Discourse in Seventeenth-Century French Antilles." *Journal of Social History* 38, no. 1 (Autumn 2004): 113–126. https://www.jstor.org/stable/3790029.

Pearson, Roger. *Voltaire Almighty: A Life in Pursuit of Freedom*. New York: Bloomsbury Publishing, 2005.

Pellegrin, Pierre. *Aristotle's Classification of Animals: Biology and the Conceptual Unity of the Aristotelian Corpus*. Berkeley: University of California Press, 2021.

Pennazio, Sergio. "Elements of Plant Physiology in Theophrastus' Botany." *Theoretical Biology Forum* 107 (2014): 97–108.

Pérotin-Dumon, Anne. *La Ville aux* îles, *la ville dans l'île. Basse-Terre et Pointe-à-Pitre, Guadeloupe, 1650–1820*. Paris: Éditions Karthala, 2000.

Petroff, Florence. "William Robertson's Unfinished History of America. The Foundation of the British Empire in North America and the Scottish Enlightenment." *Transatlantica* 2 (2017). https://doi.org/10.4000/transatlantica.10326.

Pettigrew, William A. *Freedom's Debt: The Royal African Company and the Politics of the Atlantic Slave Trade, 1672–1752*. Chapel Hill: The University of North Carolina Press, 2013.

Phillipson, Nicholas. *Adam Smith: An Enlightened Life*. New Haven: Yale University Press, 2012.

Plissonneau-Duquêne, René. *Un Essai de contingentement d'importation au XVIIe siècle*. Paris: Recueil Sirey, 1935.

Pogliano, Claudio. *Brain and Race: A History of Cerebral Anthropology*. Leiden: Brill, 2020.

Pomeau, René. *Voltaire en son temps*. Oxford: Fayard and Voltaire Foundation, 1985–1994.

Popkin, Jeremy D. *A Concise History of the Haitian Revolution*. Malden: Wiley-Blackwell, 2012.

Popkin, Richard Henry. *Isaac La Peyrère (1596–1676): His Life, His Work, and Influence*. Leiden: E. J. Brill, 1987.

Popkin, Richard Henry. *The Third Force in Seventeenth-Century Thought*. New York: Brill, 1992.

Prior, Sir James. *Memoir of the Life and Character of the Right Honorable Edmund Burke*. London: printed for Baldwick, Cradock, and Joy, 1826.

Pulteney, Richard. *A General View of the Writings of Linnaeus*. London: Mawman, 1805.

Quatrefages de Bréau, Jean Louis Armand de. "Les Arguments zoologiques du polygénisme." *Revue des cours scientifiques de la France et de l'étranger* 12 (1869): 202–225.

Rae, John. *Life of Adam Smith*. London: Macmillan, 1895.

Rahmatian, Andreas. *Lord Kames: Legal and Social Theorist*. Edinburgh: Edinburgh University Press, 2015.

Rasmussen, Dennis C. *The Pragmatic Enlightenment*. Cambridge: Cambridge University Press, 2014.

Rasmussen, Dennis C. *The Infidel and the Professor*. Princeton: Princeton University Press, 2019.

Rawley, James A., and Stephen D. Behrendt. *The Transatlantic Slave Trade: A History*. Lincoln: University of Nebraska Press, 2007.

Reader, John. *Missing Links: In Search of Human Origins*. Oxford: Oxford University Press, 2011.

Régent, Frédéric. *La France et ses esclaves de la colonisation aux abolitions, 1620–1848*. Paris: Grasset, 2007.

Rennard, Joseph. *Le P. Labat O.P. aux Antilles*. Paris: Editions Spes, 1927.

Ribot, Théodule. *Heredity*. New York: D. Appleton and Company, 1875.

Riley, Philip F. "Louis XIV: Watchdog of Parisian Morality." *The Historian* 36, no. 1 (November 1973): 19–33.

Roe, Shirley A. *Matter, Life, Generation: Eighteenth-Century Embryology and the Haller Debate*. Cambridge: Cambridge University Press, 2003.

Roger, Jacques. *Buffon: Un Philosophe au Jardin du roi*. Paris: Fayard, 1989.

Roger, Jacques. *Buffon: A Life in Natural History*, edited by L. Pearce William. Ithaca: Cornell University Press, 1997.

Roger, Jacques. *The Life Sciences in Eighteenth-Century French Thought*, edited by Keith R. Benson. Palo Alto: Stanford University Press, 1998.

Rogers, Ethan S., and Stephanie L. Canington. "Lemurs before Lemur: Depictions of Captive Lemurs Prior to Linnaeus." *Notes and Records of the Royal Society of London* 77, no. 1 (2023): 19–48.

Roget, Jacques Petitjean. "Les Femmes des colons à la Martinique au XVIe et XVIIe siècles." *Revue d'histoire de l'Amérique française* 9, no. 2 (1955): 176–235. https://doi.org/10.7202/301707ar.

Rolland d'Erceville, Barthélemy Gabriel. *Mémoire sur l'administration du collège de Louis-le-Grand*. Paris: chez Pierre-Guillaume Simon, 1778.

Romero, Aldemaro. "When Whales Became Mammals: The Scientific Journey of Cetaceans from Fish to Mammals in the History of Science." In *New Approaches to the Study of Marine Mammals*, edited by Aldemaro Romero and Edward O. Keith. Rijeka: InTech, 2012, 4–30. https://academicworks.cuny.edu/bb_pubs/371/.

Root, Elihu, et al., eds. *The War of the Rebellion: A Compilation of Official Records of the Union and Confederate Armies*. Washington: Government Printing Office, 1902.

Rosenthal, Angela. "Raising Hair." *Eighteenth-Century Studies* 38, no. 1 (Fall 2004): 1–16.

Rugemer, Edward B. "The Development of Mastery and Race in the Comprehensive Slave Codes of the Greater Caribbean during the Seventeenth Century." *The William and Mary Quarterly* 70, no. 3 (July 2013): 429–458.

Rupke, Nicolaas, and Gerhard Lauer, eds. *Blumenbach and Natural History*. Oxfordshire, UK: Routledge, 2019.

Rupke, Nicolaas, and Gerhard Lauer. "Introduction: A Brief History of Blumenbach Representation." In *Johann Friedrich Blumenbach: Race and Natural History, 1750–1850*, edited by Nicolaas Rupke and Gerhard Lauer. London and New York: Routledge, 2019, 1–13.

Sainton, Jean-Pierre. *Histoire et civilisation de la Caraïbe: Guadeloupe, Martinique, Petites Antilles. Le Temps des matrices: Économie et cadres sociaux du long XVIIIe siècle*. Paris: Éditions Karthala, 2012.

Saville, Richard. "Scottish Modernisation Prior to the Industrial Revolution, 1688–1763." In *Eighteenth-Century Scotland: New Perspectives*, edited by T. M. Devine and J.R. Young. East Linton: Tuckwell Press, 1999, 6–23.

Scarth, Alwyn. *La Catastrophe: The Eruption of Mount Pelée, the Worst Volcanic Disaster of the 20th Century* (Oxford: Oxford University Press, 2002).

Schiebinger, Londa. "The Anatomy of Difference: Race and Sex in Eighteenth-Century Science." *Eighteenth-Century Studies* 23, no. 4 (1990): 387–405. https://www.jstor.org/stable/2739176.

Schiebinger, Londa. "Why Mammals Are Called Mammals: Gender Politics in Eighteenth-Century Natural History." *The American Historical Review* 98, no. 2 (April 1993): 382–411.

Schliesser, Eric. *Adam Smith: Systematic Philosopher and Public Thinker.* Oxford: Oxford University Press, 2017.

Schmitt, Stéphane. "Voltaire et Buffon: Une 'Brouille pour les coquilles.'" *Revue Voltaire* 8 (2008): 227–239.

Schönfeld, Martin. *The Philosophy of the Young Kant: The Precritical Project.* Oxford: Oxford University Press, 2000.

Sebastiani, Silvia. "Race, Women, and Progress in the Late Scottish Enlightenment." In *Women, Gender and Enlightenment*, edited by Sarah Knott and Barbara Taylor. London: Palgrave Macmillan UK, 2005, 75–96.

Sebastiani, Silvia. *The Scottish Enlightenment: Race, Gender, and the Limits of Progress.* Basingstoke: Palgrave Macmillan, 2013.

Sebastiani, Silvia, and Jean-Frédéric Schaub. *Race et histoire dans les sociétés occidentales (XVe–XVIIIe siècle).* Paris: Albin Michel, 2021.

Sepinwall, Alyssa Goldstein. *The Abbé Grégoire and the French Revolution: The Making of Modern Universalism.* Berkeley: University of California Press, 2021.

Seth, Vanita. *Europe's Indians: Producing Racial Difference.* Durham, NC: Duke University Press, 2010.

Shank, John Bennett. *The Newton Wars and the Beginning of the French Enlightenment.* Chicago: University of Chicago Press, 2008.

Shapiro, Celia D. "Nation of Nowhere: Jewish Role in Colonial American Chocolate History." In *Chocolate: History, Culture, and Heritage.* Hoboken, NJ: Wiley, 2009, 49–64.

Sheshadri, Kalpana. *HumAnimal: Race, Law, Language.* Saint Paul: University of Minnesota Press, 2012.

Sinha, Manisha. *The Slave's Cause: A History of Abolition.* New Haven: Yale University Press, 2017.

Sloan, Philip R. "The Buffon-Linnaeus Controversy." *Isis* 67, no. 3 (September 1976): 356–375.

Slotkin, James S. *Readings in Early Anthropology.* London: Taylor and Francis, 2012.

Smith, Justin E. H. *Nature, Human Nature, and Human Difference: Race in Early Modern Philosophy*. Princeton: Princeton University Press, 2015.

Smitten, Jeffrey R. *Life of William Robertson: Minister, Historian, and Principal*. Edinburgh: Edinburgh University Press, 2016.

Smout, Thomas Christopher. "A New Look at the Scottish Improvers." *The Scottish Historical Review* 91, no. 231 (April 2012): 125–149. https://www.jstor.org/stable/43773889.

Soll, Jacob. *The Information Master: Jean-Baptiste Colbert's Secret State Intelligence System*. Ann Arbor: University of Michigan Press, 2009.

Stalnaker, Joanna. *The Unfinished Enlightenment: Description in the Age of the Encyclopedia*. Ithaca: Cornell University Press, 2010.

Stearn, William Thomas. "The Background of Linnaeus's Contributions to the Nomenclature and Methods of Systematic Biology." *Systematic Zoology* 8 (1959): 4–22.

Stem, F. D. "The Unity of the Human Race." *Mercersburg Review* 3 (1851): 129–143.

Sternberg, Robert J. "It's Time to Move beyond the 'Great Chain of Being.'" *The Behavioral and Brain Sciences* 40 (August 2017).

Stevens, Cara Rogers. *Thomas Jefferson and the Fight against Slavery*. Lawrence: University of Kansas Press, 2024.

Stewart, Dugald. *The Works of Dugald Stewart*. Cambridge: Hilliard and Brown, 1829.

Stewart, Dugald. "An Account of the Life and Writings of Willliam Robertson." In *The Works of William Robertson D.D.* London: T. Cadell, 1840.

Stewart, Dugald. "Account of the Life and Writings of Adam Smith LL.D." In *The Collected Works of Dugald Stewart, Esq., F.R.SS.*, edited by Sir William Hamilton. Edinburgh: Thomas Constable, 1854, 265–351.

Stuckenberg, John Henry Wilbrandt. *The Life of Immanuel Kant*. London: Macmillan, 1882.

Stuurman, Siep. "François Bernier and the Invention of Race Classification." *History Workshop Journal* 50 (Autumn 2000): 1–21.

Svenbro, Anna. "Linné et la France: Entre botanique et politique." In *La Revue de la BNU* 8 (2013): 26–37. https://doi.org/10.4000/rbnu.1961.

Terrall, Mary. *The Man Who Flattened the Earth: Maupertuis and the Sciences in the Enlightenment*. Chicago: University of Chicago Press, 2002.

Thérenty, Marie-Ève, and Adeline Wrona, eds. *Objets insignes, objets infâmes de la littérature*. Paris: EAC, 2018.

Thompson, Peter. *Heir through Hope: Thomas Jefferson's Lifelong Investment in William Short*. Oxford: Oxford University Press, 2023.

Tucker, George. *The Life of Thomas Jefferson, Third President of the United States*. Philadelphia: Carey, Lea & Blanchard, 1837.

Turnbull, Paul. "British Anatomists, Phrenologists and the Construction of the Aboriginal Race, c. 1790–1830." *History Compass* 5 (2007): 26–50.

Tytler, Alexander Fraser, Lord Woodhouselee, and Henry Home Kames. *Memoirs of the Life and Writings of the Honorable Henry Home of Kames*. Edinburgh: William Creech et al., 1817.

Tytler, Graeme, and Melissa Percival, eds. *Physiognomy in Profile: Lavater's Impact on European Culture*. Newark: University of Delaware Press, 2005.

Valdez, Inés. *Transnational Cosmopolitanism: Kant, DuBois, and Justice as Political Craft*. Cambridge: Cambridge University Press, 2019.

van der Woude, A. M. "Population Developments in the Northern Netherlands (1500–1800) and the Validity of the 'Urban Graveyard' Effect." *Annales de démographie historique* (1982): 55–75. https://doi.org/10.3406/adh.1982.1528.

Vartanian, Adam. "Voltaire's Quarrel with Maupertuis: Satire and Science." *L'Esprit créateur* 7, no. 4 (1967): 252–258.

Vergés, Françoise. *Le Ventre des femmes. Capitalisme, racialisation, féminisme*. Paris: Albin Michel, 2017.

Vermeulen, Han F. *Before Boas: The Genesis of Ethnography and Ethnology in the German Enlightenment*. Lincoln: University of Nebraska Press, 2015.

Villiers, Patrick, and Jean-Pierre Duteil. "Les Compagnies des Indes au XVIIIe siècle." In *L'Europe, la mer et les colonies (XVIIe–XVIIIe siècle)*, edited by Patrick Villiers and Jean-Pierre Duteil. Vanves: Hachette, 1997, 188–205.

Wade, Ira. *Intellectual Development of Voltaire*. Princeton: Princeton University Press, 2015.

Wall, John. "Human Rights in Light of Childhood." *International Journal of Children's Rights* 16, no. 4 (2008): 523–543.

Walton, Guy. *Louis XIV's Versailles*. Chicago: Chicago University Press, 1986.

Wauters, Éric. *Les Ports Normands, un modèle?* Rouen: Presses de l'Université de Rouen, 1998.

Wiencek, Henry. *Master of the Mountain: Thomas Jefferson and his Slaves*. New York: Farrar, Straus and Giroux, 2012.

Wills, Garry. *Negro President: Jefferson and the Slave Power*. Boston: Houghton Mifflin, 2005.

Wilson, G. S. *Jefferson on Display: Attire, Etiquette, and the Art of Presentation*. Charlottesville: University of Virginia Press, 2018.

Wolf, Eva Sheppard. *Race and Liberty in the New Nation: Emancipation in Virginia from the Revolution to Nat Turner's Rebellion*. Baton Rouge: LSU Press, 2009.

Wulf, Andrea. *The Brother Gardeners*. New York: Random House, 2008.

Yab, Jimmy. *Kant and the Politics of Racism: Toward Kant's Racialised Form of Cosmopolitan Right*. New York: Springer International Publishing, 2021.

Zammito, John H. *Kant, Herder, and the Birth of Anthropology*. Chicago: Chicago University Press, 2002.

Zimmer, Amie Leigh. "Kant's Conjectures: The Genesis of the Feminine." *The Journal of Speculative Philosophy* 36, no. 2 (2022): 183–193.

Zuckert, Rachel. "The Momentary Inhibition and Outpouring of the Vital Powers: Kant on the Dynamic Sublime." In *Kant and the Feeling of Life: Beauty and Nature in the Critique of Judgment*, edited by Jennifer Mensch. Albany: State University of New York Press, 2024, 129–152.

Zysberg, André. *Les Galériens: Vies et destins de 60.000 forçats sur les galères de France 1680–1748*. Paris: Seuil, 1991.

ILLUSTRATIONS

p. 51 Map by Nicolas Sanson, c. 1656. Boston Public Library, Boston.

p. 53 Engraving, anonymous, in Jean-Baptiste Labat's *Nouveau voyage aux isles de l'Amérique* (Paris: chez Pierre François Giffart, 1722). Courtesy of the John Carter Brown Library, Brown University, Providence.

p. 54 Drawing by Louis Boudan, 1704. Bibliothèque nationale de France, Paris.

p. 56 [top] Seventeenth-century ruins. Photograph by the author, 2022.

p. 56 [bottom] Chapel built by Jean-Baptiste Labat, 17th century. Photograph by the author, 2022.

p. 62 [left] Engraving, anonymous, in Jean-Baptiste Labat's *Nouveau voyage aux isles de l'Amérique* (Paris: chez Pierre François Giffart, 1722). Courtesy of the John Carter Brown Library, Brown University, Providence.

p. 62 [right] Engraving, anonymous, in Jean-Baptiste Labat's *Nouveau voyage aux isles de l'Amérique* (Paris: chez Guillaume Cavelier, 1742). Courtesy of the John Carter Brown Library, Brown University, Providence.

p. 72 Engraving by C. Mathey, in Jean-Baptiste Labat's *Relation historique de l'Éthiopie occidentale* (Paris: chez Charles-Jean-Baptiste Delespine, 1732). Courtesy of the John Carter Brown Library, Brown University, Providence.

p. 76 Painting, anonymous, c. 17th century. Smith Archive / Alamy Stock Photo.

p. 78 Oil painting by Beaubrun Workshop, c. 1680. Château de Bussy-Rabutin, Bussy-le-Grand. Photo copyright © Benjamin Gavaudo / CMN 2019.

p. 85 Engraving by Claude Mellan, c. 1637. Metropolitan Museum of Art, New York.

p. 87 Engraving, anonymous, in John Ogilby's *Africa: Being an Accurate Description of the Regions* (London: T. Johnson, 1670). New York Public Library, New York.

p. 90 Painting, anonymous, c. 1653. Metropolitan Museum of Art, New York.

p. 92 Engraving, in Romeyn de Hooge, *Les Indes Orientales et Occidentales et autres lieux* (Leide: Chez Pierre Vander, 1708).

p. 106 Marble sculpture, anonymous, c. 200–100 BC. Museo Archeologico Nazionale di Napoli, Napoli. Photo copyright © ho visto nina volare 2012.

p. 193 Oil painting by Nicolas de Largilliere, c. 1718–1724. Musée Carnavalet, Paris.

p. 197 Engraving by Louis-Simon Lempereur, 18th century. Bibliothèque municipale de Bordeaux.

p. 203 Pastel painting by Jean-Baptiste Perronneau, 18th century. Nationalmuseum, Stockholm.

p. 213 Colored engraving by Jan L'Admiral, in Bernhard Siegfried Albinus's *Dissertatio secunda de sede et caussa coloris Aethiopum et caeterorum hominum* (Leiden: Theodorum Haak, 1737). Wellcome Collection, London.

p. 216 Engraving by Jean Charles Baquoy, in Voltaire's *Œuvres complètes de Voltaire* (Kehl: Imprimerie de la Société Littéraire-Typographique, 1784). ETH-Bibliothek Zürich, Zürich.

p. 221 Etching and engraving by Charles-Étienne Gaucher, 1778–1782. The Art Institute of Chicago, Chicago.

p. 224 Oil painting by Allan Ramsay, 1754. https://www.nationalgalleries.org/art-and-artists/60610, National Galleries of Scotland, Edinburgh.

p. 226 Engraving by Johann Christian Püschel, in Burkhard Gotthelf Struve's *Bibliotheca iuris selecta secundum ordinem litterarium disposita et ad singulas iuris partes directa: accessit bibliotheca selectissima iuris studiosorum* (Jena: Christian. Henr. Cuno., 1756). Courtesy of Yale University Library.

p. 238 Oil painting, anonymous, c. 1760. Victoria and Albert Museum, London.

p. 241 Engraving by Bosselman, in Charles Coquelin's *Dictionnaire de l'économie politique contenant l'exposition des principes de la science* (Paris: Guillaumin, 1854). Baker Library Special Collections and Archives. Provided by Harvard University, Cambridge, MA.

p. 248 Engraving by John Buego, 18th–19th century. Collection of the author.

p. 251 Oil painting by Sir Joshua Reynolds, 1772. https://www.nationalgalleries.org/art-and-artists/3580, National Galleries of Scotland, Edinburgh.

p. 255 Title page in William Roberson *History of America* (New York: Blakeman and Mason, 1759). Courtesy of Wesleyan University Special Collections and Archives.

p. 260 Engraving by Simon Charles Miger, 1764. Courtesy of the National Gallery of Art, Washington, DC.

p. 266 Oil painting by Johann Gottlieb Becker, 1768. Schiller-Nationalmuseum, Marbach am Neckar.

p. 290 Engraving by Johann Elias Haid, c. 1762–1809. Rijksmuseum, Amsterdam.

INDEX

Note: Words with several hundred occurrences—such as Africa, America, Black, Europe, History, Race, Slave, War, or White—appear under more specific categories.